Finola

Louise Gherasim

Finola

Louise Gherasim

This is an original work of fiction. Except for actual historic figures, events, and places, all characters in this book have no existence outside the imagination of the author.

Copyright © 2000 by Louise Gherasim

First Edition

All rights reserved. No part of this book may be reproduced or utilized in any form or by any means, electronic or mechanical, including photocopying, or by any information storage and retrieval system without permission in writing from the publisher.

ISBN: 1-58721-595-0

Library of Congress Catalog
Card Number: 99-97676

1stBooks – rev. 07/05/00

Acknowledgements

To Kate Miller and Katie Hagen
of the Tigard Literary a go raib mile mait agut
(a thousand thanks) for your patience
and cheerful assistance at all times
especially with finding rare copies of out-of-print books for
my research.

To my ever encouraging and eternally
courageous husband, Teodor, who continually
brightens and fills my days with his optimism, a
loving thank you.

Dedication

To the millions who suffered, and died not only during the Famine years in Ireland, but down through the centuries because of brutal oppression, injustice, and the atrocities of war. May peace and prosperity henceforth be Ireland's destiny.

November 1999

Ill fares the land, to hast'ning ills a prey,
where wealth accumulates, and men decay...

Oliver Goldsmith
The Deserted Village.

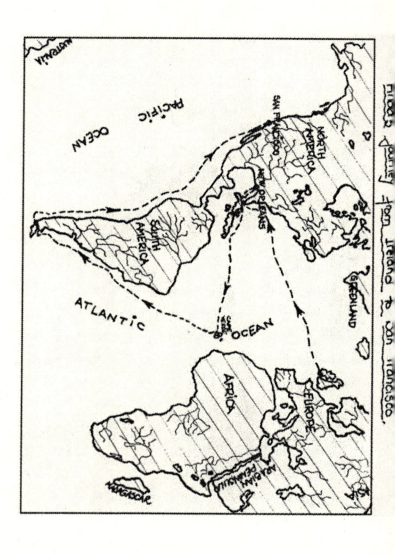

Part I
Glencarrow

And, long, a brave and haughty race
Honoured and sentinelled the place -
Sing oh! not even their son's disgrace
Can quite destroy their glory's trace.

Thomas Davis (1814-1845)

Preface

**Persecution is not wrong because it is cruel,
but cruel because it is wrong.**
                                        Whately

Get to work, boys," shouted Patrick Dunne, overseer for the estates of Lord Sutherland. No sooner were the words uttered than three rough looking men sprang to obey. Insolently, they entered the rude hut and started dragging out the occupants. At first, the screams of the terrified children pierced the damp air; then, as their mother's frantic cries penetrated their confused minds, the little ones grew silent. They stood wide-eyed, mouths gaping, their small hearts visibly palpitating in their emaciated chests, for each wore but a single thread-bare shift.

Maeve O'Donoghue's voice rose first in prayers, "Mother o' God have mercy on us. God Almighty spare us." She importuned heaven with raised eyes, then turning to the man whom she considered the cause of all her sufferings, she begged, "My little children! In God's name have pity …" Her words fell on deaf ears. She threw herself on her knees in the mud in front of Dunne's horse. Beating her breast with her fist, she started to keen. The mournful sounds, begun as a low supplication, grew steadily into a mighty crescendo rising above the agent's harsh commands and the cursing of his men.

Finola O'Donnell was twelve when she witnessed the scene. Her mouth was dry and a gnawing feeling grabbed at her stomach. She leaned against the low stone wall; the hard cold surface seemed to lend her its strength, the strength she needed to remain in an upright position. Her great luminous green eyes stared in disbelief. She knew well she should have run straight home at the very first sign of trouble, but despite the warning voice within, she couldn't drag herself away.

A wee girl, not much younger than Finola, herself, was standing in the yard in front of the one roomed thatched hut. Tears were streaming down her pale cheeks. She wiped them with the back of her hand and looked up at her mother's distraught face. Her mother, a woman young in years but old in body, held an infant to her breast while two little boys in tattered rags clung to what remained of her red skirt. The pathetic father, stooped and crushed with grief, held fast to the jamb of the door. His breeches were torn, his flimsy shirt in shreds, his head bare, the remnants of his boots barely covered his calloused feet.

An iron pot, a small table, two three-legged stools, an assortment of rags, a rough blanket, and some wooden bowls were thrown pell-mell into the mud in front of the kneeling woman as again the agent raised his voice, "Finish the job."

Finola saw a weak puff of smoke rise from the doomed cabin. Two men had climbed up on the roof and with very little effort, had located the supporting beam. Fastening a rope around it, they dropped it to the floor below and then they weakened the beam with a saw. This done they jumped down and pulled the rope through the door and in this way the roof was wrenched and torn from its bearing.

Finola watched it fall in a great grey cloud of dust. The blackened broken gable ends stood stark and defiant against the misty sky; in the mud below, the agonizing mother sought to raise bare, white skeletal arms heavenward.

No longer a child, Finola had grown old in those fearful minutes, matured beyond her twelve years. She had seen, witnessed with her own eyes, human nature at its worst - cruelty and indifference, utter barbarism. She would never again trust the Sasanach or their representatives.

As the dust settled, smoke began to rise from the ruins where the fallen thatch now rested on the still smoldering embers of the turf fire. For a few moments the smoke continued, then, in a burst of flame, the whole interior was ablaze.

She waited a little longer. It had started to rain, a cold rain that would surely turn to sleet before the night was spent was driving across the hills. When she turned to go a piercing cry rent the air. She closed her eyes and made a hurried sign of the cross as her mother was wont to do in times of crisis. Sure, 'twas the banshee! The fear gripping at her heart, she slowly reopened her eyes and beheld a strange sight; out of the grey mists grotesque forms seemed to materialize. At first, one specter appeared and straddled the fence behind the ruins of O'Donoghue's cabin, then, a second ghost-like form shrieked into view... a third, a fourth, and as quickly disappeared. Terrorized, Finola was rivotted to the spot and in the ensuing pandamonium, became completely disoriented. Even the cries of the ghosts were lost in the melee as the angry agent picked himself up from the muddy mess into which his horse had thrown him before it took off at a gallop across the adjoining fields. He had lost his top hat, his greasy grey hair fell in wisps about his haggard face. "Damnation! Blast it!" he cried as he looked at his clothes. His black boots, knee-high, woolen, ribbed stockings, loosely fitting black breeches, and even his coat tails were covered with a putrid slime. His hard-bitten face was screwed into deep lines and ridges and a nervous condition, exaggerated by the trials and tensions of the moment, was an added botheration. He tried to clean off some of the muck, but 'twas no use.

"Shit!... God damn it! Pure, unadulterated shit!" He shook his hand but the muck persisted clinging to his distended fingers. Livid with anger, he sought a clump of grass and aggressively fought with it in his efforts to be rid of the dung.

One of Patrick Dunne's men had left in a terrible hurry while the two others were too terrified to make such a rational decision.

"Blast ye! Ye God damn fools, catch 'em! After 'em, I tell ye!" But the two stood as though paralyzed still gaping at the place where the spectacle had been enacted on the stone wall not fifty feet away.

At length, the angry command penetrated their numbed brains. "Jesus, Mary, and Joseph!"... cried one man making the sign to the cross. His companion answered, "Christ Almighty, 'twas a bloody ghost!"

Dunne tore into the men shaking them to action. "Ghost be damned! After 'em, I tell ye." He was trembling. A cold sweat covered his face and the twitching made it more hideous and ghastly. Fuming, his raucous voice bellowed and stuttered. "A good ... . good floggin'... is... is what them ruffians need. Scoundrels all of 'em. No... no doubt... that... that Dara O'Rourke is... the ringleader. I'll... curse him to hell... I'll break every bone in his bloody body if ever... I lay me hands on that bugger... spookin' me horse like that. Damn bastard." By this time Dunne's face was beetroot red. The ghosts had long vanished, and his men were equally long passed being effective.

A strange and eerie silence followed the departure of Mr. Dunne and his accomplices. Dazed by what had taken place, the unfortunate family of Sean O'Donoghue clung to each other, mute, beaten, desperate, they stood huddled in a dejected little heap.

Finola's tender heart ached. Such cruelty! The injustice of it. Young though she was, she swore to herself that she would never allow such a thing to happen to either herself or her family. How she might avert such a catastrophy she had no notion at that time, but the sight of the Donoghue family's destitution and dire misery was so seared into her mind and heart that she knew she would scratch, claw, and even kill the landlord who dared to evict those she loved.

Chapter 1

"Know how sublime a thing it is to suffer and be strong."
- Longfellow.

Finola lived with her parents, fivebrothers and an infant sister in a two- roomed cottage near the brow of Carrow Mór. The growing family strained Owen's limited resources to the extreme; his meager earnings from the sale of his crops and animals did not always meet the needs of his wife and little ones and many's the night both parents and children went to bed hungry.

Until the Spring of 1845, Owen and Deirdre O'Donnell eked out an existance on their four acre farm. Most of the land was rocky and the soil poor, but, due to hard work and careful planning they managed to feed and clothe the family. But luck had run out that fateful Fall, for the potato crop caught the blight and the harried father of seven was forced to buy Indian meal to suppliment the meager diet of old potatoes from the previous year.

Finola had just turned fourteen; tall for her age at five feet five, she was too thin. Her school days had come to an abrupt end as the old teacher had died and there was none to take his place. She had been a good student - bright, eager to learn, easily gaining proficiency in the three R's. Able to read and write in her own language, she soon attacked the fundamentals of the foreign tongue, for Liam MacSweeney was well versed, and those who were privileged to be tutored by him fortunate, indeed. He had been Master of a hedgeschool in the not so distant past, when the Sasanach were determined not only to keep the Irish poor but illiterate also.

Finola knew well the list, though it was long, of the inhuman and intolerable codes called the Penal Laws, that forced her grandparents into abject poverty and destitution. She had learned that the aim of these laws was threefold: (1) To deprive the Catholic population, at least ninety-five percent of the nation, of all civil rights. (2) To reduce them to extreme ignorance. (3) To devest them of all claim to the land.

In pondering some of these laws, so brutal and repressive, Finola wondered how the race had survived at all. A glance at her mother told her that it would not take much to wipe out the entire population at that moment in time.

What could a people do without food, without work, without education? The people, her kind, were forbidden to hold public office, to have a profession. They were not allowed to live within five miles of the nearest corporate town. They were not permitted to own a horse of greater value than five pounds, nor were they free to own arms even for their own protection. Listening to her father, in his sober moments, she learned that the Irish race could not long endure. He was fond of recalling the story of The McCarthy who had been robbed of his estate. As an old man, he sat under a tree sobbing. When the English 'gentleman' who had received the estate saw him, he ventured to ask the cause of his grief. "These lands," answered the heart-broken man, "and that castle were mine. This tree under which I sit was planted by my hands. I came here to water it with my tears, before sailing tonight for Spain."

But Finola also knew that these injustices, these laws of which the French jurist, Montesquieu, wrote: 'laws conceived by demons, written in blood, and registered in

Hell.' - were, at every opportunity circumvented. Thousands went to the Continent to be taught in colleges and universities set up especially for them by friendly countries; France, Spain, Italy. While those who could not leave were tutored by learned men who gathered the children of the area together in make-shift hovels; by the side of the road, in the hedges, and in dugouts, they congregated and there, these indomitable mentors risked their lives to impart knowledge. So receptive were their pupils that besides the fundamentals many acquired skill in several languages including Latin and Greek. Thus, ever faithful to a long tradition of learning, did the Gael resist this injustice as firmly as they fought the tyrannical laws against their faith.

During the winter of 1845, Finola remained at home helping her mother who was pregnant with her eighth child. The previous pregnancy had been difficult and her present condition did not bode fair for this one either. Seven months along, Deirdre looked like a skeleton except for her protruding belly. Exhausted most of the time, she had taken to her bed a week before and was now unable to rise even for the most basic human necessity. Her frail body rejected the watery vegetable soup Finola had prepared especially for her. "If, only I could have a wee sup o' milk," she sighed and her oldest girl child felt a sharp pain in her heart for she was unable to fulfill her mother's simple wish.

Owen, like others in Glencarrow, had gone to the city hoping to find work. As the outlook for the tenant farmer became bleaker, due to more extensive failure of the staple crop, the government, under pressure from America, set up a public works system. Roads and bridges were built to no purpose save that of giving employment. Thousands applied, but it was only a temporary affair, a stopping off place on the way to the poorhouse.

Finola knew her mother could not survive without more food. Leaving the younger children in the care of a neighbor, she went in search of work, a futile if not impossible task at that time. Yet, she was determined to do her part - albeit a self-imposed part - to augment the slim wages of her father.

Rural Ireland in the early to mid 1800's was made up of settlements called clachans. These communities were self-sufficient. They may have lacked shops, markets, churches and other public buildings, but they had all that was necessary for a frugal yet satisfying life-style. Within these clachans there were weavers, thatchers, woodworkers, shoemakers, smithies, and sometimes a priest or minister. The old traditions and customs were faithfully carried on because there was no shortage of musicians, singers, dancers, poets, and story tellers. Life may have been difficult but it was not without its joys and the ancient beliefs and culture were fostered and preserved.

Finola was, finally, forced to accept the fact that only at the Manor, called locally the 'Big House,' the residence of Lord Sutherland, an absentee landlord of all the lands in and around Glencarrow, would she find some kind of employment.

She approached the huge iron gates leading into the long driveway; they were locked but to one side a small gate swung back and forth on rusty hinges. Slipping through, she started towards the Manor barely visible for the large oak trees that stretched ahead on either side of the driveway. With each step forward her anger grew, a feeling of deep resentment. She, who was Irish, who could trace her ancestry back for hundreds of years, was forced to seek employment from the strangers now in possession of what rightfully belonged to her people. Were it not for the Sasanach, all the sufferings, the hardships endured by her family and those around her, would never have been. The insults, humiliations, and cruel evictions she had so often witnessed now crowded her mind with vivid pictures and strengthened her resolve. Gritting her teeth and clenching her hands as she neared the end of the driveway, she halted momentarily. At this juncture the avenue divided to form a circular area planted with shrubs and flowers, before sweeping to the main entrance. She allowed her eyes to travel the length of the massive exterior and again the resentment boiled in the depths of her being ... stolen, confiscated ... all ... and by whom? Common, illiterate soldiery who, having killed and raped and looted, were honored by the crown with the lands and homes of their victims.

She reached for the heavy iron knocker, raised it and let it fall ... once, twice, three times, then waited. A hollow shuffle on the wooden floor within, then a bolt was withdrawn, and Finola stood facing Patrick Dunne.

He looked her up and down, his bleary eyes uncertain, suspicious, "An' what would you be wantin' eh?" His voice was almost a growl.

"I've come looking for work. I'm a good cook and I've heard ..." she swallowed hard.

The word cook was enough for Dunne. Since Mrs. Mulvaney was laid-up with a broken leg for the past week, he hadn't had a decent meal. "Well, if you can cook ... but it 'ill only be temporary, mind you." He opened the door just wide enough to allow her to enter, then bolted it again.

At that moment, Finola experienced a strange feeling of apprehension. She wanted to turn around and leave and never return. Filled with trepidation and not understanding why, she faltered, unable to follow the overseer.

"Are ye comin' or aren't ye?" he rasped from the far end of a long corridor leading off the main entrance hall.

Shaken, she tried to throw off the feeling and hastened to catch up. He led her through several other long hallways, the walls of which were hung with massive oil paintings chiefly of animals or country scenes. Finola had time only to glance at them as she hurried along. At length, they arrived at the back of the house and entered the large kitchen where a rosy-faced, plump woman in her mid-fifties sat beside a dying fire, her left leg resting on a stool.

Without so much as a nod in Finola's direction, Dunne launched forth, "Here, see if this one can be of some help ... says she can cook. Devil o' much ye've been able to do of that yerself this past week."

"Now, Mr. Dunne none of your impertenence, if you please." And the housekeeper lifted her head and sniffed the air as if his very presence were odious.

Dunne didn't wait to hear anymore; he tolerated Mrs. Mulvaney only because she was the best cook in the county, and his first and only love, his stomach.

As soon as Dunne had left, Mrs. Mulvaney put Finola at ease. "Don't pay too much attention to him. He's a rough hard man. Now put your things over there behind the door and come see what you can do with this fire."

Finola got to work instantly and in no time had the fire roaring, the pots steaming, and a batch of oatmeal bread ready for the oven.

"You're a veritable gift, girl," the housekeeper said, observing her as she kneeded and shaped the last batch of dough, sprinkled a tray with flour and with a flourish, confident that her work was good, she wiped her hands on a clean towel. Then taking the tray with the ends of her coarse apron and with agile energetic steps, she set it in the oven.

Meanwhile the housekeeper thought: This one will go places. Then her curiosity got the better of her and she asked: "And where, might I ask, did you learn to make bread?"

"My Mam," came the quick reply, almost defiantly. "We weren't always so poor, you know. Dad worked hard when he was younger and we had oaten meal and barley bread for supper on Sundays. An' plum pudding and pies for Christmas and for Easter lamb meat with lots of gravy." There was a ring of triumph in her voice.

"Well, faith an' ye were better off than most, then. Your mother must be from a good family, I'm thinkin' if she knew how to make such fancy dishes."

"I doh know about that, but she is a determined woman. She always worked hard and has a great respect for learning. I remember when my Dad wanted to stop me from going to lessons with Mr. Sweeney, said there wasn't any reason for a girl to be getting all that learnin'. Mother got cross and told him a girl had more reason to be educated. 'Who is responsible for the learning the children will get if it doesn't come from the mother first?' she asked him. Dad didn't say another word after that and I attended school every day until the old master died. I prayed that someone would take his place but no one ever did. So I was forced to stay home and help with the children after that. But I put my knowledge to good use because I taught my brothers to read and write also." The pride in her tone and demeanor was obvious. And the cook could scarcely hide the smile that slowly lit up her grey-blue eyes.

"Well, seems you're well equipped to make your way in life, then, Finola. Thanks to your mother's foresight."

"Aye. She's a fine woman. But I'm terrible scared she'll not be around to see the little ones grown up. She's awful sick an' she expecting another baby an' all." Finola hastily wiped the tears that clouded her eyes.

"Now, now child, God has His ways of takin' care of mothers and children. An' there's nothing you or any of us can do to change things if it's His Will." Mrs. Mulvaney was groping to find words to distract Finola for she knew comforting was not her task nor her forte. The simmering porridge drew her attention. "You might give that pot a stir. We don't need burnt gruel and I can tell you Mr. Dunne most certainly doesn't favor it." She smiled and motioned to the bubbling stirabout.

Instantly Finola set herself to the business of making sure that all was right with the cooking food.

"Well, that's done," she said turning to face Mrs. Mulvaney with a happy smile. "And now, what's next?"

She scrubbed the backstairs; the boards never looked so clean, almost white. She cleaned the grates and blackened the fenders in several of the adjoining rooms. Then she turned her attention to the silverware in the dining room, standing back from time to time to admire the different pieces.

"One day I'll have a collection as good if not better than this," she said giving a last rub to a particularly beautiful silver salver.

Realizing it was getting late, she hurried down the back stairs and prepared the table for lunch. Having served Mrs. Mulvaney and Mr. Dunne, she hastened back to attend to the bedclothing in the master's bedroom. They felt damp. At that time of year it was necessary to air the blankets and sheets when they were not in use.

"Yes," she concluded, "This is a magnificient room. And it truly was when Finola had finished dusting and polishing. A white marble fireplace was the eye-catching feature. Above it hung an old French tapestry. The huge, mullioned windows were flanked by bright gold velvet hangings setting a frame, not only for the windows themselves but for the lime-green walls. The landscape from that vantage point was spectacular affording an expansive view of the hills and the valley stretching for miles below the Manor. Against the wall facing the handsome oak bedstead was a tall secretary with a superb pediment fashioned from mahogany. The chairs, of which there were four with white horse-hair seats, Finola did not know then, were 18th Century French, but having sat on each one in turn, she decided they were an item she might like to have in her own future mansion.

Quietly and efficiently she went from one task to another, stopping only to have a cup of soup and a taste of her own fresh bread, and that at the housekeeper's bidding.

It was well into mid-afternoon when Mrs. Mulvaney called her.

"It's time you had something more substantial to eat, my dear. Come, you can't work on an empty stomach. Why didn't you eat at noon?

"I just didn't have my work done, Mam."

"Oh, the work is never done here. So you must take your food at the appointed time in future."

"Yes, Mam. Thank you."

When, finally, the long day ended, Finola was tired but content that she had done well. Her first day at the Manor had been a success. She had earned Mrs. Mulvaney's respect and had been rewarded with a loaf of bread and a jar of soup. At first she protested. Proud, never one to look for handouts, to consider charity was beneath her dignity, she refused the offer. But when the good woman explained that it was part of her wages, servants had to be fed, and she had merely partaken of one meal that day, Finola graciously accepted. She thought of how welcome such a treat would be at home, especially for her sick mother and thanked Mrs. Mulvaney so profusely that the housekeeper feigning a sneeze hastily pulled out her pocket handkerchief to wipe away a tear.

"Now, you be off with you. It's getting late. And mind you're here on time in the morning." Her tone was firm, authoritarian, but Finola knew she had a good heart. She had found a new friend.

"I will, I will," said Finola as she snatched her shawl from a peg on the back of the kitchen door. Then gathering the precious food in her arms, she hurried out and into the gathering dusk.

Though the slim wages scarcely increased the family's slender resources, the regular, and at times, generous leftovers from the Manor kitchen were a Godsend to the undernourished O'Donnell family.

"Mammy .... you awake?" Finola called softly as she opened the bedroom door. Her mother didn't answer. She hesitated not wishing to disturb the sleeping woman for she knew how badly she needed rest and how poorly she had slept the night before.

Her father, Owen, had come home in the wee hours of the morning and, for what seemed an eternity, had fussed and shuffled about in the kitchen with a din and clatter that awakened all but the very youngest children.

Weak from hunger, he hadn't eaten a decent meal in several weeks; he was 'under the influence'. Managing somehow by the faint glimmer of the smouldering peat fire to find his way about, he groped until he had discovered the potato sack, the last of their stock. He dug into it with both hands, but the effort to balance himself and carry the potatoes to the iron pot hanging near the fireplace was too much. He stumbled. The potatoes fell and rolled around the hard earthen floor in all directions. "Christ... Lord Almighty can't a man get something to eat in his own house?" he raised his voice in anger.

The frightened children cowered in the loft. They had, of late, grown to fear their father's homecoming... the outbursts of anger and the unpredictable behavior when the drink was in him.

He called to his wife. "Deirdre... Deirdre... Come woman... I... I," then he collapsed, too weak to get up and cook himself a few spuds... . He couldn't fill the great void, the emptiness his stomach continued to feel despite the raw whiskey he had downed hoping to drive away his disappointment, the feelings of inadequacy. He had been 'let go'. 'Unable to keep up with the work', they had said. He had seen it coming ... had tried so hard. A man couldn't do much road building on an empty stomach. So Owen, always frail, was one of the first to succumb to the drudgery. Guilt, frustration, and sheer desperation drove him to do that which he swore he'd never do... drink. He had failed... failed in his duty before God... the breadwinner unable to feed his wife and little children. He, Owen O'Donnell, was useless.

Until recently, he'd been a good husband, father, provider, always managing, somehow, to furnish the necessities for his growing happy family. But the last two years of high rents and poor crops had got the better of him. No matter what he did, for he had taken odd jobs here and there, he couldn't make ends meet. If only he could be sure of a healthy crop of potatoes this year, he'd at least save his loved ones from starvation. It was with this specter in his mind that he had set off the week before, walking five miles to the City of Limeriek to find work. But his strength was gone; the hard labor had done him in. Like so many others he now faced the inevitable, eviction and the slow death of starvation in some muddy ditch.

"A lot o' good I am... Christ, what's a man to do?" Then he cursed himself low and vehemently and the sweat broke out on his furrowed brow and ran in tiny droplets down his hollow cheeks and he joined the others as they piled into Murphy's pub.

It hadn't always been so. In their long history, the Irish had never been known as an intemperate race. Their endurance, their long suffering is legendary, but ordinary men have a breaking point. The misery of the famine years: the inexcusable neglect by the English government of the starving multitudes; the inhuman disregard for the sick - those suffering from typhus, dysentery, and fevers. Added to these cruel negligencies were the heartless evictions of starving families unable to pay their rents.

Their rude hovels were burned even as they watched in disbelief and their small holdings given over to the raising of sheep - so much more profitable.

Facing such hardships and conditions, a demented father might well try to forget his misery, if he had the strength, at the local pub.

As time passed and no help was forthcoming, those still able to support a long journey sought escape from their miseries by leaving for America. But, here again, the unfortunates, having scraped together the enormous sum to pay for their passage, were lucky to arrive at their destination. Many caught "the fever" on board ship and were buried at sea. Others were immediately deported upon landing in the New World because they were too ill to enter the "Promised Land". Stories of the crowded ships, the lack of all necessities: privacy, sleeping space, toilet facilities, cooking conditions, and absolutely no medical assistance, reached Ireland and inevitably had its toll on the national morale. The whole country, it seemed, sank into a deep depression.

Yet, through all this suffering and death, there were adequate supplies of food in the country. Ireland still exported grain, and livestock to England.

Witnessing such scenes daily, Owen's heart sickened, and despair took possession of his mind. There was no escape. Hopelessness and certain death was his lot and that of his family. . . the last resort, the only escape for his inevitable depression was the local public house.

And, sad to say, he was not alone. A new and ruinous scourge had now gripped Ireland and a once proud and noble race sank to an even more despicable level.

Finola heard her mother stir. "Mammy, stay. You stay in bed, you hear, I'm coming." She quickly pulled a thin woolen shawl about her shoulders and clad in her long white nightgown hurried down to the kitchen. Lighting a small tallow candle and looking around, "Aw!" she gasped. "Dad! Are you sick?"

Slouched in the corner near the fireplace still clutching one miserable potato, Owen O'Donnell cut a wretched figure. She wasn't sure whether he was dead or alive as she bent to listen to his breathing. "God!" she wanted to take him in her arms. In his early forties, he appeared to be an old man. She wanted to take care of him, tell him everything would be all right but as she bent closer, the smell of the liquor still heavy on his breath caused her to pull back. "How could he? How, in God's name, could he spend good money on drink?" She turned her attention to the fireplace. 'Twas no time to be feeling sorry for oneself and that's what her dad was doing. She clenched her teeth and set herself the task of getting the fire going. She adjusted the kettle over the flame. A cup of tea for her mam was more important now, her father would sleep for several hours. Deep down in her heart, Finola pittied him. Yet she despised and resented him for spending his hard earned money on drink. He was weak. She was determined to be strong. Only those who were strong would survive.

She would not just survive, she resolved there and then, she would achieve, accomplish, rise from her present impoverished position and ultimately prosper.

But those days were in the future and Finola was of a practical turn of mind. Gritting her teeth again, she turned her attention to her sick mother who so badly needed nourishment.

"Mam, Mammy," she called, listening intently, straining to catch the slightest sound, she waited at the bedroom door. All was as still as the village church within and almost as cold. A shiver ran through her body as she crept on tip-toe over to the side of the bed. "Mammy, you all right?"

Deirdre stirred and a low moan escaped her purple lips. "God! She looks like death," mumbled Finola under her breath. "Mam, do you want your tea now? I've got it ready."

The pregnant woman turned with difficulty from her side to her back and opened her tired eyes. "That you, Nola? Is it morning already?" She yawned. "Can't be, child."

"Aye, Mam, that it is." Finola peered into the semidarkness trying to determine for herself her mother's true condition.

A shaft of light filtered through the small opening that was once a fairly large window but now boarded up. There was no money for glass, and the cold of winter had to be kept without.

By this faint light Finola was able to make out the delicately chiseled features of her mother's face. The roses had long ago faded from her wax-like cheeks. Her shapely nose, always slender, looked pinched, and around the eyelids, the crowsfeet were indelibly stamped, but they were momentarily overlooked because the great greyish blue circles under the eyes were so obvious. The thin purple lips were expressionless and the once flaming hair, the envy of many a young lass, clung in damp discolored tangles to her moist brow and tumbled in disarray across her bare shoulders and the crumpled soggy pillow beneath her head.

Yet, despite her deplorable condition, there was still a quiet beauty about Deirdre O'Donnell. The ravages of poverty and the exhausting incessant struggle for survival had robbed her early of youth's vitality. The bearing of one child after another had not contributed to her general well being and had stolen her once shapely figure. At thirty five, Deirdre's life was spent. Finola knew she would not live to bear her eighth child.

In the drab cold sickroom there were few comforts let alone beauty. The crude bed was the principal article of furniture and it occupied most of the space. A wabbly side table, showing the scars of many generations of rough treatment, was in a corner near the bed. On the table, a glass jar tilting in a rather precarious position still held the withered bluebells Finola had gather for her several days before. A wooden trunk stood against the whitewashed wall facing the bed; in it Deirdre kept her Sunday dress, her winter cloak which had been a wedding present from her parents, and a few other small items of clothing. The same acrid smell, a mixture of peat smoke, the odors of dry straw and earth and now and then a whiff from the pig pens on the other side of the wall, permeated this room as it did the rest of the cabin.

Fear gripped Finola's heart as she bent towards her mother's emaciated form, touching the one cold hand that lay outside the coarse blanket. Drawing the cover over it, she uttered a silent prayer, "God in heaven, please spare our Mammy."

"Where's your father?" There was concern in her grey-blue eyes.

As if she hasn't enough to worry about, thought Finola. "Oh, he's without... by the fire... asleep."

"He's all right then?"

"Sure. He's fine." Finola tried to make her voice sound unconcerned. "Just tired."

"Don't be too hard on him, lass." Her mother made an effort to rise.

"I... I won't," a slight edge to her tone of voice. "Now, are you wanting your tea, Mam?"

"Aye, lass. That I do."

"Anything else? How about a little slice of Mrs. Mulvaney's soda bread. I buttered it 'specially for you before I left the Manor last night."

"Sure, 'tis you're the good girl… thinking so much… of… of your poor sick mother…. Yes, love,… I'll try a wee bite."

* * * *

April, the month of many moods: sunshine, showers, scudding clouds, darting sunbeams, blustering breezes, gentle zephers. April, the time of verdant fields, vivid flowers: dancing daffodils, tinkling bluebells, shy swaying cowslips in the short grasses. April: days of perfumed breath and music; the singing of blue-tit and finch, of thrush and yellow hammer. And the incessant hum of the bees above and around the fragrant willow catkins. April, with nights of crisp clean air and a shy moon that reluctantly peeps from behind scudding fluffy clouds.

The month had only just begun to live when they sent for her. Little Patrick, sure of foot and fleet as a wild deer sped down the bóithrín and across the lush meadow. At the door of the Manor he waited only long enough to take a deep breath before raising his trembling hands to the latch. As the door swung open, Finola looked up from her work. Fear grabbed her heart when she beheld her small brother. Standing speechless, his large blue eyes told her all she needed to know." "'Tis Mammy…."

The child at the open door nodded. Finola didn't even take time to snatch her shawl from the peg but grabbing her little brother's hand, she ran from the kitchen.

Mrs. Mulvaney stood looking at the fleeing figures a moment, then feeling the awful impact, sat down. "Glory be to God on high, what's to become of them?"

Deirdre O'Donnell and her stillborn son were laid to rest among the wild bluebells in the old churchyard while her weeping children stood by the graveside as the priest prayed over the mortal remains. Finola looked at each one in turn and the pain that showed on her pale face was only a shadow of that felt in her broken heart that day. Her beloved brothers, her little sister, her distraught father... helpless, uncertain, broken...

* * * *

Shouldering the responsibilities and caring for the large family more like a mother than a sister, Finola worked early and late. She managed the household, as she did everything else, with energy and determination. It was imperative, she reasoned, for her to keep her position at the Manor and since it was impossible to do everything herself at home, she delegated specific chores to each child, thus ensuring that things would run smoothly.

Patrick shrank from his older brother, Mikey, who growled at him in derision. "Coward, ye're a snotty nosed coward, Patrick O'Donnell," and he poised for a fight.

Patrick had retreated to the other side of the kitchen table, a safe distance by the calculations of an eight year old. He depended on speed and agility to get him out of a tough spot, for strength and brute force he certainly didn't possess.

"I'll get ye. I'll skin ye alive ye yella' belly." Mikey was about to plunge headlong across the table having jumped first on a stool and from that vantage point might have done himself and his timid brother bodily harm had not Finola swiftly intervened.

Coming into the kitchen with a bucket of fresh water, she sized up the situation. "Mikey, you at it again! I'll tan your hide, m' boy, if you don't stop your fighting this instance."

She had put the bucket down and with quick sure action pulled Mikey from his perch. Off balance and restrained by Finola's firm grip, the nine year old wasn't as tough and formidable a force as he had imagined himself. She shook him then with both hands. "Now you listen an' listen good. I've had enough of your bickering. Your incessant haggling and hounding of Patrick is going to stop. Yes, stop right now. Do you hear?"

"I'll tell me da on ye." Mikey answered in defiance. His head was bent low, his eyes averted from his sister.

"You'll what! You'll do no such thing an' you know it. For if your dad is to hear of this carrying on it's from me he'll hear it. And, believe me, the consequences you'll not enjoy."

So saying, Finola lifted the short shift and administered several wallops on Mikey's bare backside. "Now get your breeches on and fetch some turf. Your dad's gone off this half hour to the corner field and you'll be catching it, m' boyo, if you don't get down there in short order."

Mikey rubbed his bottom. Then, casting an embarrassed glance in Patrick's direction, he mumbled, "Didn't hurt a bit. She can't spank."

Finola had turned her attention to Patrick. Although she favored the younger child, she didn't want the others to notice her preference, hence, she chided Patrick also. "For shame, Patrick, fighting first thing in the morning. An' your mammy hardly cold in her grave. 'Tis right cross she'd be with you, lad... ."

"Oh, Finola. I'm sorry... I... I... ." Little Patrick rushed to his beloved sister and threw himself into the folds of her long grey skirt.

"There, there, a grá. Sure you didn't mean it." Finola raised his golden head and looked into the tear-filled blue eyes. Had she seen the cherubs in Michael Angelo's frescos she might have known that such beauty is captured once in a thousand years and then only by a great master. She bent and laid a kiss on his satin cheek and with the tips of her fingers, carefully brushed away his childish tears. "Come, I've a treat for you. Here, sit down by the fire till you see what I've got."

When Finola had seated her little brother on a stool in front of the bright turf flames, she went to the dresser. This, the only other furniture in the room was a rather rough looking cupboard consisting of three narrow shelves above and a larger more spacious compartment below. Upon the upper section a few pewter mugs, two cracked earthenware plates, some jugs, jars, and a tin canister were displayed.

She stretched to reach the top of the dresser and pulled down what looked like an old dish rag. Placing it on the table, she carefully unfolded it. Patrick's eyes grew wide with excitement. He was familiar with Finola's special treats by now, but the anticipation of some tasty morsel was always a glorious experience. In rapt silence, the small boy watched his sister's every move until at last the treasure was uncovered.

"Mmmm..." Patrick's mouth was partly open and a trickle of saliva had slipped from behind his lower lip.

"Now, since you're really the best boy in the house, you deserve a nice breakfast," Finola held up a thick slice of Mrs. Mulvaney's brown soda bread. It had been generously buttered and spread with blackberry jelly. The child took it in both hands, as he would a gift of great value, with care and gentleness.

"Now while I'm warming a mug of milk, a grá, you eat up every bit of that."

Later, when Mikey returned with the turf, Finola found an excuse to reward him in like manner. Mikey wasn't a bad child, just mischievous, a happy-go-lucky type with a quick temper and an equally quick smile.

As soon as little Colleen awoke, Finola washed, fed, and ushered her off in the company of Patrick to the care of a neighbor. With the two youngest safely lodged and the older ones in the fields in the custody of their father, Finola turned her thoughts to herself.

It was after seven, she must be getting a move on; already Liam Nolan's cows were straggling down the bóithrín. She could hear them as she hurriedly changed into her black dress. Quickly, she rearranged her hair into two thick braids encircling her shapely head and casting a final glance about to see that all was as it should be, she closed the cabin door and started off for the Manor.

The O'Donnell family paid several more untimely visits to the village graveyard during the next few months. The first to follow her mammy was little Colleen. Never very healthy, the tiny creature caught 'the fever' and quickly succumbed to its ravages. Mikey, the bold one, and Sean, a lad of eleven, both died within a week of each other. They started vomiting one morning at breakfast and were unable, thereafter to keep any food in their stomachs. The six year old twins, never parted in life, were found dead in each others arms a short time later.

The house was strangely quiet after that. Finola became more protective of little Patrick but wasn't always on hand to comfort him. Often coming upon him in an off-guarded moment, his great blue eyes rimmed with tears, she'd ask, "An' what's the matter, now?" His invariable monosyllabic response was, "Mikey."

Finola didn't intend for things to continue as they were. Somehow, she must and would change the improverished miserable conditions in which she and what remained of her family now lived. She couldn't look to her father for help, he was weak; weak physically, that was obvious but also weak-willed. All ambition had left, he lacked aim, drive, and even the will to live. Finola could see him steadily growing more lethargic as if a great burden weighed heavily upon him, gradually but surely draining his every last ounce of energy. With bowed head, dull unseeing eyes, and hunched shoulders, Owen O'Donnell shuffled through one weary day after another.

At times, Finola was exasperated, at times frustrated. She so needed his help. Then she'd remember her mother's words, "Don't be too hard on him, lass." Still, inside, she rebelled for she didn't understand. Indeed, Finola didn't understand; she was too young to understand that when hope dies there's nothing left for a man. Owen O'Donnell had lost all hope.

So, she pushed herself day and night, night and day and carried on as best she could; at home, trying to maintain a semblance of order and continuity, sustained by the thought that her mam would want her to do so, caring for the needs of her father and little Patrick. At the Manor, she worked methodically, efficiently, and with determination. She had much to learn nor did she intend to dawdle over the process. The sooner she acquired the necessary skills, the sooner would she be able to move on and up.

Chapter 2

"There is nothing half so sweet in life as love's young dream."
- Moore.

She heard him long before she saw him. The clear flute-like sound ascended on the warm air then floated, it seemed, in her direction. Fergus O'Rourke, known as Dubhdara or Dara thrilled the heart of every young lass from the Cliffs of Moher to the banks of the Shannon River. But Dara had eyes for only one, Finola O'Donnell, and it was her heart he was hoping to captivate on this bright spring morning as he whistled his way down the hillside. For her part, Finola wanted nothing more than to be on her way. She had a job to do and she intended to do it so well, she would make herself indispensable at the Manor.

She quickened her steps along the narrow bóithrín and when she reached the stile, the only entrance to the meadow behind the Manor, she stopped before mounting the three stone steps. Why?... She wasn't quite sure. Not unmindful of Dara's good looks, nor the fact that he was greatly attracted to her, she tried to stifle the surge of emotion within her breast. The sound of his whistling was close now... Her heart started to pound, a flutter... a moment of anticipation... Did she really feel something for Dara? she asked herself. Then, just as the dark youth rounded the bend, Finola picked up her long skirts and tripped nimbly and daintily over the stile and into the meadow. She was well on her way before he reached the spot where she had been standing.

Somewhat crest-fallen, Dara mounted the stone steps where he had an unobstructed view of the meadow and watched as she hurried on. When she didn't look back, he waited only long enough to see her reach the gate that led directly into the yard behind the 'Big House'. Disappointed but undaunted, he jumped from the stile and sauntered leisurely toward his fields at the lower end of the valley. He'd try to catch up with pretty Finola later, on the way home. The thought of her sweet face would keep him going that day, and the determination to rescue her from slavery, from the employ of an Englishman, goaded him on.

Dara was nineteen. Standing over six feet, he was a powerful young man, —broad shoulders, strong shapely body all muscle and sinew. Exuding vitality, virility, and robust health, he was known far and wide as the handsomest man in the County Clare. His nickname, Dubdara, (black oak) was acquired quite naturally, for Fergus had a thick crop of jet black hair that fell in soft waves on a broad, lightly tanned brow, and his robust physique was obvious. His eyes, the color of ripe sloes were set wide apart under dark brown brows. And in those dusky pools the temper of Dara O'Rourke's soul was mirrowed. They could be soft and loving when his thoughts were of Finola or blaze like hot coals in moments of anger. At other times, they betrayed his Celtic nature, his melancholy side. But most often, those sultry orbs were filled with a merriment that was irresistible and contagious. His nose was straight and flared slightly at the tip, giving his face an aristocratic touch. He had a fairly wide mouth, the upper lip well defined. And when he laughed, as he often did, Dara displayed a set of regular sparkling white teeth. To his great physical attributes were added those of a uniquely forthright personality. He was an honest man, a just man, a man of integrity. In one so young such traits might lead one to think of him as a dour, serious, perhaps quiet person but

Dara was quite the contrary. He was, by nature a happy boisterous youth ready at the drop of a hat, to play a prank on his friends of which he had plenty. He could always be relied upon for a joke, for his wit was as keen as his tongue was sharp. He was self-confident and invariably optimistic. It seemed that the fear and hopelessness gripping at the heart of every other man in Glencarrow had not even touched Dara O'Rourke.

Despite the loss of most of his potato crop the year before, Dara managed to provide for his widowed mother and young sister, Una. He refused to be beaten. His indomitable spirit rose above all obstacles, simply rejecting all thoughts of defeat. He would live up to the name he so proudly bore. He would weather whatever storm blew his way. Just as the old oaks, clinging tenaciously to the rugged hillside had defied the onslaughts of a hundred years or more, Dara would survive.

Was it the brashness of youth that gave him such confidence or was there something hidden in the inner recesses of his nature? He had no father to emulate, no living male relative on either side of his family. His mother was a mild-mannered, rather retiring person and his only sister, younger by three years, favored her personality. Whence then came this tower of strength, this tenaciousness, and will-power? The only explanation that seemed plausible at the time was that although Dara had lost his father at a young age, the man, a power-house of moral courage and rectitude, himself, had left an indelible mark on the eight year old boy. For until his dying day, Dara would remember the words uttered by his father before they led him away to execution. 'I have lived my life according to the Christian principles handed down to me by my parents. I have never intentionally harmed any man, but if as a patriot I have used a weapon against despotism, I deem it my duty to have done so. Nor do I repent of my actions.'

During his trial, Denis O'Rourke appeared calm - his mouth, and the features around which defiance was a constant - though immobile, firm, and grave - had an air of conscious superiority. His head was erect, his eyes were focused. A man of purpose and determination.

The image of this indomitable man as he stood in the dock that morning more than ten years before was still fresh in Dara's mind. Nor did a day pass that he was not mindful of it.

In the ten years since his father's death, Dara had never reaped the full reward of his labors. The blight had claimed part of his potato crop for the last three years. But, by diligence, good management, and frugal living, he not only provided for himself and the family, he had even succeeded in saving.

The year 1845 had seen his total potato crop fail miserably. The following summer showed promise, all that Dara could ask. The fields bloomed in profuse splendor and the wise nodded and commented, "Sure 'tis a bad year indeed, that isn't followed by a good one." But, by the middle of August the hopes and expectations of many were as blighted as their fields. Dara was downcast but not defeated, for he had planted more grain than potatoes on his twenty acres. He had doubled his production of pigs and poultry and by clever buying and selling would make do. He congratulated himself on his good judgment. He had but to look around him to see what he had been spared. The charred shell of O'Donoghue's rude shack was a stark reminder of how Agent Patrick Dunne dealt with the tenant farmers under his charge. Those who were unable to pay for what was rented to them were swiftly and mercilessly evicted, and, lest they return to the scant shelter from which they were cast, it was instantly put to the torch.

Dara felt the blood in his veins run cold as he recollected the treatment that was meeted out to Sean O'Donoghue, his wife, Maeve, and their four small children. Forced to seek shelter in a damp, dirty hollow in the side of a hill, the three youngest soon succumbed to cold and hunger and within two weeks Sean had lost his entire family.

The injustice of it gnawed at Dara's guts; a sweat covered his broad brow and spread over his handsome face. It was a cruel thing. The civilized world had long ago thrown off the bonds of the despot, yet, here in Ireland that tyrannical form of government still prevailed with ninety-five percent of the population at the mercy of the other five percent. The only defense the tenant farmer had was precarious at best, a good harvest. Dara set his mind to his labors; he had much to do. The long drills of potatoes stretching out before him were in need of hilling. He noted the fresh green shoots. "Thank God," he murmured, "for a good crop."

As he spaded the soil up around the young plants and tapped it firmly in place, his thoughts again turned to the girl of his heart. The lovely face of Finola O'Donnell captivated his imagination. As yet, Dara had not dared to approach her. 'Twas a splendid day, indeed, if he managed to catch her eye and steal a smile from her pretty lips. But he had come to the stage where this was not enough. "Aye," he said to himself, "it's time I made known my real feelings to pretty Finola."

* * * * *

The following morning, Finola was late. She hurried down the bóithrín thinking only of getting to the Manor as quickly as possible. Then she heard it. The air was filled with the sweet clear sound of Dara's whistling. The most glorious sound Finola had ever heard. And she thought, no linet, thrush, or even lark could sound so sweet.

He was waiting at the stile. As she approached, the whistling stopped. He stood a moment as if transfixed. Then, collecting himself, he strolled toward her, "Sure 'tis I'm the luckiest man in the County Clare. No mortal girl am I beholding on this beautiful spring morning." Then he poured forth his admiration and love in his favorite song and the velvet liquid of his tenor voice stilled all other sounds.

> "By the short cut to the Rosses
> A fairy girl I met.
> I was taken by her beauty
> As a fish is in a net.
> The ferns uncurled to look at her
> So very fair was she.
> With her hair as light as seaweed
> Upon the deep blue sea."

Before he could continue, Finola interrupted. "Oh, Dara O'Rourke, you're teasing." Then she tossed her proud head back. "But, I like it all the same." Having said that, she blushed. Perhaps she was too bold, she thought. Ach, what matter, she told herself, I'll speak my mind come what may.

"So the fair creature likes the teasing but says nothing at all, at all, about the one doing the teasing. Isn't there a wee soft spot in your heart, pretty Finola, for Dara O'Rourke,, then?" Dara feigned a grieved expression as he awaited her answer.

"Maybe…" Finola shrugged her shoulder but didn't look at him.

"Then a poor boy can be hoping?" He would play along and his voice grew more excited. "Sure, a maybe will keep me going for a year and a day."

Before Finola knew it, Dara had stolen a kiss and was on his way. Blushing with the excitement of the bold act and the clever way he had cheated her of a wee peck, Finola hesitated a moment longer watching him stalk off in right royal mien. Then, as he disappeared behind a large clump of fuchsia bushes and his happy whistling burst again upon the still air, she lifted her long skirts revealing a pair of slim white ankles and tripped joyously across the meadow. It felt nice to be admired. And even the fact that he had cheated her of a kiss only added to the excitement, the thrill of the moment.

The sun was low in the heavens when Finola left the Manor that evening. She hurried to the stile where she promised herself a moment of quiet, a time to catch her breath and admire the evening sky.

A cuckoo called softly in the distance. Over the hills where she knew the great Atlantic swelled, then dashed against the jagged black rocks, Finola saw the sunlight streaked with pearly shafts fan out across the purple hills. The air was pungent - full of the scent of primrose and cowslip; its stillness shattered only by the chatter of crows seeking space in the beach tree.

"Ahhh…" She released a long sigh of weariness. Then, in whispered tones "Aw! Sure 'tis a vision of heaven I'm seeing." her words were spoken to the soft breezes tossing the flaming strands about her gentle face.

"Isn't that the truth," came the rich resonant voice of Dara O'Rourke. "For the vision I'm beholding is that of an angel." He came from behind the low stone wall where he had been awaiting her coming for the past half hour or more.

"Oh, Dara!" She turned her head quickly. "What on earth are you doing here? You startled me."

"Then 'tis right sorry I am, sweet Finola, for there's naught in the whole wide world I'd not do to spare you that."

She looked up at him as he towered above her. "Oh, forget your flowery words and sit awhile?" She would remind him that she was a plain-speaking young woman. She knew her own mind, knew what she wanted and no flattery or sweet-talk would deflect her from that which she had set her will and heart to accomplish.

"Sure, there's nothing I'd like better."

She moved over a space and Dara quickly climbed up beside her. For a moment, all was silent between them; she continued to contemplate the changing patterns in the western sky. Dara watched the play of the golden lights as they assaulted the brilliant hues in the silken waves cascading to Finola's slender waist.

Then, as the first dusky shadows crept across the damp grasses and over the willow trees near the trickling brook singing its way down the hillside, Dara leaned over and encircled that slender waist with his strong right arm.

"Finola m' darlin', I've been waiting a long time for this moment. You're the only girl I'll ever love an' I want you to know it."

"Dara-a-." He barely heard the whisper, but he felt the fire in his veins.

She looked up as he was about to speak again. Then raised a slender arm, placing her index finger against his mouth. His lips were soft and warm and moist to her touch. "You needn't say anything else, Dara; I know how you feel about me. But... " She hesitated "I... well... I've my plans, you know." She looked straight at him, a touch of arrogance in her tone.

"Plans! What kind of plans? Am I included?" he asked.

"Mmm... that depends." She spoke in an off hand manner.

Dara withdrew a little, showing concern. His dark eyes grew wider but she noted the twinkle still lingered.

"So, it depends... well now... An' could a man be knowing the reasons why it depends?" he fixed his gaze on her beautiful face.

"Yes, indeed." she said without hesitation.

Again his eyes widened. He was seeing a side of Finola O'Donnell he hadn't known existed. She was strong, he knew. The way she had taken over and handled the household after her mother's death was evidence enough, but that she had future plans, ambitions, that might not include him never occured to him.

"I've a mind to better myself. I'll not be satisfied with a life of toil and drugery such as my mother settled for. A life that robbed her early of her youth and brought her to an untimely grave. No, I mean, Dara O'Rourke, to be someone... to make something of myself."

"I see... ." Dara admired the spunk, but he wasn't too sure how all those high- flown words might materialize into something concrete. "And might I ask how you intend that all this should happen?" For a moment he thought he'd trapped her, for she hesitated, but it was only for a moment.

"Well, I've made up my mind to learn as much as I can while I'm at the Manor. I'm not going to be a scullary maid forever, you know." And he noted the look of pride. Then she continued, "Already I've learned how to make sweet breads and to cook several fancy dishes. Aye, Dara, but it's not to be a cook I'm aiming either but a lady's maid and then... well... who knows." She didn't intend to give all her secrets away even if the recipient was the tall, dark, handsome Dara O'Rourke.

Dara, though still taken aback by this revelation of Finola's ambitions, did not see that there was any real obstacle to their personal relationship. He was a man of ambition himself. He, too, intended to better his lot. Wasn't that the sole reason why he had delayed so long to make his feelings known to her. Sure... He became more aggressive. "Well, indeed, it's a fine thing entirely, Finola, that you've decided to do, and I, for one, would be the last to dissuade you. But you're not telling me, I hope, that these plans of yours are going to be keeping us from seeing each other?"

For the first time, Finola saw a cloud cross Dara's face. There was more than concern imaged in his dark smoldering eyes. As he awaited her reply, his heart knew a moment of trepidation. He, who feared no man, felt fainthearted, even timid, in the presence of this frail slip of a girl. He hung on her every word. Yes, Dara O'Rourke was concerned that she might not have time for him.

Finola knew she had the upper hand; she felt it, and it was a good feeling. For the first time in her life, she experienced the sensation of power. By being evasive, she could play for time. She needed time to put her own plans into operation. "Oh, I'm sure I can find time now and again to see you, Dara." Her tone was casual, her attitude noncommittal.

He grasped at the straw like a drowning man; at least, he hadn't been rejected. He could still hope. "Oh, Finola m' darlin', you've made me very happy. Sure, it warms a man's heart to know that he can steal a wee moment now and again to be with the sweetest most beautiful colleen in all Ireland."

She felt the warmth of his body, his nearness. She was, in spite of herself, flattered by his attention, for Dara O'Rourke was a man with whom any girl would be proud to associate.

As she didn't appear disturbed by his advances, he drew her closer. She looked into his face. A fine face, carved to perfection were his manly features. She felt her heart miss a beat. He bent his head and gently lowered his lips to her upturned mouth. Slowly, tenderly, but deliberately he moved and played with those trembling lips, demanding a response. For the first time, womanly instincts were aroused. Dormant embers fanned into flame, a warm glowing feeling quickly spread through her. She trembled. A little moan escaped; then, as he released her, she sighed, "Oh, Dara, Dara... you mustn't."

"Ah, sure a wee kiss never did anyone any harm." he assured her.

"That very well may be... but... ."

"Please, Finola, I've waited a long time for this blessed moment. I'll not harm you. Just let me hold you an instant longer."

Before she could object, Dara pressed his mouth to hers again, a long lingering kiss that sent shafts of fire through her delicate frame. Then, as suddenly, he released her and gazing with love-filled eyes into her beautiful face, he said, "Finola m' darlin' I love you... I love you so much."

Her heart fluttered. She was deeply affected by his outpourings, even troubled.

He saw the anguish in her emerald eyes. Like a mist stealing over fair Glencarrow Valley obscuring the beauty he loved so well, was the frown on Finola's pretty face. This, Dara couldn't endure. "Sure an' I don't want to hurt you, love? I was only telling... ."

"I know... I know, Dara. It's... well, you see, I can't allow... ."

"You mean your plans won't allow... Your plans don't include me, then?" Dara was agitated.

"I didn't say that, Dara."

"Well, what did you say?" His voice was sharp, but there was a concern in it too deep for her to ignore.

"Dara, perhaps this is not the time. I... I told you I've made up my mind to better myself. I have much to do. So much to learn. Yesterday, I had to clean and dust the library at the Manor. So many beautiful books. I mean to read them, all of them. Don't you understand? I must know. I just have to learn, so much, oh so much."

Dara didn't answer immediately. He was thinking. This is no ordinary young girl beside me. She's a lass with ambitions I can hardly fathom.

He felt a cloud, a heaviness descend on his spirits. What was a gassoon like himself, doing in such company? Could he ever make such a young woman completely happy? he asked himself.

But no sooner had these thoughts entered his head than his old self-confidence returned. Of course, he could provide for her in a suitable way. He would work hard. In time, he would, somehow, acquire more land, build a decent house, he would test the new Emancipation Bill. He, Dara O'Rourke, would achieve great things too, and with pretty Finola at his side... He became troubled. How long would he have to wait? He turned and faced Finola. She had grown into a beautiful woman in the past year. The limpid pools of aquamarine fringed by long silken brown eyelashes held him bound an instant. Then his glance lingered, in turn, on the slender straight nose, the sensitive nostrils, then the shapely full lips begging to be kissed. Oh Finola, Finola you're the most beautiful woman I've ever seen, his heart told him. What can I do, at all, to change her mind, he asked himself. But aloud: "So because pretty Finola O'Donnell wishes to become a lady, Dara O'Rourke must be content to wait... must bide his time... is that it? An' how long might that be, may I ask?"

"I don't know... a year... or... ."

"Say no more. I see your mind is set," and as Dara contemplated his beloved Finola, he had a vivid and sudden intuitive glance into her inner soul. Gazing at the thin flushed face of extraordinary beauty, he realized that, behind those gleaming pools of blue-green fire, there lay a fierce determination, an implacable will. And, for a split second, he again felt fear, not for himself this time but for her. His Celtic intuition and innate sensitivity alerted him to the mysterious, the other worldly forces that he divined were working, affecting the destiny of this young woman.

Was it possible that one so young could be so strong, so adamant... from whence came this determination? And Dara's emotions spun, whirled like the dust-filled eddies on a summer afternoon that suddenly and for seemingly no reason disturb the tranquil air, he was instantly filled with a wonderous new pride in her, but, strangely, it was coupled with uneasiness.

He studied her a moment as she sat looking off into the distant mists. A dreamer or a visionary? he asked himself. Here, beside him, he saw a half-starved girl, frail, needing protection. What foolish ideas filled her mind, what unrealistic, unattainable yearnings crowded her brain? Yet when she again turned to address him, he saw a face so determined, so resolute that he was forced to admit despite his inner feelings that if anyone could accomplish, could achieve the impossible, it surely would be Finola O'Donnell.

"You understand, don't you, Dara?" And the green eyes, deeply in earnest, searched his face.

Dara didn't answer. His mind was still occupied with his own thoughts, and the sense of fear still lingered gripping at his heart. He just could not shake off the feeling that her unfaltering strength and her fierce will-power might lead to her ruin. This strong will, this independent nature would surely be her undoing. As she mounted the ladder of ambition there would, undoubtedly, be someone waiting to break her. Someone who wished to prove himself her superior. And, for a poor girl of her class, there would be no mercy. She would be crushed, mercilessly crushed. And, Dara knew that would be the final undoing of Finola. He considered her his girl. To see her brave spirit broken would be devastating. He couldn't allow that to happen. What he might do to prevent it, he didn't know. Not just then.

Continuing to gaze at her, he contemplated again the stark contrast between her superior will-power and her frail physique. How frail and undernourished! His heart ached, for although she held her head high, it was upon a very slender neck.

The bones of her shoulders were clearly outlined beneath the light summer bodice. Yet, despite the seeming fragility of the obviously deprived body, she had a beauty that challenged those deficiencies. Her skin was white as the driven snow. Her eyes, unlike any Dara had ever seen, were sparkling orbs of emerald brilliance. And Autumn's richness could not rival the vivid tints in her flaming hair. No one could look at Finola O'Donnell and not see the promise of a rare beauty, a bud which would one day burst forth into a perfect rose.

"Oh, Finola... Finola... m' darlin' Finola." Then he noticed she was shivering. It was getting late. "You'll catch your death of cold, a stoirín óg mo croí. Come, I'd best be taking you home."

It seemed Dara's only weakness, if weakness it could be called, was his love for Finola O'Donnell. At sight of that pretty maid, he was a different man. His mind in a whirl, he was easily aroused, and his friends soon learned to avoid any controversial topics. This fact Big Rory O'Connor learned the hard way.

Dara had joined a group of his friends, young men from all over the valley, on their way to a crossroad's dance. It had been a glorious day, and the golden rays of the waning sun promised several long hours of an even more glorious evening. Dara, as usual, was in a jovial mood. All dressed up in his Sunday best: black woolen breeches and white shirt, the sleeves of which were neatly rolled back above the elbows, his black boots sparkled almost as brightly as the twinkle in his sultry eyes.

"Sure 'tis a fine evening, lads. One to bring the colleens flocking, I'm thinking."

"Aye, flockin' about you, no doubt," answered Big Rory, for he too had set his hat for Finola.

Dara instantly jumped onto a tree stump. Then, with arms akimbo and legs spread wide apart, he responded with his customary élan. "Well, m' boys, we all can't be tall, dark, and handsome, ye know."

There was applause from his friends, but Rory responded with a saturnine, "An' a womanizer."

Dara turned on the speaker. "What's that? What did you say?"

"Oh don't deny it. Sure, didn't I see you with me own two eyes. Aye, a rollin' an' a tumblin' with that Finola O'Donnell in the ditch not a week ago."

Before Dara, himself, knew what had happened, he had struck out at Rory sending him sprawling in the dust.

"Now... now... that's enough o' that." Colin Flanaghan tried to intervene, but Dara's dander was up. No one was going to drag Finola's name in the mud and get away with it. He swung right and left and delivered two resounding blows to Rory's jaw as he regained his feet. This time he remained where he had fallen.

Dara brushed the dust off his clothes with the back of his hands and issued a final warning, "If I ever again so much as hear you mention Finola O'Donnell's name, I'll break your bloody neck, Rory O'Connor."

Among the men the feeling was that Dara had sufficient provocation for his action. So discussion of the incident was dropped with Seamus Hickey's remark, "It isn't the size of the dog that counts in a fight, it's the size of the fight in the dog."

* * * * *

Finola O'Donnell sat on the stile overlooking the meadow behind Glencarrow Manor to catch her breath, as she so often did. She had run all the way from her home in the hills; those hills rising out of the undulating terrain to dominate the village of Glencarrow. She was out of breath and must rest awhile, but she mustn't be late. Patrick Dunne, that oaf of a man who oversaw the Manor and all within for the absent Lord Sutherland, would be furious. Finola could not afford to make him furious. It might mean her position. There were two mouths to feed at home and having this post was a Godsend. The little she earned, together with the left over scraps from the dinner table at the 'Big House,' meant the difference between life and death for her sick father and hungry brother.

* * * *

It was late summer in the year 1846. Ireland, ever beautiful, a gracious lady decked in shimmering shades of green, was dying. Slowly, as a consumptive in the last stages of that dread disease, the strength and vitality of the once smiling land was wasting away. The tenant farmers, called 'peasants' by their English overlords, were not of that class; many, in fact, were descended from the noble families that once ruled the land. Now, suffering greatly from the failure of the potato crops over a period of several years, entire families were lost. Others, like Finola's, had seen weaker members succumb to 'the fever' while those who remained were frantically clinging to life by a mere thread.

For generations, the vast majority of Ireland's subjugated people had come to rely on the potato as their staple food. Potatoes yield more per acre than any other crop. Consequently, the tenant farmers were relatively well fed. With a pot of potatoes, some fish, and a little milk, they needed nothing else. Ireland always produced an abundance of food: rich crops of grain, lavish supplies of milk products, meat, and poultry. Yet, for generations, the people had very little variety in their diet. Most of the income from the produce was handed over to the landlords or their agents to satisfy exorbitant rents for meager shelter and for the use of the land that was once their own.

Rumors had reached Glencarrow that were even more devastating than the tales of the numerous deaths and the mass graves. At every port in Ireland, English soldiers with drawn muskets supervised the loading of thousands of bushels of grain, hundreds of pounds of Ireland's best butters and cheeses, and countless sides of beef and bacon. These foods were shipped to the overfed in England, while Irish men, women, and little children starved. They were seen dropping like diseased animals by the side of the road. The exact number that had perished during the past two years would never be known. Whole villages were wiped out, and the homes left deserted were quickly pulled down to give place to the sheep which could survive better on the lush grasslands.

So it came about that Ireland began to export more than food at this time. Those who had the strength to survive the hunger and who had escaped 'the fever' were fleeing to whatever fate awaited them in England or America.

The thought of leaving had often entered Dara's mind, but his mother had not been well during the winter months of 1845 - 1846. He would not, could never, abandon her or his sister even if for him, it meant a slow death by starvation. And, besides, there was Finola… He knew what her answer would be. Still, he hoped she might change her mind. So he hung on. Hoping, waiting, waiting... .

Chapter 3

"We should believe only in deeds; words go for nothing everywhere."
- Rojas.

In late October of 1846 the weather became unseasonably cold and was the most severe in living memory, for although the prevailing wind in Ireland comes from the West, that year it came from the North-East blowing across Russia; it held the entire continent of Europe in an icy grip. Bitterly cold gales, howling snow storms, hail, sleet and torential rain made the roads impassible. Transportation came to a standstill.

Reports of numerous evictions not only in and about Glencarrow but in other areas of the country had been the central topic of conversation around the turf fires for the past several months. But by mid-winter rumors of typhus, 'the fever', soon took over the discussions. This was not a matter of another poor family being thrown out of their home; this was personal. No one was safe. The fever did not discriminate; everyone rich and poor, weak or strong was susceptible to the ravages of this dreaded disease. Then added to this hysteria which was gripping the community, the distressing stories of those dying of starvation reached the valley.

From the town of Skibbereen in West Cork, the following accounts written by a Mr. Cummins to the Duke of Wellington, himself an Irishman, were recounted.

Upon arriving in the town, Mr. Cummins noticing that the place seemed deserted went to find out the reason. 'I entered some of the hovels... the scenes which presented themselves were such as no tongue or pen can convey the slightest idea of. In the first, six famished and ghastly skeletons, to all appearances dead, were huddled in a corner on some filthy straw, their sole covering was a ragged horsecloth, their wretched legs hanging about, naked above the knees. I approached with horror, and found by a low moaning they were alive - they were in fever, four children, a woman and what had once been a man.

In another case, decency would forbid what follows, but it must be told. My clothes were nearly torn off in my endeavor to escape from the throng of pestilence around, when my neckcloth was seized from behind by a grip which compelled me to turn, I found myself grasped by a woman with an infant just born in her arms and the remains of a filthy sack across her loins - the sole covering of herself and baby. The same morning the police opened a house on the adjoining lands, which was observed shut for many days, and two frozen corpses were found, lying upon the mud floor, half devoured by rats.'

Fired by such reports and the fact that an eviction had occured the evening before in a remote corner of the valley the young men of Glencarrow gathered at the crossroads; gaunt haggard for the most part, they no longer walked with light steady steps but shuffled as old men. Big Rory O'Connor was there and Colin Flanaghan. Seamus Hickey stood beside Dara, their faces grim, their mouths set; they listened a long time in silence to the speaker.

Sure, he's out of his mind, thought Big Rory. Finally, he could stand it no longer. "Arrah, it can't be that bad! God Almighty! Sure no Christian would... ."

"Is it soft you're gettin' Big Rory? It wouldn't be the first time one of them blackguards thought more of their animals than a poor Irish family." It was Seamus who spoke and as he spat the venom from his mouth, his voice was hard, bitter.

"'Tis time to act." Dara was thoughtful. His words spoken calmly. "Someone must be taught a lesson, boys." He looked at his companions, his gaze steady.

"Aye, you're right, man," answered Hickey.

The others nodded assent.

With the failing health of the national leader, Daniel O'Connell, whose policy had always been moral force versus revolt, a new political party, radical in nature, which called itself Young Ireland, arose. The Young Irelanders founded by the poet, Thomas Davis were extremists, advocating violence to attain their ends. Although Davis himself was a poet, philosopher, journalist and barrister from Cork, an educated man, nevertheless, he realized that force was the only way.

Almost all the local lads had joined this new movement. It was the thing to do and gave them a sense of purpose, a new determination to fight for their rights as human beings, to be once more a proud and free nation. The Penal Laws had done much to subjugate and repress not only physically but they had also left their marks psychologically - the once strong, intelligent, learned, nay distinguished men of letters, proficient in the arts, and the sciences, who were known as 'Saints and Scholars' by the rest of Europe, now considered themselves inferior, lesser men of no importance, backward and ignorant. What was the use in trying to improve oneself when there was nowhere to go, no way out of poverty, ignorance, and serfdon as established by English rule and enforced by English law.

To strengthen the new fire that had been enkindled in the minds and hearts of the youth, Davis, together with Charles Gavan Duffy and John Blake Dillon launched the newspaper, The *Nation*, a national paper which supported the Young Ireland Movement and propagated patriotism and a love of Irish culture - literature, art, and music in particular. In his many journeys throughout the country, he was constantly on the look-out for snatches of old traditional melodies, or verses and eagerly recorded them from wayside musicians or wandering Seanchai. One poet described Ireland:

> 'More dear in her sorrow, her gloom and her showers,
> Than the rest of the world in its sunniest hours.'

And in speaking to his followers, he would fire their spirits with words glowing, burning with the fervor and warmth of his own ardent heart. 'I have prayed that I might live to see the day when, amid the reverence of those, once her foes, her sons would-

> Like the leaves of the shamrock unites
> A partition of sects from one foot-stalk of right:
> Give each his full share of the earth and the sky,
> Nor fatten the slave where the serpent would die.

But not only by her sufferings does Ireland call upon you: her past history furnishes something to awake proud recollections. I speak not of that remote and mysterious time when men of Tyre traded to her well-known shores, and every art of peace found a home on her soil; and her armies, not unused to conquest traversed Britain and Gaul. Not yet of that time when her colleges offered a hospitable asylum to the learned and the learning of every land, and her missionaries bore knowledge and piety through savage Europe; nor of her gallant and romantic struggles against Dane, and Saxon, and Norman; still less of her hard wars, in which her interest was sacrificed to a too-devoted loyalty in many a successful, in many a disastrous battle. Not of these. I speak of sixty years ago. The memory is fresh, the example pure, the success inspiring. I speak of "The Lifetime of Ireland."'

The *Nation* quickly became an inspiration and produced a blossoming of such talent that later generations would look back with pride on its masters of literature, and by publishing the works and spreading knowledge of the gifted minds the country had somehow managed to produce: Denis Florence McCarthy, Samuel Ferguson, Michael Doheny, John Fisher Murray, Clarence Mangan, D'Arcy McGee and "Speranza" (Lady Wilde) would raise the morale and lift the hearts of a whole generation.

Determined to survive, Dara would not give up even if others were prepared to do so. In late September of 1846, he had joined the Young Irelanders and quickly rose in the ranks to become a local leader.

Unfortunately, the brave young Davis died in 1845. So great was his loss that the whole country wept. So well-loved was he and with such promise for a brilliant future that his passing was not soon forgotten. It was an irreparable blow to Ireland.Dara had met the great man the year before his untimely death and was smitten with his poise, his courage, and especially his great learning. Although a young man, himself, Davis was extraordinarily well-versed in many subjects and commanded the attention of his audience young and old. His ideas, his aspirations eagerly and quickly became those of Dara and his friends and were often repeated in those tragic days that followed his death.

'This country of ours is no sand-bank, thrown up by some recent caprice of earth. It is an ancient land, honoured in the archies of civilization, traceable into antiquity by its piety, its valour, and its sufferings. Every great European race has sent its stream to the river of Irish mind. Long wars, vast organizations, subtle codes, beacon chimes, leading virtues, and self-mighty men were here. If we live influenced by wind, and sun, and tree, and not by the passions and deeds of the past, we are a thriftless and hopeless people.'

Dara had lost a good part of his potato crop that Fall of '46, but with God's help, and the inspiration of the great Thomas Davis, he'd pull through to spring. Naturally optimistic he believed that plenty would surely follow scarcity. But if worse came to worst, he would be prepared to fight for what was rightfully his. No food would leave Glencarrow while the people of the valley were hungry.

November's skies had not been friendly. A biting wind with the breath of frost caused the hill people to stay closer to the peat fire. The view from Carrow Mór was more expansive at that time. Even the Manor could be seen at the other end of the valley, for the last of Autumn's colorful canopies had been displaced. And, in their stead, gaunt and knarled branches wove a filigree through which the grey-blue countryside appeared. The only adornment was clusters of shriveled crab-apples bobbing to the tempo of irratic gusts. In the distance the grove of oak and elm stoutly refused to be disturbed.

As stories continued to trickle into the Glencarrow valley, Dara became more incensed. He heard that two troops of Dragoons had galloped through the town of Longford to repel a group of 300 starving men. 'The British government is not prepared to supply food but very eager to call out the army!' Dara scoffed when he heard the details. Unarmed, weak from hunger, the men of Longford had gone in orderly fashion to the home of Lord Crofton to protest the huge shipments of food from the area. Instead of meeting with his lordship, they were confronted by British soldiers and driven mercilessly to their homes.

In Mayo, a large but orderly body of people marched to Westport House to see Lord Sligo and when he came out to meet them they knelt in the dirt before him pleading.

Having received assurance of help, they betook themselves peacefully to their homes, but nothing was done to alleviate their sufferings. Yet, for all the indifference and callous disregard by the English authorities, protests were few and violence rare in the stricken country. In general, despair prevailed. The proud and noble Gael had sunk to his lowest.

But as the phoenix rises from its own ashes, so from the dying embers of Ireland's starving masses strong spirits arose; Spirits who would not be broken, who refused to be vanquished. Dara O'Rourke was one of these. Finola was another.

Old Sean was usually pottering about the yard as she went by of an evening. In warmer weather he sat on a low form near the door and pulled on his clay pipe. As soon as he saw Finola, he would remove the pipe from between his broken black teeth and, while still holding the bowl in the hollow of his palm, he'd raise his right hand to salute her.

"Dia guit, Nola," the friendly Gaelic words never failed to greet Finola as she hurried home. Of the foreign phrases, he knew a few, but was loath to twist his mouth to give them voice. A wisend little man in his late sixties, he lived all his life in the same place and had brought his wife, Briget, there forty odd years before.

Strange, thought Finola. "I wonder... " Then retracting her steps she decided to take a look. Could the old couple be sick? She approached the door. It was closed. She knocked but got no answer. Lifting the latch, she pushed hard. The heavy door creaked on rusty hinges. The interior was dark but as her eyes grew accustomed, she became aware of the huddled forms.

"Aw!" Finola put her fingers to her lips and took a step back.

There on the straw near the still smoldering turf fire lay the pair, fully dressed, wrapped in each others arms.

Instinctively, Finola knew they were not asleep, yet, she called softly to them.

"Sean, are you awake? Briget are you all right?" Receiving no answer, she stepped closer as if to confirm her initial instincts. Then making the sign of the cross, she withdrew closing the door behind her.

Instead of going home, she retraced her steps towards the village. Tired though she was, she could not rest until Fr. Quinn had been informed.

"Wisha, they're better off, child. God rest their souls." The priest tried to comfort her. "Thank you for coming back all the way to tell me, Finola. Now take care of yourself, child." He opened the door and bade her, goodnight.

Once again she climbed the hill that led to her home. By now it was almost midnight. Before entering the house, she glanced back across the valley.

Leaping flames lit up the night sky and huge columns of black smoke obliterated the half-moon. Finola stood looking at the spectacle. Her heart-beat quickened. So that's where the men had gone, she thought. Dara had told her he had some business to take care of and would not see her that evening but that was all she could get out of him. Now, she realized he was out there leading a group in a very dangerous business, indeed.

It had to be Lord Killary's home. What a shame, she thought. So much destruction and yet, for all that, she couldn't really blame the men. Lord Killary had asked for it. Three evictions in as many days... horrible rumors circulating, whole families dying by the wayside. No more tenant farmers on Killary land. "Sheep, only sheep, more profitable, less trouble," was his Lordship's arrogant retort when asked about the evictions. He had decided to turn his whole estate into a sheep farm and be rid of the wretched Irish 'peasantry' once and for all.

As Finola watched, a shiver of fear, an inexplicable dread akin to that experienced when first she set foot inside the 'Big House' set her heart pounding and a cold sweat covered her entire body. She felt limp, and drew her cloak closer to ward off the sudden chill. She knew she should not tarry. Her father and little Patrick would be none too pleased to be left to their own company in an empty cabin with a lifeless hearth. For a moment longer, she lingered... Then a shot... a second... and in quick succession, two more struck terror to the very core of her being. The blast shattered the black stillness that had descended with the heavy darkness of the Autumn night and completely shocked Finola's sensibilities: "Great God Almighty!" she cried, and her thoughts were only of Dara.

When finally, she entered the small, two-roomed thatched cottage, her father was seated on his favorite stool, legs apart, head resting in the heels of both callused hands, shoulders hunched, he was gazing into the lifeless sods with unseeing eyes. Without moving, he addressed her. "No need to have witnessed that fire, Nola. The authorities will be rounding up anyone and everyone for questioning; the less you know the better."

She didn't answer him as she caught sight of little Patrick huddled near the cold hearth, but set about rekindling the fire. Soon the meat and vegetables she had salvaged from the Manor were bubbling in the iron pot. A warm stew would afford her father and small brother, at least, one more night of peaceful sleep.

The morning was blacker than the previous night when Finola reached the stile;she wanted to be sure to see Dara before going on to the Manor. Anxiously she waited, alert to every stir, her heart pounding so loudly she had difficulty hearing any other sound. "Oh, Dara, I must see you, I must," she murmured.

After what seemed an eternity, her patience was rewarded. The silvery melodious whistling barely audible at first, alerted her to his coming. Her heart pounded even louder and she felt the blood rush to her neck, her face and the very roots of her hair. "Oh God! dear God, thank you... safe... alive." She murmured and jumped up, smoothed her flaming tresses on both sides of her pretty face and shaking out the creases in her long skirt, anxiously peered down the bóithrín awaiting the first sight of him.

As he turned the bend a little gasp escaped. Then she gathered up her skirt and ran to meet him.

"Tis you're the prettiest sight ever to gladden a man's heart." Dara greeted her, caught her about the waist and lifting her off her feet twirled her around.

"Put me down, put me down," she cried but her happiness was obvious. Once on her feet, she took Dara's face between her hands saying: "Let me look at you; all in one piece, are you?"

"Dara frowned, "Why do you ask?"

"Och, weren't you out with the lads last night, Dara O'Rourke? Do you think I don't know what it is your up to? Is it playing me for a fool, you are?"

"Shhhh... not so loud. Is it the whole county you'll be telling?"

"So, you don't deny it, then?"

"An' why should I? Isn't it proud I am to strike a blow for freedom, not to talk of the poor starving creatures evicted two nights ago. Killary got what he deserved."

"But you can't go on like this! Sooner or later the authorities will... ."

"Don't you trouble your pretty head, now. Dara O'Rourke can take care of himself. But I'm in dire need of a wee kiss this morning." Dara encircled the slender waist once more with his strong right arm and drew her to himself.

She trembled. There was a fierceness about his action, a new boldness; he hadn't dared embrace her in such bold fashion before.

"Tis you're the reckless one; what's with you, at all?" her voice was concerned.

Then remembering her own experience of the night before, she quickly told him of the O'Malleys.

"Starvation... Too proud to ask for a miserable spud. May God rest their souls." Dara's thoughts turned to his own mother. "The old ones won"t be able to resist. May God protect us all." Then realizing he held the girl of his dreams in his arms, he declared: "Oh, Finola, Finola m' darlin' I need your soft sweet kisses. It's been a long hard night, that I'll confess." Then reconsidering what he had said, he quickly hastened to add, "but I don't want you worryin', a grá. Dara O'Rourke won't take any foolish risks; he's got too much to lose." He looked for a moment into her luminous green eyes as the sun broke through the morning mist, and seeing how the pure light of her soul was mirrored in their limpid depths, his heart quickened and he seized upon her full moist lips and hungrily took possession of them.

Finola was so relieved to have him in her arms, to know he had escaped unscathed from his night's escapades that she temporarily let down her guard. Reaching up, she encircled his neck with her snow white arms, savoring the while the sweet warmth of his eager kisses.

Dara's passions quickly aroused, he thrust his tongue between her pearly teeth. Instantly, tingling sensations, feelings hitherto undrempt of, fired Finola's body. Her knees grew weak as she yielded to his ardor... It was utter bliss.

"Oh Dara... Dara," she whispered and pressed her body closer. She became aware of his strong masculinity. The warmth of his flesh suffused a radiant glow enveloping her straining, aching, womanly body... a sweet draught only lovers can taste.

Inflamed by her nearness and grown brash by her seeming willingness, Dara skillfully maneuvered his left hand till it rested on the firm roundness of her young breast. Gently, he kneaded and stroked sending tantalizing shafts of fire through her sensitive body. She clung to him and desire awakened so strongly that she thought she would die from the sheer ecstasy of it.

The familiar sounds of awakening day alerted the young lovers to the fact that soon their solitude would be disturbed. They must part ere their amorous dallying be witnessed. He stepped back the better to capture and retain the image. That image which would carry him through the coming day... the flashing emerald eyes, the slim delicately shaped nose, the soft expressive mouth. "Oh, Finola O'Donnell, you'll be the undoing of me, entirely. You're my life, my only love. My thoughts will be of you all day... An' mind you think only of me." he cautioned.

Finola laughed at his warning. "Indeed, Dara O'Rourke, I have other things to do with my time." She tilted her head in an offhand gesture. But there was a twinkle in her eye.

He pretended to be hurt by her seeming indifference. "Oh... so... there's someone else! Just let me get my hands on him. I'll tear him limb from limb."

"Dara!"

"Och, sure I'm not meanin' a word of it. I just love you to distraction an' I'll not have another set eyes on you, Finola m' darlin'."

"Sure, I know. Now will you be off with you."

She shooed him as she would the ducks in the barnyard, flapping her white apron, then turned and hurried off to her day's work.

Spring brought new hope to some parts of the country. The tenants on Lord Fitzwilliam's lands, however, some five miles east of Glencarrow, grew desperate. Those who hadn't been able to pay their half yearly installment, who were under a 'hanging gale', were the first to be evicted. No mitigating circumstances were considered. Neither the aged nor the very young, the sick or dying, were shown mercy. As many as fifteen families were driven from their rude hovels and turned out into the raw cold of early spring.

Word reached Dara and his friends. That same night the stables on the Fitzwilliam estates were put to the torch.

* * * *

Chapter 4

"Hunger is the most degrading of
adventures."
- Josue de Castro.

Despite the blight of the previous year and the scarcity of food, the farmers planted more potatoes than ever that spring of 1847. The weather had been exceptionally bad, with frost and snow that lasted even into April in some parts. But with the coming of June, there was a complete change. Warm balmy weather produced a bumper crop. The plants grew to enormous size and the foliage looked healthy and luxuriant. Up and down the valley there was an air of expectancy. People strode with a firmer step and their lightheartedness was obvious in their laughter and song.

"Sure God never closes a door but he opens a window." The words were those of Mick Cullen, a tenant farmer on the lands of Lord Sutherland, as he spoke to a neighbor, Brian Casey.

"Yes, Mick. Looks like we'll be havin' lashins and leavins come winter this year. Praise be to God." He had twelve mouths to feed not counting himself and the missus.

The bonfires were lit according to the ancient custom on St. John's Eve. Then both men and women grabbed faggots and burning sods from the fires and carried them around the edge of their fields to ward off the evil one from their crops. Everything looked good. Contentment rested on quiet if gaunt faces.

Even though a few cases of potato blight had been reported, the country seemed, at that time, to be comparatively free of the disease. Dara joined with the rest of the clachan in celebrating the obvious end of their extreme suffering.

Summer had settled into the valley. The scent of mint and thyme mixed with wild roses and woodbine. The hedges swelled with bright red berries. Poppies streaked the yellowing corn. And across the lonely marsh that stretched beyond the lower hills, the scarlet specks of kingfishers or bitterns showed stark against the dun sodden earth.

The weather during the early summer of '47 had been good. The crops grew lush and looked healthy in hundreds of small fields dotting the countryside around the mouth of the Shannon River. Dara exulted; he had a winner this time. A good harvest of grain, a bumper crop of potatoes, and fine fat sheep and pigs promised a heavy purse and, best of all he told himself, he now had the means to propose to Finola.

The dry hot weather at the beginning of July had been a great boon to the growth of all the crops but particularly to the potato. It promised a remarkable harvest. The feeling of euphoria was widespread. Towards the end of the month, however, an abrupt change occured. Even in the unpredictable climate of Ireland, this sudden change was unusual and brought, for a period of about three weeks, continuous damp gloomy weather which engulfed the entire country. The temperature dropped and a constant, steady, chilling drizzle accompanied at times by thick fog settled upon the land. Yet, despite the weather, the potato crop still looked very good at the end of the month. The *Freeman's Journal* reported that "The poor man's property, the potato crop, was never before so large and at the same time so abundant." In *The Times* of London similiar accounts were given, some announcing that from the four provinces of Ireland an early and productive harvest was everywhere expected.

Dara pulled his frieze coat about him as he strode through his potato field, the one on the brow of the hill behind the house. His heart was filled with pride and gratitude, "Twill be a grand crop, thanks be to God," his words half prayer, half congratulatory comment upon his own handiwork. He bent to examine the leaves and stalks of the plants at his feet. "Healthy, aye, fine an' healthy. God be praised." Then his thoughts turned to Finola. "It's asking her hand I'll be and that before the summer's out," he announced with finality to the straight long drills that spread out before his appraising eyes. He pondered the thought a moment as a complacent smile worked its way into a broad grin. And then, as if the reality had just dawned on him, Dara O'Rourke gave vent to an uproarious shout, scattering the crows chattering on the low hawthorn bushes and sending a wee grey rabbit scurrying to his burrow. Then, leaping for joy from drill to drill, he set off on the run for home.

Full of confidence, he announced the good news, "Mother mo croí, we're set for the coming year."

"Praise be to God," Ellen O'Rourke looked proudly at her fine strong son, her wistful blue-grey eyes searching his dark ones. Slowly and deliberately, she blessed herself, making the sign of the cross and, in a soft lilting voice, thanked her Maker again. "May God an' His Holy Mother be praised and glorified. Sure, 'tis great news entirely, you're bringing this day, my son." And the pride brightened her pale wan face.

Dara didn't move. He watched as she pressed a stray wisp of silver into the coil encircling her shapely head... Surely she had been a beauty. Now in her mid-forties, she was already old, worn with toil, hunger, and childbearing. Having lost her husband almost twelve years before and five children, she now depended entirely on her only surviving son, Dara. She moved to touch the strong line of his jaw, "'Tis good God has been to me to give me such a fine son."

Dara's heart welled up with a surge of emotion, "Ach, Mother, sure 'tis you, yourself, are the one to be thanked for all I am."

"Ach now, you've always been a good lad," she replied.

He smiled, happy with her compliment then added, "Mother, I've something I'd like to say... It's about Finola and me."

A warm smile lit up Ellen's gaunt face as she looked up into the handsome countenance of her tall son. "So . . o . . o . .you've set a date!" There was genuine joy and excitement in her voice. "Sure, 'tis real happy, ach, what am I sayin'? It's delighted I am entirely to be hearin' such news. Finola's a grand girl. She'll be makin' you a fine wife, Fergus O'Rourke." And she wiped the tears from the corner of her tired eyes.

"Mother, you're sure? I'm... I'm not asking too much? Una's a big girl now an'... an' you... ."

"Now will you whist, lad. O' course it won't be too much. I'll be moving my bedthings to the settle. 'Tis only looking for an excuse I've been this long while to get to sleep by the fire. My old bones need the heat, especially on the long cold winter nights. So, tell me, lad when's it to be?"

"Oh Mother, mo croí," and Dara threw his arms about the frail shoulders.

"There, there," she patted him on the back as if he were still her little boy. "Sure, 'tis only fitting that the old give place to the young. An' 'tis mighty proud I'll be o' my new daughter. Can't think of one I'd be more happy to have in my house than Finola O'Donnell." She paused to let Dara see by her expression that she really meant what she said. "Now, when will we be having a wedding?"

"Arrah, I don't know yet but... but I'd like to be getting engaged before Advent. By that time, I'd... well the crops would be sold an' I'd be able to have a bit put by... an'..."

"Ah, 'tis the fine celebration we'll be having, then."

"Mother, I don't want the word of it to be spread about. Not just yet. There's a fair time between now an' then an' I wouldn't want... well you know things can happen... an' people talk. An' besides, I haven't asked herself yet... ." Dara fumbled with a loose thread in his course frieze jacket.

"Whatever you say, son. Whatever you say," she interjected, coming to his aid and wishing to spare him embarrassment. "It won't be from me the neighbors will be hearing the good news. But I can't keep it to myself forever. 'Tis news like this we've got little enough of, God knows; sure, in these times 'tis small wonder there's anyone left alive to get married."

"Get married?" Una entered hearing her mother's last words. "Who's getting married?"

"I was just sayin' that it's a wonder, with the terrible times and troubles we've seen, there's anyone left to get married, lass." Then turning quickly Ellen gave her full attention to the stew pot bubbling over the peat fire. The matter was dropped but Una wasn't fooled.

Unable to restrain himself any longer, Dara pulled several stalks early the following morning and filling a crail he carried it on his shoulder to the house. There he emptied the lot on the earthen floor to the joy of his frail trembling mother.

Wiping the rheum of sleep from her puffy semi-transparent eyelids, with the end of her apron, the 'old' woman threw up her hands and cried: "May God in His Mercy be praised and blessed. He has not turned his face from his suffering people." She then went to the fireplace and started to caress the smoldering embers. "We'll have a good breakfast this morning, a mhic." Immediately, she bent down, picked up the potatoes and placed them carefully, reverently in the iron pot. She then took them outside; poured water from the rainbarrel over them loosening the light soil. Then disgarding the dirty water, she replenished the pot with fresh spring water and carried it to the hearth. Hanging the pot on the crail, she swung it over the bright turf flame which had meanwhile sprung to life.

With a little salt fish, the family enjoyed a plentiful meal for the first time in many months. The usual mug of milk was supplied by the one cow left on the farm. It was a glorious occasion, a joyous meal. God had indeed blessed his people.

But their joy and contentment didn't last long. Early afternoon brought a sudden change in the weather. The bright sunlit sky of morning had become dark and threatening. Soon streaks of lightening light up the darkness. The rain, in torrents, poured from the black clouds as if the floodgates of heaven had suddenly been opened to disgorge their pent-up waters without any consideration for the havoc they might cause. The earth shook with the terrible grating peals of the raging thunder and, almost instantly, the temperature dropped. It became cold in a relatively short period of time. All conversation in and around the houses stopped abruptly. People stared at each other, awe-stricken. Some crossed themselves, others too frightened to act just stood as if petrified.

In the O'Rourke cabin, Dara was the first to find his tongue.

It's here again. In God's Name! That's exactly what happened last year."

They fell on their knees beseeching God to have mercy. Dara and his sister, Una, bowed low, their heads in their hands listening as the Litany of the Blessed Virgin was recited by their trembling pale-faced mother. Then the prayer to which they had grown accustomed in the past few years was added. "Mother of God pity your poor children, save us from all harm but particularly the blight."

The storm did not last long, but the rain continued — a drizzle, dense and penetrating, it seemed, to the very bowels of the earth.

As if in answer to their prayers, the next morning dawned bright and fair. A dazzling day with the dew-drenched fields, each droplet glistening like so many jewels in the early sunshine.

Dara did not wait for Finola but went immediately to check his fields at the lower end of the valley. It was in these that he first caught sight of a minute whitish growth, resembling a fringe, surrounding the leaves on several potato plants. Since it was so small and not wide-spread, he still hoped for the best. What a glorious crop it now appeared! Surely, God in his infinite mercy would spare them this year, he mumbled to himself.

Faithfully, each day for several days, Dara went to inspect his fields. All seemed well and his heart swelled with pride for he felt he had done the right thing in sacrificing by selling his pigs during the spring to have more seed potatoes to plant. Some there were, he knew, who had eaten even their seed spuds. But not, he, Dara O'Rourke. He would show them how foolish they were. He pulled up a stalk. Then taking his spade, he dug. Big, round, and beautiful they looked. He bent to touch, then caress the blessed fruit of the earth. They were solid, firm, and, oh, so big. How many bushels would he gather? He tried to calculate. He'd have enough, more than enough for the family, and with the sale of what was over, he could put aside, some money for his wedding. Aye, he'd delay no longer; Finola would see the sense of it. He knew she didn't relish her position at the Manor. But she was a brave girl and did all she could for her family. 'Twas time he rescued her from that incessant drudgery.

So it was that Dara returned home that day happy, eager to see Finola and anticipating a bright future.

Then, on the last day of the month, another violent storm vent its fury on the land.

"'T'ill pass. Sure it's nothing - much the same as the storm around St. John's Day," was Dara's answer to the troubled expression on his mother's face.

But the rumors were coming. County Cork had the blight and no mistaking it. There was a hue and cry throughout the whole county. Starvation, for sure, would be theirs this coming year. Dara still hoped that the cruel fate of the people of Cork would not be his. Surely, the curse would not fall on his beautiful fields, would not strike his lovely valley.

It was about the middle of July when Dara, upon leaving the house early bent upon seeing Finola, stopped suddenly in his tracts. Over against the western sky a thick white cloud hung low to the ground. Like a great bank of swirling snow suspended by invisible hands, it appeared.

At a loss to know what on earth it could be, Dara dismissed it for the moment; he had to get to the stile before Finola. But as he hastened along the bóithrín, he became aware of the awful stillness. A hush had descended on the whole countryside. Where were the birds? The air seemed heavy, dense.

Dara haulted again. The cloud began to move, slowly at first, in a great mass. Then, as it gradually spread over the lower end of the valley, obliterating all in its path, he became aware of a horrid stench. He hastily crossed himself. "God Almighty!" his words were scarcely audible.

Soon the whole valley was engulfed in a whitish vapour, and it looked as if a fine drizzle of tiny white particles was gently falling from the cloud. The stench was now stronger and more pervasive - decay, rot, the noxious odor of corruption and death. Then as the cloud neared the field close by it formed wraithlike vapors which floated in aimless wanderings over the drills of drooping stalks, filling the low soggy hollows, then rising in swirling columns that clung to the tangled grasses and overgrown shurbs at the edges of the field. A weak, sickly sun pierced, with silver light, the curling ghostly shapes from time to time adding an etherial, other-worldly diminsion to the scene.

Dara, instinctively, covered his nose and mouth with his hand. For several minutes he was unable to move. Fear and anguish gripped at his heart. The blood drained from his handsome face. Then a loud wailing, as if the Banshee had suddenly found her voice, startled the still air, arousing Dara. The valley was now completely shrouded in a thick mantle of fog; no sun shone through the dense clammy drizzle. It was almost dark, yet it was only noonday.

Dara sprang to action. He leaped ahead and ran in the direction of his distant fields stumbling several times. For, although he knew the way blindfolded, his legs seemed to deny him their usual strength. Suddenly, he felt weak, sick.

Arriving, at what only a few days before was a beautiful healthy field of potatoes, he was aghast to find that all the plants had grown limp and had become discolored. Some were black and had already withered, were obviously dead.

But, ever optimistic, he reasoned that the distruction of the leaf didn't necessarily mean that the tubers were lost. He had tried cutting off the infected stems the year before and, in some instances, had harvested a crop of dwarfed potatoes the size of walnuts. But they were food and he had been able to feed them to the pigs.

He sprang to action once more. Taking his fork he plunged it into the slimy soil. As he hit the tubers, a putrid gush of sticky liquid spued out in all directions. He ran from one drill to another at times snatching at the limp stalks with his bare hands but continually plunging his fork in desperation to right and left into the slimy drills.

Surely, there were some good ones left. But each time he dug, he was confronted with the same result. Destroyed! All destroyed! And in a single night!

He stood motionless, a sharp pain in his heart, as he studied the long straight furrows — his pride and joy only a few days before. Then his stare grew cloudy, his eyes darkened. In utter anguish and despair like a cornered animal, his vanquished wail reverberated with a flat hollow sound, closing in on him - heavy, unfeeling.

How long he remained thus, he didn't know, but at length, as if awakening from some terrible nightmare, he jerked himself back to reality. Averting his eyes from the earth and all its loathsome ugliness, he looked up into the murky skies allowing the soft drizzle to mix with the moisture on his clammy cheeks and cried out: "Almighty God! Father in heaven, how could you allow this thing to happen?" This time the sound of his agonized voice rang through the silent valley and, as from a great scornful giant, his words came back, floating back to mock him.

'God — Father — Father — heaven — happen — happen —'

His head throbbed, his heart ached. He bent over and heaved his scant breakfast unto the stricken stalks. In the terrible silence that surrounded him, only his palpitating heart thumped in rapid pounding beats. Like a great war drum it tormented his tortured brain. Then, as if unable to endure more, he broke lose from the invisible bonds that bound him to the slimy earth and, springing like a wild thing, he brought all the force and power of his young body down upon the rotten plants, crushing, stomping out the last remnant of life. The stinking juices oozed slowly onto the damp earth as Dara continued until the putrid tubers were ground into slime and the stench about to asphyxiate him. In paroxysms of rage and anger, he beat the air with splaying arms, howling the while as a raving she-wolf who had lost her cub.

Finally, in desperation and utterly dejected, Dara slowly sank to his knees. Low, pressed to the stinking earth, in the murk and mire, he gave vent to the excruciating pain and anguish that knawed at his body and soul. Into his upturned hands, his livid face streaked with the slime of the putrid soil and wet with the cold tears of heaven, Dara O'Rourke shed the burning tears of his own bleeding heart. Great sobs wracked his powerful frame. Writhing in agony, he beat his dripping locks into the rotten earth. "'Twere better to die . . ," he uttered as he collapsed on the vile and rank soil.

Dara lay prostrate in the slime, in a stupor, semi-conscious for several hours. Eventually, dragging his wracked limp body to an upright position, he pushed the clinging matted hair from his stained forehead and once more looking heavenward, uttered in broken whispers a contrite prayer. "Merciful God, forgive my arrogance — my pride — my lack of faith. Father in heaven, have pity on me. Help me accept this cross. Show me the way."

Chapter 5

"He who is firm and resolute in will moulds the world to himself."

- Goethe.

Finola had been working at the Manor for almost a year. Responsible, dependable, and efficient, she had proved her worth.

"Can't, for the life of me, tell how I ever got on without you, Finola," commented Mrs. Mulvaney. "You're sure a blessing, child."

Finola smiled as she remembered the words spoken only a few days before when Mr. Dunne asked why her services were still necessary. The housekeeper was adament. She would leave that very day she told Dunne if he decided to let the girl go.

The compliment was, for now, her assurance that she would have a job despite the Agent's objections. Little by little, she was making progress. Her plans were, slowly but surely, materializing. She would make good. She would be someone. She could now turn her hand to anything she was asked to do.

"No doubt you'll be the one in charge, one o' these days, Finola." Mrs. Mulvaney smiled as she spoke.

"Oh no, Mrs. Mulvaney. I'm not looking to be taking your position here. But I would like to be bettering myself. Maybe I'll go to Dublin next year." She shrugged her shoulders. She wasn't sure, yet, what her next move would be.

Although Finola did not like working at the Manor for many reasons, chief among them being that it was the home of an Englishman and he a Protestant, she, nevertheless, felt it was her duty to do so. It was the means of keeping herself and little Patrick alive. Her father, by this time, was beyond her help.

In a year or so, she figured, she would be able to leave home altogether and find better employment perhaps, in one of the big cities. Her present position was a mere temporary one, of that she felt certain. It would not be her lifetime career as was the case with Mrs. Mulvaney.

Apart from the fact that Mr. Dunne, the overseer, or agent, was a gruff, harsh man, even cruel at times, Finola had no real fears. She was getting three square meals, upon the insistance of the good housekeeper, and she rarely left for home without something for her small brother, at least.

She made sure to keep a safe distance between herself and Mr. Dunne, for sad experiences had taught her that he was not beyond lashing out at her verbally and physically when the humor was on him.

The old rambling house itself ceased to hold the sinister, eerie fears of the early days. Upon entering the large entrance hall on her daily rounds of dusting and polishing, she never tired of admiring the shiny wooden floor with its sheepskin rugs spread, at intervals, upon its smooth surface. Then her eyes invariably rested on the oak panelled walls and followed them to the great staircase. The banisters were delicately carved from mahogany. She noticed how the colored glass panels in the front door cast rainbow shafts on the white rugs. She moved toward the heavy oak hallstand and her hand fondled the pegs as she wiped away the invisible dust. Then she glided to the center of the hall, spread her arms wide and twirled in a burst of exuberance.

"One day, yes, one day, I'll own a home like this. I'll have servants of my own. And I'll dress in the finest silks. There'll be a carriage and four to drive me wherever I wish. Oh, yes!... "

Finola heard a door slam. She paused... listened. Then with head held high on her slim shoulders, she mounted the stairs holding her skirt up with the tips of her fingers as she imagined a fine lady would do. She reached the landing where the stairway branched off into two sections. Standing in the center, she turned around and looked back. She had a good view of the expansive hallway below.

"I say, Samuel, fetch me my shawl. It's rather cool this evening." Finola's imagination was running away with her. Her clear voice rang through the empty hall and drifted, it seemed, back to her. There was a squeek below, as from an opening door.

"Oh Lord! Has someone heard me?" she mumbled under her breath.

She didn't wait. But hurrying on up the stairs she went about her duties.

Since coming to work at the Manor, she had learned much. Sensitive as well as perceptive, she had been outraged by the discrepancies that so blatently existed between those who claimed ownership of the land - the English, and those to whom it rightfully belonged - the Irish who now merely worked it. She was continually troubled by the question, why should the foreigner have so much while the native people had so little? These strangers, these Sasanach, lived in luxury, in splendor, completely removed from the cruel realities of the everyday existance of those living in such close proximity to them. They squandered, wasted, and destroyed and laughed at their wanton excesses.

Finola couldn't help comparing the crude living conditions of her own home with the expansive well-aired rooms of the Manor. She thought of the mud floor, uneven and forever dusty; the small cramped living quarters where little light penetrated the one-paned windows, and the discolored walls desperately needing a new coat of limewash. And as she thought of the drab, harsh, and impoverished surroundings in which she and her family were forced to live, her determination to somehow, escape them, to improve her lot in life, became all the more steadfast.

She clenched her hands and gritted her teeth. What did these English care about the poor long-suffering Irish who worked from dawn to dusk to eke out an existance under inhuman and intolerable conditions, and that in their own land, so that the overlord, the usurper, the invader might grow fat, lazy, and indolent. Insufferably arrogant, even cruel and inhuman, Finola knew what they were capable of. And she shivered as she remembered the risk Dara had taken not too long ago.

The entire valley was becoming a wasteland. There was nothing left for the inhabitants but to further cut back on their scant food intake and hope for some assistance from the government. Most, by now, were down to one miserable meal a day.

The Parish priest, Father Pat Quinn, old and infirm in body but alert and keen of mind called for a meeting of the able bodied in the immediate vicinity, despite the new Treason Act. Her Majesty's government had just enacted this law making it an offense punishable by death or life imprisonment for anyone to hold meetings under any circumstances whatsoever, unless it were for public worship once a week and the conducting of approved schools.

But Father Quinn was a rebel at heart, which trait had from his earliest years as a priest, placed him at loggerheads not only with many of his colleagues but, also, with his bishop. Hence 'his banishment' to the ends of the earth - Glencarrow - although he had shown signs of great promise as a young man. But his ambitions lay not in the glory of this world, nor might one conclude that his thoughts were unduly on the next, for in truth, he had little time to think of himself at all. Those who knew him best described him as a humble, down-to-earth man, a man of the people, who knew their ways and was one of them. His old soutane, faded, green-streaked, glossy and badly frayed at the cuffs, elbows and collar wore the telltale spots of candle drippings removed by scraping with a knife. Those who knew him not at all, nor cared to bear him company - the Reverend Harry Wilson, Vicar of St. Andrew's Anglican Church is the nearby town of Ennis, among them - considered him uncouth. But unlike the new curate, Father Tom Grogan, in that same town, who was a product of the recently founded Maynooth College, set up by Her Gracious Majesty to stop the flow of young men to the Continent for eccliastical studies, Father Quinn's services were rarely if ever rewarded with money or kind. Whereas the former felt himself duty-bound to accept the half-crown proffered reluctantly by the oldest son from a family of twelve for the funeral and burial of his father, the late Mr. Fagan, Father Quinn was never known to have accepted even a penny from the poor.

Father Pat heard the details in due course. He made no comment, but mentally reflected upon the values and philosophies being taught in Maynooth. What would become of Ireland, of the Irish poor, he asked himself, if the next generation of priests considered only the value of money . Who would enter the lice-infested dens, the foul-smelling hovels to minister to their needs. For word had been noised abroad; the younger men kept a distance; they did not mingle; they did not agree with the ideas and ideals of the ignorant masses. Well so be it, as long as Father Pat had breath, he would listen and learn from even the humblest of his parishioners. The meeting was held, but few came because they were unable - sickness and death were guests in every hovel, starvation had claimed half the parish. He might well have been the pitiful figure described by Yeats in later years:

> 'The old priest Peter Gillegan
> Was weary night and day;
> For half his flock were in their beds,
> Or under green sods lay.
>
> Once, while he nodded in his chair,
> At the moth-hour of eve,
> Another poor soul sent for him,
> And he began to grieve.
>
> 'I have no rest, nor joy, nor peace,
> For people die and die;
> And after cried he, 'God forgive!
> My body spake, not I!'

At the meeting the decision was made that Fr. Quinn would appeal to the representatives of the absentee landlords on behalf of their tenants. No rent should be collected at this time and the families who still possessed a cow, a pig or any other animal should be allowed to keep them until such time as things returned to normal.

It was insane, the priest had argued, to take the last bite from the mouths of the poor and send it off to feed the well-fed in England.

And Mr. Matt Foley's retort backed up the good priest's statement when he said: "How can any Christian, or Godfearing person allow such a thing to happen?" Foley, the mill owner, was one of the few Catholic propriators in the area. His respectable position and holdings having been inherited from his Protestant grandfather.

About this time the public works project, which had been set up to give some relief, came to a sudden and unexpected halt. What were the starving supposed to do? Surely, the English government and its henchmen didn't intend that the hardworking laborers on the rich lands of Ireland should die. There was so much food being shipped out daily, why not allow it to remain in the country.

Fr. Pat spoke up. "Before you leave, men, I would like to show you an article I received in the mail yesterday. It's enough to make my blood boil." He unfolded a newspaper clipping and slowly read aloud the offending paragraph.

'A valuable cargo, borne by the steamer Ajax which sailed from Cork, consisted of: 1514 firkins of butter, 102 casks of pork, 144 hogshead of whiskey, 844 sacks of oats, 247 sacks of wheat, 106 bales of bacon, 13 bales of feathers, 3 casks of magnesia, 8 sacks of lard, 296 boxes of eggs, 30 calves, and 69 miscellaneous packages.'

"And besides this, my good men, you might like to hear what Mr. Jonathan Swift has proposed be done to solve a similar situation in his time."

Here, Father Pat read aloud from A Modest Proposal: 'I have been assured... that a young healthy child well nursed is at a year old a most delicious, nourising and wholesome food, whether stewed, roasted, baked, or boiled, and I make no doubt that it will equally serve in a fricassee, or a ragout . . .

...I grant this food will be somewhat dear, and therefore very proper for landlords, who, as they have already devoured most of the parents, seem to have the best title to the children'

"So there you have it, now. I need say no more," with that the old man sought the comments of his guests.

Foley again spoke "It's beyond belief. It's appalling! 'Twas only this morning that Mrs. Dwyer told me her oldest girl child hadn't long to live. Starvation slowly but surely is taking the whole family. There won't be one of them alive by Christmas."

"It's sacrilegious. All this good food leaving the country an' our own people dying of starvation." Fr. Pat was outraged. "There's only one thing for it, the annual six million pounds in taxes and rental fees as well as the tax grants to the State Church must cease at once. Which of you can support these enormous taxes at this time?" Fr. Pat was furious. He would sever the ties with England at the risk of his life if he could. "Sure 'twas only last week that I saw in that bloody *London Times*, accusations of improvidence hurled at our people. An' our rival brethern keep reminding us that the famine and all its devastating pestilence are a curse from Providence," he was referring to an encounter he had had with the Reverend Wilson.

Every day stories of the horrors suffered by the people of the small seaports in Cork, came to be told in Glencarrow. In a once prosperous home, a widow and her three children lay dead for a week before anyone was aware of their condition. When, finally, the doctor on his rounds came upon them, he discovered their poor swollen bodies half-eaten by rats. Those evicted from their crude shelters lasted only a few hours. Yet, despite this, the evictions and tumbling down of scant shelters was commonplace and was going on at a mad rate. The misfortunate families thus treated were often brutally beaten or even killed if they resisted. At times they were not even given notice or warning.

In this merciless fashion, without food or shelter, thousands died through exposure to the harsh weather. It was particularly cruel for the many little children who were sacrificed in this way.

Fr. Pat got small comfort when he approached the authorities the following morning.

"More's your shame, Father," said the burly, rosy-faced Mr. Simms, chief agent for the estates of Lord Killary. "You, who should be showing the example. You expect me to believe that you really mean what you say?"

"Of course I mean what I say. God in heaven, man, don't you see with your own two eyes the condition to which these people have been reduced?" By this time Fr. Pat was red in the face and perspiring profusely. Trying to impress his audience, comprising not only Mr. Simms but some official government representatives and the Protestant clergyman, the Reverend Wilson, from a neighboring town, he was quite beside himself when he realized he was having no positive effect whatsoever upon them. On the contrary, they seemed to become more fixed in their determination to thwart him every step to the way.

Eventually, Father Pat lost his temper. "Not even Cromwell's butchery compares with this. It's nothing but genecide. Don't you fellows stand there and tell me any different." Then slowly but deliberately he withdrew from his pocket a neatly folded sheet of newspaper. With trembling hands he opened it and began to read: 'They are going! They are going! The Irish are going with a vengence. Soon a Celt will be as rare in Ireland as a Red Indian on the shores of Manhattan. Law has ridden through Ireland: it has been taught with bayonets, and interpreted with ruin.

Townships leveled to the ground, straggling columns of exiles, workhouses multiplied, and still crowded, express the determination of the legislature to rescue Ireland from its slovenly old barbarism, and to plant there the institutions of this more civilized land.' The priest then threw the paper down on the table in front of him. "This is how the English government and the *London Times* views our desperation!

This, gentlemen, is the truth of the matter, then!" With that Father Pat took up his hat, slapped it on his head, and stomped out of the meeting.

* * *

After Fr. Quinn's run-in with the local authorities, he sat down and wrote a couple of seathing letters, one to the representative of Her Majesty's Government in Dublin and the other to Lord Sutherland, himself, in Hartfordshire, England. From the former he received no reply and from the latter, a brief note regretting that since his Lordship would be away on the Continent for several months, it would be better if all matters regarding the affairs of the estate be taken up with Mr. Patrick Dunne, his competent agent.

Fr. Quinn threw up his hands in despair. "My God! Is there no solution to be found for the neglected, forgotten Irish poor? And don't forget, Lord, there are millions of them, in fact, the whole population in one way or another is suffering under this foreign yolk." He put his head in his hands and wept. "I've failed them. What can I tell them? How can I face them? Nothing to offer. No hope, no prospects of relief, nothing."

While in this state of utter dejection, Fr. Quinn was suddenly aroused by a knock on his front door. He hastily wiped his eyes with his stained pocket handkerchief and called, "Come in, come in."

The housekeeper, Moll Folley, stuck her head around the door as she opened it. A fussy little woman, she was irritated to have to disturb his Reverence again. "The man gets no rest," was her constant response to the many callers and requests that came to the priest's house at all hours of the night or day.

"Beggin' yer pardon, Father," she began, "there's a man outside who says that he just now found the bodies of Mrs. O'Rourke and her daughter in a ditch yonder and them stone dead. Doesn't know how long they've been lying there." At that point she waited for Fr. Pat's reaction.

"Glory be to God! Not Mrs. Ellen O'Rourke and that darlin' girl of hers, surely?"

"The same. And that son of hers on the run. Not hide nor hair of him since the burning of Lord Killorgan's place last month. What's becomin' of the young a tall."

"Ah, sure, hasn't the man a price on his head. "'Tis Australia for him or maybe the jibbot if he's found. Now, out o' me way, woman, I've a job to do." And with that Fr. Pat left the house.

Things had gone from bad to worse. The evictions had increased. No clemency was given to those who could not afford to pay their rent. Hundreds of families were without food or shelter wandering the roads, dying in the ditches. In order to be rid of the shame of such vagabonds and refuse, several landlords came up with a brilliant scheme whereby all their problems would be solved. They called their idea The Emigration Plan. It was decided that all the old, the sick, and the very young should be transported to Canada and in exchange for their tiny plots of rented land, they were promised acres of free land in the New World.

Reluctantly, the people began to accept the treacherous solution to their problem. What was better - to die on the side of the road or clutch at a chance to find work and food in a foreign place? They had no alternative.

Thus began the flood of Irish emigrants from the fertile lands and the quiet homes of their ancestors to a strange, alien country ruled by the British Crown. Thousands died before they ever set foot on Canadian soil, while thousands more, sick and starving, died shortly after disembarking. Those few who did survive faced discrimination and hardship in cities like Toronto where there was a large population of English people. But, at home in Ireland, these facts were, as yet, unknown.

Finola had not seen Dara since mid-September when the estate of Lord Killorgan had been razed to the ground. He was immediately implicated and a price put on his head. As a Young Irelander, he had no alternative but to flee into the mountains with some of his friends. In brutal retaliation, the authorities evicted his mother and sister and burned their home.

It was a bitterly cold evening. The rain and the gusting wind tore at their wretched clothing and hampered their progress. They must find shelter before nightfall. But where? All were forbidden to offer comfort or protection to those who had been evicted. To stretch out a hand in pity or kindness meant certain eviction for that person or his/her family.

Finola heard the news as she neared her home the same evening. "Glory be to God! You're not making a mistake, now are you?" she asked her friend, Sive, who lived not too far from the O'Rourke home.

"How could I be mistaken, now. Didn't I see with my own eyes them murderen' devils set fire to the cabin," answered Sive indignantly.

"And where have Una and her mother gone, in God's name," Finola asked fantically.

"Not far, I'm thinkin'. But I don't rightly know where . . .' She lowered her voice, "if ye get me meaning." Here Sive pointed towards the distant hills.

Then as she turned to leave, she mumbled: "They're beyond in the ditch . . . go see for yerself." She pulled her cloak about her and walked away afraid lest some conniving neighbor wish to profit from her indiscretion.

Finola portioned out the food she had received from Mrs. Mulvaney into four small equal parts. When little

Patrick and her father were asleep, she crept out with the remaining food in the hope of finding the O'Rourkes. Sive knew Finola would try to help her friends, for it was not the first time that the young woman had laid the thought of her own safety aside to help the destitute.

About a quarter of mile up into the hills behind her home, Finola found Una and her sick mother shivering in a make-shift shelter by the side of the road.

"Mother o' God, child," the feeble voice was that of Mrs. O'Rourke. "Is it, . . . is it out of your mind, you are . . . coming out here after us? Don't you . . . know what they'll do to you when they find out?"

"Now, I'll not hear you talking like that. You and Una are coming home with me this very minute. But first eat this." She handed them a little bread and some milk.

"The blessings of God on you, child." Ellen took the milk but gave the bread to Una. "Here, you . . . eat it, a grá. It won't sit well on my stomach at all."

It was obvious to both Finola and Una that the older woman was, indeed, very ill.

"As soon as you finish, we'll be walking home."

"All right, all right, I won't fight you on it. I'm awful tired." Ellen began to cough and again started to shiver. "To tell the truth I'm not myself at all."

It took both young women a considerable effort to finally get Dara's mother to Finola's home. Una, too, was in poor health and Finola didn't know how long she would be able to hold on. She lit a fire and dried out their clothes, heated some milk and then, exhausted herself, fell asleep in front of the hearth.

The following morning, she told Patrick to stay in the house and not allow anyone inside while she was at work. He was to try to keep the fire going and help Una and her mother until she got home in the evening.

By the time Finola did get home, she found that Mrs. O'Rourke had died a few hours earlier and Una was fast following her - that was certain.

"They wouldn't have lasted the night had you not taken them in, Finola, so don't go blaming yourself now. You did all you could. Una isn't going to get better either, I'm thinking. It was a cruel thing, to send these two out into the cold. No way could they stand such treatment," her father tried to comfort her.

A few hours later, as Finola slept, her father, though weak and sick himself, removed the bodies and placed them in a protected place by the side of the road, not far from the house. What else could he do, he asked himself. He had to protect his home, his daughter. Could he allow the authorities to evict them also - merely for harboring two unfortunate starving women.

Thus it was that Mike Slattery found them the following day and hastened to inform 'his Reverence'.

"Go fetch Michael Folley and tell him I want the loan of his cart." Father Quinn ordered Mike.

"Yes, Father," and Mike tottered off to do the priest's bidding.

Father Quinn sent word to Finola in the meantime knowing she would want to attend the burials. Father Pat marvelled at her strength and courage and prayed silently that she would escape the ravages that surrounded her. Ireland needed women of her caliber, spirit, and determination if the country were ever to overcome the destructive forces now assaulting her.

Finola feared for Dara's survival in the boglands and bleak mountainous areas. But she feared, especially, for his safety. Sooner or later the agents of the English Crown would hunt him down. Those so-called custodians of the law who, in reality were cut-throats and hired assassins would stop at nothing to capture him. If he were not shot on sight, he would, surely, be done to death in some cruel way.

But much as she fretted about Dara, Finola had other worries more immediate and pressing. Her father was sick, very sick. Little Patrick was growing more frail despite the food she managed to carry home for him. He needed three good meals a day, not the left-overs from the Manor kitchen.

It had been a bitterly cold day. As the shadows lenghtened and the drip, drip, drip of winter's rain gradually gave way to a howy frost, her small brother came to fetch her.

"Dad's real sick. Fr. Quinn's beyond now. I ran for him when Dad's cough got terrible bad. The doctor was out." He panted as they raced across the field behind the Manor.

"You did a good job. Patrick." Finola wanted to reassure herself as much as her young brother. She always felt bad leaving them both alone and her father that sick, he could hardly stand. Now she felt guilty that she wasn't there when… She knew in her heart his time had come.

They were met at the door by Father Pat. The sleeve of his threadbare soutane did not protect her from the sharp angles of the boney arm that encircled her shoulder.

"Your father is dead, my child. We'll have to bury him right away. We fear it's the fever." He looked at her with pity and kindness. "You two ought not to stay here any longer. The sickness is in the house. I'll take young Patrick here, to stay with me for a while. Perhaps Mrs. Mulvaney would find a corner for you at the Manor. I'll have a word with her."

"Can't I see him, Father?" Finola asked, her eyes wide with grief and anguish.

"I think it's better you not go near him. Not now. For your own sake, lass."

Finola turned to go. Then she caught sight of Patrick. Shivering, his gaunt cheeks wet with hot tears, his golden hair clinging in tangled clammy strands around his delicate pale face, his large blue eyes beseeching, begging her attention. She opened wide her arms and drew him to her warm embrace saying, "Patrick, a leanbh, don't be afraid. I won't leave you. I'm here. I love you. I won't let anything happen to you."

They clung together for a few moments. Then Finola took his hand and they both walked away towards the clachan and the priest's house in the half-light of that raw December evening.

Chapter 6

"Love looks not with the eyes, but with the mind."
- Shakespeare.

One evening about a month after she had laid her father to rest, Finola's little brother came to the back door of the Manor. Mrs. Mulvaney answered his knock.

"Well, if it isn't himself. Come in lad. Come in and warm yourself, Patrick, a grá." Looking at the purple lips, the pinched face and the great sad eyes - eyes no little child should have, she felt sorry for the wee fellow.

"I...I doh know, Mam, if I should. I...I must go."

"Yerrah, what's your hurry. Is the old boy, himself - after you, now?" Mrs. Mulvaney was not one to be put off. She took hold of the skeletal arms and fairly lifted the small boy into the kitchen. Soon she had a large slice of bread and a cup of hot soup before him.

"Now while your 'puttin' that inside your shift, I'll call Finola." So saying, she disappeared down a large passageway and was gone for several minutes.

Patrick looked around the large kitchen. Although he had been there before, he never had time to take it all in. Now, while he thoroughly enjoyed the unexpected treat, he had the whole place to himself. His large blue eyes focused on one object of wonderment after another. The beautiful dresser hung with an assortment of delft the likes of which he had never seen in all his life. Pots and pans - surely, he thought, there weren't so many kinds in the whole world. Then his eyes lifted to the ceiling. From the high, black wooden rafters hung a vast array of cured meats, fish, and puddings. His mouth dropped open - so much food, never could he have imagined, even in his wildest dreams, such a vast amount of food in one place.

As he was trying to figure out who would eat all this lovely food, he heard Mrs. Mulvaney coming. She was telling Finola that her little brother badly needed looking after.

"Oh, I know. Indeed, I only wish I could find a good home for him," came the answer.

That was not his Finola speaking! Surely she wasn't thinking of giving him away. Suddenly, he didn't want anymore of the delicious soup and the fresh brown bread seemed to sour in his mouth.

"Ah, there you are, a grá." Finola came towards him all smiling. "An' to what do I owe this honor, darlin'?"

"Sure, let him finish his soup, first," interrupted the housekeeper. "He's only half-done."

"I can't eat anymore." And Patrick looked sideways at Mrs. Mulvaney, his long golden eyelashes shading his downcast eyes.

"Come on now, surely you can eat some more," she coaxed.

"Aren't you hungry, a leanbh?" asked Finola. "I never knew you to refuse food before." Then she thought of her father and how he refused to eat when the fever was on him. "Are you sick?" The alarm sounded in her voice.

All this unaccustomed attention was too much for little Patrick. He had no refuge except in tears. Large drops fell from his eyes and ran down his cold cheeks.

Finola instantly hugged him close, pulling his small face against her rough apron. "What ails you at all, at all? Tell me, tell your Finola."

For a moment there was no answer. Then, as she lifted his golden head and gazed tenderly into his upturned face, he answered. "You want to send me away."

"Oh, darlin' what are you talking about? Of course I don't want to send you away."

"But, - but you told Mrs. Mulvaney…"

"Oh, you silly boy. I was only talking. Only wantin' the best for you, a grá."

"I want to stay near you. Father Pat says I can stay."

"And so you shall. Now, no more worrying about such things." She smoothed his rumpled quiff. "Perhaps, you can eat another little bit now?"

Patrick nodded. He was reassured.

"An' while you finish your soup, maybe you can tell me who sent you. You must have a message or something?"

Patrick had forgotten. "Oh, yes," he answered, his mouth full of bread. "I have it here all right." He stuck his hand deep into the pocket of his frieze breeches and pulled out a tattered note. Handing it to Finola, he said: "Sean Hogan gave it to me. Said 'twas important." He resumed his eating, determined this time to finish the lot.

Finola glanced at the writing. A hasty scrawl: "Come to Dara's old house tonight - 9:00." For a moment, she didn't know what to make of it. You say Sean Hogan gave this to you. But - I . . I don't -"

Mrs. Mulvaney had left the kitchen allowing the two to have a little time together. At this juncture she returned. Noting Finola's perplexed expression, she asked: "Anything wrong?"

"No." Finola's reply was too hasty. "Well, yes and no," she tried to soften her voice. She didn't want the housekeeper who was always so good to her, to think that she didn't trust her.

"I got a note from Sean Hogan asking me to meet him tonight. I don't know what to make of it. I haven't spoken but two words to the same Sean."

"Sean Hogan. Well now, from what I know of that young man, I'd say you were in good hands. He's one of them Young Ireland lads, that I know. But I wouldn't be telling that around," and she lowered her voice and looked across the kitchen towards the back door.

"Then you think I should go?" Finola sought reassurance in the older woman's eyes.

"Yes, I can't see the harm that's in it." She thought perhaps that there might be news of Dara but she didn't want to raise the poor girl's hopes so decided to keep her mouth shut.

Having taken Patrick back to the priest's house, Finola quickly wound her way to the now tumbled-down ruins of Dara's home. She picked her steps among the stones and sought shelter from the chill air in a corner already overgrown with brambles. She pulled her shawl about her and prepared to wait.

Scarcely had she seated herself on a large stone, when she heard a footstep. She got up thinking it was Sean Hogan come to meet her. Before she really knew what was happening, she found herself in the arms of her beloved Dara.

"My God! Oh, it can't be true." she managed to say, at last.

"Sheee - Not so loud. You want them to know in Dublin that Dara O'Rourke is risen from the dead." He kissed her smothering the last word as he did so. Then releasing her, he said, "Now, I don't have long. But I had to see you to tell you…"

Looking down into her anxious, frightened but beautiful eyes, Dara's heart missed a beat. How could he leave her. How could he expect her to go on alone. He again gathered her to himself. With deliberate care and the utmost respect, he lowered his mouth and covered hers with a slow sensitive kiss that persisted unrelentingly until her fears and anxiety were banished to the furthermost regions of her consciousness. He continued to play in tantalizing subtleties demanding a response. Finola was not insensitive, and as her lips yielded to his ardor, they tasted the depths of their youthful love.

"Finola, my darlin', my heart breaks to have to leave you. But I don't have much time," he said as he drew reluctantly away. "First, I want to thank you for what you did for..." Here he choked back a sob, then continued "for what you did for mother and Una. It was a brave and noble thing, Finola and I want you to know that I'll never forget it."

Finola didn't answer. She, too, was overcome with emotion. Life was so difficult, so cruel. Oh, why had things got to be so hard. Her disturbed mind and emotions cried out for answers but none were forthcoming.

Dara continued: "As I said I don't have a lot of time, darlin' but you must know my plans."

"Your plans! My God, Dara! don't you know they're looking for you everywhere - A man with a price on his head!"

"'Tis well I know it. But, I have my plans all the same. Now listen an' I'll tell you."

"I'm listenin'," answered Finola anxiously.

"In two days there's a boat leavin' for New York. I aim to be on it."

"Ahh!" Finola put her hand to her mouth.

"Now don't be fretten' darlin'!" Dara put his arm around her shoulder. "I'll be all right. An' when I'm settled in the New World I'll be sendin' for you, Finola O'Donnell."

"Oh Dara, I'll never see you again." She buried her head against his broad chest as the tears welled up in her sad and worried eyes.

"Now, don't you be sayin' such things, a grá. In six months, maybe less, I'll have the price of your passage. Aye, you and little Patrick. An' - "

"Six months! 'Tis dreamin', dreamin' entirely you are."

"Is it doubtin' my words you are, then?" Dara seemed hurt.

"Oh no, but - " she felt ashamed.

"No buts or anything else now," he answered.

The cry of the curlew alerted Dara.

"They're callin' for me, a cuisle mo croí. Tell me you'll be waitin' for me and I'll go with a stout heart."

Finola clung to him a moment longer. "I'll be waitin' Dara."

"Then, I'm off." He kissed her tenderly for the last time. And quickly getting to his feet and without looking back was lost in the twilight.

* * * * *

Finola sat some moments longer on the cold damp stone listening... half hoping to hear his departing steps, a last lingering sound that would be an echo, a small hint of his presence. But only the croaking of the frogs in the rushes, the gentle swish of the night breeze in the elms, and the splash of water over the rocks in a nearby stream could she hear.

She shivered as the dampness around her sought to enter her sparce thin clothing. The reaction of her body turned her thoughts inward. What would she do now that Dara had gone out of her life, for she had no doubt that such was the case. She had heard the stories recently come from across the Atlantic...thousands dying at sea, thousands too sick to work and those who were fortunate to find employment had fought discrimination. "No Irish need apply," were the words too many had read. Was Dara making a mistake? Brave and strong and handsome though he was, he, too, was not immune to sickness and death and, being Irish, to unfair employment practices in a so-called free society. But then, Finola deduced, the English had set foot in America first and their ways had been established there before other European people arrived. Could the Irish expect any better treatment there than they got at home? Only by dint of their wits and hard work would they overcome these handicaps. At least the country was a big one, she had heard. In time, the Irish might even outnumber their enemy some said.

Again, her mind returned to her own situation. She would wait to hear from Dara. He loved her; of that she was sure. He would stand by his word; of that she was, no less, certain. In the meantime, she could only continue on at the Manor and save all that was possible from her small salary. She thought of the old home, her family, her mother. How the years had changed her fondest hopes for them. She remembered the eviction of the O'Donoghue family and how she had felt on that occasion. She had sworn to protect and fight for her family; to never allow them to be driven from the hallowed walls of their tiny cabin. But time, sickness, and poverty had taken all. There was nothing left now for her in Ireland. And yet, the thought of leaving her native land and going out into the unknown, was a sobering one. She loved Ireland. She loved its people - the roots from which she and generations upon generations before her had sprung. She loved this land which in olden days had a culture and a standard of learning the envy of Western Europe, and that in a time when England was an island of illiterate tribes. How could she leave it, this land, this soil. The very rocks spoke to her, were part of her. And then, as never before, she understood what her people called the 'American wakes'. The wakes that had become all too common during these past few years, so many leaving their homes, their farms, their country. Of course it was a dying; a parting worse than death with no hope ever again of a reunion. Death offered more, she concluded drawing on her Catholic faith.

The tears flowed, and Finola allowed them to course down her cold cheeks. It had been a long time since she had known the luxury of tears. But even as she sobbed, she knew she would have to gather herself together and face the world. Whatever lay ahead, she would overcome. She would stand strong and use her wits, her courage, and her will. She would succeed, come what may. She would rise as so many of the great men and women of her land had done before her, overcoming all obstacles, proving beyond a doubt to the whole world that the Celt was not a coward, was not a sluggard, or a dullard but strong, courageous, intelligent and hardworking with a spirit that would never die.

Yes, she would go when Dara sent for her. She would join him, marry him, and raise up a family which would be proud of its Irishness, its culture, traditions, and all that the ancient heritage had given.

* * * * *

'They are going, going,
going from the valleys and the hills,
They are leaving far behind them heathery moor and mountain rills,
All the wealth of hawthorn hedges where the brown thrush sways and thrills.
They are going, shy-eyed cailins,
and lads so straight and tall,
From the purple peaks of Kerry,

from the crags of wild Imaal,
From the greening plains of Mayo,
and the glens of Donegal.
They are leaving pleasant places,
shores with snowy sands outspread;
Blue and lonely lakes a-stirring
when the wind stirs overhead;
Tender living hearts that love them,
and the graves of kindred dead.
They shall carry to the distant land a tear-drop in the eye
And some shall go uncomforted
- their days an endless sigh.
For Kathaleen Ni Houlihan's sad face, until they die . . .
Oh, the cabins long-deserted! - Olden memories awake -
Oh the pleasant, pleasant places! Hush!
The blackbird in the brake!
Oh, the dear and kindly voices!
- Now their hearts are fain to ache.
They may win a golden store
- sure the whins are golden too;
And no foreign skies hold beauty
like the rainy skies they knew;
Nor any night-wind cool the brow as did the foggy dew.
They are going, going, going, and we cannot bid them stay;
Their fields are now the stranger's,
where the stranger's cattle stray
Oh! Kathaleen Ni Houlihan, your way's a thonry way!'

Ethna Carbery
−"The Four Winds of Eirinn."

Chapter 7

"The Virtue lies in the struggle, not in the prize."

- Milnes.

The months were slipping by and still Finola had not heard from Dara. "It's been so long," she muttered. "Not a word of his whereabouts."

"What's that you're saying?" Mrs. Mulvaney caught her off guard.

Finola was having her usual morning bowl of porridge and her thoughts were faraway. She looked up at the housekeeper but didn't answer.

Then suddenly, both were disturbed when the back door was roughly thrown open and Patrick Dunne's huge frame filled the entrance.

He ignored Finola and addressed Mrs. Mulvaney. "Breakfast ready?"

"The porridge is, but I waited to put on the rashers and eggs fresh for you. Finola, will you be helping Mr. Dunne to a bowl o' porridge while I fix the bacon?"

"Sure," answered Finola. She didn't relish the privilege of serving Mr. Dunne, but she wouldn't show it. Although her knees wabbled and her heart missed a beat, her hand was steady as she served a large bowl of stirabout to the overseer, the master she hated even more than Lord Sutherland, himself. To Finola's relief, she was completely overlooked that morning. Patrick Dunne had more important things on his mind. As soon as he had gulped down a mouthful or two, he broke the silence which had descended like a heavy shroud on the otherwise warm and cheery kitchen.

"His Lordship's expected." He shoveled another couple of spoonfuls into his mouth and swallowed them instantly.

Finola watched as she awaited Mrs. Mulvaney's further orders.

"Oh Lord Almighty! When?" asked the housekeeper, a large carving knife poised threateningly in her right hand as she turned to look at Dunne.

"Doh know for sure. Probably in a day or two. He's in Dublin already."

"Do you know if he's coming' alone or . . . ?"

Dunne didn't wait for Mrs. Mulvaney to finish. "The letter says he's comin' with his son."

"Well, I'll be needin' help around here, Mr. Dunne." The anxiety was quite obvious on the housekeeper's face. "Saints alive, the whole place will have to be gone over. And then there'll be provisions needed. An' . . . "

Again the overseer interrupted. "For the love o' God, woman, will ye hand me m' breakfast an' put that idle girl there to work. Seems to me all she does is stand around gawkin'."

"The girl does her share," came the quick retort. Then turning to Finola she said, "Start washin' up, lass, there'll be extra chores for you today." Again she confronted Dunne. "I'll be needin' help. The house needs a thorough over hauling and there's silver to clean an' china, and bed linen to air an'…"

"All right. All right! What a fuss ye make, woman. For Christ's sake, whist, will ye. I'll send for Bridie Roark."

"'Twon't be enough at all, at all. At least two women, otherwise I'll just throw in the towel and walk away altogether."

Patrick Dunne's face blanched and then turned red. He was angry with the housekeeper. She was too demanding.

But he knew there was no one like her in the whole county. If she left, the burden and blame would be all his. He couldn't afford that problem at this time.

"All right, all right. Cool down. No need to get excited. Just get things in order for his Lordship. Ye know how particular he is."

"Particular!" Finola thought. "God, the English sure had gall. Coming over to a country that wasn't theirs, to an estate they had unjustly appropriated, and then ordering, nay demanding that everything be to their particular specifications. Well, let them come. She'd do her job because it meant that she'd earn a living, but she'd not stoop to subservience, to slavery. There would be no bowing and scraping on her part.

Mrs. Mulvaney's voice interrupted her thoughts. "Things 'ill be in apple-pie order if I get the help." She'd had the last word. Finola knew she was satisfied. Setting her chin and jaw with determination, the older woman concentrated on poking the fire.

Patrick Dunne had been in Lord Sutherland's service for fifteen years, long enough to assess his position realistically. Shrewd in his evaluation of his own chances to survive if Glencarrow failed to make a profit, he also carefully weighed the chances of others, paticularly those over whom he had control. He knew that the fruits of his labors were not for him; but he was, in his own dour way, genuinely consoled when he reflected, to his own amusement, that 'fruits' were not to his liking anyway. He was, first, last, and totally, a meat and potato man. He had no palette for side dishes or desserts. Plain and practical, he'd existed all his life on what he termed 'the bare necessities.' He'd looked out for himself. Others be damned.

A tall man with broad shoulders, Patrick Dunne's skin was deeply bronzed. His black hair and brown eyes accentuated his dark looks. A hard-bitten face with brooding severity was etched into pessimistic angles. A nervous twitch near the corner of his left eye became more noticeable when he was excited and being an excitable man by nature, the twitch was more often conspicuous than not. Unmarried, the man had only himself to account to and for. He was, as a consequence, selfish, unreasonable, and intolerant. He suffered from a bad stomach, and his gastric belches were as lusty as his foul language, and as odious.

As soon as Mr. Dunne had left the kitchen, Mrs. Mulvaney set about making the list of provisions she would need for the lavish meals she'd have to prepare as soon as Lord Sutherland was in residence. It had been over two years since his last visit, she recollected. She was not looking forward to the experience - constant demands, continual vigilance in all matters, and the never ending preparation of exotic foods, savory dishes 'fit for a king' as the good woman was often heard to say.

Mrs. Mulvaney had held her position since before young Robert was born and that was neigh on twenty-five years. In all that time she had been reliable and efficient. She knew exactly how to please the gentry, although she didn't have occasion to do so too often. During her long service at the Manor, the lord and master had visited the estate about five times and only once with his wife and child. Although those visits were of short duration still they had entailed considerable alterations in the life of the Manor and caused quite a stir, not only in the whole household but in the entire neighborhood.

Before noon, two extra women were found to give a helping hand with the major overhaul that Mrs. Mulvaney declared was necessary for the reception of Lord Sutherland. Finola's sole occupation during the following days was to help with the cooking for the good housekeeper knew that when the master was in residence, there would be much entertaining. The larders had to be full at all times, the cellars well stocked with French wines, Spanish ports, and Irish whiskies.

By the end of the day Mrs. Mulvaney had made a long list of all the provisions she would need and presented it to Dunne. He protested and fumed but in the end he was obliged to travel to the town of Killrush to purchase all that was required.

Finola had, as yet, never laid eyes on the master for whom she really worked.

What of it? He couldn't be much worse than Dunne. She had managed, so far, to avoid an outright confrontation with that individual, although there had been several times when she was sorely tempted to let him have a piece of her mind. This she came perilously close to doing only a few days before when Dunne, in what appeared to her to be a needlessly bad humor, had growled a command in her direction. Finola managed with quiet diplomacy to mollify the overseer. She felt, therefore, that she was adequately qualified to handle her foreign overlord in much the same fashion if any similar unfortunate occurance should arise.

"What kind of man is his Lordship?" Finola enquired of Mrs. Mulvaney as she carefully chopped nuts in preparation for a mince pie.

"Och, no better or worse than the rest of his kind, I'm thinkin'. Still an' all, I wouldn't like to be in his bad books, if ye get my meaning?" The housekeeper paused long enough to give Finola a glance.

"You mean, God help the tenant farmer who can't pay his rent on time." There was a fierce glint in Finola's green eyes.

"You might put it that way, child. But then it's none o' our business. Those of us who work in this house, I mean. An' you'll do well to remember that, m'girl."

"Oh, I'll remember it," said Finola. "I'll remember it well. But the day Lord Sutherland lays a hand on me or what's left of my family, I swear, I'll scratch his eyes out."

"Careful now. Them's harsh words, a grá, an' walls have ears," warned Mrs. Mulvaney.

At that moment, Finola didn't care who heard. She was determined that anyone, be he native or foreign, who sought to harm herself or her little brother would rue the day.

It was long past the hour when Finola usually left for home. Seeing Mrs. Mulvaney's fluster and agitation, she volunteered to remain longer. There was still so much to be done. Eventually, as the first stars appeared in the night's sky, Finola yawned. "I must be off if you don't mind, Mrs. Mulvaney. I can hardly keep my eyes open."

"Aye, you've put in a mighty long day. 'Twas right decent of you, Finola, to stay on." She reached for a slab of the cured bacon hanging from the low beamed kitchen ceiling. Here, take this. You deserve it. 'Twill make a grand Sunday dinner with a couple of turnips or a head o' cabbage. Do you have any spuds left?" Without waiting for a reply, the housekeeper shoved two potatoes imported from England into Finola's hands.

"Thank you. Thank you kindly. You're so good to me. I . . . I . . ." Finola was at that time staying with her friend, Sive, so the extra food was a boon to her also.

"Now be off with you before himself comes in." She gave her a little shove as she opened the door.

A full moon shone in a cloudless sky as Finola hurried across the meadow. The stench of rot and pollution still hung in the air. She could never get used to it, but at that moment she was happy. She had eaten well that day, and, besides, she had a substantial parcel of food to share with little Patrick.

Just as Finola was about to cross the stile, the sound of galloping horses caused her to draw back to the shelter of the nearby bushes. Almost immediately two riders drew level with the stile and reined in their animals. In the clear moonlight, Finola could see that they were strangers. She crouched low, but as she did, a dry branch snapped.

"What's that?" The voice was that of a young man.

An Englishman! thought Finola.

"What's what?" an older man asked. His accent was English also.

"That noise. I'm sure I heard a noice, Father, over there."

"Very well, son. Draw your gun. We're in Ireland now, and in these parts the natives could be hostile."

Finola decided she'd best show herself. "No need to be alarmed, gentlemen." She stepped into the clearing in front of the riders. "Perhaps I can help you?"

"Ah ha! A peasant girl. You got a young man with you? How many more behind those bushes?"

"No one else, sir. No one at all." Finola's voice was firm.

"You're out late, miss. Aren't you afraid?" The older of the two men continued to do the talking.

"I work, sir. Work at Glencarrow Manor."

As soon as the Englishman heard the familiar name, he relaxed. "Then you must be one of my own servants. Perhaps you can direct us to the Manor. I'm Lord Sutherland and this is my son. Seems we have taken the wrong road. It's been several years. One dirt road looks the same as another at night."

"Yes, I suppose so. It's not far. Just beyond the trees... Across this field is the quickest way." Finola replied pointing towards the Manor.

"Fine. Well, Robert, I wasn't too far off. Come on, son." Lord Sutherland ignored Finola, put spurs to his horse which galloped off, leaped the fence, and crossed the meadow before she had time to gather up her skirts to mount the stile.

Before following his father, Robert urged his horse closer to Finola. He looked down at her with a superior but curious air, then as he turned his horse, he spoke: "I hope we didn't frighten you."

"No, we Irish girls are made of stronger stuff." Finola looked the young man straight in the eys.

"I see." A cynical lear belied the soft words. "Hah! I must remember that." Then pointing his mount in the direction of Glencarrow Manor, he followed his father.

Finola stood for a few moments longer looking after the riders. So his Lordship and son had come. Life would surely be different at the Manor, from now on. His Lordship was stern and aloof; no doubt about where one stood with him. She decided that his son was of a more brash nature; she must be on her guard. She did not like either of them. However, it wouldn't really matter to her in the long run. "Probably never lay eyes on one or other again anyway," she said to herself as she hurried home.

The following morning Finola arrived at the Manor bright and early. In a frenzy of excitement, Mrs. Mulvaney addressed her as she entered the kitchen. "Praise be, Finola. I've been havin' palpitations for fear you wouldn't be here on time. What with you workin' so late an' all last night. You're a good girl."

Finola smiled and the dimples at the corners of her mouth grew deeper.

"His Lordship's come, lass. Aye, an' his son. Came last night . . . shortly after you left." The housekeeper fussed with several pots and pans as she spoke.

"I know, I had the misfortune to meet the pair as I was about to cross the stile last night.

The housekeeper paid no attention to Finola's response.

"They'll be sleepin' late, no doubt, this mornin'. But that doesn't mean we can afford to dawdle. His Lordship's the demandin' type. Mrs. Mulvaney looked confused. "Where in tarnation did I put that knife?"

"This the one?" Finola picked up a large carving knife which was lying close to a side of bacon.

"Aye, that's it," answered Mrs. Mulvaney. Then raising her plump arm to wipe away the beads of perspiration which had accumulated on her anxious brow, she said, "Lord Almighty I almost forgot. You'll have to be doing the serving this mornin' Finola."

"Me! Mrs. Mulvaney! Do you really mean it!" cried Finola.

"Yes, girl, I do. There's no one else."

"Oh Lord! I... I... doh know." Then Finola pulled herself together. Why not, she thought. This is my chance! My chance to better myself! "You'll show me what to do, then?" And her self-confidence reasserted itself.

"But o' course, I will. That's the spirit, the determined spirit I detected the first day you set foot in this house. You're a bright girl. Always knew you'd go places. See here." She went to the upper drawer of the huge dresser that stood against the wall opposite the fireplace. Opening the drawer she took out a starched white apron and a small lace-fringed cap. "Here put these on. Then, I'll show you what to do when you go upstairs."

"Now, when I was a slip o' a girl like yourself, I started off the same way. The only blunder you can make, child, is to forget which is your right an' which is your left hand."

"What do ye mean, Mrs. Mulvaney?" Finola looked surprised.

"Well, sit down here an' let me show you."

Finola sat on a stool which was drawn up to the table.

"Now pretend you're his Lordship. I'm about to serve you breakfast."

Finola decided to act the part. She sat rigid, not a muscle moved in her body.

She had never seen the gentry eat, but judging from what she had observed of Lord Sutherland the night before, her notion of how he might behave was not too far-fetched.

Mrs. Mulvaney couldn't help herself. She burst out laughing and the corners of her grey eyes fanned out in a multitude of crows feet. "Oh child, you do strike quite a pose. As stiff as a ram rod, you are. I've me doubts that his Lordship would appreciate your perception of him."

Finola relaxed. "He does have what you might call a poker face, though." She joined the housekeeper in the light-hearted banter.

"Well, this carrying on won't get us very far, an' time's a wastin."

Then, as Mrs. Mulvaney, serving cloth in hand, placed a plate in front of Finola, she said, "Serve from the left, take from the right. That's the most important rule to learn. Other mistakes will be ignored, but for a serving maid to break that rule is unpardonable."

For the rest of the morning, Finola kept on repeating the words... 'serve from the left, take from the right'. Although she felt a certain apprehension in confronting his Lordship on her own and some fear of making a mistake, she was remarkably cool, calm, and collected when her moment of trial came. She even felt a surge of excitement. She knew, somehow, that she had reached a turning point in her life. She had surely started on the road to bigger and better things.

Mrs. Mulvaney had seen possibilities in her right from the start and now it was her chance to prove once and for all to Mr. Dunne that the girl was capable of more than washing dirty dishes.

So, at precisely eleven o'clock, Finola mounted the stairs with a large tray, entered the dining room, and prepared to serve late breakfast to Lord Sutherland and his son. She placed the silver covered serving plates on the broad oaken side-board and the cosy-covered china tea-pot on its fancy earthenware stand. "There, now everything is in order." She stood back to admire the snow-white linen cloth, the sparkling silverware, the shiny rose-patterned china. Then, from the table, her gaze traveled about the room. The beautifully carved oaken side-board on which were placed a huge crystal flower bowl now displaying a perfusion of colorful blooms, and a wine decanter surrounded by several wine glasses. She noted how the sun's rays drew forth a spectrum of colors that danced and shimmered in the massive mirror behind. The garnet colored velvet chairs were showing signs of long years of wear to be sure, but still looked grand. The rose colored carpet was thin in places, but to Finola's inexperienced eyes, it was a luxury she could only wish for in her wildest dreams.

The door opened. Lord Sutherland entered followed by his son.

Finola dropped a half curtsy. "Morning your Lordship." Her voice was firm.

He nodded his head in her general direction. "Breakfast ready?"

"Yes, m'Lord." Finola held her head high.

"Good. This Irish air puts an edge on the appetite." He spoke to his son who had by that time seated himself and was shaking out his serviette in an unhurried manner.

Finola brought the dishes one by one to the table. First the fish, then the eggs, and finally the bacon. When she had returned all again to the sideboard she waited a moment to see if there was anything else needed of her. From that position, the gentlemen having their backs to her, she could observe without being observed. She tried to evaluate the two men before her, the so-called gentry, products of

England's elite society. She would note their weaknesses as well as their strong points, she decided, and when the appropriate time came, use both to her own advantage. Finola had grown old in the ways of the world since her mother's death. No English landlord would use her to further his own ends. She did not intend to go to an early grave like her mother. The image of the poor woman's last days still haunted her. Lying weak and sick, slowly starving to death while the inhabitants of houses like this feasted sumptuously and wasted more food at one meal than would feed a family like hers for a week. At such moments, Finola vowed that she would avenge that untimely death as well as those of the other members of her family.

"I'd like my tea now." Lord Sutherland spoke but did not address Finola directly.

Instantly diverted from her thoughts she answered: "Yes, certainly." She then approached the table and lifting the teapot proceeded to fill his Lordship's cup. As she stepped close to Robert's side and was about to pour some for him, he raised his hand to protest.

"No, not yet. I'll tell you when I want it." As he spoke, he looked up at her and Finola saw the hate in his cold blue eyes.

She instinctively withdrew a few paces but remained where she could better observe the pair.

She judged that his Lordship was a man in his mid-forties. Slender and well proportioned, he was not a tall man. Of a sallow complexion, his features were regular, but nondescript. No scar, blemish, or other telltale mark marred the soft lines of that inscrutable face. His well-manicured hands knew not the touch of the black earth, Ireland's richest resource, which had given so lavishly to sustain him in his idle, useless lifestyle. To Finola, he was a parasite. She despised him. Having seen the hardness in his steel-blue eyes when he condescended to even acknowledge her presence, she resolved to avoid him, to steer clear of him, when and if, at all, possible.

Then Finola's eyes searched the face of young Master Robert. He appeared to be a man in his early twenties. His blond hair fell in a boyish, rakish quiff over his right eye. As he spoke to his father, his light blue eyes never left his plate. His voice was resonant and he appeared to have even white teeth. His slender nose drew attention to his full shapely lips. He's actually quite nice looking, almost handsome, she thought.

Lord Sutherland emptied his tea-cup.

Finola stepped to the table again. "Another cup, sir?" She could scarcely believe her own poise and confidence. This serving business wasn't so hard after all. She'd make sure she'd keep this job until something better came along. It was far better than the pots and pans. But she'd have to help with them, too, she knew.

His Lordship looked up. "Ah, you're the peasant girl we met last night," he addressed her with disdain an air of contempt.

Finola bit her lip. How dare he! "My name is Finola, sir."

Lord Sutherland noted her reaction. She either didn't like him or . . . yes, that was it, she resented being called what she obviously was - a peasant. What next? These Irish. Who could understand them? He chose to ignore her emotions after that. She was, after all, not much more than a mere child. "An' a good thing it was too. We might have ridden on by the Manor and not found our way for hours."

"I'm glad I was able to help, sir."

"So... " He took stock of her. She had beautiful eyes, emerald? No, too light, but no jewel sparkled any brighter. And the color of her hair! Her skin! My God, where did she come from? It was an enigma his Lordship had long ago given up trying to unravel, but he never ceased to be amazed. From whence came such beauty? That such a damnable race of people could produce such loveliness baffled him. He looked at his son. The boy was obviously not unmindful either. When the eyes of father and son met, the latter blushed slightly.

As Robert lowered his eyes and concentrated on the remains of his breakfast, Finola asked, "Will there be anything else, sir?"

"No, I don't think so. What did you say your name was, girl?" He had a rather harsh precise voice which varied little in its intonation.

"Finola, sir. Finola O'Donnell."

"Very well, Finola. That will be all. You may leave."

"Yes, sir." Finola dropped a half curtsy as she had been taught and quickly left the room.

Outside she stood a moment. She found herself shaking. It had been an ordeal after all, but she felt sure she had carried it off. The important thing was that she was learning how the so-called upperclass lived. She noted the manners and deportment particularly at meal time. One day, she meant to put all this knowledge to good use.

Chapter 8

**"When passion rules, how rare the hours
that fall to virtue's share."**
- Walter Scott.

He watched her come across the cobble stone yard on her way to collect the eggs. On her slender white arm she carried a basket. Strands of rebellious flaming hair escaping from beneath the lace of her stiff cap played about her face. The flashing eyes, the slim straight nose, and the shapely, full, expressive mouth aroused him. She wore an old, grey, muslin dress, but over it was a fresh white apron. As she approached, Robert heard her hum a little tune.

He had been watching his chance, seeking an opportunity to meet Finola alone. A pretty little thing, naive, innocent - maybe a virgin. "'Begorra', as they say in this godforsaken hole, I can still have some fun," and Robert chuckled to himself.

The journey to Ireland, undertaken by Lord Sutherland, reluctantly accompanied by his son, was not strictly business. Like most absentee landlords, he detested 'the bloody Irish', and hated the necessity of having to monitor the activities of those barbarous 'peasants' from time to time, especially in such a faraway corner of that infernal land. On this occasion the visit was twofold. First, and most important, was the fact that he had to sequester his incorrigible son in some remote place lest his conduct completely ruin the family's reputation and blight the chances of a decent marriage for his only daughter. The second task, Lord Sutherland expected to accomplish was the extraction of his annual rents and other fees in cash or in kind, that were long overdue.

In all, an annual six million pounds of taxes and rental fees as well as State Church taxes were collected from the now impoverished land. And while these monies were wrung from the nearly penniless, ships and merchant vessels laden with the choicest food products were daily leaving Ireland's shores giving the lie to the world at large that the people were starving.

Having spent a year at Oxford, young Robert had failed miserably in all his examinations. But by subtle persuasion and other sundry means on the part of his father, the Dean had reluctantly agreed to allow Robert to return for the next school year. Although the young man had sorely tried his father's patience as well as his pocket, Lord Sutherland was determined to make something of him.

For a time, he had allowed the young 'buck' his latitude. He remembered his own youth. 'A gay blade', they had called him, and a wry smile spread across his lean face. He felt he was a broadminded man. He did not object to the servant girls - so long as his son's philandering was discreet. He could even deal with his gambling bouts, the drinking, and the opium fad, but - his mind reeled. He shifted his weight and fumbled. "Damn it," he pounded the desk at which he was seated.

The sordid scene was reenacted many a time before his mind's eye. The squalid street, the evil-smelling, dingy apartment, the filth, - It was all too bloody awful. An' just as he was consolidating his own position for a seat in the House. The boy had such bad timing. Blast him! Damn to hell the churlish fag! Then, suddenly, His Lordship threw his head back and laughed aloud. "Poor bastard - not more than a child." He recollected the slim nude buttocks of the fleeing youth - the peevish rebellious posture of his shocked son as he confronted him. It was then that he lost his temper, removed his coat, hat and gloves and — He didn't want to remember the rest of that evening.

The following day he had withdrawn all monitary gifts, closed his son's bank account and ordered him to leave London. He must not return home. He would not hear of it. He would betake himself to their small property in Kent while preparations were made for his departure for Ireland.

Robert stepped from behind the shed where he had been watching her. Her basket full, she was at a disadvantage.

"Oh, beggin' your pardon, sir. I didn't see you." Finola haulted abruptly and tried to sidestep as she came smack up against him.

"No need to beg pardon, pretty Finola. I came here on purpose to meet you. I have been watching you now for several days.

"Sir!" Finola blushed and lowered her shapely head. "I hope, sir. I haven't. . ."

He ignored her embarrassment. "There's something in yonder shed I'd like to talk to you about.

She became alarmed and drew back a pace. Her beautiful eyes wide with fear, she blurted: "Oh no, sir. I don't know anything about things in that shed. That's Mr. Dunne's business. You'll have to ask him. Now, if you'll excuse me, I must be . . . "She didn't wait to hear more. But gathering up her long skirt in one hand she ran quickly back to the house. She was trembling as she entered the kitchen.

"Lord Almighty! Have you seen a ghost, child?" Mrs. Mulvaney was alarmed.

"That, that fool gander fairly took the leg off me." She stammered and she knew her words sounded flat.

"Since when have you ever let that crazy bird get the better of you?" She hadn't convinced Mrs. Mulvaney.

"Ach, I wasn't mindin and he came on me sudden-like." She was in control again. "An' what with the eggs an' all."

"I see. Well, let's have them, then." Finola still stood just inside the door clutching the basket close to her. "Or do you intend to stand there all day?"

Finola walked towards the table and laid the basket on it. Her whole body trembled but she steeled herself and lifted her head high. "I'll be off to do the upstairs chores now, if you don't need anything else," she said, her voice steady, determined.

"No, I can manage the rest, answered the housekeeper as she turned her attention to her pots and pans.

Finola was still trembling when she arrived at the top of the stairs. What was she going to do? She sat for a moment to compose herself and to try to resolve the problem she now faced.

Did he really want to harm her, she asked herself. What fool idea had he in his head asking her into the shed if he didn't. What did he take her for. She realized she was only a poor servant but she still had her pride and her morals.

From this day hence, she would have to be on her guard. Life at the Manor had suddenly taken on a more sinister aspect. She could have taken Dunne's harsh words and cruel blows but the threat that now hung like the sword of Damocles over her head was far more cruel. And if the young man were to take up residence permanently as she had gathered from conversations between himself and his father, there would be no peace for Finola.

She thought of Dara. Where was he now. Had he arrived safely in America. When would he send for her.

Going about her chores that day her mind was travelling even faster than her feet. She would have to change her plans. She would have to leave the Manor sooner than she had intended. She just couldn't wait for Dara to rescue her. She, instead, would have to go to him.

With no use now for the family home, she could, doubtless, save the few shillings Lord Sutherland was demanding in rent if she were to abandon it. With these thoughts in mind, she decided to wait a few days before addressing his Lordship about the matter. In the meantime, she would be vigilant with regard to Master Robert. And, at the first opportunity, she would discuss the prospects of obtaining passage for herself and little Patrick with Fr. Quinn. Perhaps he could help in the purchasing of the tickets. Authorities would be less apt to cheat a man of the cloth in such matters. Cautious and shrewd beyond her years, Finola calculated and formulated her strategies, as skillfully as any major general on the battlefield.

For the next few days Robert would be kept busy. His father had demanded that he accompany Mr. Dunne on his rounds of the estate. He would be the one to make the decisions regarding evictions and such like.

After the first day he had had enough. At breakfast the next morning, she was to learn his opinion first hand.

"It's incredible. I had heard that the Irish were no better than animals. Now I believe it. My damn horse has a more comfortable and cleaner living space than any I saw yesterday."

"Now that you have seen with your own two eyes, you can understand what the landowners in this country are up against. I was talking to Lord Fitzgibbon when you were away and it is his opinion that we will have to band together to rid ourselves of this enormous problem.

"Hah! Have you any idea how many tenants we have on our lands alone?" he snapped. "We're talking of thousands. In one hut alone, I found a family of twelve children. Never in my life have I seen such faces - gaunt, listless, starving creatures. While the mother, dirty and weak lay in a corner on a stale heap of straw, the oldest girlchild was trying to get a miserable fire started. There was nothing to eat; they barely had any clothing - miserable rags for the most part.

"They're a lazy bunch," interjected his father.

"Dunne told me that lot wouldn't last long. Said he knew the look."

"So, how many are on your list for eviction?" There was no sign of emotion on his Lordship's face as he asked the question.

Finola was appalled. She could barely keep her mouth shut. What did these so-called gentry expect when the unfortunate people were taxed beyond endurance, when their food and animals were taken from them. With nowhere to turn, no help of any kind, and no reprieve from greedy landlords, there was only one solution - death, the slow death from starvation.

She was interrupted in her thoughts by yet another alarming pronouncement.

"This very day you'll remove that refuse from our lands. Draw up a list of all those living on the east side of the valley as far as the Carrow Hills and we'll be done with this once and for all. A good flock of sheep will bring more income in a short time." His Lordship dabbed his thin lips with a white linen serviette, then pushed his half-finished breakfast to one side.

Finola looked at the food - an egg, two large sausages, and a thick slice of bacon, and gritted her teeth. Within, her sensitive heart ached for those like herself who could live for a day on the left-overs on that plate.

Robert caught her eye as he answered his father's decision. "We'll squeeze them off the land, then, just as the guts of a louse are squeezed between the fingernails."

Finola could take no more. She stepped up to the table. "Beggin' your pardon, sir, will you be wantin' anything else?" She felt she was about to get sick. She must get out of that room immediately.

"I'll have another cup of tea."

"And I'd like another helping of bacon." Robert smiled showing his even white teeth as he looked her straight in the eyes.

But Finola knew it was just a mask. He enjoyed torturing her.

A miserable dreary day with a cold gusting wind had set in. Lord Sutherland left his place at the table and went to stand by the large mullioned window. He drew the faded velvet drape aside and looked out across the sodden lands. "God, what a dreary bloody place this is. What's a man to do in such a desert spot?" Then he turned and looked at his son who was still hacking away at a piece of bacon.

"Don't dawdle, Robert. Get a move on, boy. The sooner this business is done with, the better. I don't want to spend the rest of my life in this damn awful country.

"An' what about me?" he asked his mouth full of food.

"Ah, that's another question. Remember you brought all this upon yourself. A year or two until your…" He remembered that Finola was still standing by the sideboard. "Well, yes." He cleared his throat. "Ahem." We'll talk later about that matter." Then without another word left the room.

Finola immediately started to stack the tray with the breakfast things. Robert eyed her every move.

As she went to open the door, he got up and deliberately barred her way.

"Now where do you think you're going?" he said in an authoritive tone.

"About my business, sir. I have a lot to do." Finola answered trying to control herself.

"Well I don't remember dismissing you."

"His Lordship has left - I'm now free to go." She faced him boldly.

"Who do you think is in charge here?"

"His Lordship," she answered.

"That old fool! Hah! He won't be here longer than a week. I'm the Lord of this stinking chateau. An' I intend to show all you lice what that means." He caught Finola by the wrist, holding her in an iron grip. He was about to pull at her long shirt, when he heard the booted step of his father coming towards the diningroom. He released her and turned abruptly away murmuring: "I'll get you pretty Finola - I'll get you yet."

Finola immediately opened the door and fled down the long hall to the kitchen. Fortunately, Mrs. Mulvaney was too busy to notice her hasty entrance or pay any attention to her. She composed herself by washing up whatever dirty dishes were lying around. But her mind and heart were not easy. She would have to talk to Fr. Quinn that very evening.

The wailings and lamentations that sounded through the valley by the end of the day were only a forerunner of what was to come. Ten families unable to pay their rent were evicted into the inclement weather with scarcely enough to cover them and no food. Their humble abodes were destroyed, pulled down and burnt before their eyes. Dazed, for the most part, they wandered about the muddy roads looking for a ditch or a grove of trees which might afford some shelter. No one was allowed to help them or take them in. Many, it was known, would be dead before morning.

Eileen Mulligan and her newborn would be among the first to succumb to these atrocities, Finola thought as she made her way to the priest's house shortly after dark. It seemed as if the whole world was coming to an end. What were her people and the country as a whole going to do.

Were the Sasanach going to exterminate every single one of them.

When she arrived at the small house owned by Fr. Quinn, she was greeted at the door by her little brother, Patrick. He was looking better - had even gained a few pounds and was wearing a pair of boots and a fine new breeches.

"My! What a fine gentleman you are, Patrick O'Donnell," she said as she threw her arms around him and hugged him tight.

He buried his head against her a moment, then raised his cherubic face and smiled. "I'm glad to see you, Nola."

"I've a big secret to tell you. But first I must talk with Fr. Quinn. Where is he?"

"He's within. I'll show you."

They entered the priest's presence without any formality.

"Sit down, here Finola. What can I do for you, lass?"

"First, I want to thank you, Father for taking care of Patrick."

"Ah, sure he's no trouble at all. He's a good boy." And Fr. Quinn ruffled the golden locks that fell to Patrick's shoulders. "Did you show her your nice boots?"

"Indeed, he did, Father."

"An' did he tell you, he even wears them to bed? Afraid someone will steal them while he's asleep he is." At this the priest laughed poking fun at the wee boy. "Well, I can tell you, they won't fit me so they're safe in this house, son." Then turning to Finola, he said: "And what it is that's troublin' you now? It's written all over your face - the worry of it."

Finola soon told him her plans. She then waited while the priest thought over her words and considered a solution.

Finally, they came to an agreement. Father would purchase, though reluctantly, a ticket and a half, Patrick was considered to be only a child. He would make inquiries regarding the next sailing for America and would try to find a good family whom she could join on her way to a new life. Much as Fr. Quinn regretted the loss of such a splendid young woman from the valley, he knew there was no future for Finola in Glencarrow.

Chapter 9

"Passion makes the will lord of the reason."
- Shakespeare.

By Gad! He'll have me living the life of a bliddering, papist monk." Robert slammed the door of the library and threw his riding crop onto the oak table breaking a decanter full of wine and demonstrating, as was his wont, that anger was his only refuge in times of frustration. Ignoring the mess he had made — the broken glass, the ruby splotches, and general disarry, he strode across the room to a sidetable and poured himself a tumbler of whiskey. Without waiting to replace the stopper, he drank the liquor in long steady gulps until he had drained the glass. Then he flopped onto the arm-chair nearest him as he poured another drink.

"Tomorrow. Yes, tomorrow, I'll have myself that pretty little wench," he mumbled in a half coherent voice. "I'll . . . I'll show him and her, who's lord . . . in this . . ." His confused mind conjured up images of his father one moment, the next the beautiful face of Finola O'Donnell. The glass slipped from his hand and the heady liquor formed puddles of various sizes on the polished wooden floor that edged the carpet. Robert Sutherland was now unaware of anything; his legs sprawled in careless fashion, his arms dangling on either side of the chair, he was sound asleep.

To distract himself from the monotonous and troublesome exercises of evicting so many families in the course of a few days, he had decided early that morning to go for a ride. The air was crisp, invigorating. And although the stench of the putrid fields had not completely left the valley, the air at the higher elevations was fresh. For several hours he galloped along the brow of the hills surrounding Glencarrow and overlooking the vast estates. He did not see the destitute families he had so lately evicted squatting in make-shift dugouts nor did he hear the feeble cry of a dying infant. Only the many wretched cabins that still dotted the far end of the valley and the westside of the estate captured his attention.

"A few more days, and I shall be finished with that lot." His words startled the magpies on a nearby bush. "Then perhaps, my father will betake himself back to England and good riddance." He thought of what life might be when he was alone. For a moment only the advantage of being far from the tiring remonstrances of his father occupied his brain and he rejoiced in the thought of a new-found freedom. But slowly the reality of his existance in that out-of-the-way section of the world, surrounded by those he considered half-savage, began to dawn on him.

"My God! I'll go crazy in this place." His voice echoed through the valley and returned to mock him ... crazy... crazy... place... place.

He shivered despite the sweat that clung to his inner shift, then, dug his heels into the horse as he again turned towards the Manor. He needed a stiff one to escape the boring unfulfilled existence he now felt was his destiny. Pessimistic by nature, there was he believed no other alternative for him.

It was a sleeping, disheveled figure, with gaping mouth and clammy brow that Finola found when she entered the library to light the lamps several hours later. At first, she was startled to find herself alone with him. But seeing he was asleep, she decided to get on with her work and leave as quickly as possible. As she advanced into the room, she noticed the broken glass and the wine stains on the carpet.

"Ah!" Her voice was no more than a sigh. I'll have to clean up this mess before his Lordship comes, she thought. She hesitated a moment ... which should she tackle first, she asked herself. Better start with the lamps. Quickly and noiselessly she set to lighting the three lamps giving the library a pleasant warm glow. As she was about to attend to the fire, she noticed the English magazine, Punch, lying open on the table. Glancing at it, her first reaction was disbelief. Were her eyes deceiving her. Indignation and utter revulsion spread across her face. Surely these hideous, grotesque caricatures were not of Irish people! Again, Finola blinked — crude ape-like faces glared at her. Ape-men dressed in ragged clothes brandishing shillelaghs at a richly dressed gentleman. Another grotesque figure had an ape-like child, complete with shaggy facial hair, by the scruff of the neck, while, at a distance, an ugly disheveled female sat cowering clutching a keg of potheen.

Never in her life had Finola seen anything so degrading. Did the English really think the Irish were such monsters. She had a good mind to throw the horrid thing into the fire... so that was how Sutherland and his drunken son amused themselves. Finola knew enough to realize that these people who now owned the land on which she and others like her lived, were once common soldiers. Many uncouth illiterates who had been sent to subdue their betters by an overbearing grasping monarch. Yes, they had become rich and powerful at the expense of her people . . . the Irish. Her forefathers had been overcome by sheer brute force and military might, driven from their lands and homes and forced to flee to the mountains to survive. Now their children and grandchildren were portrayed thus. It had to be from men like Lord Sutherland who rarely set foot in the country, let alone visit the tenants on his large holdings, that the writers of such a base, insensitive magazine got their information. Of course, she reasoned, having spent a week or two in the country, these absentee landlords, as they were called, would return to their fine homes in England and gloat over the poor wretches they had chanced to catch sight of from the comfort of their carriage windows as they hurried by. These roadside beggars represented the Irish as a whole in their minds. It never occured to them to look further, to meet and mingle with the vast population of intelligent hardworking people that were Finola's friends and neighbors.

Seething with rage, she flung the tabloid on the table and gave her attention to the embers on the hearth. As she brushed the ashes and pieces of unburnt turf into the grate, her thoughts fanned the flames in her own heart. What could she do to tell the world that her beloved Ireland was not a land of freaks. How could she open the eyes of these foreigners, the Sasanach, to the truth about the Gael. Certainly, at that point in time, Ireland and her people were fallen into destitution. It would take much more than her poor efforts to convince the world at large, but especially England, that all those with whom she was acquainted, though starving and wretchedly poor, yet possessed hearts of courage, intelligent minds eager for knowledge and learning and souls of moral rectitude and character.

Her image of her own self-worth, her ideals and aspirations which had been handed down from countless generations, she felt was a mirror of Ireland as a whole. All that was needed, she reasoned, was to inform and instruct the unbiased, the open-minded people of the rest of the world to the truth about Ireland and the Gael. One day, with God's help, her people, her land would be second to none among the nations of the earth.

Finola, young though she was, now realized that she had a mission. Instinctively, she knew that somehow she would eventually find a way to do what her heart inspired. The day would come when she, Finola O'Donnell would tell the world about the atrocities done in a land which once flowed with milk and honey, to a people who blazed the trail of Christianity and learning across the unlettered lands of Europe from Bangor and Clonmacnois in Ireland and Iona in Scotland to Kiev in Russia.

Finola recalled the words of her old school master when speaking of the Saxon, Aldhelm who had been educated by the Irishman, Maeldubh. 'Ireland is a fertile and blooming nursery of letters: one might reckon the stars of heaven as enumerate her students and literature.' How did the suffering, depressed country that she knew compare with those golden days of yesteryear, she asked herself. Was the present state of affairs the recompense due this once proud and glorious land. What of the sacrifices, the toil, the courage of thousands of Ireland's sons and daughters who had gone forth, generation after generation, to teach, preach, and educate. Who in their efforts to eradicate ignorance, to uplift and civilize the illiterate and uncultured masses of Europe had not only worked unceasingly to establish schools, monasteries and universities, in England and the continent, but had also founded settlements such as Brandenburg in Germany (St. Brendan) which were to become in time a beacon of light for the German people. These intrepid missionaries did not fail in their efforts, some even gave their lives for their beliefs, but they eventually succeeded in saving Western Civilization and passed on the light of knowledge and learning which, otherwise, would have been lost forever.

Finola knew the lists of Ireland's saints and scholars and their achievements were long. Hadn't her beloved land been known on the Continent, as 'The Island of Saints and Scholars.' She could recite the names of the towering intellects of their day. Men such as Sedulius, John Scotus Erigina, and Marianus, the Tutor of Pope Adrian, were known for their extraordinary learning and were greatly honored and celebrated throughout the whole of Europe. And to them the whole world was indebted for the introduction of scholastic divinity and the application of philosophical reasoning to illustrate the doctrines of Theology.

Filled with pride and inspired by the example of so many - thousands of gifted and learned men and women over the centuries who had gone forth from this, her beloved land, to do so much good, she had decided that she also had an obligation, a duty to herself and her country. She would become an educated woman, a woman of standing and culture. For she knew that nothing in the achievements of her forefathers shone so brightly as the establishment of centers of learning and culture in the many lands they had visited during the centuries called 'The Golden Age of Ireland'. Yes, by their erudition and holiness they had saved Western Civilization in a time when all seemed lost. Now, it would take the young people like herself to save the Irish race and preserve for posterity all that was noble and exhalted in the oldest culture of Western Europe.

She stacked the fresh turf on the fire and was about to rise, satisfied with the goals her mind had set, when Robert staggered from his chair and caught her about the waist with one hand while the other he pressed tightly over her mouth.

"Don't you make a sound, you little Irish bitch or I'll…"

Helpless and taken by surprise, Finola, at first, offered no resistance. Then as Robert dragged her across the floor and pushed her roughly onto the couch, she fought back. Clawing, biting, kicking and scratching, she ran her fingernails down his face.

"Aw! You bloody whore. I'll... I'll make you... you pay for that." He slapped her across the face knocking the wind out of her.

Immediately, he took control. Frail and undernourished, Finola was no match for him.

She looked into the cold, hard, lustful, bloodshot eyes of Robert Sutherland and her heart seemed to freeze within her breast. God! What am I to do? She prayed silently.

He tore at her coarse blue flannel gown ripping the bodice. And before she could regain strength to repulse him, he pushed himself upon her with such force, sheer physical power, that she screeched in agony.

"Ha, ha." he laughed. "I was right. A virgin!" He flung himself upon her again and plunged into her a second time.

The act did not take long, but the ravaging was cruel and the pain excrutiating.

When Robert had spent himself, he rolled over and Finola availed of the opportunity to escape. She ran from the room as quickly as she could clutching at her torn bodice, and descended the back stairs towards the kitchen. Her only thought, at the moment, to put as much distance as possible between herself and Robert Sutherland. When she had reached the ground floor she halted and sat down on the bottom step of the stairs trying to steady herself. She was trembling, her teeth were chattering and the excruciating pain in her loins past bearing. She had to get control of herself. Slowly, and with determination, she regained a semblance of her natural calm composed demeanor. Then she deliberately set her mind to work on a solution to her present dilema.

The consequences of what had just taken place she weighed with a maturity far beyond her years - the future she could not control but the present demanded action. She would inform Mrs. Mulvaney; she needed her advice and assistance.

Again she shivered from head to toe, but she would not allow herself to cry, although, within, every fiber of her being sought that outlet.

She got up. With decisive step and head held high, she entered the kitchen.

"An what in tarnation has kept you, girl? I've been waitin' here for the last half hour for your help." Mrs. Mulvaney rarely got upset with Finola, but at that moment she was preparing to make a souffle and needed fresh eggs. Not receiving an answer, she momentarily ceased all activity, and looking up from her work, knife poised over the chopping block and mouth open, she stared at Finola. There was a momentary silence, then the housekeeper found her tongue. "Now what in the name of God has happened to you?" She paused but receiving no reply, continued: "An' don't tell me it's the auld lame gander, again, for I won't believe a word of it."

Finola sought the nearest stool, for her trembling legs would no longer support her. "Mrs. Mulvaney, I . . . I've got to tell you."

The housekeeper laid down her knife and faced Finola. It was then that she noticed the torn bodice and the red and blue marks under her right eye. Her whole attitude changed; she closed her lips tight and waited for an explanation.

"He... he raped me." With eyes full of pain, never leaving the housekeeper's face, Finola stammered.

"He... who?" cried Mrs. Mulvaney, "What are you talking about?"

"Robert... the young..." she couldn't continue. "Please... please... water," she gasped.

Seeing that the girl was about to lose balance, Mrs. Mulvaney quickly caught hold of her and drew her closer to the open hearth. Her hands were icy cold, all the color had left her cheeks. "Here, lie down awhile, maybe we can get to the end of this," she said trying to be patient with Finola but knowing that if lunch wasn't served on time there would be no patience shown her.

"Seems you're all washed-up child. You're doin' too much. I've said it often, but there's no use in talkin' to some people. You know that, don't you. 'Tis to his Lordship, himself, I should be addressin' my demands." Mrs. Mulvaney not bothering anymore to address her words to Finola, instead, half mumbling to herself, set about making a cup of tea for the girl. As soon as that was accomplished, she sweetened the strong brew with a generous helping of sugar and then added a little milk.

"Here take this. It'll do you good," she said as she placed the mug of hot tea on the floor beside Finola. Then leaving the room Mrs. Mulvaney went outside to collect a few eggs. Upon her return, Finola revived, somewhat, by the tea and the warmth of the fire, had propped herself against the wall. Some color had returned to her pale face. Obviously, the girl was not well . . . but had she heard correctly? Rape! . . . Robert! She continued to mumble to herself. Wasn't the young master out? She was sure Dunne had saddled the grey mare that morning for him.

While Mrs. Mulvaney mulled over these things, Finola's strength and courage returned. She sat upright and in her usual forthright manner addressed her friend. "Mrs. Mulvaney, 'tis awful sorry I am to be causing you trouble especially now when there's so much work to be done. But,... but I can't stay another day in this house. I... I tell you again, I've been raped and 'tis Robert Sutherland that's done it to me. He's above in the library drunk, or half drunk and in a raging mood. I can't stay here with that loutish brute another minute."

"An' what will you do? Where will you go, child?" Mrs. Mulvaney was by now convinced that something did happen. Whether she was raped or not was another story.

Did the girl know the meaning of the word? she asked herself mentally.

"I'll be going to Father Quinn's. After that..." Finola hesitated. She didn't want to tell anyone, not even Mrs. Mulvaney about her plan to go to America.

"Well, if your mind's made up, there's nothing I can do to stop you. But since I'm in such dire straights right now, I'll be needing Kate Malone or Molly Duggan to take your place." She looked sideways at Finola trying to gauge her present condition. "Faith an' sure neither one of them will ever fill your place, I'm thinkin'." Then as Finola rose to her feet, Mrs. Mulvaney threw her arms around her and pressing her tightly to her large bosom gave vent to her maternal feelings. As she released her, she hastily wiped her eyes with the end of her apron, sniffed loudly, and went to the dresser. There, from an old tin box, she quickly withdrew several coins and thrust them into the cold hands.

"Take these child." There was a quaver in her voice. "You well deserve them and more. An' may the good God go with you. Now be off before I change my mind." Emotions were getting the better of her. She could take no more. A blessing of a girl she had been and now God alone knew what would become of her, she thought as she watched her gather her few belongings together.

Finola stopped only long enough to place a kiss on the old lady's cheek. "Thank you, thank you for everything." Then lifting her shawl from her shoulders, and placing it over her beautiful hair, she turned once more and with a little sad smile closed the door.

She walked slowly and with difficulty around to the front of the house. A harvest moon scattered silver dust on satin oak leaves and velvet pines. The night air was cool and a whiff of air carried the fresh pungent smell of the drenched needles. There wasn't a cloud in the sky, only a million diamonds in a cushion of ebony. No breezes caressed the lilies or played with the ferns. The moist earth breathed forth a sweet perfumed breath and from the damp grasses croaking frogs serenaded the Autumn night. Finola still weak and in pain was determined to see once more the graceful exterior of the house. She wished to remember the sweeping avenue and the gate through which she had entered into adult life. Although finding it difficult to proceed, she urged herself forward; she knew it would be the last time she'd see the Manor.

She had spent almost two years behind those walls. How quickly they had passed. How many things had befallen her and her family. They were all gone... Only little Patrick... Oh, where was Dara? Now, when she needed him most, he was, God only knew where.

She returned to the back of the house and made her way as she always did across the meadow. She shivered. The going was slow but she forged ahead ever determined to overcome... even now when it meant conquering physical pain.

What a moon! It was almost as bright as day. She had reached the stile. How often she had waited there for him... anticipating the sound of his whistle, the warmth of his loving embrace, the tenderness of his kisses. And again her heart cried out. Oh, Dara, Dara where are you? And, for the first time, there was doubt. A little doubt, like a tiny worm knawing at her heart's core. She did not doubt that he loved her, or had loved her when he held her in his arms, when he told her so face to face here in this very spot. But who could tell what snares and temptations awaited him in the New World... so far away, so very far away. It had been such a long time since she had heard from him - not since that night, the night he had come to say goodbye. Not a word from him... not a sound, not even a wee whisper. No one knew where Dara O'Rourke was and if they did they weren't saying.

Now she too would have to go. She would have to flee like a hunted animal from the land and the home she loved. She would have to face the world, a world of strangers and strange ways, all alone. She would have to fend not only for herself but for her small brother. There would be no one to advise her, no one to help, no one on whom she could depend. She would be solely responsible for little Patrick as well as herself. She would have to be strong, determined, steadfast. Finola sighed... a long slow sigh. She was tired. She hadn't realized how tired until now. Then she looked about her again, as if savoring for the last time the beauty that lay before her. So lovely... so very lovely.

"And I must leave it all. Leave the fields and the streams, the song of the thrush, the lark, and the blackbird. Never again will I see the fat robin redbreast building her nest in the spring. Never will I see the young lambs playing in the lush meadows; nor will I smell the fragrant flowers of woodland and hedge... snowdrop, cowslip, and primrose." Finola spoke her thoughts as the golden moon rode high in the evening sky. Soon her cheeks were wet. She placed her head in her hands and allowed the fountain of her sorrow to break lose its bonds. She was alone; she could endulge herself a little after the horrific evening she had endured.

Then she prayed to God, to His Blessed Mother, to all the Saints she had ever heard of, to her dead mother and father, her sisters and brothers asking their protection in the new life she was about to embrace, for the long hazardous journey she would soon undertake and the strange faraway land she would, in the near future, call home.

Cold and feeling miserable, she finally got to her feet. She would have to tell her friend, Sive, the reason for leaving the Manor but her only hope for help was the old priest, Father Quinn.

Chapter 10

"Where there is sorrow, there is holy ground."
                                         - Oscar Wilde.

With no hope for the potato crop, the winter of 1847 would be a catastrophy. By mid- October, Fr. Quinn had succeeded in contacting a friend, the Reverend Con O'Hara who had organized a party of about a hundred families wishing to leave Ireland for New Orleans. Father O'Hara's plan was twofold: to save as many Irish families as he could from starvation and to found a strong Irish Catholic community in the State of Louisiana. To the care of this saintly man Finola and her brother were entrusted.

As Fr. Quinn bade them and others of his parish farewell, the words of Lady Speranza echoed in his brain.

> "Weary men, what reap ye?
> Golden corn for the stranger.
> What sow ye? Human corpes for the avenger.
> Fainting forms, hunger stricken,
> What see ye in the offing?
> Stately ships to bear our food away,
> Amid the stranger's scoffing.
> There's a proud array of soldiers,
> What do they round your door?
> They guard our masters granaries
> From the thin hands of the poor."

And the priest could not help contrasting the pitiful concourse setting forth that day from Ireland's shores with those of a bygone era. The time Finola was so recently reminded of. The time when Europe, sunk in the depths of ignorance and despair, was saved through the efforts and sacrifices of saintly souls, stout-hearted, valiant men and women who journeyed far and wide to spread not only Christianity but a love of learning.

From her schools and monasteries Ireland sent her monks and nuns, her poets, bards and musicians to preach and teach, to plant and sow to build and nurture. Wherever they went, whether to the fertile valleys of France or the flat lands of far off Russia, to the cold northlands of Germany or the mild Italian climate, the Irish taught by word and example. They founded centers of culture and learning which helped shape the future of Europe and set the stage for the glorious reawakening that was to come.

Fr. Quinn could only pray that Ireland, his beloved Ireland would somehow survive. Though beaten and humliated, she would rise again; that one day her people would again be free, free from oppression, injustice and greed.

Finola stood on the quay in Cobh, harbor for Cork, awaiting with so many others the boat from Liverpool. She wore her mothers black woolen shawl. It covered her head and wrapped her frail body against the cold sea breezes and reaching to her ankles it also covered her long red woolen skirt allowing only the tips of her black leather boots to be seen. Beside her stood little Patrick. He had a woolen cap and a new freeze coat the color of slate, a white linen shirt and corduroy breeeches, woolen stockings and black boots. Though fairly well dressed, for Fr. Quinn saw to it that the two had, at least, the bare necessities, Patrick was shivering. They had been out on the open quay all night and now towards noon had eaten only a piece of bread and cheese.

Finola looked at him and her heart bled. His little face was set against the cold blasts but his teeth were chattering. He gazed up at her with questioning sad eyes, but didn't speak.

She squeezed his hand. "It won't be long now, a grá. We'll be going aboard in a little while." She tried to reassure him, to calm his unspoken fears. "An' then we'll get something hot to eat."

She was unable to secure a place below deck due to the fact that her passage was obtained at a very late date. But she did succeed in finding a little nook between an assortment of casks and barrels near the stern on the upper deck; a canvas covering protected the area. Here, at least, she thought they would not be completely exposed to the elements. Each passenger was legally supposed to be provided with thirty-three inches in width of sleeping space, but, in reality, only got about half that.

Two days rations of sea biscuits were passed out, most of which were already stale. Each passenger was given a tin cup of water. Cooking was restricted to certain areas on the main deck and people had to wait their turns to avail of the spots.

The ship, called the *Chasca*, no more than a tub of a vessel, was fitted out to accommodate three hundred. But there were more than five hundred on board that morning. No one bothered to count the exact number.

As it eased out into the Atlantic, its creaking timbers struck terror into little Patrick. He looked anxiously at his big sister.

"It's all right. Don't be afraid. It will take us to America; you'll see."

Sailing along the coast of Cork and Kerry, Finola kept her eyes on the green hills of the country she loved so much. Would she ever see this dear land again, she asked herself. And in her heart there was a great void, one she knew would never more be filled. Nor was she alone in her thoughts. For not an eye on board that day was dry. Old men and young, women and children wept to see the verdant fields of their native land slipping farther and farther away into the distance Soon the mists and the clouds swallowed up the last vistages forever.

"She's gone, our beautiful country is gone. How peacefully I could have spent my days there if only our enemies hadn't destroyed everything." A man, hat in hand, as if showing respect for a great lady or a dead friend, thus bade Ireland farewell.

Finola looked at him as the tears streamed down his pale face. Then she turned to comfort and protect Patrick who was still shivering. She placed her hand on his forehead. God! she cried within, he's burning up. What could she do. If he had the fever, all on board would shun them They would be outcasts, as lepers to be avoided at all cost. Even if such a thing were nigh impossible in those overcrowded conditions, there would be some who would make her life miserable.

She pushed her way back to the protective area she had claimed for herself and fixed a little bed for Patrick, using whatever she could find in her bundle - her mother's winter petticoat and part of an old blanket to make it comfortable. She took off the cloak she, herself, was wearing and wrapped his emaciated body in it. Then she went to get something for him to drink.

All this time Patrick never asked for anything, not even a drop of water. Used to hunger and want, he merely looked with great, haunting, blue eyes at his sister and knew she would do whatever she could to help him.

A few minutes later, Finola returned to his side with a tin-cup of water already discolored and foul tasting. She raised his head and tried to coax him to swallow a few drops, but the effort was too much. He lay back and closed his eyes. He was very tired.

Finola sat beside him and took his small hand. Gently, she carressed it as softly she sang:

> 'O swan of slenderness,
> Dove of tenderness,
> Jewel of joys, arise!
> The little red lark,
> Like a soaring spark
> Of song, to his sunburst flies;
> But till thou'rt risen,
> Earth is a prison
> Full of my lonesome sighs;
> Then awake and discover
> To thy fond lover
> The morn of thy matchless eyes.'

Her voice soft and sweet as the lark itself caught the attention of those in close proximity and when she had finished, there was grateful applause even from the sick; for wee Patrick was not the only 'fever' stricken passenger on the *Chasca* that evening.

The conditions on board were indiscribable. A mug of water and some salted meat was supplied once a day. The poor passengers were unable to partake of the meat for it caused an unquenchable thirst. Those on deck were exposed to the elements and those below to the noxious fumes of the unsanitary and unventilated hold, for the ships which crossed and re-crossed the Atlantic with the Irish emigrants were, for the most part, cargo vessels quickly converted to house the thousands seeking escape from poverty and starvation, after they had unloaded their cargoes of timber or other merchandise. There was no medical care whatsoever. The only release from pain, the only comfort for the dying was death, itself.

Finola was awake most of that first night applying a cold cloth to Patrick's burning forehead. Towards morning, she dozed off dreaming of happy days when they were small and the family was together. When Dara strong and handsome and so much in love with her came strolling down the bóithrín. His lively whistling filling the air with sweet music, how eagerly she looked forward to his happy greeting, his warm embrace. Then he was before her, his arms outstretched waiting at the dock as her ship pulled in. She heard him call her name, "Finola, Finola m' darlin' I've waited a long time... so long... long... long...." She was about to walk down the gangway when she was rudely awakened.

A red-faced sun had appeared on the horizon, the winds had picked up and the seas were choppy. Finola tossed about, awoke with a start. She heard her name. It was Mrs. Bridie MacMullan who was speaking. She had taken possession of the only space left between Finola and the side of the ship.

"Ah, sure let her alone. Why disturb the poor thing? Sure, there's nothing she can do now."

Somehow, Finola knew the woman was talking about her. She sat up and looked around. "Where am I?"

"It's all right, a grá. Take it easy now," said the same voice.

Then Finola realized that Patrick was no longer beside her. "Patrick! My little brother, where is he?" she cried out.

As she got to her feet intending to go and look for him, a hand was laid on her shoulder. "Wait, wait a moment, Finola." The voice was soft and full of concern.

Finola turned and looked into the sweetest face she had seen in a long time.

Brenda Gallager, a woman of about thirty-five with a small baby in her arms was seated not too far off.

"Come and sit beside me a grá." She shifted the baby who was asleep to one arm and made a place for Finola beside her. "There's no use hidin' the truth from you. Your little brother is gone to God."

Finola remained mute for a moment, as if trying to comprehend what had happened. She had seen enough of death and dying in her short life to know that there was nothing she could do when the final hours came.

"Aw!" Finola gasped when the reality dawned on her. Then opening her beautiful eyes wide in disbelief she jumped to her feet. "No, it can't be. He was -" Then her thoughts turned to the shivering, trembling little form of the night before. He must have been far sicker than I realized. "Where is he now?" she asked. "I want to see him."

"You won't be able to do that, a grá," answered Brenda.

And Finola understood. And the tears began to fall. She sat down again burying her face in her hands. "Oh God! You have taken them all. I thought you'd leave me poor little Patrick." And she cried bitterly.

Brenda did not interfer but allowed Finola to give full vent to her sorrow.

After a few minutes, Finola again addressed her new friend. "When, when did it happen?"

"As you were sleepin', lass. The little one had no pain. I heard him cough, once, an' as I was awake myself feedin' this one," here she nodded towards the infant in her arms, "I happened to look over at him. Shortly after, he gave a little gasp and I knew his precious soul had gone to join the angels."

* * * *

Each and every day on that seven week voyage, Finola was to witness the same ghastly scene as the wretched ill-clad bodies were confined to their last resting places in the depths of the Atlantic ocean

The days following Patrick's death were long and lonely indeed. Finola tried to distract herself by lending a hand to the distraught and harried young mothers around her. But her heart ached with a fierce and gnawing pain and her mind anguished and was tortured by the uncertainty of her own physical condition. What if she were pregnant? She had been grievously violated and the dire consequences might be more than she could bear.

With no one to whom she could turn, she kept all hidden deep in her heart and tried to face each new day and every waking hour with a firm resolve that come what may, she would find a way out of her dilema, a solution to her problems. She consoled herself in her bleakest moments with the thought that, somehow, she would find Dara. He would be waiting for her and together they would overcome all obstacles.

Having no idea of the great distances that separated the port of New Orleans, her destination, from New York where Dara was supposed to have landed, it never occurred to her that she might not find him when she arrived in America.

Grappling with the alternatives her mind presented for nigh on four weeks regarding the possibility of pregnancy, she woke up one morning to the realization that the problem no longer existed. Tears of gratitude welled up in her beautiful eyes. Those who were closest to her observed her confusion but they dismissed her apparent dilemma as embarrassment or the keen sensitivity of a young woman of her age.

* * * *

About six months after Finola left on her long journey to America, a letter arrived for her in care of Mrs. Mulvaney at the Manor.

The Bronx
New York U.S.A.
Sept. 24, 1848

Finola m'darlin'

Since I left ye, my mind knows no peace. Your beautiful face is ever present and I await the day when we can be together.

I got me a job. Sure, it's not what I would be callin' great but it keeps a roof over me head and gives me two square meals a day. So I can't complain. But I'm aimin' to do better. If you can hang on a little longer, I'll be having them tickets for you.

With the help o' God we'll be together come Christmas even if I've to beg, borrow, or steal.

I love you with all me heart and not a day, ah, what am I sayin, at all, not even an hour goes by that I don't be thinkin' of you.

And, as you would say: 'I have me plans,' plans for the both of us. So darlin', a cuisle mo croí, think of me sometimes. The day is coming when we will be able to live in peace and comfort.

Your ever loving
'Dara'.

Mrs. Mulvaney looked at the address when she had wiped her eyes. She had heard that New York was a terrible big city. Dara didn't say what kind of work he had or where he lived. But, she concluded, maybe The Bronx was an important residence like the Manor and if she were to reply telling him about Finola's departure he would surely get the letter just as she had received his. Who could tell, maybe New Orleans wasn't too far away from New York and if so, he could get in touch with his previous girl. So without delay, the good woman took on the formidable task and that very day mailed her response making sure to give the details of Finola's hasty departure.

About four months later, Dara wrote again, and true to his word, sent the tickets for Finola and little Patrick but never a mention as to whether he had received Mrs. Mullvaney's letter. However, as she reread the short note that accompanied the tickets, she realized that this time the address was much longer.

Again the good woman put pen to paper, reiterated her previous story and enclosing the tickets mailed them to the new address.

It was well after Christmas and into the New Year before a reply came from Dara. He thanked her for returning the tickets but said little about his grief. He'd follow her lead and search New Orleans till he found his Finola. It was all he could do, but he was sorely disappointed to hear the news of her early departure from Ireland.

Part II
New Orleans

When I remember all
The friends, so link'd together
I've seen around me fall
Like leaves in wintry weather;
I feel like one
Who treads alone
Some banquet hall deserted,
Whose lights are fled
Whose garlands dead,
And all but he departed!

Thomas Moore (1779 - 1852)

Chapter 11

"They can conquer who believe they can."
- Dryden

The New Orleans to which Finola was introduced was a world so exotic, so colorful, that her wildest imaginings could never have conceived such a fantastic place.

New Orleans! Gateway to the Mississippi. Sparkling gem of the mighty Delta. Growing in leaps and bounds, it was a curious mixture of cultures, a mingling of colors and customs as varied as the flotsam and jetsam of the muddy river that hugged its banks.

A surge of excitement swept through the newcomers. They were caught up in the frenzy, the flurry, the hustle and bustle that was the everyday life of the busy wharfs. The noise was deafening - rasping voices hollering orders, whistles and huge belching smoke-stacks, braying mules hauling wagons laden with cotton bales, barking dogs, and screeching urchins, and among all the hullabaloo the constant cries of aggressive vendors plying their trades.

The air was heavy with the super-sweet odor of molasses, the pungent smell of mixed spices and a curious tangy aroma she did not then know but later learned was coffee. As Finola awaited her turn to disembark, she noticed how the gentle warm breezes carried flecks of cotton from the bales piled high on the levee and few in the bustling crowds escaped the tell-tale signs.

At the time, New Orleans was considered the richest city in America. And those who held this belief stoutly defended their claim with facts and figures showing it had the country's greatest per capita wealth. These facts, at least, were true, its banking capital had soared higher than New York City's even in the 1830's. Its exports often exceeded its rival and its port easily competed.

As the forth largest city in America, it was attracting people from all over the world as well as from all over the country. Thomas Jefferson had said that: 'The position of New Orleans certainly destines it to be the greatest city the world has ever seen.'

This was the city into which the *Chasca* sailed in the winter of 1847. Vessels of all sizes, shapes and colors crowded the wharf-sides. Perhaps the grandest of all were the new steam-packets - white and proud and clean, they were moored along the walls of Canal St., once an outlying wasteland; it was now busily astir as a commercial center. On one side, just fronting the French Quarter, the ocean-going vessels with their gray sails furled disgorged the new immigrants and following them the gangplanks unloaded sailors in wild and gaudy garb from a multitude of nations all around the world. On the other side, where the American section was growing rapidly, flatboats, keelboats, and all sorts of smaller river craft fought and jostled for space. The area nearest the waterfront was known as the "Irish Channel". Here thousands of Irish immigrants had made their homes and gave their names and customs to the surroundings. And, as always, they kept a fierce independence, and never lost their love for Ireland. They clung closely to their own kith and kin. The men worked on the river, the cotton presses, and all related tasks. They drove the cabs and the drays and quickly added the flavor of French phrases to their own special turn of the English language. And as they did elsewhere, they soon worked their way up on the social ladder and into the political positions of the day holding posts of power and authority.

The highlight of their yearly calendar was the annual St. Patrick's Day parade. To this event, they all turned out despite the weather. However, to keep things livened-up throughout the rest of the year, the inevitable wakes, of which there were all too many, were conscientiously and dutifully attended. These shindigs, which lasted until the corpse was taken to the church yard, were sure to provide entertainment go leor. Starting with the keening, gradually the talking and drinking would take its place. Then eating, drinking, and storytelling interspersed with jokes, cursing, and the odd fight, the Irish Wake continued well into the wee hours of the morning.

It was the time when cotton was king and its power growing steadily, but sugar was trying desperately to catch up. This waterfront in New Orleans was called 'the master street of the world'. Not even in London, it was said, could one find so dense a crowd, so congested a dock.

Although the bulk of the trade was in cotton and sugar, there was a great variety of goods to be bought and sold - coffee, rum, barrels of pickled foods, kegs of salted meats and fish, hemp, tobacco, and skins.

Into this maelstrom Finola was hurled and as she gaped in awe and wonder at the sights, the sounds that reached her sensitive ears were no less bewildering. Speech and accents were distinct not only among the newcomers but even among the Americans themselves. They came from all parts of the land and their lingo betrayed their origins - whether it was the Carolinas, Kentucky, Georgia, New York or as far away as the cold remote regions of Canada.

Father O'Hara eventually found a safe place for Finola. It was late evening when she was entrusted to the care of Mrs. O'Grady who kept a boarding house in a lane off Canal St. The building was similar to the line of houses stretching ahead and rose directly from the sidewalk - the banquette. The only difference was the color of the painted plaster exteriors, for the pinks and blues, and even purples were quite individual. Although unpretentious, Mrs. O'Grady's establishment was adequate. It served its purpose and made its proprietor a comfortable living.

Finola shared a room with a young woman of great beauty. Her skin was light brown, her eyes darting orbs of blackness dancing in the lamplight, her hair blue-black and falling to her hips, her lips rosebuds of the brightest hue. Finola never saw anyone so beautiful before. She noticed her slender frame, and the energy with which she sorted her worldly goods.

Mrs. O'Grady introduced Finola. "Madeleine, this is Finola O'Donnell. She'll be your roommate for a few days. She's from Ireland."

Madeleine stepped towards Finola and acknowledged her with a slight bow of her head. She quickly made an appraisal of her feminine charms and then nodded approvingly. "Enchanté, ma petite. You very pretty. Welcome."

"Thank you," answered Finola.

At this point Mrs. O'Grady withdrew. Alone together, Madeleine soon started up a conversation. She told her new roommate she had come from Paris, that she would not be staying long with Mrs. O'Grady. She had, in fact, a much better place to go to. She knew Monsieur Bernard Marigny, and although Finola had never heard of the gentleman, everyone in New Orleans considered him one of the richest men in the city.

As Madeleine spoke she raised her dusky head and assumed a proud pose while her delicate hands moved in fluid artistic gesticulations.

"You mean you have found work already?" Finola asked incredulously.

"Mais oui, cheri. I know Monsieur Bernard a long time - I meet him in Paris. He love me very much. He ask me to come America . . . So, I come." She paused a moment and a smile of pleasure and contentment spread across her sallow face and lit up her gorgeous black eyes.

Finola was fascinated. She had never before seen anyone so enchanting. Yet, there remained a puzzle, a question, in her mind. Why, she asked herself, why then hadn't Monsieur Bernard, whom Madeleine professed loved her so much, come to meet her at the ship, taken her to his home? She was about to ask but was interrupted with another confidential snippet.

"Finola, " Madeleine looked at her new friend in an appraising way. "You like to meet with Monsieur Bernard? I think he like you."

Finola wasn't assured and decided to play it safe. "I'll take a look about myself, first, thank you." She would talk to Mrs. O'Grady in the morning and find out exactly where the better homes were located. A well-to-do Irish family would be her first choice, she inwardly concluded.

Accordingly the following morning after breakfast, Finola confided in Mrs. O'Grady. She told her of the conversation with Madeleine and her offer to introduce her to Monsieur Bernard.

"Glory be to God, child! 'Tis you're the innocent one. Sure that Madeleine, a Creole from the West Indies, is no more French than you or I. Paris, indeed. Huh. No, Finola stay far from that one and her likes . . . Says she's movin' out in a day or two, well, I'll be lookin' for a replacement, then. She's no more than a strumpet, child, if you get me meaning. And Mrs. O'Grady screwed up her face in a grotesque manner confirming her disapproval of Madeleine and the French in general. Then assuming a more protective and motherly attitude, she placed her arm around Finola's shoulder and drew her into the kitchen.

"Come, child sit down here a moment. I can see you need to be told the facts of life . . . well, at least, as they pertain to this mighty metropolis, before you set out to find yourself a job." Mrs. O'Grady's round rosy cheeks relaxed and there was a twinkle in her grey-blue eyes. "We may as well have a cup of tea." She stoked the grate and put on a kettle of water. "No turf in these parts, but the bit of coal does the work just as well. Aye, there are many things different in this country, lass. An' the way of doin' things is also different. No doubt you saw all that for yourself as you came off the boat yesterday." The good woman stopped to take a breath but she wasn't finished.

"I did, indeed. Never before saw so many strange people - all colors, shapes and sizes and so many languages . . ." Finola managed to get a word in edgewise.

"That's it. You've said it, girl. Different people. You've got to be very careful, especially with the colored folk. Mind you, I'm not sayin' they're all bad, but their ways are very different from ours."

"How so?" Finola asked.

"Well, take Miss Madeleine for instance. Now I know for a fact that she's one of them 'Sirenes'." Some call them the 'serpent women'. Many of them live quite well off in little houses near the ramparts. Some are very pretty, with good figures, fine features; they carry themselves with much grace and dignity but their desire is to lure a wealthy man from his family. So when Miss Madeleine tells you she is loved by Monsieur Bernard you can be sure she's out to get herself a little house and freedom from want and toil. So be careful, child. You don't want to get trapped in that kind of a life."

Finola had to agree. She had no intention of becoming someone's mistress.

"I'd advise you to seek employment in the American section. There are some fine homes being built there and I'm sure a good reliable young woman like yourself will be appreciated in one of them.

Armed with Mrs. O'Grady's advice and her own indomitable will, Finola set out an hour later. She made her way, first, towards the French District. For despite Mrs. O'Grady's warnings, Finola was drawn to the exotic Madeleine and wanted to see firsthand the surroundings and lifestyle this young damsel was about to embrace.

Crossing Canal St., she quickly walked along Chartres St. and soon came to the Place d' Armes which was the city's center. The old square was used as an assembly place, for parades, and such like and came into being with the birth of the city itself. It remained the same down through the years. It had a central area planted with grass and shrubs. To one side stood the Cathedral which had been completed in 1794, a completely Spanish structure with a pair of bell-shaped towers. Along side the Cathedral the massive three story state house with its unique architecture - grandiose Spanish below and delicate French above. The stuccoed massive exterior walls were broken by fanlighted windows, and wrought-iron balconies added the Creole dimension. As her eyes travelled upward, she noted the royal arms of Spain emblazoned on a pediment on top of which was a balustrade.

Finola stood a moment longer to take in the sights. Across the square on the other two sides ran long brick buildings with stately galleries decorated with wrought–iron work which contrasted beautifully with the crimson background for the walls were a bright red. She drew in her breath. She had never seen anything so lovely. And all around her the gaiety and activity of the city was utterly captivating. She was spellbound, rivetted to the spot. She noted the conglomeration of people - French, Spanish, American, Italian, Irish, German, Chinese, Greek, Filipino and Negro but most prominent and certainly most attractive, in Finola's eyes, were the Creoles. She was fascinated by the variety of their coloring especially of the young women - from the light coffee color to dark olive. She was soon to learn they had a variety of names to go along with their coloring, not always quite accurate - mulatto, quadroon, octoroon, tierceron, griffe and there were more. She liked their gay, and happy dispositions and stood fascinated by their dress. Some wore beautiful robes of velvet, others damask lavishly trimmed with lace or expensive ribbons. Their faces were brightly painted with rouge and several sported small beauty spots. The tinkle and merriment of their laughter rose above the chatter of the crowds. And there was music everywhere. From an upstairs window the crystal clear notes of a truely superb soprano practicing an area for that night's performance at the opera floated to the street below. Across the boulevard a little marchande with a basket of fruit on her head sang snatches of favorites from Carmen. A big Italian fixing his vegetable stall tried to drown out the female voices with his redition of Figaro's aria from *The Barber of Seville*. Astonished, Finola noticed how two Frenchmen were arguing over the vocal accomplishments of the latest Diva to grace their operatic stage.

"So Charmante!" said the first man enthusiastically waving his arms as he spoke.

"Mon ami, I disagree. Too big, too fat, too ugly." Then he thought the better of his remarks and tried to make amends. "But her voice!" he nodded his head and there was tenderness in his dark eyes as he remembered the performance. "Yes," he continued, "what a voice!"

Soon Finola's natural lively disposition caught the spirit, the joie de vivre of sultry, seductive New Orleans.

She skipped towards the Cathedral. A little prayer to the Blessed Virgin would surely help her in her quest for work and a new life in this wonderful city.

On her knees in the great church with its golden icons and gaudy display of clothed statues, she felt very out of place. Never having seen the interior of a Spanish church before, all the glitter, the pervasive smell of incense, and the hundreds of lighted candles were more a distraction than a help to her devotions.

Thoughts of little Patrick - his trusting blue eyes seeking reassurance as they boarded the *Chasca*, his raging temperature, the fever, his shivering small body appeared and disappeared troubling her mind and imagination. She thought of Ireland - the beautiful green fields, the flowers, the cool air, the fresh smell of the brown earth. She brushed a nagging noisy mosquito from her face. "These horrid things." How painfully they bit leaving marks and welts and nasty red spots on her pale white skin despite the net curtain she was obliged to use the previous night - such a disagreeable and confining way to sleep.

"I expect there will be many more strange and unusual things I'll have to do in this strange and unusual city before long." she mumbled to herself.

A candle hissed and sputtered in its sconce reminding her that she had come to pray. "Holy Mother, I'm all alone in this world now. Not even Dara can find me here. Please help me. I need a good home. I need to make something of myself."

Then again thoughts of Dara came rushing into her mind. She sighted. Her heart felt heavy. Would she ever see him again? How far was it to New York? She would have to find out. Perhaps she could go and search for him. But the more she thought about that idea the less she liked it. She compared what she had seen of New Orleans to what she had heard about New York. It would never work. She concluded it would be like looking for a needle in a haystack.

The sounds of a band, strident, loud and off key penetrated the cool dark interior of the church. Finola was again distracted. She had been out since before noon and as yet had not even spoken to anyone about employment. She had no idea how far away the Garden Section was but she knew she had deliberately chosen the opposite direction. Now that her curiosity about the French Quarter has been satisfied and that she had learned how the people lived, she decided it was best to be on her way. She certainly didn't want to be out after dark in a strange city.

You didn't come here to find trouble, she warned herself. Then making the sign of the cross she got up off her knees. Looking around the huge church once more, she genuflected towards the high altar, and left its dark confines. She emerged into the bright sunshine and for a brief moment was dazzled by the glare. It was hot and humid. She wiped away the beads of perspiration that had gathered on her upper lip with the back of her hand.

"I must get to the Garden District as quickly as possible," she mumbled urging herself foward.

On her way she saw many more examples of the ironwork for which the Orleanians had a penchant - patterns in grapes and cornstalk, or delicate intertwining lattice work - in fact any design or shape the proprietors seemed to wish. She noted how the more affluent citizens liked their privacy, for always a carriageway or gate separated the house and inner courtyard from the street. So elegant were the dwellings that Finola hastened her step; she would find a position in one such house, come what may. But then a warning voice within said, "No - the Garden District for you."

Reluctantly, she heeded the inner voice. "I'll check out the American area first, anyway. Better be sure than sorry," she encouraged herself.

Upon turning into a very large, straight, wide street, she came upon a house that really impressed her. Built in the tradition of the great homes of the South with Grecian columns and wide verandas, the New Orleans wrought-iron touch added for flavor, this mansion was magnificient. It stood three-stories high and had a stuccoed exterior.

Inquiring regarding the occupants of such an impressive home, Finola was told it belonged to Mr. Sheridan and his family.

"Is he Irish, then?" she continued.

"Can't rightly say, Miss." answered the stranger. But there are many here from the old sod."

She thanked the man and decided to try her luck. Lifting the latch on the huge iron gate, she entered the carriageway that lead to the impressive front door. Immediately she was back in Ireland to the time when she first set out to find a job. She pictured the driveway leading to the Manor and felt again the fear she had experienced within those cold unfriendly walls. How naive she was then. Had she known what was to happen to her in that house she would never have darkened its doors. She stood looking at the Sheridan mansion wondering... "But I'm here now. God alone knows what's in store for me in this place. I must go forward no matter what the future brings." Thus armed she tilted her head in her own inimitable way and boldly stepped forward walking straight up the steps that led to the enormous entrance.

* * * *

Everything about Mr. John Francis Sheridan was large. He was a big man standing over six feet tall with broad shoulders, large hands and feet and a florid high- cheeked face. He had happy grey-blue eyes, a rather prominent nose and a wide mouth that never seemed to be shut. Not to be overlooked or obscured by the other features, his ears were especially large and red and sticking out from his head like two great cabbage leaves. His one redeeming grace was his fine crop of wavy, sandy hair of which he was very proud. He wore a mustache and kept his whiskers well waxed.

In keeping with his own personal and physical dimensions, John Francis had a large family - twelve children ranging in ages from twenty to three. There were eight boys and four girls. A rowdy but not unmanageable bunch over whom his roar always had the desired effect - instant and complete silence.

John Francis hailed from Irish Catholic stock, but that was several generations back and although he was proud of his heritage, he now considered himself a full-blooded American Yankee. He had made his name and fortune on the cotton market while still young and built himself a mansion in the growing city of New Orleans. He then married the homely daughter of a prominent Protestant New Englander, Annabella Tillbury, and thereafter settled into a rather placid and, I may add, at times boring family life. A humdrum existance, one might call it, except for his infrequent little visits to the French Quarter. Although Annabella knew of these escapades, she never hinted of them to anyone, least of all to her husband, for she had been taught that a dutiful wife paid attention to the running of her house and the upbringing of children and did not meddle in her husband's affairs.

Annabella was a rather plump woman. In her early forties, she was already showing signs of premature aging. Her dark brown hair was streaked with grey and no amount of powder could camouflage the crows feet that framed her eyes. She had a double chin and a small mouth. Her skin was sallow, no doubt the result of the French connection some three generations back. Her great-grandfather had married several times and was not particular about the background of his wives. His excuse: "White women are a scarce commodity in this country. A man must have a woman to warm his bed so he does the best he can."

Annabella was taciturn by nature and rarely raised her voice above a whisper.

She, therefore, had very little trouble with the servants who went about their work in a happy-go-lucky way. There were several colored hands for the hard outdoor work but they were free men for Mr. Sheridan didn't hold with slavery. All the servants in the house were white with the exception of Mammy who ruled the nursery and at times the rest of the house. Gracie, the scullary maid was Creole.

The children were tutored at home, a separate area of the house having been set aside for their school rooms and recreation. Children were to be seen not heard and they were rarely seen by John Frances except on special occasions or before bedtime when they dutifully filed into the sittingroom to bid him goodnight or, in the case of the young ones, to deposit a kiss on his shiny forehead accompanied by the usual prodding and coaxing from Mammy.

It was understood that John Francis Jr. the oldest son, would follow in his father's footsteps. He would learn as did the 'old man' by getting involved and working his way up in the business. However, Frank, as he liked to call himself, was not given to hard work. And since his father had so much money he didn't see why he, the first born, should have to associate with the mulattos and negros on the wharfs and in the warehouses in order to learn how to run a thriving business.

This was the home and family for whom Finola aspired to work on that sunny afternoon in December 1847. The door was opened by a young woman with a bright cheery disposition.

"I'd like to talk to the lady of the house, please." Finola was encouraged by the friendly atmosphere.

"An' who shall I say wishes to speak to Madam?" asked the maid.

"Say Finola O'Donnell, please. I'm lately come from Ireland where I was employed in Lord Sutherland's Manor and now seek work here." Finola carefully enunciated every word and drew herself up to her full height. She would make a good impression even on the servants.

"Come in, then, Finola. My name is Monica. You might be in luck. 'Tis only this mornin' that the parlor maid, Nelly, left. 'Twould be nice to have someone my own age." Monica was evaluating Finola's attributes and liked what she saw, particularly the age factor. "Why don't you sit here, till I go and tell Madam."

"Thank you," said Finola as she seated herself on a plush velvet chair near the hall-stand.

As Monica hurried along the hallway towards the back of the house, Finola had time to look around. In the middle of the hall, the hard, teak floor was covered with a rich dark burgundy carpet, the center of which displayed a large cluster of multicolored flowers. Several other chairs similar to the one on which she was sitting were placed at intervals along the side of the hall. There were many plants, especially palms scattered around.

Several large mirrors with golden frames decorated and contrasted with the black flocked wallpaper. A few pictures, mostly landscapes of European origin were also visible from where she was sitting.

To her limited and untutored mind in such matters, this home seemed to be very beautiful and she hoped she would be lucky enough to be hired. Her thoughts were interrupted as she saw Monica coming towards her.

"Madam will see you at once," she said, as she approached, a smile on her pretty face. "Follow me, Finola."

The room into which she was shown was sumptuous. Her imagination could never have envisioned such grandeur. But before she had time to take it all in, the lady of the house, Mrs. Sheridan, spoke.

"Sit down, Finola. Monica tells me you have come seeking employment."

"Yes, Ma'm."

Monica withdrew closing the door behind her and suddenly Finola felt a little scared. Yet, the woman before her was anything but threatening.

"Come now, tell me what experience you have. I hear you are but lately come from Ireland."

Finola's old courage returned. She had plenty of experience she told herself and she was determined to make the most of it.

A half an hour later, she left the room in triumph. She had completely convinced Mrs. Sheridan of her worth and was told to go fetch her things and move into the upstairs room with Monica that very evening. She would be paid $5.00 a month all-found. For such a sum she would be expected to act as personal maid to Mrs. Sheridan as well as attending to guests and serving at table. She was elated.

Her hard work and perseverance at the Manor had paid off. She would now learn all she could in this situation and who could tell what she might be able to achieve at some future time and place.

* * * *

Finola settled into her new home and position without much difficulty. She soon became a favorite with the whole household. Even the three year old toddler, Amy, refused to eat unless Finola served her. Rowena, the oldest girl, she would celebrate her seventeenth birthday with the coming of April, became deeply attached to the new Irish serving girl. This unusual friendship developed, it was thought, because of several quite plausible reasons. To begin with, the two young women were close to the same age, Finola being about a year younger. Both had a natural happy disposition, and while Rowena had the good fortune to have had a tutor all her life, Finola was not without some education. In fact, she found she was far superior in her knowledge of Latin and Greek. From Rowena, Finola would learn how young ladies of the South behaved in society - from the gowns they wore to certain functions, such as the theater, the opera, or a ball, to the way they painted their faces, wore their hair, fluttered their fans and glanced coyly above them at the elegant youths they fancied.

"Oh, Finola, I don't know how I ever managed without you." Rowena looked at the pretty face of her friend, for she did not consider her as one of the servants. Even to visitors she spoke of her as a companion. Now that she was all grown-up, she reasoned she needed someone in whom she could confide, someone to share her dreams, secrets, and plans.

Rowena was not a pretty girl. She was, in fact, quite plain. Her mouth was too big, her eyes small and an insipid grey-blue, and her nose had a pinched look. Her skin was clear and creamy-white, her best feature. And although she didn't pay too much attention to her figure, at that time, she did have a good one. With her hair, however, she was unduly occupied. It was dark-brown and cascaded in silky waves to her waist and surrounded her round face with teasing tendrils. She was a naturally happy carefree young lady, enjoying life and all it had to offer to one of her station. She hadn't been a particularly bright student, but then she hadn't particularly liked to study. One accomplishment, however, in which Rowena was acceptably proficient was playing the pianoforte. This skill her mother had insisted she acquire as no household worthy of the name could be without such an instrument, and no daughter of any respectable family without that accomplishment.

Now that her student days had come to an end, her leisure hours were many and since she was the only girl among the older members of the family, the company of her brothers was not one which she enjoyed. Except, of course, when they brought home male friends; at such times, Rowena became quite ostentatious and very attentive to her brothers.

Finola's duties were light in comparison with what was demanded of her at the Manor. Answering the hall door, showing ladies and gentlemen to the waiting room, serving at dinner, she was expected at all times to look clean, neat, and cheery. With a long blue gown perfectly fitted to her beautifully shaped body, a spotless apron trimmed with a ruffle and a starched white ruffle on her gold-red hair, she was a delight to behold not only to the family but to all who came to call on the Sheridans. Many were the compliments paid her as well as Mrs. Sheridan on her account.

"You seem to have a knack for finding pretty housemaids, my dear Mrs. Sheridan," said the bank manager, Mr. Horace Cadwell, a frequent visitor - making sure to keep on good terms with the Sheridans, as he shrewdly kept an eye on the growing bank account of his favorite client. And, being a bachelor, he kept a shrewd eye on the maturing eldest daughter of that same client.

So Finola became a favorite, an almost indispensible part of the family. She, herself, was more than satisfied and happy to have found such a position so quickly. Immediately, she started to save, keeping her money locked in a small box which she purchased for that purpose. Now, if only Dara were near, she would be completely and truly happy.

But she was a realist; she would not spend her days moping nor would she be content to waste too many years of her life listening to Rowena's daydreams and foolish musings. Somehow, she felt she was meant to gain a place of some consequence in society. She would not be fully content, she knew, until she had reached her full potential and that Finola O'Donnell realized would indeed lead her to achieve great things.

Chapter 12

"The human heart, at whatever age, opens only to the heart that opens in return."
- Maria Edgeworth.

John Francis sat watching his children as they romped on the beach. His attention was especially drawn to the twins. The nineteen year olds were horsing about by the edge of the lake like two young colts; their bronzed bodies wet and slick gleamed in the sunlight. He could not but admire the flexing of strong muscles as they wrestled and tossed around. They would soon be a problem, he thought. He had no qualms about their cavorting with the pretty young Creole gals in the French Quarter, but he had no stomach for the equally pretty and far more vunerable white servant girls in his own household. He was not blind to the goings-on at the dinner table. He saw how the two eyed young Nelly Flynn and tried to embarrass her as she served the food and took away the empty plates. Though he perceived she was handling the situation with tact and maturity, yet he was not foolish enough to think that the young bucks would not sooner or later outwit, or outmaneuver her.

He turned to his wife sedately seated under the protection of a large sun umbrella, although she had already taken precaution by applying large quantities of perfumed oil to her 'fair' skin. For added protection she wore a long gown, sunhat, and veil. Southern women did not expose their creamy white skin to the sun. "My dear, I think we ought to consider sending that pair," he nodded in the general direction to the twins, "to some school or other."

His wife raised her eyes from the book she was reading, adjusted her spectacles and looked at him but she did not speak.

"There must be a lawyer in this family." The bright idea occured to him at that moment. "Yes, by Gad, and since those two are inseparable, why not have two for the price of one." Having uttered the words, he thought them funny so he laughed aloud at his own cleverness.

It was a long established custom in the Sheridan family to spend the last two weeks of August in a rented house near Lake Pontchartrain. That time of year was particularly trying on everyone's nerves and tempers. The heat of the city was partially the reason for the frayed nerves; but the yearly exodus of Miss O'Connor for the North where she dutifully and unfailingly spent two weeks with her mother caused the whole family such consternation and 'upsetment' to use Mammy's word that there was nothing to do but bundle all up and transport them to a far-away place, a spot where they could run wild and free without disgracing themselves and the family name.

So on that sultry, lazy day in late August it had been decided, decreeded would be the better word, that the twins, Eoin and Liam, would read Law at Georgetown University. And between them, perhaps, make one respectable business lawyer. How, in fact, such a feat might be accomplished Mr. Sheridan had no idea, but given his money and influence he had no doubt that it would.

* * * *

The Sheridan household was a fever of activity - washing, dusting, sweeping and cleaning; it seemed the whole house was being turned inside out. Preparations for the Christmas season were afoot. Happy songs were being sung in the nursery__

> "Christmas is coming
> The Goose is getting fat
> Please put a penny
> In the old man's hat
> If you haven't a penny
> A half-penny will do
> If you haven't a half-penny
> Well, God bless you."

"What's a half-penny, Finola?" Little Anna, who was six and the oldest in the nursery, asked.

"It's money, Anna." Finola who had taught the youngsters the Christmas carol now had the task of trying to explain the strange new words while she attended to her chores of dusting and decorating.

"An what's this we have here?" shouted Eoin as he entered sweeping his little sister into his strong arms but completely ignoring her otherwise as his eyes devoured Finola's beautiful face.

Anna noticing that her big brother's attention was elsewhere, spoke: "This is Finola," our new maid. She's from Ireland and she teaches us songs. You want to hear?"

"Some other time, Anna." Eoin put his sister down. "So you're Finola."

He struck a pose, raised his head and slowly, deliberately placed his right hand with index finger extended under his jaw. For a moment he did not speak but with the eyes of an experienced philanderer studied the curves and maidenly form of Finola's body. At length, taking a step backward and cocking his head at another angle, he declared: "Not bad, not bad at all."

At that juncture Liam bounded into the room; he sized up the situation and word for word, as so often happened with the twins, he repeated what his brother had said. "Not bad . . . not bad at all." Then, with a sly glance at Eoin, he continued, "I hear you're Nelly's replacement."

"Yes, sir. Now if you'll excuse me." Finola made as if to leave the room.

"What's your hurry? We've only just come," said Liam pulling a pout. "It would be nice to get to know you."

"I've got a lot to do, sir. I'm already late with Madam's afternoon coffee."

"Don't tell me we've got another Nelly." Liam was irritated. He stepped closer to Finola and was about to grab her arm when Mammy came into the room. She immediately took command.

"Yo' shu is no gemppmum. Ain' got no mo' manners dan a fe'el han'. Ah ain' nevar figger out, mahself huccome yo all doan got no manners. Miss O'Connor shu try she bestest fer so many year."

"Oh, Mammy. Yo' shu nevar change." Liam answered mockingly, half teasing her. Then he went towards her, and giving her a peck on her big round black cheek pretended to be hurt by her scolding. Better to keep her on his side; she wasn't beyond using a whip on him nor was she afraid to expose his behavior to his father. He just didn't want any trouble this first day home. After that, both boys apologized and left Mammy and the nursery. They meant to have a good time this Christmas and were ready to do whatever it took to ensure the desired outcome. But, as Mammy would say, 'de devil alway find work fer dem no good idle han's.'

Having tasted liberty and the complete freedom and independence of college life for three months, the twins were not about to lose it during the Christmas vacation. They had escaped the eagle eyes of Miss O'Connor and the shrewd calculating gaze of Mammy, not to mention the prying eyes of younger brothers and sisters now that they were mature college students. And they intended to flaunt that independence and their self-envisioned superiority during the Christmas break.

Mammy knew all the children from the inside out. She had been there when they came into the world. She, it was, who soothed their aches and pains, who rocked and petted them when they had coughs and colds. She knew their good points and their not so good. It was she, alone, who devined the real reason for Nelly's speedy departure when news of the twins homecoming was announced. She had watched the pair grow and develop. She had tried so hard to curb and mold them the best she knew how according to the standards of "de decen' white folk." How often over the years had they heard her repeat: "No, yo ain'. It jus' ain' fittin'. Yo all ain' no white trash," or, "what yo ma tink. Ain' got no manners. Ah cun' never figgered dat out."

And as they grew older, the twins loved to ruffle her feathers. Scurrying behind her huge frame and hiding in the great folds of her long black skirt laughing and making fun and never paying her any mind until she was forced to reach for the strap. Then she would beat the air and stomp and the pair would take flight knowing full well that Mammy could never catch up with them, even if she wished to do so.

Now at six feet one and one and a half respectively, Eoin and Liam were still the same - carefree, irresponsible, full of devilment. They were not unattractive but certainly no one could call them handsome. They had inherited too many of their father's traits for that. But, fortunately for them, the New England blood had modified in them the size of the paternal features. They were fair haired and had clear blue eyes with a ruddy complexion and they had inherited their mother's mouth and square chin.

Although they refrained from harassing Finola during the days that followed, they went out of their way to tease and make fun of Frank, their older brother, using every opportunity to 'get his goat'.

At first, Frank took their teasing as a joke, but as time went on and there was no end to it, he became irritable, then angry, and finally, he struck out at Liam. Eoin, at once came to the rescue of his twin brother. A fight ensued and though no real harm was done, Frank, nevertheless, emerged with a bloody nose and a bump on his head which resulted in a blazing headache. It was in this condition that Finola came upon him stretched on a sofa in the blue upstairs hallway. His eyes were closed.

"Master Frank! What on earth happened to you?" she asked startled by his appearance.

Frank groaned and opened his eyes.

"You look awful!" Finola continued.

"Be a good girl an' fetch me a cold towel. I'll be all right in a moment."

Finola went at once to do as Frank asked. Returning with a basin of warm water and a towel she gently wiped his face and when he complained of a headache, she folded the towel and placed it on his forehead.

"That's so much better. Thank you, Finola. I'll sleep a while and then I'll be fine." He closed his eyes again completely ignoring her.

Finola lingered a moment and for the first time since the death of little Patrick, she felt emotion. Something deep within her stirred. She looked at Frank but she saw Dara. Oh, Dara, where are you? Her whole soul cried out and she felt an ache in her heart. Why haven't I heard from you? And then she knew, as surely as she had the night she had said goodbye to him, that she would not see him for a very long time, if ever. Yet, she could not resign herself to the thought. She would hope - hope against all odds. He was the only love of her heart - Dara, Dara, Dara....

Frank stirred, then turned on his back. Still Finola tarried. She had an opportunity to study the features that had, in a flash, reminded her of Dara. He was not as tall as Dara, nor indeed his own twin brothers. Probably not more than five feet ten, Finola conjectured. He had a delicate frame, a comly youth with a fair complexion. It was his hair, she decided, that caused her to think of her beloved. Yes, his thick dark-brown hair, although not so dark as Dara's, was the attraction. Strangely enough, it was parted in the same fashion and had a wavy forelock that hung down over his left eye. Finally, she studied the prone figure longer, examining the reclining body more carefully, she decided that the likeness began and ended with the hair. Nevertheless, Frank had pleasing features. Dark long lashes cast shadows on his clear skin. He had a firm mouth, the same square jaw as his brothers but his nose was slender and flared at the tip. One would hardly consider him a handsome man but his was a pleasing face. Then she remembered his smile, fetching is how she described it to herself and his even white teeth were very attractive.

Finola, however, knew other things about Frank that did not please her and only helped to elevate Dara higher in her estimation. Frank was lazy; there was no two ways about it. But if this was his most flagrant flaw, he did have some appealing, face-saving qualities. He was generous, warm-hearted, and generally good-humored. It was his easy going nature, she conjectured, that allowed his younger brothers to take advantage of him.

She tiptoed away assured that a short rest would set Frank on the mend. If she could only be so sure that Dara was so healthy. Her thoughts and her heart were with him as she passed the large sittingroom. where the door was ajar and from within she heard voices.

"Have no idea." It was Eoin's voice.

"Then you'd better read it. Both of you." Madam sounded angry.

There was a short pause, then Liam spoke: "The old biddy. We merely paid a brotherly visit to the... ."

"That's not what I heard." His mother raised her voice.

Finola was startled. She shouldn't be listening but... Mrs. Sheridan's voice changed. "I know you're on vacation and you feel you should be having a good time but I won't have you disturbing the whole house. You'll both have to find something useful to do. I'll talk to your father. He may have a job... ."

"Ah, no Ma," they spoke together.

Finola heard the pleading in their tone. Merely little boys again, she thought.

"Look, Ma, we promise not to upset the old . . . old Mammy again. And we'll... ."

"Can I depend on that?" interrupted Mrs. Sheridan.

"You bet." Again they answered in unison.

"Don't let me see or hear of you again until dinner," were the final words.

The two were dismissed from their mother's presence and as they walked across the hardwood floor, Finola decided she had better knock on the door. It was past time for Madam's afternoon cup of coffee.

Not receiving an answer, she was about to knock again when the door was flung open and Eoin exited closely followed by Liam. She stood back to allow the pair to pass.

"Well, well!" Eoin's eyes opened wide. "If it isn't little Miss Ireland!"

"Been listenin', have ye, then?" His tone was sarcastic as he mimicked the Irish accent.

"That you, Finola?" Mrs. Sheridan's voice interrupted any further comments and Finola was allowed to enter the room.

"Mischievous from the day they were born," she said, half to herself and half to Finola. Then looking her full in the face she continued: "It seems they'll find trouble where trouble was never meant to be. I apologize for what happened this morning. It won't happen again, I assure you."

"Thank you, Ma'm." A slight blush tinged Finola's cheeks.

"I'll have my coffee now, if you please, Finola."

"Certainly, Ma'm."

There was peace in the house for several days. The twins had found a new diversion for they were nowhere to be seen between the hours of 10:00 A.M. and 6:00 P.M. No one asked where they spent their time or how, for sooner or later the truth would be known.

Finola was happy to be able to go about her chores unhampered by their unwanted attentions. However, she was causing quite a stir in another quarter. From the day that she had attended to Frank's bruised face and bloody nose, she could not help but notice that he was extremely kind to her. Often offering to carry what he considered a heavy tray or open a door.

At the dinner table, she was aware that his eyes followed her as she served the many dishes and he actually got to his feet one evening when she was having difficulty with a large soup-tureen.

This action did not escape the twin's ever critical eyes but they did not comment at that time. A nudge under the table sufficed. It would be a savory morsel to chew upon later.

As they never had had the opportunity to get to know the city and all its attractions while they were growing up, their new freedom now opened up all sorts of possibilities. So instead of tantalizing the housemaids and their younger brothers and ruffling Frank's feathers, they sauntered forth to sample the sights and sounds and even the smells of the bustling metropolis.

"The French Quarter. We've got to taste the jambalaya," said Liam.

"I hope that's not all we'll taste." Eoin's blue eyes brightened and his fair brows arched, questioning, anticipating.

Liam was quick to respond. "Capital old boy!" He sealed his approval with a brotherly slap on the shoulder.

Chapter 13

"Love reasons without reason."
- Shakespeare.

Bougainvillea blooming profusely, magnolia, oleander, red and white, large cannalilies, and an assortment of palms decorated the spacious enclosed patio at the back of the house. The fragrant air was soft and warm against her creamy cheeks. Distant bells summoned monks and nuns to their evening prayers. As yet the plague of the city, the mosquitoes, miniature vampires, had not started on their nortural quest for blood. It was in this setting, in a shaded arbor that Finola liked to spend a quiet time alone with her thoughts at the end of her busy day.

During those precious moments, she usually allowed her mind to race across the wide Atlantic to the small green valley, and the quiet countryside she once called home. The pale face of her dying mother, her frail young body bathed in a feverish sweat as she struggled to cling to the miserable existance she called life, for the sake of her starving children. Her father, head bowed in shame, blaming himself for what he couldn't possibly achieve - a decent living for his family. Her brothers, eager, anxious to help but unable because youth's vitality and strength had been drained from their once healthy limbs. 'Man does not live by bread alone', but man cannot live without it. She thought of her baby sister - the little one who never had a chance to prove herself. Where were they now - All gone!

Why was she the only one to survive. At that moment, she felt she was carrying a great burden. She owed it to her family to make something of herself. She the last living member would not allow the name, the blood-line to die out forever. She came from good stock.

For countless generations her people had lived and died in that little corner of heaven. The very soil was made up of their flesh and bones. How could she possibly not feel that part of her was still there. Then it occured to her that her true mission, her real purpose in life was not only to achieve for herself alone but to set her goals so high that she, Finola O'Donnell would be able to carve out a place in history, in the history of her adopted country and thus be in a position to influence the course of events in her native Ireland. This then was the reason why she survived. This was the purpose of her existance.

How all these high-flown ideas might become a reality, how a poor servant girl, like herself, could possibly climb to the heights of American society, she had no idea. But in the depths of her heart, she had a strange but compelling feeling that somehow it would come to pass. She was reminded of her mother's words in those far off days of her own childhood when life was good and no one went hungry. 'Remember Finola, a grá, that whatever you can imagine can be accomplished. Hold on to your dreams.'

Finola sighed and raised her beautiful eyes to heaven. "God, Almighty, Heavenly Father," she prayed aloud, "if you have placed these ideas in my mind, then you will undoubtedly, see that they are brought to fruition. "

In the west a crimson sun fringed with fuschia and gold lingered bidding farewell to day as night gradually drew her deep-violet curtains blocking his view. In a little while it would be dark. She missed the long twilights of the Irish spring and summer. How very different this world was. It overwhelmed her to make comparisons. No lush green fields, no songbirds, no running streams and cascading waterfalls and no surcease from the heat - so overpowering at times. She wiped the perspiration from her face with a pocket handkerchief and was about to settle down to a book she had borrowed from Rowena, when Frank came towards her down the path.

He could not have seen her for she was hidden by the thick growth. Probably taking a walk in the cool of the evening after his day's work, she thought. Yet, as he drew nearer, she couldn't help the stirrings that seemed to race through her body. Her heartbeat quickened; she felt flushed. Excitement chased other thoughts from her mind, but she did think of Dara. It had been so long. Where was he now? What was he doing? Was he thinking of her?

"Well . . . Hello there." Frank was surprised but there was also pleasure on his dark face and in his smoldering brown eyes. "You aren't afraid the fairies will run off with you, alone... out here all by yourself?"

"Huh! Sure they'd bring me back again in the morning, I'm thinking." She knew she was blushing and was glad it was almost dark.

"Oh, I'm not so sure about that." He was now standing beside her looking down on her beautiful face. "Do you mind if I sit a moment?" He didn't wait for her to answer but seated himself beside her.

Finola was uneasy and made as if to rise. Of a sudden, a fear and trembling took hold of her. Her mind conjured up scenes she thought she had completely wiped from her consciousness. She saw herself confronted by Robert Sutherland, realized she was cornered, in his power. She heard herself scream; then all went blank. It was a momentary impression; but it left her feeling faint and bewildered.

Are you all right? Frank's anxious voice caused Finola to focus on the present. She, then, realized she was seated on a wooden bench looking up into his face.

Things seemed to be different in America - the chasm between master and servant didn't appear to be quite so deep. Yet, Finola was wary.

Frank repeated himself.

"Oh please, just a moment. I have been wondering when I might be able to talk to you, alone." There was pleading in his voice and now that he was so close, she could see the emotion in his eyes.

Finola waited. She could feel his nearness, smell the eau-de-cologne he liked to wear.

"You're a special young woman. I've watched you. You're not like the other servants. You have a mind of your own. There's a certain something about you that makes you stand out as intelligent, courageous, and . . . and yes... self-sufficient.

"Thank you, sir. I take that as a nice compliment," answered Finola. He seemed sincere but she wouldn't let down her guard.

"Please, Finola, let's drop the sir. I would like to be your friend." He again looked into her eyes sparkling like glistening jade in the dusk.

"I don't think that's a wise thing. You are..."

Frank interrupted. "Finola, don't say anymore right now. I have grown to admire you over the past few weeks and I want to get to know you better."

Finola was growing uneasy. What if someone, a family member happened by and saw them together in the dark? She would surely lose her job. She thought of the twins. They would be home soon if they were not already in the house... "I must go now, sir... Please."

"Very well, but I mean what I say. In fact, Finola, I... I'm... ."

She heard no more. She was running up the path Frank had only a few minutes before followed, leading from the consevatory to the patio and beyond.

When she reached the house, she was shaking. What had he said? Could she believe him? Her all too recent experience in Ireland had unnerved her. Yet when she compared Frank with Robert Sutherland there was an enormous difference. In fact, she concluded at length, there was no comparison. But, to be sure, she would bide her time. She would observe . . . watch, listen, and deduce from what she saw and heard and then draw her own conclusions.

The next few days were a continuous round of activities. It would soon be Christmas and all that it entailed - festivities, parties, shopping, giving and receiving gifts. There was never a free moment for any of the servants. Finola was going from morning until night.

* * * *

The Christmas season came and went. The twins returned to school and the Sheridan household resumed the usual routine. Finola and Rowena's friendship continued to grow as did the relationship between herself and Frank. Although it had, of necessity, to be a clandestine affair, they did find some time to enjoy each others company.

The most exciting news to reach the city early in the New Year was the discovery of gold in California. 'One rainy morning in January,' the local newspapers reported, 'John Sutter, a Swiss landowner in the Sacramento Valley, heard an urgent knock on his door. It was James Marshall, his foreman. The man immediately unrolled a piece of cloth containing several nuggets of yellow metal which he had found along the American River northeast of the small settlement called Sacramento.'

With this news, the entire city of New Orleans, it seemed, went completely wild. Everyone was talking about gold and within days thousands of young men were preparing to go West, particularly those who were single, but the lure of gold was no respector of persons and soon married men also joined in what was to become known as the Great California Gold Rush, the largest and wildest mass movement of people the world had ever known. Few women joined in this histeria as it was considered unladylike. But there were those intrepid ones like Marie Suize Pantalong, Luzena Wilson, Margaret Frink, and Lucy Cooke, pioneers with stout hearts and steadfast wills who strode forth to seek their fortune also.

In the Sheridan household, the New Year brought its own changes. Frank actually showed some initiative in the warehouse organizing the men into smaller groups and staggering the work load. This move eventually led to more effective methods and greater efficiency. John Francis was pleased. At last his son was maturing. True, it had taken a long time but . . .

However, the spurt of energy and the brainwave that had accompanied it, didn't last. Frank fell back into his old habits, becoming listless and careless. And the tiresome arguing and haranging resumed between father and son.

The Lenten season was fast approaching and all in the Sheridan household had caught the 'fever', the annual two day sickness of Mardi Gras, which was highly contagious and spread throughout the city at that time of year. The only exceptions were Finola and Mammy. Finola didn't understand what was going on and Mammy was above 'all dat foolishness'. Of course it hadn't always been so with Mammy, but for the past few years she had grown tired; she was in the words of Mariah, the cook, 'slowin' down.' But rather than admit to it, Mammy cocked her nose in the air, squeezed her thick lips together, and shaking her head remonstrated in her quaint southern drawl. 'Ah ain' neva figger out, mahself huccome dey all make so much fuss ova nothin'. It shoo beat me. All de young folk aimen' to go straight te Hell one o' dees days.'

Despite Mammy's words the frenzy of activity, the anticipation of free time took over in the kitchen, but Mariah's forsight and persistence during the days prior to Mardi Gras had assured the family of regular and sumptuous meals despite the desertion of the entire kitchen staff.

Finola whose ignorance of what exactly was going on, remained at her post but she was upset when so much of the work was left to her already full hands, With all that she had to do, Rowena was constantly calling upon her for little jobs of a different kind. Her mother had ordered several new dresses, all of which must be fitted perfectly. Not content with the assurance of the dress fitters and couturieres, she wanted Finola's opinion also. She trusted her friend would tell her the truth as to how she really looked in the different gowns.

Then one evening while the two young women were alone together, Rowena, who was almost Finola's size, suggested that she try on one or two of her new gowns. At first she refused arguing that they were made for Rowena and that she didn't think Madam would approve.

"Oh, fiddle sticks. Nobody will ever know. And even if they do, they're my dresses. Surely I can do what I like with my own gowns." Her voice was defiant but reassuring.

Finola stood admiring the beautiful crinolines with their billowing twelve yards of muslin, silk, cotton and velvet. She had once or twice imagined herself in such a gown.

"You're sure?" she arched her brows as she looked Rowena straight in the eyes.

"Of course I'm sure." Then she stepped to the door and turned the key in the lock. "Now, that should settle the matter," said Rowena as she again faced Finola. When Finola was decked out in a pale-green muslin dress,

Rowena loosened her beautiful hair from its confinement. It cascaded in flowing waves to her waist.

"Now you slip your dainty feet into these leather slippers, and voila! You're the prettiest young lady I've ever seen." Rowena stood back to admire her.

Finola ran to the long mirror to see for herself. She was totally transformed and could hardly believe her own eyes. "It's so pretty! It's a beautiful dress." She twirled to feel the full effect of the soft cloth about her body. Then she ran to Rowena and threw her arms around her. "Thank you, thank you so much for allowing me such pleasure."

Rowena was touched. In her heart she envied Finola's beauty. She would never look so pretty no matter how many beautiful gowns she put on.

A knock on the door sent Finola's heart into a flutter. Rowena asked, "Who is it?"

"Frank," came the answer.

"Oh, you're home early. Just a minute, I'm changing." She made a sign to Finola who quickly slipped out of all the finery and into her own dress; then she swiftly caught her russet tresses and bound them into a chignon and thrust her feet into her own boots.

Rowena opened the door for Frank, he stood figeting, an anxious expression on his boyish face.

"I'd like to . . . ." He blurted out but catching sight of Finola, stopped.

"Afternoon, Master Frank," said Finola. She could feel a blush mounting to her cheeks. "Must be getting back to my chores. I'll never be finished otherwise." She gathered her skirts about her as she hastily left the room.

"Talk to you later," said Rowena with a smile as she made way for her to exit and Frank to enter the room.

"To what do I owe this honor?" She smiled as her older brother lowered himself onto a chair close to the large bay-window which lent a view of the back garden.

At first, Frank looked sheepish, fumbling with the edge of his jacket. I... I don't know where to begin... I... well I thought, you being a woman an' all..." There was consternation written all over his face.

Rowena was a little taken aback by his obvious predicament and was at a loss as to what to do. "I... I can't help you if you don't tell me what's troubling you."

"It's something personal. I just can't go to mother, and father certainly wouldn't understand." He raised his deep brown eyes and looked into his sister's face seeking the assurance he so ardently desired. "You see, Rowena, I think I'm falling in love."

Rowena eyes opened wide. Then she laughed outright.

"Oh, I shouldn't have confided in you." Frank was visibly hurt.

"Nonsense, Frank. On the contrary, I was laughing only because you're so serious. Love can't be that bad." Rowena said in a practical off-handed way.

"But... but you see, it's not likely the young woman I wish to marry is... well, is from the class mother would approve."

"Ah, hah! Frank I do believe you're in love with Finola. Mother may not approve but father will. She's Irish and you know how proud he is of his Irishness."

"You think so? How did you know... I mean that it was Finola?" He was taken aback. 'Love is blind,' and Rowena sighed - an exaggerated sigh. 'And lovers cannot see the follies they themselves commit.' Huh! See how well I can quote Shakespeare". She tried to make light of his embarrassment.

"That bad, eh?" There was a twinkle in Frank's brown eyes.

"There have been little signs," said Rowena teasing. "But I'm happy for you. I like Finola very much. And I must say you've got good taste. She's by far the prettiest young woman I've seen in these parts." She didn't add that of course she had no way of judging since as yet she had not been introduced into society. But her next birthday was to take care of that deficiency.

"I'd like to take her out. Get to know her better —" He hesitated. "But —"

"But she hasn't anything to wear. I know. Leave it to me. Now stop fretting, Frank. You can be so charming when you try." She kissed her brother lightly on the cheek.

Frank's eyes brightened as he exclaimed: 'Love sought is good but given unsought is better.' See, I've learned a few quotations myself," he quipped. Then in a more serious vein: "You're an angel, Rowena. I'll not forget you for this." He then returned her kiss and hurried from the room.

* * * *

Finola dressed with care. Having bathed in rosewater, she reverently lifted the exquisite dress Rowena had given her from the chair. Was this really hers? Was she, indeed, going to the theatre? She had not expected to find herself escorted by a son of the wealthy Mr. Sheridan to the opera. She knew she would look ravishing in that green velvet gown. She also knew she would be the envy of many and she intended to show that she was inferior to none. She might be a poor girl working as a servant in the Sheridan house but she never considered herself inferior. She knew, eventually, she would rise from her present position and find her true place in this world. She would be a person of influence, someone others would appreciate and admire. For unlike many young women in her station, Finola knew she had qualities far greater than money - in fact, money could not buy intelligence, courage, strength of character, and rectitude. She would advance her education - read more in her free time she told herself. One could never have enough knowledge - learning. Yes, she would acquire whatever knowledge and learning it took to be a worthy and respected citizen of her new country as well as a credit to the land of her birth - her beloved Ireland.

She took a last look at herself in the mirror. Then a knock on her door startled her for a second.

"It's Rowena," responded the voice from outside.

"Oh come in, come in," came the excited reply.

Rowena opened the door and gasped. "Finola! You're absolutely beautiful." And she ran to her and hugged her close. "You'll be the envy of all." She started to laugh. "I can just see Madam Rouquette's face when she sees you, especially if she is accompanied by her frompy daughter, Colette."

"You really think I have done justice to your lovely dress, then?" Finola asked.

"Done justice to the dress! Why, it's quite the contrary. That dress has never looked so good, so exquisite."

Rowena helped her with the long black cloak she had borrowed from her mother's wardrobe. "You must not be seen leaving the house." Rowena opened the door and glanced outside. All was clear. "Bye, have a wonderful time. I'll be waiting to hear all about it," she whispered as Finola slipped quietly down the back stairs and out into the side garden where Frank was waiting for her.

Once the carriage left the American section, the whole city seemed to come to life. The streets were crowded with gaily dressed people, many of whom were in costumes so lavish they fairly dazzled Finola's eyes. There were bands and parades, groups and couples dancing, singing, laughing, shouting and, in general, all were having a hilarious time.

"It's wonderful! I feel like joining in the fun myself," cried Finola catching the spirit of the moment.

"I have something far better planned," said Frank, and he settled back in his seat to feast his eyes on the vision of lovliness beside him.

At Bourbon and St. Louis streets, the grey walls of The French Opera House were visible from the carriage window. The queues outside the door for the troisiemes and quatriemes levels were already reaching halfway down the block. It was quite obvious that the opera was not for the rich, the affluent, or for the educated; it was for all. It was an event which the whole family and every level of society attended. Life without l'opera was not worth living. In fact, the Orleanians were so much in love with the opera that not even deep mourning, which required the wearing of black for a year, kept them, especially the Creoles, from this form of entertainment. It was sacred to them. The loges grillees were at the disposal of these and other participants such as enceinte ladies who did not wish to be closely scrutinized. They could enjoy the music from their inconspicuous boxes decorated with latice work without the intrusion of prying eyes. A story is told of one such lady who thoroughly enjoyed the first act, but shortly after said to her husband: "Jean - I'm so sorry, but I cannot stay for the ballet!" The baby was born in the carriage on the way home.

A man or woman might go without a meal but never could miss the opera.In the midst of such excitement and anticipation, the air was electrified. There was music everywhere. Snatches from the current season's billings were heard floating from open windows or balconies. The youngsters in the street belted forth the role of the street boy in Carmen. They were ready at a moment's notice to fill in if required.

Finola was caught up in the enthusiasm. "I'm so excited. My first opera! How wonderful! And you've made it all possible, Frank."

"I'm happy to be able to do this for you, Finola." And he looked into her emerald eyes lovingly and saw such innocence that his heart was fairly melted in his youthful chest.

They had passed down Bourbon Street. Its assortment of shops were all connected one way or another with the opera. People of various colors, shades and tones milled about. The air was vibrant. Individuals shouting, calling to friends, saluting in so many different languages.

"I believe our fair city holds the honor of being the first in the United States to have established a permanent resident opera company." Frank was happy and proud to impart this bit of information.

"That's something to be proud of. I would have thought New York might like to hold that honor." Finola replied.

They had arrived at the entrance and her first glance rested on the large poster screaming the name Julia Calve. She would be the leading lady for that night's performance.

"We will hear the very best tonight." Frank observed. "They call her, 'La precieuse cantatrice,' 'la belle Calve'. You're in for a treat. They say Rossini, himself tutored her. She not only sings beautifully, she is beautiful - petite, with a glorious head of black hair and "the most beautiful eyes in the world." But you know, Finola," Frank turned and looked into the wonderous green eyes dancing so full of life. "You know, I wouldn't exchange your loveliness for all the dark beauties in the universe."

Finola blushed and lowered her eyes. "Thank you, Frank."

Frank took her arm and led her across the threshold into the sumptuously carpeted foyer. Removing her cloak, he handed it to a colored man in the cloakroom, who in return gave him a ticket.

Gazing on her now for the first time in all her glory, Frank was speechless for a moment. Then collecting himself, for he noticed he was not the only one fascinated by the lovliness in the green velvet gown, he bent to kiss her finger tips. "Finola, you're beautiful! Enchanting."

Indeed, she was a picture of grace and beauty. Her auburn tresses were caught up by a rich green velvet ribbon. Her elegant gown which was cut low revealing shapely, creamy breasts, a slender swan-like neck, and perfectly smooth sloping shoulders was fitted to her delicate body. She wore a string of pearls. "God bless Rowena," Frank murmured. "Come my dear. I'm afraid this vision of lovliness will vanish before my eyes have time to appreciate my good fortune. An Irish fairy-girl you surely are, Finola O'Donnell."

"Well, thank you, Frank. I've never been admired so much in all my life." But scarcely had she said the words when she thought of Dara. If only he were here to see her. If only he were here in Frank's place. Dara - Dara, where are you? And a little sigh escaped.

"You are sad, my lovely Finola." Frank exclaimed. "Are you all right?"

"Oh, perfectly. It . . . it was just a passing thought . . . Ireland, home, little Patrick." How could she tell him about Dara. That secret she would keep forever deep within her heart.

Once again taking her arm, Frank proudly led her into the family box which they would have to themselves for that evening. His father had business matters to attend and his mother would not go to the opera without him.

Heads turned. Remarks were made.

"Who's that beauty?"

Haven't seen her before. Must be a relative from the North," concluded Madam Rouquette. "Pretty little thing," she admitted to her oldest son, Edmond, as she fanned herself. "You might find out at intermission who she really is."

"That Frank's the sly one. Never fear I'll pry it out of him," answered the youth.

Finola was enthralled. The costumes, the settings, the music above all cast a spell. She was transported to worlds of such beauty that she never before could imagine existed.

At the end, when the curtain fell for the last time, bouquets of fragrant flowers were hurled at the stage. There was wild applause.

It was an experience Finola would not soon forget.

"And now, my dear, I want to take you to one of our famous French restaurants." He took her small white hand firmly in his gloved one and led her from the theatre. Hailing a carriage, he gave the order "To Antoine's." As they settled into their seats for the short drive, Frank asked: "Well, my dear, what was your impression of your first opera?"

"Never, in my whole life, have I heard or seen anything so wonderful. I was transported to heaven. I can't imagine heaven can be any more beautiful." There were tears in her luminous green eyes. "You've opened up a whole new world for me. I'm walking in a dream. Hoping I'll never wake up."

They had already reached Antoine's. It was bursting at the seams.

Antoine's was one of the restaurants Frank liked. It was located at 713 Louis St. and was a family owned enterprise. Old Antoine had started working when he was only twelve in the kitchen of the Hotel de Noailles in Marseille. At sixteen his preparation of an order of beef for Monsieur Talleyrand which won him high praise. When the statesman asked him what he called his creation, the youth immediately answered: "Boeuf Robespierre". As the roast was served very rare, the boy could think only of the bloody execution of Robespierre.

From New York, the young man eventually made his way to New Orleans, worked for a while at the St. Charles Hotel and eventually opened a pension. Soon he became known for his uniquely seasoned turkey dish called Dinde Talleyrand.

The delicious odors wafted from the open shutters as Frank and Finola drew near.

"What a marvelous aroma!"

"Wait 'till you taste the house specialty." Frank was excited also. He noticed the way people looked at him as he led Finola to the reserved table by the window. Heads turned. Comments were made.

"Who is she?" asked a rather plump matron to his left.

"You sly old bird, Frank Sheridan. Your lady companion - aren't you going to introduce me?" An old friend of the family stepped to the table.

Frank arose, bowed as he saluted Mr. John J. McCarthy, and then presented Finola. "I'd like you to meet Miss Finola O'Donnell."

"Irish! Well, well, I might have known. Where else in the world do they produce such beauty? Sure, I'm half Irish myself. Please to meet you, Miss O'Donnell." He extended his hand and as soon as Finola's was secure in his great palm, he held it captive. For an instant he stood looking deep into her beautiful clear green eyes. "My, my, my . . . the French say it best - Enchanté." Then he thumped Frank on the shoulder and said. "Don't let her out of your sight, my boy, if you know what's good for you."

After a few more platitudes, Mr. McCarthy left saying: "We must meet again… soon." After bowing in Finola's direction, he turned and disappeared into the crowded room.

"Word of this wonderful evening will soon be general information," Finola said as she watched Frank's reaction.

"Who cares. I love you, Finola. I want to… ."

"Frank, please. We barely know each other, and besides you have to consider your family, your mother…" Finola knew Mrs. Sheridan would never accept the notion that her son, her eldest son, could be in love with a servant in her own household.

"Finola when are you going to believe me? I mean to marry you…" he hesitated, "that is if you'll have me."

She gave him an endearing smile, but would not commit herself. "Let's wait and see, Frank." She knew he was not a man of purpose. His indecisiveness, his lassitude and indifference were common knowledge - a sore point with his father, the brunt of jokes with the men at the warehouses, and a source of unending teasing with his brothers, particularly the twins.

"When will you pull yourself together? Make something of yourself? You've got to show those fellows on the docks who's boss," invariably the unfailing introduction to the family dinner.

And invariably, Brian, the seventeen-year-old, brash, brawny, and overbearing would interject, "Allow me Papa. I'll show them… ."

"In time, son. In time," the 'old' man would answer and as always his brow creased with long horizontal furrows as his gaze rested in thoughtful anticipation of the day when young Brian would join him in the business.

Yes, Finola knew, even in the short time she had been in service at the Sheridan house, how Frank's father ranted and raved when his oldest son failed to live up to his expectations. She calculated. Would this be another blunder? She did not want to be part of it, then. Yet, the last few weeks seemed to have changed him. He was punctual at table, was more alert, more attentive to his father and mother. She had actually heard his father praise him for his handling of the workmen. Perhaps Frank could change. Maybe he needed encouragement. 'With a purpose in life, a goal, he might put forth the effort, might find the willpower and drive to make something of himself,' as his father put it.

At that juncture, the waiter interrupted their thoughts. Frank ordered the meal, the house specialty, Dinde Talleyrand, and a bottle of the best French wine. The dinner was everything the palate could imagine and more and concluded with a café brulot. This aromatic beverage was prepared in a silver container. It consisted of sugar, orange and lemon peel, cinnamon sticks, cloves, allspice, and brandy. These ingredients were set on fire; then the coffee was slowly added with a ladle while it was lifted blazing into the air.

"Simply tantalizing!" Finola remarked. But when she tasted the heavenly mixture, she couldn't find words to describe it.

"Mmm . . . indiscribable," she murmured and her eyes lit up with pleasure.

The whole evening had been a dream Finola would never forget. And now it was nearly 1:00 A.M. Where had the time flown? She had waited, anticipated, so looked forward to this evening. But her mind had never dreamed it could possibly be so wonderful.

As they returned home, Frank pressured her further for an answer to his proposal.

"Please, Frank," she pleaded. "You must give me time. Easter is almost upon us. There is much to be done. When the festive season is over, we'll talk. In the meantime I think you should consider approaching your father, discussing the matter with him."

"Very well. As you desire, my dear." He seemed content and clasping her hand, slim and delicate, he held it firmly in his. Then he lay back against the plush upholstery, his boyish face relaxed, a smile in his dark brown eyes.

It was the first time Finola had seen him thus. She would await the outcome patiently. But whatever future lay ahead for her, she realized one thing. She would not remain as a servant for long. She had tasted the better side in life. She always knew she was destined for greater things but she had not expected to gain position and prestige quite so fast. Now that she had experienced what it felt like to be a lady and realizing that the role held no inhibitions or difficulties for her, she determined she would take the opportunity to better herself in whatever way fate ordained. But, no sooner had she made the decision, than her heart ached. There was a tugging at her shapely breast, and her conscience fought back troubling her inner being. Dara, Dara — the cry arose from the very depths, from her heart's core and she sighed. A long low sigh that seemed to weigh her down.

"What is it, my dear?" Frank was alert and attentive instantly.

"Oh, nothing, Frank. Just thinking of Ireland." A mist covered the green of her eyes much the same as the mists in her homeland shrouded the emerald fields there.

"Don't be sad or lonely for Ireland, Finola. One day we'll visit it together. I'll take you back to see again the home of your childhood, the green fields, the rivers and streams that father so often talks about." He placed his arm around her waist and drew her close. "I love you, Finola. Remember that. We will be happy. I will talk to father tomorrow. Everything will be fine, I know.

They had reached home. Frank paid the cab-driver and then led Finola to the side-door. A light kiss on the forehead and then he said, "Good night, Finola. I love you."

"Thank you for the most wonderful evening of my whole life," she said and opened the door which Rowena had made sure was left unlocked.

Chapter 14

"Hasty marriage seldom proveth well."
- Shakespeare.

The morning of March 8, 1848 was beautiful. A golden glow suffused the garden; the sky was a clear azure blue, the air mild and laden with the heady scent of magnolia. A great calm seemed to embrace the whole world - at least that on which Frank gazed. But he himself was anything but calm.

His thoughts and emotions were in turmoil. He had enjoyed the previous evening. In fact, he had felt happier than he had been in a long time as he escorted Finola to the opera and to the late dinner afterwards. But when they had returned home and he was left alone with the prospects of having to confront his parents, of having to bare his soul to his father, he wasn't at all happy. He tossed and turned all night. Sleep finally came in the early hours of the morning - a fitfull restless sleep. He knew his mother would not approve of his decision to marry Finola. But his father - he hoped he, at least, would not turn his back on him. The young woman, after all, was Irish. That did hold weight with the 'old man'. And it wasn't as if she were an ignorant girl, ill-bred, who didn't know how to conduct herself. On the contrary, the previous evening had proved beyond the shadow of a doubt her true worth. She had been admired by all who laid eyes on her. She had been in the spot-light, yet she did not flinch. She knew instinctively what was required of her in polite society. She had passed the initial test with flying colors. He felt sure that at that very moment her name was being noised abroad. Word of her charm and beauty would soon reach the ears of his father. Mr. McCarthy for one wasn't going to keep his mouth shut. Frank knew he had been fascinated by her. He would have to know all the details - wherever did Frank find such a beauty? O'Donnell... he didn't know any family of good standing by that name. But obviously she was quality, from some prosperous home up north, no doubt. Who better than John Francis himself could answer his many questions. Yes, Frank knew he would have to lay the whole matter before his father and that without further delay.

He paid unusual attention to his toiletry. This aspect of his personality change added to what his father had already observed, he figured would do more for his cause than many words. It was all Finola's doing. He could envision the 'old man's' brain working. Her influence, he would contend, had such beneficial and positive effects that his son had changed his ways and habits almost overnight. How could a union with such a strong and positive young woman be anything but a blessing to himself and his family. Thus Frank speculated as he put the finishing touches to his rebellious hair.

"Good morning, Father." He wondered what humor the 'old man' was in. "Market prices good today?" That should get a tell-tale reaction.

His father looked at him over the top of the morning newspaper. "You're early. Interested in the market, eh?" He was about to add a disparaging remark when he checked himself. The boy had obviously changed his ways, why not play along, ride the tide of good fortune as long as it lasted. It had taken a long time for this, his oldest son, to mature, but better late than never. "Yes, son, the prices are good. We'll finish loading the Caroline today. Get rid of that lot before the next consignment comes. Help yourself to some coffee. Damn good stuff this morning. That Irish girl...

what's, what's her name?" Can't ever remember it for some reason."

"Finola," Frank interjected.

"Yes, Finola... seems to know a thing or two about making coffee."

Frank wasn't about to enlighten his father on that point. He knew Finola didn't make the coffee but she did serve it with efficiency and charm. "Yes, Father." He poured himself a cup and sat down on the opposite side of the table. A moment of silence ensued. "I'd like to talk... to talk to you, sir."

"Eh? What's that?" John Francis raised his head and again looked at his son. He studied the pale face before him, questioningly. "Fire away, lad," he finally said shaking the newspaper irratically as he tried to turn a page.

"I... well, I want to tell you..."

"You need a raise - is that it?" He hurried on. "Well if you think you're foolin' your old man by..."

"Father, I'm getting married."

"What, what's that you're saying?" It took a second or two for the notion to sink in. "You're getting married! Well I'll be..." He put down the paper, took off his glasses, rubbed his eyes, put the spectacles back on his nose and looked Frank full in the face. "Have we met the young woman? I... I don't remember. Who is she?"

"Yes, you've met the young lady. It's Finola."

"Finola... Finola who?" John Francis never for a moment considered his son's future wife would be the little Irish girl who attended his table.

"Finola O'Donnell, Father. The... the... young woman who..."

"You mean... you mean..." he pointed towards the door, his face having taken on a rosy hue and his eyes a glassy glaze.

"Yes, Father, that Finola."

"Don't tell me you've been carrying on with that little filly under my very roof? Have to marry her, eh? Is that it?" Without stopping to look at Frank again or listen to what he had to say, John Francis got to his feet. He had to pour himself a drink. Why had this to happen? And just when he thought things were going well... Confound the boy. He'd never amount to anything.

Frank waited until his father had taken a gulp of Scotch.

"Look, son. There are many ways of dealing with these things besides..."

"Father I'm going to marry Finola not because I've... I love her. Can't you understand that... I love her!"

"Love, I see." John Francis thought a moment. He would try another tactic. "And when do you intend to... to have the wedding?"

"We haven't decided. Finola won't...."

"Ah, a smart girl." The matter was obviously not pressing. He looked at his gold watch. Yes, the matter could wait. He would discuss it further but not this morning. "It's getting late, son. We'll talk about this matter again. I wouldn't mention it to your mother, yet, if I were you... Lent an' all that. You know..." John Francis wanted a pleasant Easter. Although it was six weeks away, he was already looking forward, as a matter of fact, to a nice lamb dinner - lamb was his favorite meat and difficult to obtain - to the usual pleasantries... greeting friends after church, rounds of toasting, the exchange of chocolate eggs with the children. At that point he was reminded that he hadn't got a gift for his wife. He liked to present her with a box of marzipan especially imported from Spain. Damn bad timing... wedding... who ever thought about such things during Lent... It was sacriligious. Love... with a servant girl - the boy was crazy. "Better get a move on and betake yourself to the warehouse. Being that it's Lenten time, the men will want some time off. Church services you know."

John Francis strode across the room, opened the door, and went out leaving Frank looking into a half-empty cup of coffee.

Could have been worse. At least he knows. Perhaps he's right about Lent. Better wait till that is over. Then he'll see the sense of it. He would say nothing to Finola, meantime. Frank's thoughts were interrupted when the twins burst into the room.

"My, my... my!... Aren't we dapper this morning." Eoin teased.

Liam winked at his twin. "Where's Finola?" He grabbed the huge drape that still partially covered the French door and looked behind it. "Not here... oh, perhaps she's under the table."

As he was about to lift the table-cloth, Frank got to his feet. Not wishing to provoke a scene, he said without ranker as he wiped his lips on the napkin nearest to him and then placed it beside his cup. "Well, if you two fellows have nothing better to do than play, I'm afraid I must leave you to it. Good morning to you both." He bowed slightly and departed, a supercilious grin on his face.

Frank's unruffled demeanor left the two nonplussed. He was gone before they again found their tongues. At first they looked at each other in disbelief. Then Liam said: "Our little brother hath changed. What think you, Sir, be the cause?" Having read a few pages of Macbeth, the twins liked to demonstrate their knowledge of old English.

"Methinks our brother is in love."

"In love! say you. Pray tell, who is the object of such favor?" Eoin's voice dripped disdain.

"None other than the fair Finola. An' mark my word, dear brother, he'll have her to bed ere this holy season is spent."

At that they both laughed aloud. It was a clever game they were playing. They were proud of themselves and their acute powers of observation. They hadn't, it was true, "ruffled Frank's feathers" as they had anticipated, but, nevertheless, they knew he had been goaded despite his seeming indifference. Soon matters of more serious import occupied their minds. Home food was considerably more tasty and of a greater variety than that served at college. The delicious aroma of the morning coffee was one indicator.

Several other family members had gathered. They had obviously missed the "old man". A pity for it meant approaching their mother who was not so lavish when it came to money - something they badly needed if they were to produce any gifts for the family that Easter Sunday.

Finola waited until she knew Madam had entered the dining room before she replenished the platters. The Sheridans liked a hearty breakfast, Irish style. They had not adopted the customs of their French neighbors and the city of New Orleans - a cup of coffee and a sweet roll would never have been sufficient for that Irish household.

As Finola was about to leave, Rowena whispered, "Come to my room about 10:00 A.M. please. I'm dying to hear all."

"Rowena," her mother addressed her. "I'd like you to accompany me this morning. I have a little shopping to do, so please be ready as soon as possible, my dear."

"Yes Mama." Rowena answered and caught Finola's eye as she closed the door. So much for her plans.

As it happened, Finola didn't have time 'to bless herself' as she would say, for the rest of the day. A hundred and one different chores still remained to be done before the usual church services at which every one attended.

* * * * *

Frank arrived home early on Holy Thursday evening and found her dusting in the entrance hall. She was standing on tiptoe on a chair her face flushed. The sight of her sent a charge of energy coursing through his body. He started to hum the Halleluljah chorus from Handel's Missiah. She had never heard him humming before.

She, a smile on her pretty face, looked down at him. There was love in his upturned brown eyes and in his hand he held a small package.

"Let me help you down. I've got a little gift for you." He was excited and so happy.

She had never seen such happiness on that face before.

"I want to wish you the very joyful Easter, Finola, my love." He placed a quick kiss on her cheek and handed her the gift.

"Oh, Frank, what have you gone and done at all?" She quickly opened the wrapping paper, then the velvet covered box and was utterly amazed when she saw by the light of the oil lamp standing nearby, the beautiful gold chain and diamond pendant that lay glistening on its red velvet cushion. "You bought this for me!" She looked into his eyes trying to read the smoldering depths. Yes, she was sure he really loved her. Again, she examined the exquisite gift. "It's... it's beautiful, absolutely beautiful. Never in my life have I had anything so lovely, so fine..." Then she though she had nothing to give in return. "But... but I can't take it."

His face fell. He was visibly disappointed. "Why not?"

"Because it's not fitting for a... ."

Frank put his fingers to her mouth. "Don't you dare say such a thing. You're the most beautiful woman in the world. Didn't you notice how people were looking at you when we walked together the other evening. I was so proud to be your escort. There's no one who deserves this more than you. I only wish I could give you what I really want to give. But at the moment that's not possible. Soon, yes, very soon, my love, I'll place a golden band on your beautiful hand. I've spoken to father."

"Aw!" Finola drew in her breath. "You told your father?"

"Yes."

"What did he say?"

"He will talk to me after the Easter festivities. I'm sure everything will be fine."

There was a moment of silence. Then a tear ran down her creamy cheek and splashed on the soft velvet. A sob, coming from deep in her breast, escaped.

"Surely, I haven't made you sad?" His concern and anxiety were obvious.

"No, no. On the contrary, you've made me very happy. But... but do you really think your father will approve?

"Of course. An' even if he doesn't when you tell me you love me and want to get married, it will be done one way or another." A new determination in his voice and demeanor convinced Finola that he meant what he said.

She looked at him a long time. "Thank you dear Frank for such a beautiful gift. I'll treasure it always. I know it comes from a sincere heart." Then a cloud of anxiety passed across her lovely face.

"What is it, my love?" he asked as he gently took her in his arms.

With her whole soul in her limpid emerald eyes, she gazed at him. "You know something... I... I feel... sure, I've nothing at all to give you in return."

"Sure, as you say yourself, you could give me a wee kiss," and his merry brown eyes twinkled with anticipation.

As Finola reached to place a peck on his cheek, she heard footsteps hurrying down the hall. Hastily she closed the box and hid it under a cushion. "I've got to get my work done, Frank... Thanks again for such a lovely gift," she whispered.

Rowena immerged from the shadows. "I've found you at last," she said smiling. Then seeing Finola's embarrassment, she continued, "Am I intruding?"

"No, I was about to leave," Frank answered. "See you later, eh?" He addressed Finola.

"Maybe," she hesitated.

Immediately Rowena spoke up. "Why don't you two use my room later, if you wish to talk." She alone had been her brother's confidant and she was completely in agreement with his decision to marry Finola. "You two have scarcely had time or a chance to get to know each other. And, by the way," she looked directly at Finola, "I'm still longing to know your decision." Without waiting for a reply, she continued. "Got to go. Mother wants me to help hide eggs for the little ones."

Finola did not see Frank alone again for more than two days. On Easter Sunday morning, she arose early and quietly slipped out of the house to attend Mass in a church close by. Her thoughts and prayers were for God's guidance. She had received an offer of marriage - a chance for a fine future. Should she accept or wait in the hope that somehow she would find her first love, her only true love - Dara? Frank loved her, of that she was sure. But in her heart there was place for only one love. She knew no matter what life brought, she would never love another the way she loved Dara.

"Oh dear God, help me to do the right thing." As the Sacred Host was raised at the elevation and the shrill sound of the bells the chubby altarboy so vigorously rung, still palled on her ears, she besought her heavenly Father with bowed head to pity her. She was alone with no one to guide her, no one to whom she could turn for advice. She must make up her mind. She couldn't go on allowing Frank to hope forever. Whether or not his parents gave their consent, she knew he intended to make her his wife. She had only to say the word. The final decision was hers. Again the altarboy sounded the chimes. And again, Finola raised her head to gaze on the elevated chalice and adore the Precious Blood of Christ. At that moment, an inner voice sounded above the echoing peals: 'Marry Frank. He is your only hope at this time.'

Chapter 15

"A perverse and fretful disposition makes any state of life unhappy."
- Cicero.

John Francis sent for Frank. He was seated on a rough wooden chair behind a desk piled high with papers and clutter. The dust was thick and particles of cotton clung to just about everything. He lit a cigar and puffed hard on it several times inhaling deeply. Then slowly he pursed his lips and blew a long grey column of smoke upward toward the dingy ceiling. It left a sweet yet tangy pundent odor in its trail.

As Frank entered his father's office the 'old man' cleared his throat and laid the cigar on the dirty ashtray in front of him.

"Sit down, son. Sit down." He waved his hand to the chair, looking at him square in the face an instant and continued. "Time you were movin' in here, you know. Taking a more active part in the business end of things."

Surprised by his father's unexpected suggestion, Frank raised his brows and seated himself in the only empty chair facing the desk having stepped over a pile of dusty faded dockets to do so.

Was his mind playing tricks or was his father setting a trap for him. Defensive, he waited trying to fathom his parent's mind.

John Francis took another pull on the cigar and immediately replaced it on the ashtray while exhaling the smoke.

"So what do you say? Eh? A desk over there by the window where there's plenty light. I'll double your salary, but on one condition..." He was watching Frank's reaction. Then he hurried on "You must forget that little servant girl."

"Father!" Frank's features were frozen in a mask of disbelief. Slowly the color drained from his face. He started to rise but found his knees buckled. He sat down again. He hadn't expected this from his father. Sure there was never any great love between them but... but not this. How often had he asked him for anything in his life. He steadied himself, only to find perspiration ozzing from every pore.

Seeing that his offers were not having the desired effect, John Francis changed his tactics. "Tell you what. Let's reconsider. Perhaps I was too hasty. Didn't realize how serious this matter was." He tried to appear concilitory. Maybe another way to resolve this dilema..." He shifted his corpulent body and the chair squeaked.

"So how are things anyway? I mean with . . . with Finola and yourself? Not in trouble, I hope. I haven't told your mother, but it wouldn't be long till she hears. It seems J.J. McCarthy saw you at the opera some time ago. Spoke in glowing terms of the elegant young woman who accompanied you. From some well-to-do family in Boston I was told. I didn't enlighten him..."

At this point Frank interrupted. "Father if your trying to tell me that you won't recognize... won't sanction this marriage then I'll have to make my own arrangements."

"Now Frank, let's be reasonable. Do you think your mother will be happy? I can hear her already. 'A servant girl and from our own house. Is he mad? What will we be telling our friends?'"

"Father, I don't care what mother thinks or says. I love Finola and I intend to marry her with or without your consent."

Seeing that reason did not pervail, John Francis addressed the little matter of practicality. "Would you mind telling me where you intend to live and on what?"

"I... I had thought... you would perhaps..." He blushed realizing he had nothing, was nothing without his father. He had hoped. "If you don't... I suppose I'll have to look for employment elsewhere, then." He started to rise.

"Not so fast. Let's keep our heads." His father raised his hand to avert Frank's hasty departure. I've been thinking about the matter ever since you broached the subject. Can't say I enjoyed the festivities much either with this on my mind. However, I have come up with a solution if you're bent on going through with the marriage. Nobody need ever know the real identity of the girl - that is outside the family... the house, if you two were to elope. Sure beats explanations and such like regarding Finola's background, etc." John Francis considered his suggestion a capital one. He pulled on his cigar and again blew the smoke towards the ceiling while raising his eyes heavenward.

Frank was speechless. Was he hearing correctly? Was his own father suggesting that he slink away, get lost, disappear rather than have him, his son, face up to the fact that he was in love with a servant girl? Was money and society all that mattered? He could think of no young woman in the stuffy crowd that gathered in his home from time to time, the so-called uppercrust of the city, that in anyway held a candle to Finola.

"Well, what do you say?" His father's question aroused him. John Francis was impatient.

"I... I don't know what to say. It wasn't an option I had considered. But... but since you've made yourself perfectly clear..." He fell silent again.

"Tell you what I'll do." John Francis hurried to bring the awkward discussion to a conclusion. "You've made up your mind to marry this little girl. Well, provided you take off, I'll make you a heafty gift... How about a $100,000? That should set you up in business and see you... ."

Again Frank interrupted and rose to his feet. "Father you've said enough. I don't want your money. We'll make out somehow. Thank you very much." He turned his back, picked his way across the floor to the door and before his father could stop him he was outside and hurrying down the steps that led to the pavement.

Once he was in the open air and alone, he stopped briefly wondering what should be his next move. Bewildered, frustrated, and completely disconcerted, he asked himself: did his father really tell him to get lost? He could scarcely believe it. Was the 'old man' so insensitive to any paternal feelings? His oldest son, did he mean nothing to him? It wasn't as if he were bringing home a... Yes, he concluded he'd sooner have him marry a quadroon than a decent Irish girl - just because she happened to be poor and alone in the world. He could not believe it. He had thought that surely his Irishness, his pride in his heritage would have excluded all such thoughts from the mind of John Francis Sheridan, but obviously he was badly mistaken.

He hailed a barouche. He couldn't stand around for the rest of the day outside the warehouse. He needed time to think, to plan, to gather his wits. He got into the carriage and told the driver to take him to the French Quarter. At the Cathedral he ordered the carriage stopped.

"Wait here I won't be long." He had decided to apply immediately for a marriage license. "Yes, by God!" he mumbled as he mounted the stone steps two at a time. "I'll take your advice, 'old man'. "We'll not be an embarrassment to the grand Sheridan family." Then his thoughts travelled back over the years to the time when he was little. He remembered his grandpa had come to visit.

He was a poor man who spoke with a strange but musical accent. His voice was gentle, kind, full of warmth. He still had a good feeling when he thought about the bent grey-haired figure who had entered his life for such a short while. He seemed poor, yet he had given him a gold piece. "Take it, laddie," he had said when he saw him hesitate. "Sure I may not get the opportunity again, Frankie, boy. I'll be off in the mornin' back to Boston. It's a long way."

And Frank somehow knew he'd never see the old man again and that the gold piece was all the money he had left in the world. But, no matter, he would make a fine gift to his oldest grandson.

What had happened in one generation? he asked himself. His own father ashamed of his roots? It just wasn't possible. What had Rowena said only a few days ago? 'Mother may not approve, but father will. She's Irish and you know how proud he is of his Irishness'. Was he merely pretending then? Putting on a front when in the company of his Irish friends? Frank was confused. Then as he entered the dark interior of the great church, he recollected himself. What does it matter. Nothing matters except my love for Finola. With that, he knelt a moment, said a short prayer, and went to look for a priest.

* * * * *

John Francis was livid when Frank walked out of his office. "Damn it. The boy's a fool. A man works all his life to see his wife and children lack for nothing and when they grow to manhood the first thing they do is throw everything back in your face. A bloody ungrateful pup, that's what he is." He lit another cigar. "This blasted madcap idea of his has cost me a day's work. Not to mention what is happening below with the men with no one supervising." He got up with a heavy heart. He'd have to go down and tell MacSweeney to take charge. His gait was leaden as he descended the wooden steps to the yard below.

"Hey, you boy," he called to a young chap of about twelve, who was hurrying towards the warehouse. "What's your name?"

"Sean, sir, Sean Quinn."

"Another bloody Irishman. Yes?"

"Yes, of course, sir."

"Who do you work for?"

"For you sir."

"Since when?"

"Oh, I've been doin' chores around here for over six months."

"Don't remember your name on the payroll."

The boy blushed. "Sir, young Mr. Frank pays me."

"He does? does he..." John Francis thought a moment. "Strange - I wonder why he... Well, no matter now. Go fetch MacSweeney and tell him I want to see him."

"Yes, sir." The boy turned to go.

"How much do you earn?"

"It depends, sir. Mr. Frank gives when he can. But he's been good to us. What with me ma sick an' three small ones at home and pa not able to do much on account of his accident. . .

"Come see me after you've done whatever it is you do." John Francis wasn't one for handouts but he was learning his wayward son had a side to his character that was completely unknown to him until that moment.

It was late when John Francis got home that evening. He was in a thundering humor and everyone knew it the moment he entered the house. The children were instantly ushered off to the nursery. Only his wife remained to see that his evening meal was brought promptly.

Finola served the meal and felt the coldness in his demeanor when she entered the dining room.

"Where's Frank? Has he come home yet?" he asked as she placed the hot vegetable dishes in front of him.

His wife, Annabella, answered. "I haven't seen him as yet. Is anything amiss?" She tried to ascertain the cause of her husband's foul mood.

"Had a run in with that fool-brained lad, today. No sense. No sense at all. An' damned ungrateful. Tried to give him a hand up, a partnership in the business. But what do you think he did?" He faced his wife and looked at her worried countenance. "Turned me down. Is he in his right mind, do you think?" He wrestled with the lamb chop but when it bested him, he pushed it to one side and took a mouthful of mashed potato instead.

"I'll take my coffee in the library," he said as he got to his feet. "Send him to me when he comes in. I'll try one last time to see if I can get through to him." He left the room having, he thought given his wife a satisfactory explanation as to his bad temper and avoided, as yet, the real issue. He intended to speak to Finola when she served his coffee.

Annabella realized he wanted to be alone, so, as was her wont, she kept her mouth shut and her thoughts to herself.

He waited until she had served him.

"Finola, sit down. I want to talk to you." He tried to smile but his face betrayed his troubled feelings and the result was a forced grin.

Finola sat in a chair at the end of the table, a distance she deemed suitable to cover the confusion and conflicting emotions, the command had precipitated.

"Ah… hem." John Francis cleared his throat. He looked over his cup at Finola an instant, then laid it down and squared his shoulders. He wiped his mouth with the linen serviette at his elbow. "Frank came to see me today… He tells me he's in love with you…" Again he hesitated. But as

Finola made no comment, he continued. "You're a very pretty young woman. You're certainly intelligent and accomplished..." He corrected himself realizing that Finola's accomplishments were not in the realm of what was expected of a young lady of high society. "I mean so far as your household duties are concerned. Mrs. Sheridan seems to be very well satisfied with your efforts. Tells me you've a fine help with the little ones, also. I would hate to have to... to let you go." He studied the effect his words were having on her.

At that point, Finola pulled herself up. "Sir, if you're telling me that unless I break off the relationship which has developed between Mr. Frank and me, I'll have to leave, then so be it. But don't try to tell me I'm not good enough for... for your son, or to take my place as his wife within this family, if I so choose. I'll have you know I have not, as yet, given my consent." There was fire in her young eyes and she lifted her pretty head high on her delicate shoulders as she spoke.

John Francis had to admire her courage, her pride and self-confidence. "You're a sensible girl. I have no doubt you'll do the right thing." He wiped his brow with his pocket handkerchief, replaced it and again addressed her. "I know it will be tough going until you get another position, so I'm prepared to compensate for this inconvenience. I'll also see to your references personally and will make enquiries among my friends on your behalf."

"The allowance is not necessary, sir. Just my wages please. Now, if you'll excuse me. I have a lot to do before I leave this evening." Finola got up.

"Certainly." J.F. was relieved. The girl was smart. The whole uncomfortable affair had gone smoother than he had anticipated. He handed her several gold pieces which Finola didn't bother to count.

After Finola left the diningroom, she intended to go immediately to the attic where she shared a room with Monica to pack her clothes. She would leave as soon as the day's chores were done. Just as she was about to mount the stairs lending to the top story of the house, Rowena came hurrying from her own room.

"Ah, Finola, I was going to look for you. Frank just came home. He's in my room. Wants to see you right away."

"I... I don't think..." Finola wasn't sure she wanted to see him. Yet, an inner voice urged her to follow Rowena. At least, she could say goodbye; he surely deserved that. He had been a gentleman, had lived up to his word. She owed him that much.

Rowena led the way, opened the door, and ushered her into the dimly lighted room. She then closed the door and left them alone.

Frank pale and troubled was standing near the French windows which opened out onto a balcony and the glorious garden behind the house. A sweet perfume from the roses and camilias pervaded the room. He was peering into the darkness beyond but saw nothing, his mind occupied with plans and thoughts of what his future would be. He turned as Finola entered.

"Darling," he went to meet her. He looked into her beautiful green eyes, let his gaze linger on the perfect features, and the crown of auburn hair framing them. "Finola, you take my breath away. You're the most beautiful woman in the whole city of New Orleans. I so love you. And no matter what they say, you will be my wife... that is if you'll consent to it."

Finola drew back a little. "What are you talking about? I've just this moment left your father. I'll be leaving this house tonight." Big tears welled up, sparkled in the dancing candlelight, then hesitatied a moment before spilling down her pale cheeks. "I was so happy here. Now I have to find work some…" She tried to wipe her face with the back of her hand.

"Shh…" Frank put his finger to her trembling lips and then patted the dampness around the limpid emeralds he so admired with his pocket handkerchief. "Finola you're going nowhere. You're staying right here. I've spoken to Rowena. For a day or two… that is until I can purchase tickets and some provisions for our journey…"

"What… what? I don't understand. What journey? Where?"

"Come sit down. And let me tell you what I've been planning."

In the dancing shadows, Frank took Finola's cold hands in his and looking into her beautiful eyes again told her of his love. He spoke in detail of his meeting with his father that afternoon and of his hurried departure and finally of his application for a marriage license.

"We will be married on Saturday in the Cathedral if you'll just say, yes, my lovely, Finola."

"Frank, it's all been so fast. I don't know what to say or think."

"I understand. It's been a hurried decision for me, too. But I know you're the young woman I wish to marry, so at this moment I have no choice. As it is I almost lost you. What if I hadn't come home just now? You might have left and I'd never find you again."

"True. I was about to pack. I intended to leave this very night." Finola again dabbed at her eyes. But, but… what will we do if we get married? Your father will not recognize me as his daughter-in-law. We cannot live in this city. Where can we go?"

"I have also though about that, my love. Frank drew closer. "We'll go West. San Francisco is growing. There's gold in California. We're young. We can start a new life in a new place."

"Oh my! California... it's a terrible long way off... I don't know... How do we even get there from here?"

"We'll go by ship. I've made inquiries. There's one leaving by way of The Cape next Wednesday. It's a long voyage. Could take up to nine months, but," he hurried on, "God willing and with good weather we could make it in six or seven. What do you say, Finola m' darlin'?"

For a moment Finola was taken aback. Nobody had addressed her with those words since... since Dara had uttered them so many long months before. Dara... Dara... Dara. Was it a sign? Was he calling to her? Or was he telling her to grasp this opportunity? She did not love Frank as she did her Dara. But she was attracted to him and in time she felt sure she could love him as he deserved. She looked again into his hazel eyes. "Frank, you are a real gentleman and I'm honored that you think so much of me as to ask me to be your wife. An' that despite what your father has said. I have only one misgiving... I do not love you as I should... I mean, at this moment, I'm not in love with you." She hastened to add: "But, I like you, you have... ."

"Finola," he interrupted. "I have enough love in my heart for both of us." He took her in his arms and covered her face with his kisses. "Please, say you'll be my wife. Please give me a life... someone to live for. I need you. We can be happy together. I will spend my every waking hour for you and you alone." There was pleading, agony and desperation in his voice, his eyes, his whole body.

Finola felt the money in her apron pocket. Her mind turned to more practical matters... money. Where would they get enough money? She didn't doubt but that Frank had some resources. But their passage would cost a lot. They would have to live in a strange city for... well until he could find some employment. She, of course, could always find work as a... Frank, she recollected wouldn't want his wife working as a housemaid.

"What kind of thoughts are troubling that pretty head of yours?" he asked studying her worried countenance.

"I've been thinking that... that we don't have an awful lot to live on."

Frank thought before responding. "No, you're correct there. But with my savings and... well, I intend to go to my father one last time and claim what is my birthright. He, at least, owes me that," he said confidently.

There was a knock on the door. Then Rowena entered carrying a tray. "I know both of you have had nothing to eat this evening. Please take this before it gets cold." She placed the tray on a side table close to where Finola and Frank were sitting.

Finola got to her feet to help her friend. "Thank you, Rowena. Thank you. You're so kind to think of this."

Both were, indeed, hungry and didn't need a second invitation to savor the delicious food Rowena had managed to coax from the cook with the assurance that the matter be confined to the kitchen and to herself personally.

Annabella was told by her husband that Finola had left the house that evening. He had dismissed her, he said because he had to protect Frank from himself. The boy was not making sense, he had fallen for the pretty little Irish girl but knowing that she, his mother, would never condone such a relationship, he had paid the girl her wages and told her to leave. Annabella although surprised and disappointed because she had liked Finola and appreciated her work and dedication, had to agree that her husband had acted in the best interests of the family.

For the next few days, Finola having packed her few belongings, remained in Rowena's room. Rowena generously added several of her own dresses to the scanty wardrobe and she spent her own money on two pair of new shoes and a woolen cloak which she felt Finola would need for her long trip. Then late on Tuesday evening when the house was asleep, Finola and Frank said a tearful goodbye to Rowena, and with many promises to write they embraced for the last time. They left quietly by the side entrance and made their way to the carriage which awaited them not far from the house.

They would sail on the *Nevada* the following morning into a life of uncertainty, into the unknown. To Frank it would be a totally new and daunting experience, and one for which he was completely ill-fitted, but for Finola only another phase in the long and difficult path to achieve complete freedom, independence and position. She had resolved as a young girl to better herself. She would not falter in her determination to win out despite all odds. That she would succeed in the end she did not doubt.

Part III
The Voyage

Come down, O Christ,
and help me! reach my hand,
For I am drowning in a stormier sea
Than Simon on the lake of Galilee.

Oscar Wilde (1856 - 1900)

Chapter 16

**"The weak soul, within itself unblest,
leans for all pleasure on another's
breast."**
- Goldsmith.

The accommodations on the *Nevada*, a two masted brig looking more like a tub than a ship capable of rounding Cape Horn successfully, were luxurious compared to the *Chasca*, so Finola did not complain. But Frank was appalled. The cramped quarters were completely inadequate. The space allowed was only six feet long and five feet two inches wide; there were no windows and no means of ventilation. To add insult to injury, they would be forced to share their miserable space with another couple, complete strangers. This was too much for him and he complained loudly and bitterly but to no avail. Captain McCullagh, a burley Scott in his late forties with sandy hair and beard, a quick temper, and a blustery voice didn't mince his words when he responded to his protestations.

"Ye can bloody well get to hell off m' ship altogether, sir, if ye nay like her. There be plenty others to take yer place." Then, as he led the way to the public living area - dark, dank, and gloomy, he proceeded to explain that although things seemed dismal at the moment, they had only to await a good storm to rip the sails away. "Then these extra sails will be used," he said pointing to the rolls of material blocking the portholes. "We'll have more light after that." He pushed on in his matter-of-fact way. No use arguing with him or trying to squeeze an extra inch of space. He had everything and everyone under control and he intended to keep it that way for the entire voyage.

To appease the grumpy Captain more than to satisfy her own curiosity, Finola asked why the route taken by the *Nevada* should necessitate their going east almost to the coast of Africa.

To this the gruff Scottsman replied, "Well, lass, ye see. . ." He called for a chart and spreading it on the circular table built around the central mast, pointed out the logic of it. "By headin' east to the Cape Verde Islands we can then take a direct southerly course, run straight for the Horn, as it were. We'll pass Brazil, Argentina, and on to Tierra del Fuego."

"I see," said Finola. "Thank you, Captain." Yes, it made sense, she concluded.

"We'll be stoppin' off in the Cape Verdes for fresh water and supplies." He continued in a more congenial mood. "By the time we get there you'll have plenty o' washin' and such-like to do, young woman." And his roguish eyes danced for the first time in her presence as if anticipating the pleasure and satisfaction the necessary ablutions would afford him rather than her.

Frank, who was still upset, turned to Finola. There was pain and disappointment in his eyes.

"We'll manage," she said confidently. Then taking his hand, she led him on deck. "We have a lot to be grateful for, Frank. Food every day. People are friendly. We'll make out, you'll see." And Finola's mind travelled back to the dreary desolate days spent on board the *Chasca*, to the starving families huddled together in far less space and in dire conditions. Sick and without any medical help, they slowly wasted away and died on the filthy lice-ridden boards they called 'bunks'.

There was no privacy in those "coffin ships". Young girls, mothers, old women, children, they were all thrown together with the men of all ages and types. The weak, the sick, and the aged fared no better than the able-bodied. Sleep came only to the exhausted. For the continuous cries of hungry children, the moans of the sick and dying, the screams of women in labor made the days as well as the nights a constant battle of frayed nerves. That no major fights errupted was the miracle of miracles.

Yes, Finola concluded anything was better than that horrific experience. And having survived it, she had no doubt she would also live to tell her children of her adventures on board the *Nevada*.

Finola and Frank were introduced to their travelling companions, the O'Gormans, shortly after. A young couple, married only six months and expecting their first child.

I'm going to have my hands full, Finola thought and hoped the pretty mother-to-be was prepared for the ordeal which lay ahead. A tossing tub in the middle of the Atlantic in the cold of early spring —no, Fall. She corrected herself remembering they would be in the Southern Hemisphere by then. Anyway, she continued, 'twill not be the most comfortable place to be bringing a baby into the world. Her thoughts were interrupted by the soft gentle voice of Una O'Gorman.

"We'll be carrying our belongings down now." She addressed her husband, Rory. "Captain says it's best we anchor the big boxes to the floor. Seems the seas can get pretty rough at times." At that point she turned to Finola who merely nodded her assent. But Frank spoke up.

"Yes, as you can see we've already tied ours down." Then trying to visualize their quarters with the extra luggage - a trunk, possibly a few boxes, suit cases, Frank's countenance showed his anguish. He was about to protest when Finola intervened.

"There won't be much room left but we'll have to make do."

Rory was a fair-haired rosy-complexioned fellow with a twinkle in his merry blue eyes and a hearty laugh. Twenty-four years old, he exuded confidence and charm.

"Sure, who could say, no, to my Rory," were the words oft spoken by Una.

The little lady herself was a delicate girl of nineteen with large hazel eyes and a flowing chestnut mane. She had small feet and hands of which she was particularly proud and a shy way about her.

Before the ship set sail that evening, Finola and Frank were to learn that their new friends were but lately come from Ireland. Rory had been working on the docks in New Orleans for a few months when he met and married his lovely Una. And as he said himself. 'The glow of the Emerald Isle hadn't left her pretty face when he proposed to her.'

Then word that a ship bound for California reached his ears. He had no love for the city life. There was land for the taking out West they told him. The temptation was too much. So he gave up his job, gathered his few worldly possessions together and with his new wife set sail.

The first member of the group to succumb to seasickness was Una and in her delicate condition this was an additional burden. As the ship ploughed through the swells of the North Atlantic with no sign of the huge waves abating, Finola's job in the stuffy cramped quarters became more difficult. She not only took care of her sick neighbor, Una, but soon, Frank also fell victim to the inevitable scourge of the landlubbers.

Finola administered to the wants of her sick husband with seemingly inexhaustible patience. She tried to make him comfortable on the hard pallet used as a bed by placing packing straw between the blanket on which he lay and the unsympathetic wooden planks. She applied cold towels to his fevered brow and fanned his face for long periods of time thereby confirming his illusion of a sea breeze.

But the stench, which by now pervaded every part of the ship, and from which she could not protect him, was his greatest tormentor. It was forever present and as the days passed into weeks became even more unbearable for him. As a result when he, finally, was able to move about he could be seen holding a perfumed handkerchief to his nose and when the weather permitted he spent most of his time on deck.

But for Finola such a luxury was not possible. There was nothing she could do but endure the unendurable one day at a time. To add to her distress, Una became dreadfully ill and her strapping young husband useless in the face of such misery. But, he wasn't unmindful of the many services rendered and the care and attention given by Finola.

"Sure, 'tis the Lord Himself that sent ye to us. What would me darlin' Una be doin' without ye, at all." And Rory looked at his sick wife. "'Tis utterly useless I am when it comes to . . . well, ye know takin' care o' the sick." He fumbled with the ends of his waistcoat and a blush ruddied his own pale face. He wasn't feeling himself of late, either, but he didn't want to admit it. He steadied his large frame against the wooden bunk. Then as soon as Finola had finished wiping the perspiration from Una's face and spooning a few drops of soup down her parched throat, he ventured to lay down beside her. There was naught else to do.

Forty days after they left New Orleans, the rugged volcanic formations called the Cape Verde Islands loomed into view.

"Land ahoy!" shouted the first-mate.

Soon everyone knew they would be landing within a few hours.

"We'll be going ashore at Porto Grande. Taking on water and supplies." Rory came back to the cabin with the news. "'T'will do you good to walk on some firm ground, again, darlin'." He encouraged his weak wife. She had lost so much weight, Finola wondered if she would be able to walk at all.

She turned her attention from Una to her own husband. He had lain now for several days with his face to the partition separating them from the next space. His appetite was poor and he seemed to have lost interest in everything. Not even the news of docking within hours evoked a reaction.

Finola, however, was elated and when word came that they had reached calmer waters and were nearing Mindelo on Sao Vincente, she suggested to Frank that they should try to go on deck for a while. Eventually, she persuaded him and after an hour in the sun his deathly pallor was diminished. If only Una could avail of the same remedy. But that was not possible. She was too weak and would eventually have to be carried aloft when they reached the harbor.

The following morning the *Nevada* sailed slowly into the largest port in the Cape Verde Islands. There were several other vessels anchored in the blue waters and the wharf was crowded with colorfully dressed Creoles. Most of the women wore bright scarfs bound around their hair and many were carrying either baskets of fruit, jars of water or cans of oil of various sizes and heights perched in the center of their perfectly poised heads. Nor were their hands empty, for usually they managed buckets or bundles in their arms as well. Finola was fascinated. How on earth could they manage such a balancing feat? And she was reminded of New Orleans and the French Quarter. And just as in the

French district, here again there was a language problem for the inhabitants of the Cape Verde spoke two distinct tongues — Portuguese and Crioulo which is the mother tongue of most of the people. But the passengers on board didn't allow that detail to deter them from going ashore.

The air was sweet and the temperature moderate — a perfect day. The feel of firm ground, the scent of ripe fruit — bananas, mangoes, limes, and, from the sidewalk vendors, whiffs of hot black coffee, roasting peanuts, and corn. The fresh water was a gift from the gods. And although it had a slightly saline taste, it was welcomed as a pure delight by the parched pallets of the miserable passengers from the *Nevada*.

Finola wanted more than anything else to bathe, to wash her clothes and those of her husband, to be rid of the body stench that clung to every thread of clothing and that had accompanied all of them almost since they left New Orleans so many long weeks before.

She tugged at Frank's arm as he sampled a mango before offering her a piece. "Let's go sit over there under that palm tree a while."

Rory had carried Una from the bilious belly of the ship. She now lay propped against the trunk of a giant hibiscus, its large showy scarlet flowers a stark contrast to her pale wan face. For this one day Finola told herself she would have to ignore her, leave her to the resources of her husband. Her own needs came first and she was determined to make use of the time allowed.

Having finished her portion of water, she returned the earthenware jar to the vendor and followed Frank to the shade of the palm tree. They sat together without speaking for sometime.

Finola's alert eyes scanned the uneven shoreline. Surely there must be some quiet cove or sheltered inlet which would afford her a place to bathe in privacy. Then she noticed a woman not too far away hanging out some rags of clothing on the rocks and tangled overgrown brush that surrounded her rude hut.

"I wonder if that woman wouldn't do some washing for us. Looks like she could use a few coins." Finola turned to Frank who was savoring the soft caresses of the gentle sea breezes. His eyes were closed. She studied his haggard face, his pale lips and worried expression. Never used to roughing it, he was no match for the vicissitudes of life that now befell them. What would it be like when they reached San Francisco? she asked herself. She began to have doubts about their hasty departure and speedy marriage.

Her thoughts turned to Dara. With him at her side she would have had no fears. He would have found a way to solve all their problems. So optimistic, so full of confidence, she knew he would not even admit to having a problem.

To him it was a matter of using the brains God had given him and then trusting in His Divine Providence. Yes, she knew without a doubt, Dara would have found a way to provide for both of them. Would their paths ever cross again? Where was he now? What was he doing? She did not doubt his escape to America. Did he ever think of his Finola now, or was there a new love in his life? The music of his voice as he called her name still reverberated in her ears, her heart, and her innermost being. 'Finola, Finola m' darlin', sure 'tis you're the lovliest flower that ever grew in Glencarrow.' Tears welled up in her eyes. As they spilled down her pinched cheeks, she quickly wiped them away with the back of her hand. No one saw her. She must forget her musings and turn her attention to mattters of immediate concern.

Again she spoke: "I'll go talk to that woman." Frank paid no attention when she arose to her feet and took off down the dusty road in the direction of the dilapidated cabin. Little children stood to look at her. Some pointed, tittered, and whispered behind cupped hands.

Then she remembered that the woman didn't speak English. How could she communicate? She looked around — no shortage of Creoles, some Africans, but... Surely there must be whites somewhere. She was about to retrace her steps when she came to a small shop — possibly a pawn-shop. Pushing aside the flimsy curtain that hung across the entrance, she came face to face with a scrawny hunchback in his early sixties. A greasy black skull-cap nestled between tufts of crinkly greying locks. Dark heavy bushy eyebrows lopped over on his silver-rimmed spectacles. He had a long nose, hooked at the end, and the rest of his face was swallowed up in a mass of black hair which reached to the pages of the ledger over which he was poring when Finola entered. He raised his head, adjusted his glasses, and tried to focus his beady black eyes on the unfamiliar customer.

"Good morning. What can I do for you?" he asked, his English betraying only a slight foreign accent.

For a moment Finola was taken aback. Then recollecting herself answered: "Oh, I'm so happy. I've met someone to whom I can speak."

The man displayed a set of broken yellow teeth in his attempt to smile. "You didn't expect to hear your native tongue in Porto Grande? There are a few on the island who speak the English."

"Sir, it's not really my native tongue. I'm Irish. We have our own language, you know, older by far than the English. But because... ."

"I know. I know. Don't tell me about an oppressed people nor the English. I know what they do to your people, Ms.?"

Excuse me. I'm Finola O'Donnell Sheridan travelling with my husband on the *Nevada*."

"Isaac Rosenthal." He offered his hand. "What can I do for you, Ms. O'Donnell Sheridan?"

"Well, I need to get some clothes washed. Perhaps you know someone who might…"

"Wash clothes? Of course I know somebody. You bring your clothes here and we'll take care of them." His dark eyes seemed to light up, the only bright spot in that otherwise shaggy heavily bearded dark face.

Satisfied with what she had accomplished, Finola left the hole-in-the-wall that afforded Isaac a livelihood. A half an hour later, she returned laden with dirty clothes and deposited the stinking bundle under the Jew's nose. He didn't flinch. But gathered up the lot, held them close to his chest, and then disappeared into another room.

Upon his return, he proceeded to make some calculations. He had counted the pieces. Before stating his price, he glanced shrewdly with narrowing eyes at Finola. Had she read Shakespeare's, *Merchant of Venice*, she would certainly have been reminded of Skylock.

"You have five pieces. Eh… for five pieces the price will be two dollars."

"Two dollars! That's quite a price! I don't know if . . . ." Finola was about to demand the return of her clothes when the crafty proprietor evaluating her reaction interrupted: "You're not in New Orleans now, Madam. Water is a very scarce commodity in these islands. You have five pieces. He stressed the number. Five pieces of clothing, Madam." He paused allowing time for due consideration on her part. Then continued: "Five pieces of clothing require much water. A boy will have to carry it from a long distance. He will have to be paid. No, Madam. It's not New Orleans . . . ." Again he waited. And again he glanced at Finola from under heavy brows and half-closed lids.

Finola was beginning to feel uneasy. Her clothes were nowhere to be seen. She felt trapped. As she looked at the crafty shrewd face and small penetrating eyes she wanted to bolt from the spot. She just couldn't stand to be in the company of this man any longer. She knew she was being weak to acquiesce so easily to his demands, but she had to get away. She could feel the perspiration oozing from every pore in her body. Little rivulets formed in the cleavage between her breasts and at the back of her neck. All at once, she was drenched in a sticky, smelly sweat.

"All right, all right." She heard her own voice as in the distance. "But I must have them early tomorrow morning."

The old man raised himself to a full standing position. "They'll be ready, Madam." He rubbed his gnarled hands together in satisfaction, looked at her with contempt, inclined in mock respect, then turned away mumbling to himself in Hebrew. She knew he hated all Christians.

Finola left and was relieved to be in the open air again. She breathed deeply and exhaled slowly as if ridding herself of the fumes, the strangling noxious vapors of a den of iniquity. Realizing that people were staring at her, she turned her steps decisively toward the stretch of beach which she felt sure must exist beyond the large outcropping of volcanic rock ahead.

It was close to mid-day and the temperature had risen considerably. She had to get relief from the heat, the smelly clothes, the sticky clamminess that seemed to suck the last ounce of strength from her whole body.

Eventually, she did find a secluded spot. Quickly disrobing, she spread her clothes on the rocks to air, then immersed her perspiring smelly body in the refreshing salt water. "This is heaven, absolutely heaven!" she said to herself. "If only I had clean clothes to wear now."

Then her thoughts returned to the grimy hovel she had just left. "What a peculiar man!" I think I'll ask Frank to pick up the clothes tomorrow. But immediately she knew she was only day-dreaming. Frank would never lower himself to such a task, besides his health, at the moment, would not permit such strenuous activities. He had to protect himself against the hardships of the coming voyage. He as much as told her so when she had asked his help for a small chore a few days before. She was beginning to realize that his father had cause when he spoke disparagingly about him. And once again the doubts, the fearful anxious doubts as to whether she had done the right thing in marrying Frank Sheridan gnawed at her heart. She sighed. A long slow sigh that even the greedy sea birds heard. "Oh, God," she prayed, "Help me in the months to come. There's nothing I can do now but take one step at a time."

She eased herself out of the water and towards a rock. There she would sit awhile and allow the sun to dry her. As her eyes scanned the horizon, her thoughts again revisited the scenes and places of the last few months. She remembered her first day in New Orleans. The sights and sounds so different from the peaceful valley she had left behind, the once pleasant and happy valley of Glencarrow. Her family — her father, loving in his own unpredictable way but utterly unrealistic and impractical. Her mother - so lovely, so gentle, lost, swallowed up by the cruelties of life. Her brothers and little sister, and lastly the trusting, innocent, small boy Patrick, whose emaciated body now lay on the ocean floor.

And Dara - her strong handsome first-love. A tear fell from her soft green eyes. Oh, why had he left her? They could have been so happy together. But then, she knew she was being unreasonable. She was day-dreaming again. He had to leave. A man with a price on his head. What could he do? Ireland seemed very far away now. She had better try to forget Dara, she told herself. She had a husband and with him she must make a future one way or another. But her head was more logical than her heart. And within that secret place she knew she would continue to hold fast to the image of her eternal sweetheart. The brave young man who had the courage to fight against overwhelming odds for what he knew was just. Oh Dara, Dara, her heart cried, and she carried a sharp ache in her breast.

Finola's body was refreshed but her mind and heart were troubled as she walked back towards the ship to join her husband. It must be meal time; her stomach said it was, anyway.

Frank still sat in the same place, but his eyes were open now and he was anxiously awaiting her return.

"You've been a long time," he complained.

"I found a little cove where the waters were calm. I was able to wash." She tried to ignore his irritability.

When she boarded the ship, the savory odor of frying fresh fish welcomed her. She secured two portions and some cassava, or manioc as the Creoles called it, and returned to the shade of the palm tree to eat with Frank.

He picked at the fish, but wouldn't touch the manioc. "God, is there nothing better to eat? No bread?"

"I'm sorry, that's all I could get." Then she saw a man lopping off the tops of some coconuts with a machete. He was offering them to passersby for a cent each.

"Would you like some of that coconut milk?" Finola asked. "I'll get some bananas for you also. You must eat something to keep up your strength." She got to her feet again without waiting for Frank to reply.

Having finished the coconut milk and eaten half a banana, Frank felt a little stronger. He continued to doze in the shade for the rest of the afternoon. Finola went to see if her friend, Una, needed anything and was relieved to find her very much better.

"I can't tell you how good it feels to be on firm ground again. I'd never make a sailor," she said. 'Twas the same story on the ship from Ireland. I'll never forget it." She paused as if her mind was reliving the horrible weeks aboard the crowded vessel that carried her and hundreds of others from the Emerald Isle to the shores of the New World. "God, it was worse than hell. But, then, you know all about it." She looked up at Finola who was still standing beside her. There was fear and anxiety in her hazel eyes. "Oh Finola, what am I going to do when my time comes? I'm so scared."

"Now, don't you be fretten' about a thing. I know what's to be done. You'll be fine." Finola's answer was reassuring and for the moment Una relaxed and smiled faintly at her.

"I'll be thankin' you for that, Finola." She then lay back against the trunk of the tree again and closed her eyes, as Rory came striding towards them, his arms full of fruit.

"The more of these you can get inside you, the better," he said as he placed an assortment of fruits at Una's feet.

Finola responded by nodding her head. "I should purchase a supply also. We'll be needing fresh fruit in the days to come."

Their stay in the Cape Verde was cut short by a day. The Captain felt there was a change in the weather.

Since Finola didn't want to return to the pawn shop, Rory obliged and picked up the clothes the following morning. By noon the brig pulled away from the wharf, slipping gently out of the quiet waters into the turbulence of the broad Atlantic.

Chapter 17

**"The miserable hath no other medicine
but only hope."**
- Shakespeare

Groaning and straining, the *Nevada* crossed the equator and into the Southern Hemisphere around mid-day on the 28th day of April 1848. The crew and some of the hardier passengers celebrated the event with a jigger of Scotch, compliments of Captain McCullagh. The captain always kept the liquor under lock and key in his own quarters, and only allowed its use on three very special occasions - the two crossings of the equator and the rounding of the Cape. Those who were in fair fit condition to do so, danced to the music of Michael O'Flaherty's tin whistle.

"Give us a good Scottish tune. A wee breath o' the highlands for a change. Enough o' ye'r Irish jigs," shouted the cocky second mate, Douglas MacPhearson, as he winked at Finola but without changing the stern expression that was his constant companion.

As soon as the whiskey was consumed, however, and there was no sign of any replenishment, the high-spirited among the crew gradually retreated, once more adopting their accustomed demeanor - sober, reticient, stolid, taking their places, as the dour cogs that they were, in the creaky wheels of the ship's life.

They made normal headway for about three weeks after they left the Cape Verde. Then all 'hell' broke loose when a gale from the southwest struck without warning. The crew and passengers were harrassed on all sides. The aft hatch was open at the time allowing gallons of cold frothy seawater to drench the cabins and all within. Everything not fastened down, including the passengers, was swept into a jumbled heap as the water continued to pour in.

Una, who was lying on her back in the lower bunk was thrown onto the floor getting wedged between the trunks. Her screams sent a cold chill through Finola. Rory scrambled to her aid and, eventually, was able to pull her free. Fortunately, she was not badly hurt - a few scrapes and scratches and very frightened but otherwise unharmed. After that, Rory decided the best place for her was the wet floor. Another fall might cause her to lose the child.

"Mother o' God! We'll all be drowned surely." she cried clinging to Rory, and putting her hand to her stomach. "Do you think he's all right?" Her large hazel eyes were wide with concern and anxiety. Rory nodded; trying to reassure her.

"If you don't feel any pain, you're fine." Finola's voice was confident and calm.

But scarcely had Una relaxed, slumped against Rory's shoulder, when another onslaught from the hatchway engulfed them.

"Great God Almighty! Why don't they secure that hatch?" Rory bellowed when he caught his breath.

At that moment, the ship's quartermaster walked by.

"Any idea how long this could last?" Rory shouted as he passed.

"Anywhere from a week to maybe four or five," came the matter-of-fact answer.

"Good God! How can we, how can my wife endure such conditions?"

"She will," came the response.

"Una darlin'." Rory cradled his frightened wife in his arms. We'll have to get you out of those wet clothes." He looked at Finola who was wringing out the ends of her own skirt. His clear blue eyes spoke volumns.

"He's right, Una. You have to get something dry on you."

"Then 'tis opening that box you'll be, for I've naught else to wear but what's within." It took all her strength to indicate which particular box. Then she leaned back once again exhausted and limp against her husband.

Finola looked at Frank hoping he might find the courage and decency to come to her aid. What a pathetic figure he cut. Like everyone else he was soaked to the skin but unlike the others he was unwilling to do anything about it. He lay where he had fallen under a heap of debris. A tiny trickle of blood marked a slight cut on his forehead.

Finola quickly checked to see that there were no more lacerations, then gave her attention to Una. Eventually, with Rory's help she managed to make her a little more comfortable.

Finola then changed her own clothes, and now that the hatch was secured, she tried to dry out their sleeping quarters. As soon as she had a dry place set up, she finally, got Frank to his feet and out of his wet clothes.

Dampness and mustiness were now added to their already unhealthy conditions. Friends were becoming less friendly as tempers and patience were sorely tried. Anger was now Frank's invariable refuge. His face bore a constant scowl and it didn't take much to call forth a barrage of explitives that further aggravated the tensions between the couples.

A strong wind helped as they neared the Falkland Islands sending them on a steady course along the Patagonian coast. These rocky, treeless islands constantly battered by wind and rain gave the weary travellers of the *Nevada* a brief surcease. Forbidding though they appeared, they were once used by whalers and when their ship anchored in a rugged inlet the ablebodied rushed to be among the first to set foot on the rough and rocky shore.

After a few hours search, fresh water was found. Driftwood was gathered and when several wild geese and ducks were captured a great cauldon of soup was prepared by Maurice. It was a gift from the gods for the famished crew and for those of the passengers who were able to partake.

Damp clothes and blankets were dried and with full bellies for the first time in seven days, spirits revived and tempers were greatly mollified.

Seated around the huge fire, the stalward members of the crew began to sing their old shanties and Captain McCullagh knowing full well that the worst of the voyage still lay ahead decided to break his own rules. He ordered a jigger of whiskey for every man. When the singing subsided, the stories began. And with the prospects of the Strait of Magellan foremost in the minds of all, it was only natural that their tales should include the feats of men like Sir Francis Drake who in 1578 negotiated the passage in seventeen days and the Frenchman Bougainville who made it in fifty-two.

"A bloody devilish trap set be the demons o' hell itself." A veteran of two trips spoke and spat tobacco juice into the leaping flames at his feet.

"How so?" demanded Rory who was seated nearby holding a blanket to the fire.

"Well," replied the sailor, the passage itself isn't too bad but it's when ye expect to be all clear o' the rocks and reefs and headin' for the open Pacific, that the trap is sprung. The Four Evangelists - them's the cause of all our trouble. Them damn islands have seen the death of many a ship, sir."

"But why? Is it fog or... ?" Rory was curious.

"Nah. It's the Westerlies. The screeching, howling Westerlies from the Pacific that pile up the waters into towering furies at the exit of the passage. In trying to break through many ships are cast upon those rocks they call the Evangels."

"So the worst is still to come, then?" Rory's scowl showed his concern. He was thinking of his Una. She could scarcely take much more rough weather and he was beginning to fear that she might not survive the journey at all.

"But then many have outwitted the acursed spirits in them waters and lived to tell their story. I've been in the very jaws of death twice meself."

"Then what's the secret?"

"Well, I'll tell ye," the sailor confided. It's that Desolation Island that's the bad one. A ship may think it has hoodwinked the Evangels and finds instead it can't keep its position. Then in panic it turns and runs and Desolation is waiting. So many fine vessels have found death and destruction in the waters around Desolation."

"But how is it possible then to escape?" Rory was determined to know if they would ever reach San Francisco or was the trip a fool's errand.

"With Captain McCullagh we'll make it. He knows what has to be done. If the Dutch and the Spaniards have made it, don't you know that a Scotsman can best the lot o' them." The sailor said with confidence and scorn in his voice.

The sojourn on the Falklands did everyone a world of good. And it was with mixed feelings that these desolate islands were vacated two days later. Then three more days of stormy wind-tossed sailing and Captain McCullagh knew they had blown off course.

When the news that Staten Island seen to port was received below deck, the cook, Maurice, immediately found a safe place for the one skillet he still continued to use. "Ah, dis is dee time, dee most bad time of all. No more cookin'. You all get dry food now, take it or leave it, till we see Pacific Ocean." He spoke to the few who had gathered for the noon meal.

Maurice was a Cajun, swarthy with heavy dark bushy eyebrows, a long straight nose, a square jaw and, if his lips could be seen, for his whiskers were thick and unkept, they would appear strong and shapely. His teeth were uneven and several were missing. His hair was long and still black despite his fifty odd years. He kept it sleeked back over his ears and tied behind with a string.

When he had finished fussing about in the small galley he sat down on a box. "Ye ain't seen nothin' yet. Wait till ye see what de Cape's got in store for ye'all. Been through them hellish waters three times, an' I'll be damned if they don't keep gettin' worse." He had been on the *Nevada* since Captain McCullagh had started his runs to San Francisco. It was his home, his family, his all. Others had come and gone, but not Maurice; he felt that his last days were somehow bound up with the Scottish Captain and his ship.

As Maurice had predicted, the next several days were almost more than the ship could sustain. There in the icy waters off the southern tip of the land called Tierra del Fuego, the small craft was cruelly tortured by thundering currents crashing in from the Pacific and equally devastating swells, turbulent and mountainous, lashing it from the Atlantic.

Finola was so sick she didn't care whether she lived or died. Frank totally removed from reality was utterly useless and spent his whole time lying flat in the narrow berth forcing Finola to find a space on the floor on which to lie down. Una was still deathly sick and continued to lose weight. Rory, who had found his sea legs, was now general factotum

Night and day for five long weary days and longer wearier nights, the *Nevada* fought her way through sheets of driving sleet and snow. The sun barely made its way above the horizon. So, it seemed, that only an ashen haze marked the difference between day and the total blackness that was night. At times the choppy seas, the avalanche of cascading water that flooded and pounded the decks so violently, and the desperate struggle the frail brig had to endure to survive caused even the seasoned sailors to wonder if she would make it this time.

To add to the misery, the weather had turned so cold that the passengers shivered continually in their damp blankets. A hot meal would have been such a relief but that was completely out of the question. Instead they had to be content with dry biscuits and cheese.

Chapter 18

"Strength is born in the deep silence of
long-suffering hearts!"
- Felicia Hermans.

It was the 17th of June. Suddenly, as if at the behest of some scheming vindictive god or goddess, perhaps even Neptune himself had provoked the attack, jagged streaks of lightening zigzagged their way across the darkening sky. An ominous bank of thick black clouds was stacked against the horizon, poised, ready to break lose on command. As the winds began to pick-up, gigantic waves buffeted the sides of the wretched miserable craft bearing the name *Nevada*. Fierce gusts and sudden squalls lashed out furiously at the sails, ripping and slashing and throwing the crew into a frenzy of activity.

Although a sudden squall was not unusual in the treacherous waters of the southern Atlantic at that time of year, this swift sneaky assault, the sailors contended, was not an accident of nature, but a calculated malicious attack, a vicious diablerie. Some of the more pious among the crew hastily blessed themselves, when this conclusion was reached. Others cursed under their breaths as they scampered to fulfill their assigned tasks.

The Captain shouted his orders: "All passengers below. Button down the hatches."

Finola and Frank had been on deck for only a short time trying to escape the buffeting below when all 'hell' broke loose. She immediately got to her feet and headed for the ladder that led to their quarters in the belly of the ship. It was difficult to maintain balance or be sure of one's footing. The rungs were already wet and gallons of salt water and foam drenched them further as they inched their way down.

When Finola reached the bottom rung a piercing cry, a shriek agonizing and heartrending seemed to chill the murky sweltering atmosphere below deck. Fear gripped at her breast and her beautiful green eyes grew wide with terror.

"My God! What is that?" were the first words she uttered as she regained some control of her emotions.

Frank was, also quite visibly shaken and unable to offer any explanation.

As they drew near their space, another heart-rending scream assaulted their already unnerved senses.

"It's Una! Holy Mary Mother of God. It's Una! Her time has come!" With that, Finola moved as quickly as she could to the side of her friend.

The ship was pitching and heaving badly. Anything not anchored was tossed pell-mell. It was utter confusion in the passenger quarters. Soon Una's cries were not the only hysterical sounds that rang through those confined cramped compartments of that fragile bark battling for its very existance in the turbulent waters off the coast of South America. Fear had gripped the entire ship below deck. In the midst of the chaos and pandimonium that now reigned, Finola, somehow, maintained an outward appearance of calm composure.

"Wouldn't you know," she mumbled half to herself, for she realized Frank wasn't capable of comprehending or being remotely in touch with such a perfectly, natural and normal occurance as the birth of an infant. "You surely picked a bad time to come into the world little one."

A moment later, her suspicions were confirmed. Una weak and pale after weeks of confinement in the squalid compartment without air or light and with little or no food because of her continuous seasickness was about to give birth to her firstborn.

"Great God in Heaven!" Finola exclaimed, "where am I to get anything or anyone to help this poor creature?" Instinctively, she knew there would be no hot water. In fact would she be able to get any water, at all, she asked herself and thought of the irony of the situation. There they were adrift in the midst of an immense ocean; there was water pouring all over the ship; they were awash in water but try to get a cup of fresh water! She knew she might as well be asking for the moon. She would have to rely on her own resources and, undoubtedly, Una would have made her own special preparations for such an important event.

She tried to make the soggy bed as comfortable as possible. Fetching the blanket from her own bed which as yet had been saved from the sloshing waters now splashing against her ankles, she propped Una on the only pillow she had till then shared with Frank. Then seizing the small suitcase that was squeezed into a space at the foot of the bunk, she quickly opened it to find a few items that would prove very useful in the next few hours - a scissors, several rolls of cotton bandages, some baby clothes, a jar of cream, and a clean nightdress for the mother-to-be.

Una had lapsed into a semi-stupor. Beads of perspiration quivered an instant on her forehead before running down the sides of her paled face. Her hair, beautiful still in color, was matted and clung to her shapely neck and shoulders, reminding Finola of her own mother in those final terrible days before the birth of her last child.

Finola crossed herself and prayed that, somehow, God would guide her to do the right thing for mother and child when the time came. She left the cabin barely able to see where she was going. Clinging to whatever she could to keep herself upright, she groped her way to the galley, eventually.

The Cajun cook, lacking all social graces - taciturn, grumpy, and cantankerous in normal times, impossible under adverse conditions, and that moment certainly claimed the latter honor, was in no mood to respond to anyone's request. He moved cautiously about his small domain gathering up the remains of the evening meal. His black eyes seemed to be closed as tightly as his mouth. His thin black pigtail bounced back and forth as he grabbed for whatever he could salvage: a hunk of pork, some salted fish. Finola saw no more. But she knew that when Maurice was taken by surprise things had to be pretty bad, indeed.

Without any introduction, apology or such like, she blurted out her request. "I need some fresh water and I need it at once," her voice was determined, demanding.

Maurice instantly stopped all activity. Then deliberately he turned his head in her direction. As if seeing her for the first time, his eyes and mouth opened wide, questioning. Surely, the storm must be getting the better of him. Who was this female to order him about? And what was her outlandish demand? Before he could voice his internal questions Finola again spoke up.

"I need some fresh water, hot if possible, immediately. You can't be deaf to the cries of that young woman down the hall? She's about to have a baby. I must have some water."

"A baby!" Who had time to think of babies at that moment? This young woman must be crazy. And as far as cries, everyone was crying, shouting, cursing. Who could tell one from another in this melee. The cook tried to ignore Finola. Perhaps when the storm subsided things would be back to normal, people would also be normal and he would be able to find his missing pans as well as his supper.

Finola was getting frantic. She was having great difficulty maintaining her balance and this stupid man didn't seem to understand or even care about her needs. "I must have some fresh water and I want it now," she demanded. "As I said before, there is a woman down the hall expecting a baby at any moment.

"A baby! Women! Of all the crazy things to happen. What a time!" was all he could say.

Finally, Finola in a desperate effort to procure what she considered to be an utmost and most vital necessity, started to pull at the casks and containers within reach.

"What ye doin'?" roared the cook ready to hit her with a frying pan if she dared trespass further on his territory.

"I've asked you several times. What do I have to do to get some fresh water from you?" Finola repeated.

By now Maurice perceived Finola to be an annoying gnat, a persistant, irritating insect that must be eliminated before he could again regain control of his environment and his life. So without speaking, he scooped up a pot, opened the lid of a large barrel and filling the pot handed it, sloshing and splashing, to Finola.

She grabbed it in both hands and quickly turned her back on Maurice without saying another word.

How Finola ever reached Una's side with her precious container of water, she didn't remember, but she arrived only to find that the baby had already been delivered. A small lifeless body, still attached to its mother, lay in a pool of blood.

Rory, a pathetic figure with head bowed and tear-stained face, huddled in the only space available between the hard pallet and the luggage.

Finola aghast at the sight was momentarily incapacitated. But a violent heaving of the ship caused her to lose balance and half of her precious water.

"Ah no!" she cried, "not now." Then realizing that her priorities were elsewhere, she pushed the container into Rory's hands and turned her attention to Una.

The young mother looked so frail. She had lost a lot of blood. Finola wondered if she would have the strength to hold on. She felt her hands; they were cold, stone cold.

"Oh God! What can I do? Don't let her die. So young... She can't..."

Then she thought of Patrick, her little brother. He was only a wee boy... her sister, a mere baby, the twins,... so many, all so young. Una was just one more in a long line... She pulled herself together and got busy doing whatever she could.

The storm had not abated. It was so difficult to do anything. She pulled at the wretched sodden sheet and tried to ease it from under the sick woman's body. When she finally succeeded, she wrapped the pathetic tiny body in it and laid it at the foot of the bunk. Then she cleaned the mother and listened to her breathing. No sooner had she placed a fresh towel beneath the sick woman than she noticed how profusely she was bleeding.

Exhausted and weakened from loss of blood, Una was barely clinging to life. Her face had assumed a ghastly greyish palor; then a little gasp, a faint sigh and Finola realized that Una's soul had left her emaciated body.

Rory buried his face in his hands and sobbed uncontrollably.

Later, when the storm had done its worst and the Captain had performed the services customary for burials at sea, Rory blamed himself for having undertaken the voyage with his pregnant young wife.

'Sure an' wasn't I the crazy fool to think that she could survive such an ordeal. I must ha' been stark ravin' mad to have contemplated the journey, at all. Me, with my high and mighty ambitions: the grand house, the fine clothes my mind fancied I'd be giving to my lovely Una. Oh, the foolishness of it all."

Finola listened and was reminded of her father. Why, she asked herself, did men wallow in self-pity. Was it the nature of the male to think only of himself. She certainly had examples aplenty to confirm such ideas in her mind and she turned to look at the miserable excuse she had for a husband before bundling up all the bed clothes and taking them topside. The fresh breeze that had arisen would help air and dry them, she hoped.

A few hours surcease and the winds picked up again. By nightfall the *Nevada* heading south was battling tempestuous waves and howling gusting winds. There was over six hundred miles to go before they would reach the Straits. Day after day the churning seas fought to devour the tiny craft, and day after day the frightened sick passengers below deck were forced to endure even more sufferings. Due to the weather, the hatches had to be kept closed, so that the foul air and damp mustiness that resulted was almost beyond physical endurance. The bed clothes had become moldy as were all the boxes and trunks wedged into the spaces designated for the passenger's cabins. To make matters still worse there was no way for anyone to exercise in those confined cramped quarters, thus everyone was constipated. One privy, so noxious it fairly sickened even the stoutest souls to use it, was all that was provided, and as the days multiplied its use became more frequent and each user remained there for longer intervals hoping for a miracle. The result of all this was that everyone on board, with the exception of the crew, was sick, gravely sick.

One gloomy dismal day followed another. Finola, although sick herself, still attended to most of Frank's needs. Her self-sacrificing nature and the long months of caring for the family back home schooled her to accept and accomplish more than her frail body should have had to endure.

Finally, the Staten Island, a desolate island off the coast of Terra del Fuego, appeared as if by magic. This wind-swept treeless rock sticking out of the angry Atlantic waters was hailed by the crew with shouts of joy and boisterous laughter.

"That's the Staten all right. Some fresh water and maybe a wild duck for supper tonight, laddie," a seasoned veteran of three such voyages trying to imitate Captain McCullagh's brogue by rolling his Rs as he spat into the foaming brine, answered a less experienced companion's question.

The novice, however, wasn't convinced. How could they land in such a place. Who could navigate a safe port in a rock-pile, he thought, but didn't express himself. This being his first long voyage, and more than he had bargained for thus far, he held a lean hope however, that perhaps the older man knew a thing or two.

A landing was, indeed, eventually made in a rocky cove. No one needed an invitation to go ashore; even Frank gathered enough strength and made a gallant effort. The outcome of this venture proved to be better than anyone could imagine. Having put together a hunting party led by the second in commend, a cocky Englishman named Winfred, the island was robbed of several hundred geese, ducks and small cormorants by the time the men returned later in the day. Another group found fresh water and before evening all the barrels were replenished, while the passengers eager for activity and wishing to help gathered all the driftwood they could. A fire was soon blazing on the stoney beach affording the womenfolk a heaven-sent opportunity to dry out the moldy bed-clothes and other garments. The washing of undershifts which had not been changed for over a hundred days, was enthusiastically undertaken despite the cold inclement weather.

For the next two days there was a flurry of activity in and around the bleak misty but relatively protected cove in which the *Nevada* was anchored.

Meantime, Captain McCullagh pored over the charts and maps he had spread out in a sheltered cave higher up on the beach. He discussed the possibilities - pros and cons of taking the northern alternative route around Tierra del Fuego with his first-mate. He had not attempted the passage before even though he had rounded the Cape several times.

The stories he had heard of the rocky islands on the Pacific side of the Strait, known as The Four Evangelists, were enough to deter even a seasoned old 'sea dog' like himself from endangering his ship and passengers by taking such a treacherous course.

"Why is this way so difficult, sir?" inquired the first-mate, a swarthy, sinewy Dutchman named Andre Van Rhur who had once been captain of his own vessel until it floundered off the Bermudas in a tropical hurricane and he was left without ship or money to replace it. In fact, he considered himself lucky to be alive, since several of his men had perished; owing to his carelessness, it was reported. He was therefore held responsible for their deaths. A long sojourn at sea as far away as possible from the authorities was his only hope and when this was offered by McCullagh, Van Rhur seized the opportunity.

"According to the tales I've heard, the Devil, himself, couldn't sail past them hellish Evangelists. Countless vessels have perished in that spot," he drummed his forefinger on the map indicating the spot as he spoke.

"Why so?" continued Van Rhur still perplexed.

"Well, it's said that the Westerlies from the Pacific are so strong that mountainous waves pile up all along the exit from the strait. As a ship tries to break through, she is, nine times out of ten, driven onto the Evangels."

"Then it's the long way around del Fuego for us, I reckon," answered Van Rhur thinking of his own experiences and how he had no mind to repeat them.

"Aye," answered the captain, a hint of hesitation in his voice.

The hot soup and roast geese were a veritable banquet that first evening on Tierra del Fuego, that lonely outcropping, inhospitable and isolated island in the South Atlantic. Even the weather cooperated - no rain, only a drizzle infrequent and light, and the wind, well, it blew in friendly teasing gusts. And when darkness, finally cast her shawl over the bleak landscape, the rain ceased entirely, the wind died down, and a myriad stars blinked at the *Nevada* and its sleeping passengers and crew. For that night, at least, the passengers on the little brig would know a modicum of comfort, a luxury denied it since first it set forth from New Orleans some three months before.

Frank, who had sampled a mug of hot soup and felt better for it, snored quietly beside Finola. She, having a full stomach for the first time in many weeks was soothed by the warmth of it and fell into a deep restful sleep. Rory, still mourning the death of his lovely Una and their baby boy took a little longer to succumb to the embrace of Hypnos, but he, too, benefited by the change, the food, and the dry bedding.

The following day brought more hot meals and clear fresh water to drink. All day long everyone pitched in, stocking the ship with meats, fish and driftwood. With another good night's sleep and a well-stocked ship, the captain gave the orders on the third day to set sail for the Cape.

Chapter 19

"The true way of softening one's troubles
is to solace those of others.
- Mad. de Maintenon.

After being buffetted for two weeks back and forth between the Cape and Staten Island, the *Nevada* finally was blown northwest towards the Falklands again, then due west to the entrance of the narrow Strait of Magellan.

The barren and bleak headland of the northern tip of Tierra del Fuego offered a sinister greeting as Captain McCullagh with his customary determination ploughed through the angry waters into the Strait and propelled by an easterly wind made thirty-five miles that day. Three days later, the vessel turned in a southerly direction, where in relatively calm waters a grey pall hung around day and night making strange eiree formations that hampered visibility and slowed progress.

"This has to be the loneliest, most God-foresaken spot on the surface of the earth," remarked Rory as he stood looking across the inky waters between the neck of land jutting out from Tierra del Fuego to the south and a promintary to the north that was part of the American continent. Finola was at his side allowing herself a brief respite from the continual administerings to the demands of Frank.

He had fallen into a fitfull sleep and she availed of the opportunity to get a breath of fresh air. Through a break in the mists, the treeless terrain of Tierra del Fuego was visible. "An' to think of the beautiful land we had to leave," she answered wistfully.

As the two young people mused about the bygone days and speculated regarding the future and what it held in store, they were unaware that Captain McCullagh had never before tried to navigate the passage discovered by Magellan.

They observed his dour countenance as he stood eyes and ears alert on the prow of the ship. He had spent many wakeful hours poring over the maps and charts left by the intrepid men who had preceeded him into these waters. Apart from Magellan in 1578, the great Sir Francis Drake successfully negotiated those very waters in seventeen days. The Frenchman, Bougainville had taken fifty-two days, but, McCullagh clenched his teeth and struck out his lower jaw as he mentally concluded if a Frenchman can do it, then, by gad, there's nay reason why a Scotman should fail.

The going was fairly easy for the first three days and the captain was well pleased with himself and the progress they were making. Desolation Island marked the beginning of what was to be the most challenging part of the entire journey.

Rory overheard the discussion between the captain and his first mate.

"What's it about them Evangels that makes the going so tough?"

Captain McCullagh responded: "Tis them that wrecks the most of the vessels that 'ave tried this route."

"Then we're lookin' for trouble by attempting this passage at all."

"Aye, ye might say that, but can ye come up with anything better right now?"

The captain, having made his point, took the helm. Rory decided to keep the information to himself; he turned and walked to the other end of the ship. There was nothing he could do. He and all on board were at the mercy of the seas and Captain McCullagh's skills or lack there of.

The search for a cove in which to land on Desolation Island proved a difficult task. No hold for the anchor could be found on the sloping shores. Towards evening of the fourth day when the winds were contrary, the captain happened upon a semi-sheltered inlet and decided to tie up for the night. The following morning, he sent a hunting party ashore hoping for some more fresh meat - fish or fowl.

By now most of those on board who had been sick had overcome that malady. Frank, alone, refused to recognize the fact and wallowed in his illusionary misery. Unwilling to accept the ship's fare and having no other means of nourishment, he became visibly weaker each day.

Finola was at her wits end to know what to do with him; she eventually gave up trying to persuade him to accept a morsel, or a spoonful of soup, and betook herself to the captain.

"Sir. I hate to burden you further. But I have a husband who refuses to eat and consequently is daily becoming more sickly. I'm afraid we'll have another death on our hands eer long if something is not done about it."

"The bloody hell! Is it a nurse-maid you think I am, then, young woman?" McCullagh roared.

"Nay, but you're a man of common sense and courage. A no nonsense man and I think a word from you would show my foolish husband the error of his ways," replied Finola.

"Hah!" at that the captain laughed - a gruff unfeeling laugh. Then without another word, he strode off to the passenger's quarters and bellowed:

"I'll not have another death on this ship - ye hear, an' I mean all o' ye. I'm responsible for the lives of all on board, an' the good name of this vessel as well as my own are important to me. The next man or woman to complain of the food will relieve Maurice in the galley for a day. An' that's an order." He then turned to Finola. "I'm thinkin' ye'll nay have to coddle him more, lassie." Then he returned to his duties on the bridge.

The captain's forthright unemotional threat shocked Frank back to reality. At heart, he was a coward and ill prepared for conflict of any kind. Finola was, therefore, not surprised when a short time later, he asked to be given a little soup.

It took another twenty-five days before the brig driven by an easterly wind swept by the north shore of Desolation Island. The sea, rougher by far than it had been, forced all the passengers below deck. By now the Magellan passage was almost conquered. All that remained was to negotiate the perilous waters around The Four Evangelists - four stark, ugly, uninhabitable rocks that stood guard at the western entrance to the strait.

Leaving the protection of Desolation Island, the *Nevada* struck out into turbulence no man aboard, including the captain, had ever before witnessed.

Towering waves from the Pacific crashed with appalling and tremendous force against the equally terrifying swells from the Atlantic resulting in gigantic mountains of surf and divergent currents and tides.

The captain's command was swift and decisive as his small craft neared this cataclysmic force: "All hands on deck, secure the hatches, then lash yerselves to the masts."

For the next half hour, the little vessel was no match for the angry waters. Tossed about like a ball at the whim of some sea monster, it was flung back and forth, up and down, set upon to port, then tossed backward. No one and nothing that was not lashed to her decks could possibly survive.

The *Nevada* struggled, fought to make her way between the northern tip of Desolation Island and the vicious rocks to the north named The Four Evangelists.

The morning hours slipped away without much progress. In fact, she had barely made any headway and was in danger of being tossed against the craggy headland of Desolation.

It was well into the afternoon, when having added but one mile to her credit that the *Nevada* felt the thunderous pounding of the mighty Pacific at its most furious. With screeching timbers and swaying masts, the tiny ship fought for her very life. Fear and trepidation gripped all on board. Even the lusty heathens among the crew prayed that their miserable lives would somehow be spared.

Captain McCullagh drew himself up to his full height and while peering ahead shouted to the firstmate.

"What think ye, is there an end in sight?"

"Aye, sir," came the calm calculated answer.

"Ye have the rocks in view, sir?"

"I do."

"Then hold her to it."

A tense two, three minutes passed. The *Nevada* shuddered, resisted a second, then leaped forward. Ploughing ahead, she held her course and cleared the last turbulence in a spasm of intense pressure. Again the timbers creaked and groaned in anguish extreme, pleading to be split asunder. But for some inexplicable reason she clung to life and held fast.

Nearing the treacherous rocks, the captain kept his eyes straight ahead. He would not be intimidated by them; with determination and statward courage, he persisted.

As soon as they had made the open sea; Captain McCullagh gave the order for the hatches to be opened. It didn't take long for those with sea legs to climb on deck. Many knelt, indifferent to the wet, the rain, and the icy winds, to thank God for their safe deliverance. The burley captain's stature; his image as a man and his extraordinary skills as a sailor were magnified a hundred-fold in the minds of all on board ship. To the pious, he was a God-fearing man and therefore under the protection of Divine Providence. To the superstitious, he possessed supernatural arts and powers and therefore had best be avoided. But those of more sober character and temperament were loud in their praise of the man and his natural abilities.

"He's one o' the best," voiced a sailor who had been on the vessel for nigh on three years.

"Aye, ye can say that without a doubt." A veteran of many hazardous voyages answered. "An' I should know for I've sailed under many a captain in m' day."

Consequently, there was an air of contentment and a feeling of expectancy aboard ship that had heretofore not existed.

Days of relatively tranquil sailing, winds with a softness in their breaths, leisurely moments spent watching dolphins cascading and tumbling in the warmer waters were a welcome respite for everyone, as the *Nevada* gently rocked its way north. Over six thousand miles of ocean still lay ahead and much could happen before such a journey was completed, but at that point in time, no one was thinking of that. This was a period of rest, refreshment, and satisfaction and everyone was caught up in the joy of the moment.

Finola took to going on deck more often. She particularly enjoyed the late evenings when the clear skies displayed their glittering treasures. After so many months of fog, dark overcast days, and pitch-black nights, this new experience was exhilarating. It renewed her spirits and vitalized her mind and body. It was good to be alive, on her way to a new and better land. Yet a gnawing, yearning feeling lurked deep in her heart - the familiar poignant motif - Dara, Dara, Dara.

Rory, lonely for a woman's company joined her one evening. They spoke of their plans for the future. She tried to console him for the loss of his lovely young wife and infant son. Their thoughts turned to Ireland, the land they had both so recently left, perhaps forever.

"It's a stone I'm carrying in my heart whenever I think of home;" an a tear moistened his palid cheek as Rory, leaning on the railing, looked off into the distance. "Sure, I wish I had never left."

"But you had no alternative, Rory," came the ever practical, realistic response.

"I know, I know." Then cupping his face in the palm of his left hand, he continued to ponder.

Silence continued between them for several seconds, each absorbed with his/her own thoughts.

"It's been an awful voyage so far," said Rory.

"Aye," answered Finola, "but we're lucky to have made it this far, all the same."

"Ah, I doh know. I often wished I had a been taken instead of me pretty Una. It's killin' me to think of her lying back there in a watery grave."

"Rory, you've got to go on. Forget this thinking of yours and remember, the real truth - she's in heaven with God yes, and the little one. They're together happy, watching over you and hoping you'll be making something of yourself and your life. We all have a different road to travel - some take the short bóithrín, others the broad road to God knows where. Yours is the latter." She looked at him then. His blue eyes soft, sad, yet serene.

"You're right, Finola, perfectly right" - he thought a moment. "It's planning my future I should be instead of moanin' and wailen' over the past. Sure, Una would want it that way."

"Of course she would." Finola shivered. A brisk breeze had suddenly made its presence known. "I'd best be going below. If Frank wakes up, he'll be wondering where I am."

"A moment, Finola." Rory laid his hand on her arm to detain her. I'm glad you mentioned Frank. You know, I've been meanin' to say somethin' for a long time. Ever since my poor Una died, I've had the time and opportunity to observe and to evaluate. Now, you may say it's none of my damn business and tell me, go to hell, but I've got to say it all the same. You're a fine woman, Finola O'Donnell Sheridan. You're young, beautiful and intelligent. It breaks my heart to see you slavin' over that lazy good-for-nothin'. Somethin' tells me, he'll amount to... well damn all." He looked at her with deep concern.

Finola was taken aback by his words and it took a moment for her to respond. "My God! Rory, he's my husband!" Her eyes were blazing and the blood rushed to her creamy cheeks. "He may be worthless but I can't abandon him. He's sick and needs me and says he loves me, an'" she hesitated, "an' I love him."

"I'm sorry, Finola, if I've offended you, but I had to say what was in my heart." Rory took her hand in his. "Tell me you'll forgive me and I'll say no more. I thank you kindly for listenin' to me tonight. You've given me back the courage I needed to go forward. I'll not be forgettin' that, I can tell you." With that, he raised her hand to his lips and placed a grateful kiss on her finger tips. Then lifting his head, he murmured: "Thank you, Finola.

Finola didn't respond. She merely turned on her heels and hurried down the ladder. Rory remained longer on deck. Alone with his thoughts, he felt satisfied that he had spoken his mind. She was too good for that lout. What future would she have with a man like Frank Sheridan. He would wallow in his own misery, feel sorry for himself; who could tell he might even take to drinking. Rory felt truly sorry for Finola. She would have a difficult time ahead, of that he was sure. Then he made up his mind that he would keep in touch when they got to San Francisco. He would be sure to know where they would be living and from time to time, would call to see her, to see that she was all right. Having satisfied himself that he was correct, he, too, descended to his sleeping quarters and lay down on the hard bunk-bed by the dim light of the oil lantern and tried to sleep.

But Finola's beautiful face, though hidden behind the flimsy curtain that gave them privacy at night, never left his mind. He turned and twisted in a vain attempt to divert his attention but all to no avail. Finally, he got up and went aloft. It was cold and the breeze of the earlier evening had picked up, now tossing and tumbling his thick brown hair across his face. He pulled his coat about him, and strode with an energetic step towards the stern of the ship then back again to the bow. Several times he made this exercise thinking to tempt sleep to his tired mind and limbs, but with nerves alert and agile brain he had to capitulate. 'Twere folly to think he could rest peacefully soon.

The second mate, was at the helm. There was a bright light in the Captain's quarters. Perhaps the old 'sea dog' wouldn't mind sharing a half an hour of his time with one of his passengers now that the treacherous waters had been safely traversed and everyone seemed reasonably satisfied with the way the voyage was going.

Rory knocked and waited.

"Enter," came the immediate response.

"Good night, Captain. May I disturb you at this hour?"

"Aye, laddie, come in, come in." The captain took his pipe from between his teeth and wiped his mouth with the back of his hand. "Ye nay can sleep, then? Nay, can get used to the tranquil waters, I gather," and he chuckled.

There wasn't much more spare room in the Captain's cabin than in any other part of the brig. Rory squeezed himself between an assortment of paper and boxes.

"You've done a wonderful job, Captain. There's nare a one on board that isn't singing your priases."

"Huh!" The captain grunted. "She did it. She hung in, despite all odds," and he slapped the wooden plants to right and left as he would a prized stallion, a live thing. "Aye, to her, the *Nevada* goes the victory and the praise. I merely guided her over the rough spots, she did the rest. Ye know, laddie, a ship's like a woman. Treat her right and she'll serve ye well. Some may think I'm crazy, but I tell ye, this brig has a spirit of her own, a will, and a temper, too. But I vex her none. I let her have her way and she does the rest."

You're a modest man, sir and it's an honor to know you," answered Rory.

"Well, thank ye, addie. But there's somethin' atroublin' ye, I'll be bound, that ye nay can sleep te night," and as he spoke he eyed Rory. Perspicacious by nature, he had divined the inner workings of Rory's mind.

"Well, to tell the truth, Captain, I doh, no. Having lost my pretty Una, the days have been long and lonely. An' now without a wife and child, my future's uncertain; perhaps that's the reason my mind's not at peace."

"A young man, full o' brawn an' in good health, like yeself will have a long an' fruitful life, I'm thinkin'. But if ye'll heed the warnin's of an old man ye'll nay have any dealin's with" - he hesitated and then looked Rory squarely between the eyes - "with that pretty young woman, Finola Sheridan. He stopped again before he continued. "Ye see, I couldn't but notice the two o' ye together earlier this evenin' an' although I'm not a religious man, yet, when it comes to a man and his wife I don't hold with compromise, if ye get me meanin'. I'll not put up with any shinanigans on board my ship."

Rory hadn't heard so many words from the captain's mouth since the voyage began five months before. For a moment, he couldn't find his tongue. Then he decided since there had been no harm done that he'd explain himself. "Well, sir, since you gave your advice with the best of good will, I'll accept it as such. But I'll have ye know that I'm a decent man and although I'm not blind to the charms of pretty Finola, I have my standards and I'm well aware of hers also."

"Fair enough, fair enough," came the captain's reply and he immediately stuck his pipe back in his mouth. He puffed on it a while. No more was said between them, so Rory got to his feet and extending his hand to the older man, said "I'll be bidding you good night, sir. An' I thank you for the opportunity of getting to know you better."

They shook hands and without another word, parted.

Chapter 20

"O, what a tangled web we weave, when
first we practice to deceive."
- Walter Scott.

For the next month, the *Nevada* sailed north-west along the coast of Chile past its innumerable rocky islands where the winds swept into narrow channels shut in by steep mountainous, snow-capped walls. Occasionally the Alaculuf Indians were seen paddling their canoes in the sheltered waters but the passengers and crew of the *Nevada* did not make contact with them. Further to the north, a whaling vessel drew along side. Both captain's exchanged some words, but, as the sperm whales were plentiful, their conversation was of necessity cut short.

Soon the temperate waters were reached and the green slopes of the distant mountains told the home-sick travellers that they were coming into a friendlier clime.

Captain McCullagh announced the news that they had arrived at the halfway mark on the Chilian coast when they proudly entered the protected harbor of Valparaiso - a huge semicircle surrounded by hills sweeping down to the shore. Ships from several lands were anchored in the quiet waters and trading was brisk. The *Nevada* pulled up close to a wooden dock and dropped anchor. All on board were invited to go ashore.

A typically Spanish-American town with a mixed population of "peon" - part Indian, part Spanish, and those of 'pure' Spanish stock. The latter were conspicuous by their attire. As Finola, accompanied by Frank stepped unto the wooden planks that formed the pedestrian's passage between sea and land, they were confronted by a man on horseback. In a red poncho striped with black, a wide-brimmed black hat, high leather boots with huge spurs and elaborate stirrups, he was an imposing figure, if quaint and rather weird in Finola's eyes.

"Bienvenidos, welcome to our fair country, my friends," he spoke the words slowly, deliberately as if searching for the English.

"Thank you, sir," Frank answered and offered his hand. The man dismounted and with a sweeping gesture, hat in hand, bowed to Finola.

"Francesco Garcia Herrera at your service, Señora. But permit me, first, to have a few words with my old friend, Captain McCullagh. It's been several years." So saying, he hitched his horse to a post and strode towards the *Nevada*, his colorful poncho flapping in the brisk breeze.

The captain was standing by the gang-plank. He hailed the Spaniard with a hearty boisterous salutation. Then a few pleasantries were exchanged. They shook hands and Francesco Garcia Herrera returned to where Frank and Finola were standing captivated by the sights and sounds around them. Valparaiso was, in the minds of the spectators, an exotic place. Vendor's stalls and businesses of all kinds came clear down to the waterfront, while the residential parts of the town were situated several hundred feet up the hillside. To get there, one had to climb a rugged dusty trail or negotiate flights of steps.

There were animals, numerous and as exotic as the town itself.

"It's settled," said Señor Garcia when he was within hearing. "You'll both dine with me and my family this evening. Captain McCullagh will also join us." He smiled broadly displaying a fine set of even white teeth.

Finola was taken aback by his forthright approach but since Frank didn't seem to be concerned, she went along with the decision. Anyway, she thought, it will be a change from the ship's fare and surely for the better. No sooner had she given her consent mentally, than she gasped at her own foolishness. Her clothes! She had nothing to wear but the filthy bundle of rags on her back. She looked at Frank; he was no better. Her obvious anxiety did not escape Señor Garcia.

"You are troubled, Señora?"

"Yes, I... I'm sorry but we cannot possibly attend your dinner, sir."

"Why not?" the Spanish gentleman asked rather surprised.

"Well, you see, sir, we haven't anything fitting to wear. What I mean is our better clothes are locked away... and..." she looked down at her faded tattered gown and then at Frank's soiled, rumbled breeches and shirt.

A smile spread across Señor Garcia's face. "We are used to such in this part of the world. We don't have many occasions to dine with equals or, for that matter, with too many of our local friends either. You see I'm a widower with only one child, a daughter, Consuela." Here he paused to consider Finola. "Yes," he concluded, "she's probably about your age, Señora."

At this juncture, Rory came sauntering down the gang plank and veered in their general direction. Señor Garcia studied the young man a moment, then addressed Frank. "Who is he?"

"An Irishman by the name of Rory O'Gorman." Frank didn't offer any further information.

"Fine, handsome, young fellow," answered, the Spaniard. Then he raised his voice. "Welcome to Valpariaso, sir. Won't you join us?"

Rory eager for conversation and the company of new people gladly accepted. "I'd be happy to do so, sir." For Señor Garcia Herrera assured all that suitable dress would be supplied for the evening's entertainment. Their proud host had made up his mind to show his foreign guests how a Chilean hacendado lived.

The spacious home of Señor Garcia was set among orchards, vineyards, carefully tended gardens and lush meadows. It was high up in the hills several kilometers from the harbor. At the appointed time four sturdy but beautiful little Chilean horses were put at the disposal of the guests and Finola understood why Señor Garcia was not concerned about her dress. For it was customary to bathe and change when one arrived at the hacienda.

'Bienvenidos, mi casa, su casa.' Señor Garcia advanced to greet as they pulled up outside the elaborate courtyard. He bowed, then extended his hand to Finola and bent to kiss hers. He clasped the hands of each of the men and then drawing them towards himself firmly planted a kiss on both sides of their faces. Finally, he indicated the direction all should take.

In the great entrance hall, they were offered a choice of drinks - fruit juices, wine and clear fresh water.

When the guests had been thus graciously received by their host, they were then conducted to their respective quarters by rather demure Peon women dressed in white flowing garb, their bright woolen girdles, the only color worn. On bare feet they glided silently before the honored company, opened doors noiselessly, bowed and departed.

All was in readiness, a ceramic bath filled with perfumed hot water, towels, combs and sundry toiletries. Clean garments were laid out ready to be put on.

Finola and Frank were overwhelmed by the hospitality. She turned to him as soon as the door was closed and declared: "Extraordinary! How fortunate we are today to have met this man!"

Frank agreed but was more circumspect. "I wonder if he has an ulterior motive in all this."

"You don't mean we're being waylaid, surely? What have we to give? Why should he bother with the likes of us?" Finola's voice reflected her alarm.

"I can't answer your questions but I think we should be alert for anything suspicious," answered Frank.

Some of the joy and excitement they had experienced to this point were diminished. But, nevertheless, the anticipation of a warm bath, clean clothes, and the alluring pervasive aroma of roses and oleander walfting from just beyond their open windows helped to eleviate their apprehensions.

For some moments, Finola paused to admire the room in which she stood. The whitewashed walls were high and for the most part bare except for a massive tapestry over the large carved bed. Other pieces of furniture included a bagueno, two tables, several chairs, and a wall comoda. The floors here as elsewhere were ceramic tile shining, spotlessly clean.

A tap on the door drew Finola's attention from the exquisitely carved furniture to the double doors leading into the galeria.

Frank who was seated near the door answered, "Come in."

A young maid-servant entered, bowing she asked, "If the Señora is ready, I will be happy to help with the bath." Finola, unaccustomed to such civilities was, for once, speechless.

Frank answered. "Certainly, my wife is ready," and he motioned to Finola to go along with the maid.

The luxury was almost too much, if only she could spend an hour in that glorious sweet-smelling warm water.

For the first time in her life, Finola felt like a real lady with her own lady-in-waiting standing by to do her every bidding.

After her bath, the young Peon fetched the light flowing gown of bright blue silk which had been laid out for her and a mantilla richly embroidered in vivid colors to ward off the evening chill, for it was as yet early spring - the second she had experienced that year.

Surprised and excited by all that had taken place in the space of one afternoon, Finola urged Frank to hasten with his toiletry. She would see as much as possible of the rancho before the appointed hour for dinner. They walked through the outer courtyards paved with ceramic tile of various intricate patterns and vivid colors. Fountains and cascading waterfalls surrounded by the most brilliant plants and flowers they had ever seen created a spectacular ambience. The roses were enormous and the perfume, in the late twilight hour, intoxicating. Beyond the gardens that surrounded the house the terraced hillsides were lush with vast stretches of grapevines. Apple, plum and pear orchards in the lower ground stretched as far as the eye could see. And swaying poplars and eucaluyptus lined the winding trails that climbed the hills. A rich and prosperous land by all appearances.

"We might do worse than settle here," Finola said as she gazed at the abundance. "It's a beautiful place. Why do we have to go to San Francisco?"

Frank looked at her as if she had completely lost her mind. "An' what do you think I could do here for a living?" he asked.

Finola didn't answer immediately. She had often, during the past few months, asked herself that self-same question. Then looking at her husband, she asked: "An' what do you intend to do when we get to San Francisco?"

"Start a business, of course."

"What kind of a business, Frank?"

"I don't know right at this moment, but when I get there, I'll see." His tone reflected his hurt pride. Was she doubting his ability? The old ghosts from the past were back to haunt him. "Let's go inside." He turned on his heel. "It must be time for dinner and we can't keep our host waiting. You do know that, don't you?"

The barb hurt. He was reminding her that she had been a servant in the not too distant past.

Finola followed saying nothing but her thoughts were agitated. What would Frank do? she asked herself and the more she saw of this new world, the more she felt, he was entirely unfit for it... Dara... Dara... Dara. A cocketoo cawed from his cage nearby startling Finola.

They again entered the house. The massive oak furniture of the dining room with its Spanish carvings and decorative inlays was a new experience for both Frank and Finola. So completely different from the French and English furniture seen in the homes of New Orleans and the Anglo-Irish houses of Ireland. But if Finola had ever visited the castle fortresses of the old Gaelic lords she might have noticed a similarity in the heavy oak chests, chairs and tables that once furnished their draughty halls.

Ceramic tiled floors were a feature quite new to Finola. She noted the spaciousness, the coolness; the hollow ring of leather boots was interrupted by rugs and carpets of varying sizes, shapes and textured, all displaying colorful patterns and floral designs which were quite unique.

Huge wooden candelabra supporting thick beeswax candles which sputtered and hissed were placed at intervals along the table and from their elaborate sconces set in the stark-white walls formed curious dancing shapes and quivering designs.

When the guests were assembled in the large dining room, Señor Garcia Herrera entered in lavish attire accompanied by his daughter, Consuela, a dark-eyed young woman with flowing black tresses, sallow-complexion and a radiant smile.

"Allow me, Señora to introduce my pride and joy, my Consuela," said Señor Garcia addressing Finola first.

Consuela waited smiling but reserved. Her natural beauty was obvious: perfect oval face and soft full lips, a delicate nose, and pearly teeth. She wore a dress of red satin, the only ornament a silver cross which hung on a slender silver chain.

"I'm pleased to make your acquaintance." said Finola as she offered her hand.

Then each of the men, in turn, was presented and shown his place at the large well-stocked table.

While the ladies were being seated, the men noticed how Finola's flawless fair beauty contrasted with the olive seductive luster of the Spanish Consuelo. They stood in awe; such wondrous lovliness, such perfection was rare.

When Señor Garcia clapped his hands several servants hurried in and while the wine was being poured into gold-edged crystal glasses, the first course of the dinner was served. It consisted of a most delectable dish of several fresh fruits. A fish pate surrounded by green olives followed; then the main course of lamb, green vegetables and delicious sauteed potatoes were served. The wines were constantly changed to suit the course and Finola found she had hardly tasted her first glass when another was substituted.

Meantime, she learned that Consuela was fluent in several languages. Her English was flawless; her knowledge of European history as well as the classics was extensive. These facts her papa made sure to detail during the course of the evening's conversations and the fact that she had recently returned home from Santiago where she had attended a convent school for several years. No doubt about it, Consuela was a very accomplished and beautiful girl with only one handicap, according to her father, a dearth of suitable suitors.

The young ladies, seated close together at one end of the table, soon fell into lively chatter; both had been deprived of female company for some time. Consuela, like the nouveau riche society of New Orleans, was captivated by Finola's beauty and grace and accepted her, at once, as a lady of standing. It wasn't until Finola spoke of Ireland and innocently revealed the circumstances of her departure from that poor sad land that the attitude of her Spanish hostess changed. She grew haughty and overbearing.

"My, my! For a mere servant girl you do very well, very well, indeed." And Consuela's flashing dark eyes betrayed the contempt she really felt.

From the opposite end of the table, Señor Garcia observed Finola's strained expression. The lighthearted exchange of only a few moments before was no more. What could have happened? he asked himself. But he knew his daughter's mercurial temperament.

"I do hope my guests are not being overtaxed by our unconventional life style." The strumming of a guitar in the background forced him to raise his voice as his brown eyes flashed her a warning.

For a moment the attention of the entire table was focused on the women. Consuelo raised her pretty head and with a dazzling smile reassured the group that she was indeed the sensitive, concerned hostess.

"The hour grows late and I fear, our sweet Finola is worn out with my prattle." She bent forward and placed her delicate shapely hand on Finola's arm. "Perhaps you would like to retire?" she enquired in the gentlest tone. "You are spending the night, you know. Father has arranged all."

At that moment, Finola felt that anything would be better than sitting in Consuelo's company. But Señor

Garcia again interrupted the charade his daughter was playing.

"I see we have done justice to the meal. If you wouldn't mind, ladies, gentlemen, I have some business to discuss with my good friend, Captain McCullagh before I retire." He then turned to Consuelo. "Perhaps our young friend, Mr. O'Gorman, would like to see the Conservatory. Would you be so kind as to do the honors, my dear?"

"Certainly, Papa. It would give me great pleasure."

Finola listening wondered how long that pleasure would last when it was discovered that Rory O'Gorman was likewise near the bottom rung of the social ladder.

"Since Señora Finola is tired," continued Señor Garcia, "I presume you would like to get some sleep, also," he addressed Frank.

"Perhaps you are right, Señor Garcia," Finola grateful to be rescued from Consuelo's palling and vexing innuendos spoke up.

"For all her education, Consuelo lacks gentility," Finola commented as she and Frank walked together toward their rooms.

"You know the old saying, 'you can't make a silk purse out of a sow's ears,' answered Frank. Then in a more intimate mood, he stopped under a burning sconce and for the first time since they had left home he looked deep into her eyes as he took her in his arms. "Finola, I've neglected you. When I saw you sitting so poised, so ravishingly beautiful at the end of the table tonight, I felt like a medieval knight ready to challenge all who'd dare cast an eye in your direction. The eyes of the men present were on you, just as they were that night I took you to Antoine's. Please forgive me. I have been so ghastly sick. This whole voyage, our lack of privacy, the stench, the filth. I just can't take it. When we get to San Francisco things will be different. We'll have our own home and…"

"I know," Finola interrupted. She knew the wine was talking, that the honeyed words would be forgotten in the morning.

He kissed her and drew her close. Then, as if it were an afterthought. "You know, darling, we've never been able to consumate our marriage.!"

"It had occured to me," she whispered timidly and she remembered she wasn't a virgin and that she hadn't told him.

They made love in the shadows of flickering candles. A cool breeze filtering through latticed windows tempered the moisture of their hot, moist brows and afterwards lulled Frank to a contented quiet sleep.

Finola lay awake for a long time, her thoughts occupied with the intimacies she had just experienced... He had been gentle. Yes, she had to concede that, but... if only it had been Dara. Oh Dara... Dara... why did you leave me, why did you go. She turned on her side away from her sleeping husband and the tears flowed freely. She realized the inner voice which had prompted her on Easter Sunday morning to accept Frank Sheridan's offer of marriage, was a shameful selfish spector of her real self, which had clouded her judgement and stiffled her true inner feelings, persuading her that she would never again see Dara and that married life with a rich man was better than servitude in a rich man's house. But what was the reality, she asked herself. She did not love Frank... Yes, she had to face that fact. Did he love her... Poor Frank... She could only feel sorry for him. He, perhaps, thought he loved her... but was he also blinding himself to the truth. Was he running from a home where he had expected encouragement and consideration and found it not. Where his father belittled him, his younger siblings taunted and teased whenever it pleased them. Rowena was the only one in that stately mansion with its lavish lifestyle, its army of servants, black and white, who understood or tried to understand Frank's lonely heart. She, alone, offered help. But she was inexperienced, and having led a completely sheltered life, knew nothing of the real world. Finola, though younger in years, considered herself to be a woman of greater maturity. She had, after all, been working since she was barely fourteen; she had taken care of the family when her mother died, and shouldered that responsibility with resolution when even her father had failed. Her horrible experience at the Manor had not broken her will or her determination to make a life for herself that would elevate and ennoble her in her own eyes and those around her. As she contemplated her present position, she reassured herself. She may have made a bad decision when she married Frank, but she would, nevertheless, make the best of it now. She would stand by him - chiefly because he needed her more than she needed him, and with God's help she would still achieve inspite of his weaknesses and failings. She would aspire to the heights and forge ahead challenging whatever lay in her path until she reached her predestined position.

Then she considered the possibility of a pregnancy. It wasn't the most convenient time for such a momentous occurance - starting a new life in unfamiliar surroundings, uncertain circumstances. God alone knew what awaited them when they arrived in San Francisco. But she was a married woman and this was what she had to expect. Well, she could only wait and see and accept the inevitable. She would find a way to meet that challenge also.

Frank stirred. Her thoughts returned to him. He was a good man; yes, he reminded her of her father - good in heart and mind, but weak physically and weak of purpose. He lacked the drive and ambition it took to succeed, the tenacity and strength of character necessary to overcome all obstacles. Frank was not a robust person and perhaps that fact in and of itself was his greatest handicap. For he was inclined to retreat from difficultires rather than face up to them. She, on the other hand had resolved to meet life and all it had to offer head on and, she concluded to her own satisfaction; if the consequence of their loving were to produce a baby, she would welcome that new life and protect and cherish it the best way she knew how.

A drowsiness overtook her and in that semi-conscious state, she once again heard the old familiar strains in the early morning air. She smelt the fragrance of cowslips and narcissi in the dew-drenched grass and then she saw him... Dara! Dara was coming, strong and brave and oh, so handsome. And... she was in his arms . .

They awoke the next morning to a cacophony of sound - bleating sheep, barking dogs, squawking birds, and as if that weren't sufficient, the parrot's continuous 'Hasta mañana. Hasta mañana, mañana' was enough to wake the dead, according to Finola. She stepped to the window and looked out, her attention having been arrested by a strange scraping sound. Beyond the courtyard women, Peon for the most part, were raking the gravel walks in the gardens, accounting for the meticulous condition she had observed the evening before.

Frank was loath to rise. A real bed after so many months of torture was a luxury he didn't want to relinquish so easily. He pulled the clothes up to his chin and turned over on his side hoping to be able to sleep some more.

A gentle knock on their door alerted Finola to the fact that there were other members of the household astir.

A little serving maid not unlike the one of the previous evening was holding their old clothes which had been washed and neatly folded.

"Oh! Thank you, thank you." Finola's words brought a smile to the young woman's face. Then in the faltering

English she had acquired over night, she asked: "You want bath, Madam."

"Yes, yes, please.

The maid smiled, bowed and quickly left.

A few minutes later, she returned, accompanied by another woman, carrying buckets of hot water.

After a delicious breakfast of sweet breads, sausages and eggs, and strong coffee, there was a tour of the hacienda. It was a glorious morning, fresh and bright. The air heavy with the perfume of a variety of flowers and shrubs. A pastoral landscape that reminded Finola of Ireland and the beautiful valley she had left perhaps forever, spread out before her. She raised her eyes to the clear blue skies and in her heart, she prayed for her beloved land and its depressed, long suffering people. And again, as always, she thought of Dara... A little sigh escaped into the scented air, which she sent on wings of love to him.

As Frank drew in his pony alongside her, Finola noticed Consuela reined in her beautiful mare close to Rory's sturdy gelding. Half hidden by a clump of tress, Consuela considered herself unobserved. Allowing her glove to fall, she waited, poised and regal, while Rory dismounted to retrieve it.

"Oh, thank you. I hadn't noticed; I'm forever losing my gloves." She feigned surprise.

"I'm at your service, Señorita," answered Rory quite proud to have been thus honored.

"I'll race you to that grove of poplars," she called as she put spurs to her horse before Rory had remounted.

"Well, I'll be... " Rory said no more, but torn off in hot pursuit.

"Wonder what she's up to now?" Finola, half to herself but loud enough for Frank to hear, asked.

Frank looked after the couple but didn't comment. Captain McCullagh and Señor Garcia who were still some distance away were apparently unconcerned.

"I suppose it's none of my business," continued Finola, "but I'd hate to see Rory hurt again."

Towards midday the group, minus Rory and Consuela returned to partake of a splendid lunch - roast duck, mountain trout, an assortment of fresh vegetables, and fresh baked bread accompanied by Señor Garcia's special blends of wine.

It was soon time to return to the ship, yet no sign of the missing pair. "We'll set sail on the morning tide," said the captain. "If young Rory isn't on board, we go without him."

"Could they have got lost?" Finola asked.

"Hah!" Señor Garcia, laughed. "There isn't an inch of this land that Consuelo doesn't know. They'll be back, have no fear."

Since Señor Garcia was unconcerned Finola put the matter out of her mind and prepared to take her departure. She thanked her host for his gracious hospitality and promised to return the favors if ever he had occasion to visit San Francisco.

The return journey to the ship was uneventful, but their arrival on board was a rude awakening. After what they had experienced, the reality of life on the *Nevada* for at least another two months was almost too much for Finola and Frank, especially Frank, to endure.

The following morning just as the ship was about to weigh anchor, Rory came running down the dusty waterfront towards them.

"Wait, wait, for the love of God," he cried as he saw they were about to pull away from the dock.

The sailors again lowered the gang-plank and Rory darted on board. "Thanks be to God, I made it," was all he said and buckled over on the deck at the feet of two husky deckhands. Instantly, they gathered him up and took him below to his quarters.

Finola followed. What could have happened to him, she wondered.

* * * * *

Rory's sleep had been long if restless. So long, in fact, that Finola feared he might have fallen unconscious, his heavy breathing, faint moaning, and occasional muscle spasms were the only sign of life. He lay on his back, his eyes closed until late the following day.

"Where am I?" were the first words he uttered when through fluttering eye-lids he glimpsed the light of day. Then as the familiar surroundings, and Finola's lovely face came into focus, he relaxed and remembered. "Thank God. I made it, then."

"Before you say another word, I want you to have a cup of soup." Finola hurried to the galley. Happily the midday meal had already been served so she had no difficulty with Maurice.

When Rory had sipped a little hot broth, he felt better.

"Oh, Finola, am I glad to see you!" He looked around again reassuring himself. "I thought I'd never again be free." Then seeing Frank sitting on a box just beyond the ragged curtain that afforded his only privacy, he continued: "Let it be a lesson to us all. Never trust any o' those foreigners."

"What are you talking about? Frank asked, utterly confused. "We saw you take off voluntarily after the young lady, you know."

Thus provoked, Rory poured forth the whole story - his contrived capture, and eventual escape.

"After Consuelo had challenged me to a race, she led me by a circuitous route to a group of small huts hidden deep in the hills. There she dismounted and while I was still a short distance off, she called aloud, hysterically, to some of the Inquilinos who were working in a quarry close by."

'See,' "she pointed at me. 'See, he's following me. Catch him, bind him, lock him up… here,' "She gestured to what was obviously a deserted hovel. 'Now go. Go quickly and tell my father. He will send help. He will know what do do.'

"These words, I heard, but it was too late for me to do anything. The Inquilinos were upon me and without much difficulty overpowered me. Having gaged and bound me, they dragged me into the hut.

"Consuela thanked her rescuers profusely and then departed. I couldn't imagine what her intentions were at that time. But I had a long night to think and only one plausible answer occured to me based on what she had said the evening before when we walked together in the conservatory.

'My father is desperate for an heir. I'm his only child. He must have a grandson. He has been hounding me about this matter for the last four years. It's enough to drive a young woman to distraction.'

"Why don't you marry, Consuela,' I asked innocently. It seemed the logical answer to her dilemma.'

"She looked at me for some time in silence. Then a sadness spread over her lovely face. 'There is no one in this land of savages that I will marry,' she angrily spat out the words and stamped her little foot on the tiled floor. Then she looked at me again - a strange searching look, as if sizing me up; there was a question in those dark eyes. But I allowed the moment to pass and did not pursue the matter further.

"You mean!" Finola was aghast and could say no more.

Then Rory spoke again: "Well, what is your accessment of my story?"

"In the light of what you have told us, I think, you're perfectly correct." Frank answered. "I did notice how Señor Garcia was particularly attentive to you that evening at dinner."

"Aye, that he was... too attentive," Rory's voice trailed off. He was still somewhat confused. Surely, Señor Garcia didn't intend to Shanghai a man to ensure that his daughter have a husband!

"In these parts, who can tell," Finola answered, shaking her head. "I suppose if one were desperate enough... But, then, Rory O'Gorman you're a fine strapping young man, you know." There was a twinkle in her eye as she tried to lighten the tension.

"Well, an' I'll have ye all know, I'm not for sale at any price; an' a slave to no man... or woman, for that matter, I'll be." Rory's sense of humor as well as his physical strength was returning to the relief of his friends. "Let this be a lesson to us all," he repeated his warning. "We three must stick together until we are safely settled in our new homes."

"It's a bargain, then," answered Finola and she looked for confirmation to Frank who nodded in reply.

The episode was not soon forgotten, but the next weeks brought changes and experiences which certainly helped dim its memory.

The weather continued to improve. Longer and warmer days and shorter balmier nights were embraced with enthusiasm and the transformation physically and emotionally was evident. Even Maurice, the cook, managed an occasional smile on his otherwise dour countenance.

"If mother nature continues to bless us in this manner, we'll make San Francisco in a month," he offered by way of a greeting as he served the midday soup about a week later.

"Do you really think so, Maurice?" Frank asked. "It will be so good to have firm ground beneath our feet once more."

"And a bath, fresh clothes! It will be a dream come true." Finola exclaimed, as she thought of the lovely warm bath she had in Valpariso now so far away and long ago. "Have you been to San Francisco?" She addressed Maurice.

"Sure, 'ave," he answered.

"Is it a nice place?" Finola continued excitedly. The anticipation of reaching their destination, of a home, a place to call her own was finally becoming a reality.

"The climate is good. Scarcely ever rains, ye know. Doh' know about dat bath you dreams of. Not much water; dat I know."

"No water! But... but how do people manage without water?" Finola couldn't believe what she was hearing. Surely, there must be some mistake. Perhaps Maurice wasn't too fussy about water and baths and clean clothes and such things and decided not to ask him anymore questions about San Francisco.

After that, the voyage was uneventful except for the understandable fact that the passengers and crew were, every day, more anxious to reach their destination.

Finally, the long awaited day arrived and the *Nevada* proudly passed through the waters of San Francisco bay through the Golden Gate Strait, passed the sandy beaches and toward the rocky promontories to the north, she slowly nudged her way. A number of ships their sails furled were anchored close by, and beyond the tents, and cabins, the stark bareness wrung an intense cry of anguish and disappointment from Finola's heart: Glencarrow, oh beautiful Glencarrow!

Chapter 21

**"There's a divinity that shapes our ends,
rough hew them how we will."**
- Shakespeare.

San Francisco was founded in 1776 and was the most northerly outpost of the California missions. Soon after, it attracted English, French, Russian, and American explorers but it was to remain a backward, lazy, unimportant and far-flung colony for the next sixty odd years.

The first Anglo-Saxon settlers arrived in 1822 when the English whaling ship, *Orion*, made port and the mate, William Richardson, deserted. The Governor, Vincente de Sola gave the twenty-six year old sailor permission to stay in exchange for his services to the colony. By 1840 about four hundred "foreigners" were established in the town, but when the American government took over in 1846, a greater number started to arrive.

Shortly before the passengers and crew of the *Nevada* had left New Orleans, James Marshall had discovered gold near John Sutter's mill. At that time San Francisco consisted of about fifty square blocks of ramshackle huts and ware houses mostly grouped about the waterfront. The few business enterprises that existed served a mixed population of about four hundred and fifty people.

But as the year progressed, San Francisco received a rude awakening, for after the news of the discovery of gold reached the rest of the country and, in fact, the world, the scene drastically changed. By the end of the year, the population had risen to over twenty thousand and a year later to one hundred thousand. Consequently, San Francisco was, almost overnight, transformed from a village to an urban and commercial center. But such rapid growth had its drawbacks, for there were neither goods nor accommodations available at any price.

Several small boats were rowed out to meet the ship. The passengers had to climb down a rope ladder and then were transported to the shore. With no place to dock, the women were carried to the beach by the sailors, while the men were forced to wade ankle-deep through the surf to the rocks.

As the forlorn group of travelers huddled together with their belongings at one end of the wooden planks that led to the Embarcadero, they looked about in disbelief. Surely, there was some mistake. How could this be considered a town? Having seen Valparaiso they had conceived the idea that San Francisco, the most beautiful seaport in all California, would be somewhat similiar. But the scene that met their incredulous gaze was anything but inviting. Shacks and tents and canvas sheds in unseemly disarray. And the streets! At that moment a furious wind blew down from a gap in the hills raising a mountainous cloud of dust which choked the newcomers and left a thick film on everyone and everything. Yet, the San Franciscans didn't seem to notice, they went about their business, these bizarre characters, with a reckless, almost intoxicated air that left the newcomers amazed by their excited fast-paced life style. Surely, never before were so many disheveled, uncouth, ill clad, dirty men gathered in one place. And besides all this, the noise, the babble of a dozen foreign languages - Spanish, Dutch, Norwegian, Swedish, Italian, German, French, even Turkish and Chinese.

Finola, Frank, and Rory were the first to move forward barely escaping a cheeky rat which had been scavenging in the rubbish, rags, and discarded debris scattered everywhere.

"Heavens above!" cried Finola.

'What a nice welcome!" was Rory's comment.

Frank was bewildered but eventually spoke. "So, this is San Francisco." His words were uttered without emotion - slowly, deliberately.

And Finola knew he was heartsick, utterly crushed. Eventually, she spoke up. "Well, we can't stay here all day. We must find somewhere to live," she addressed Frank. And deep in her heart she thanked God that there would be no baby as a result of their love-making some six weeks before.

"Of course," he answered, "but where are the cabs?" He looked around expecting a horsedrawn carriage at any moment.

Rory, who was just as baffled as everyone else, overheard Frank's remark. "Well, I'm thinkin' there won't be any carriages here for some time to come. It's a more backward place than my own little clachan in Ireland. Just look around, for God's sake."

Frank's face showed his utter confusion. Taken completely by surprise, he was unprepared to act or even give a suggestion as to what to do next. Rory, on the other hand, had formulated a plan of action and was eager, even anxious, to put it into operation.

"I think, now is the time for us to work together, at least for the present," he addressed the Irish settlers in the group. A muted assent met his statement. "Some of us men will need to look around and find out exactly where one gets the ordinary necessities. I'll go myself and check out living conditions. We'll meet here in… say an hour."

"I'll take care of food supplies," Frank had found his tongue.

"An' I'll see if... if there's any 'public facility'. I... I can hold it no longer," Colm, a young man of about eighteen, bushy-haired and bleary-eyed, stammered. His confusion and embarrassment brought a smile to the otherwise glum faces.

The tension was broken; people began to laugh and joke and Mary O'Duffy offered advice.

"Facilities, is it yer seekin' young man? Well, all ye've got to do is take a look around, I'm thinkin'. Behind that old shed yonder with ye m' boyo," and she pointed to a tumbled-down lean-to.

Rory again spoke. "The women should stay here with the luggage until we return." Then realizing that not only was the luggage in danger of being carried off but the womenfolk themselves as well; he had noticed how the passing men stared, their eyes fairly bulging in their sockets, their mouths twisted into wry smiles, some making lude gestures, others crude remarks, he addressed Colm, for by this time Colm had rejoined the group. "Stay with the women, lad." Then to demonstrate his personal confidence in the young man, Rory drew him aside and whispered: "Don't like the looks o' them fellas, if ye get my meanin'. They're an unsavory bunch as ever I've seen." He winked, squeezed the lad's shoulder, and then strode off towards the nearest tents.

Finola and the other women sat down on their boxes. She was prepared to await the return of the men, but she wouldn't stay idle for long. Her mind was working as she surveyed the barren hills and dusty surroundings. She, like all the others, was visably very disappointed and concerned.

"I should never a' left New Orleans. We were doin' just fine, but no, Owen would be doin' better. 'There's land, lashin's and leavin's,' he said, 'out West. We'll be rich in no time at all. An now look at us here in a desert with not a decent house in the whole place.' The woman, Maeve Killeen took up the tail of her long skirt and blew her nose, then wiped her eyes. She was not a young woman; it would be hard to start over and she having three small bewildered children clinging to her.

Finola tried to comfort her. "Oh, I'm sure it won't be as bad as you think. We're only seeing the wharf now. There must be nicer places up on those hills." She pointed towards the bare hills hoping that her words might be true. Surely there were some decent homes hidden away somewhere.

"What a difference from dear old Ireland with the lush green grass and the drills of flowering potatoes," Maeve again spoke.

"Ach, ye can't have forgotten so quickly, woman. Sure, there was nare a spud would grow in them fields the last time I saw them," The words were spoken in derision by Dan, a tall gangly lad with a pinched freckled face and swollen red eyes.

Having traveresed the town from one end to the other and finding nothing but scatterings of canvas, wooden shacks and a few adobe structures sprawled helter-skelter along the waterfront and up the chaparrel-studded hills, Rory returned to inform Finola and the group that there were no accommodations whatsoever to be had.

Frank had not returned.

"In the name of God! Rory, what are we to do?" Finola asked incredulously.

"Well, the only thing I can suggest is that we start building a place." He pointed to the rude huts and tents. "We can do as the rest have done." And by way of a little comfort, he added: "They say it never rains and the temperature is always warm, so we'll put some sort of a contraption together before nightfall, don't fret."

Rory rented a cart and helped by Colm, Dan and the women they moved bag and baggage from the wharf to a scrub-covered spot about halfway up the side of a hill. Then he went in search of whatever he could find by way of covering and building materials, while the women started to clean away the stunted growth with their bare hands. It was their first encounter with cactus and not a happy meeting.

Afternoon had come before Frank, eventually, found them. He had managed to buy three eggs, a loaf of corn bread, and a fish. "It's all I could find," he said as he laid his purchases down on one of the boxes. "An' you wouldn't believe what I had to pay for them." He was visibly shaken and the perspiration was heavy on his creamy forehead. "We'll all starve here when our money runs out. I paid a dollar each for those eggs! It's highway robbery!"

Finola was so shocked she could say nothing. But as she gathered the scrub in a pile, intending to make a fire she thought - I'll start with a few hens. Aye, an' one thing leads to another.

She soon realized, however, that it wouldn't be that easy. Hens needed to be fed also, and where would she keep them. More than likely they would be stolen when she turned her back.

Undaunted, she immediately considered other options. There was a need for everything in that obviously primitive corner of the world… the possibilities were endless.

By nightfall their tent was erected chiefly through the exertions and ingenuity of Rory; but, to give him his due, Frank did help. They were happy for the protection for despite Rory's assurance of continuous fine weather, the evening had turned cold and a heavy fog cloaked the entire area.

As they sat together around the weak flame of a tallow candle that first evening their thoughts and expectations were quite different. Frank was downcast, thinking seriously of making the return trip on the *Nevada* back to New Orleans. He was the first to speak his mind.

"While we still have the price of our tickets and some extra money, I think we should get out of this Godforsaken hole." He addressed Finola.

"You can't be serious!" Her beautiful eyes opened wide in dismay; she continued: "In Heaven's name, Frank what would we do and where would we go in New Orleans? Do you honestly think that either your father or mother would welcome us?"

Frank lowered his head. What could he say. Of course she was right; they would be the laughing-stock of the city were they to return.

Rory offered some constructive suggestions. "As I see it we can either make it here in a big way or we can sit around and feel sorry for ourselves. With a cart, a donkey, or burro as they call them here, and a little determination we can have a successful business in... My God! In practically anything we like - food, clothing, housewares, wood... It goes on and on. Look around. There's absolutely little or nothing available." He faced Frank and rubbed his hands together, excitement and anticipation in his face. "You saw for yeself, Frank. Eggs a dollar each! Surely, we can do better than that with a little luck."

"It's all very fine to talk... Talk is cheap. Where in God's name will we get supplies, even if we could set up a place?" Frank obviously hadn't a notion.

"Ah, Frank, use your eyes, man. Down in the harbor today, did ye see the number o' ships? Sure, if you take a walk by the wharf in the morning ye could probably do business with one or half a dozen of those ships' captains. Think, man, think of what we could do with a boat load of timber, or flour, or potatoes?" Rory already saw his name on the biggest and best store in that miserable one horse... no, it wasn't a town, he checked himself, hole in the wall called San Francisco.

Finola, for once, didn't say much, but she thought a lot. Rory's ideas weren't too far-fetched. The skills she had learned in Mrs. Mulvaney's kitchen would stand her in good stead, she realized. Her mind leaped ahead to the day when she, too, would own her own store - maybe a bakery, even a restaurant, one like Antonio's. And she would walk among her guests as the propritor, an important and respected lady of an important and growing city. Yes, she told herself if Frank didn't do business with one or other of those captains in the port the next morning, she would definitely not let this opportunity escape.

Thus began the little enterprise of Sheridan & O'Gorman which was to grow as quickly as San Francisco, itself, almost over night.

Within a year, Finola and... yes, Frank was there, but it was on Rory's stout shoulders that the brunt of the work fell - had built a small but sturdy adobe house high on a hill, Nob Hill, overlooking the harbor. It was not what she intended would be her real home; she had dreams, big dreams, but they would have to wait. So day after day, six days a week she and Rory spent long hours working at their store. She quickly realized that she possessed an inborn business acumen - her natural friendly disposition and fair dealings with the customers soon brought the men of San Francisco flocking around her.

Perhaps it was the attention given his pretty wife by so many stalwart single young men who were starved for female companionship, that provoked Frank's jealousy. Since he couldn't always be within ear-shot of her conversations and dealings with these hardy pioneers, gold-seekers for the most part, he grew restless and suspicious especially as they waited patiently for her service rather than seeking his when it was quite obvious his was available.

He had worked hard, pitched in and did his part for about six months but the effort was not sustained. The monotony, the drudgery, the sheer physical exertion as well as the will-power and determination to keep going despite all obstacles were too much. He gradually slipped back into his old ways - indifferent, careless, and unwilling or unable to shoulder his share of the work, he sought to excuse his behaviour by lashing out at Rory and blaming Finola for what were in reality his own shortcomings.

"I couldn't find any soap this morning when Chang Lee came by for his usual supply. I thought we made a promise to keep a certain amount in stock for him. He can't run his laundry without it." Frank snapped. "He was very upset."

"Frank I have told you several times that Mr. Lee's order is kept in a special place." Finola went to check on the large containers, the chinaman's standing order which she made sure would not be touched and had placed at the far end of the store out of harm's way, she recollected as she strode off.

"If you will get a cart we can load the containers on to it..."

"I'll not do a lackey's work around here any longer," he barked back at her.

Rory had just returned from delivering a large order to a new construction site high up on Nob Hill. He overheard the remark and could not resist the challenge it offered.

"Faith an' I'm thinkin' its' been a long time since ye did any work at all around here, never mind the lackey's as ye call it."

"An' who the hell was talking to you?" came the firey response.

"Well if you're shouting is loud enough for all to hear, one can only surmise that anyone who has a mind to do so can answer your rash statements." By this time Rory was red to the roots of his hair and ready to have it out with Frank.

"I'll not hear anymore o' this from either of you," Finola exclaimed. "Tomorrow's Christmas eve and we've so much work to do before then. Rory will you please go and get a cart for me. I'll deliver the soap, myself, to Mr. Lee and be done with it."

Frank took off after that and no one saw him for the rest of the day.

Rory was so exasperated with his conduct and lack of responsibility that he wanted to be shut of him altogether, but Finola wouldn't hear of it.

* * * * *

Rory was about to close up for the evening. It was Christmas Eve. Finola had left some thirty minutes before and had just reached her home when it happened. As she turned to look back at the town and the wharf before entering the front door her heart missed a beat. In one brief moment, it seemed, the whole center of the business section as well as the flimsy shacks of cloth and canvas, the tents and wooden structures and other sundry dwellings in the center of town had become a blazing inferno much like oil-soaked kindling. Soon the clamor of bells, gongs and the cries of human voices were deafening. It had been a calamity waiting to happen and long ago predicted but largely forgotten or ignored in the insanity - 'Gold fever' which had overtaken the town.

"My God, Rory!" were Finola's first words; then Frank's whereabouts was questioned in her mind. But she knew she was fooling herself. He was where he always was lately - spending her hard-earned money in that sleezy salon on the Embarcadero. She was disgusted that he could allow himself to stoop so low. And suddenly, the image of her father in those final days of his life came back to remind her that some men did not have the stamina or the will-power to forge ahead despite difficulty. She knew her father had every reason in the world to succumb to such a deplorable state but Frank - he seemed to have everything going for him - youth, health, wealth, no real responsibility except to try to do a full day's work. Yet, despite all the advantages, he had failed miserably not only as a breadwinner but as a husband and companion.

It had occured to Finola that, perhaps, he was impotent. When she saw how quickly the business was growing and that the possibilities for further growth seemed endless, she reconsidered the idea of having a child. But when she approached Frank on the subject his reaction was quite unexpected.

"You don't want my child. You know quite well I can't give you a brat - Rory's your man. Why don't you do what you really want?" he snapped and then left, banging the door behind him.

The clanging of a bell in the immediate vicinity roused Finola to the proximity of the raging flames. She left her home and ran farther up the hill.

Then she saw him. "Rory!" A ghost-like figure racing out of the darkness and the heat. "Rory," she cried again. He came bounding toward her.

"Better get to hell out o' here, before this inferno engulfs us." He reached out to grab her by the arm in an effort to drag her away from the raging flames that seemed to be gaining on him no matter how fast he moved.

'Where's Frank?" she gasped.

"I haven't seen him all day," shouted Rory above the mellee.

They both reached safety just out of reach of the flying sparks and blowing flames. In what appeared to be only minutes the whole of San Francisco lay in ashes at their feet.

Frank had been marooned in the east end of town; he and some of his drinking friends had been whiling away the afternoon hours of that otherwise busy Chrismas Eve when they were caught by the flames. They made for the water and the rocks nearby.

Fortunately, there were no deaths and in three days all the rubble was cleared away. Everyone pitched in and before long San Francisco was off to a fast start of rebuilding.

Within six months, the city was losing its most prosperous proprietors. Word of what was taking place in the 'gold fields' made many envious and they moved themselves lock, stock, and barrel to these more lucrative markets. As a result the few stores left in the city had no alternative but to raise prices to what many considered outlandish. A loaf of bread cost $2.00, potatoes $1.25 a pound, a pair of shoes which cost $2.00 in New York cost $20.00, no wonder the phrase 'mining the miners' was in common usage. And it was only a natural and logical result that consequently very few miners made money. The vast majority became homesick and many turned to drink, gambling, fighting with each other and all too soon even murder was occuring on a regular basis. Almost overnight the crime rate increased - looting, stealing and knifing leading the list.

By 1849, California had a population large enough to apply for statehood and by September 1850, President Fillmore signed the Bill of Admission - making the state the 31st of the Union. The first governor was Peter H. Burnett and Captain John C. Freemont one of its senators.

During these years Finola's business grew and prospered despite Frank's indolence, neglect, and at times abusiveness. Rory had by this time built his own home close by and intended to bring a wife into it one day but, as yet, no one he had met could take the place in his mind and heart of his lovely Una.

Finola had built her dream house atop Nob Hill and had become the mistress of three servants and the hostess on special occasions to several of the city's finest and most ambitious citizens.

Jessie Freemont the beautiful and talented wife of John Freemont had spent many pleasant evenings in 'Liafail'. She, like Finola, had interesting tales of adventure and hardship to exchange. She told of her first encounter with San Francisco, the weeks she had spent with her small daughter, Lily, in the Parker House awaiting her husband. How she shivered in that damp miserable shelter as the wind blew across the bay and seeped through the hastily erected walls and cracks around the windows. She told of how they had been disappointed when the Santa Cruz ranch for which her husband had paid an agent three thousand dollars was not purchased for them but in it's stead the Mariposa, a wild and mountainous track, overrun by hostile Indians, and of their surprise when the wilderness turned out to be a gold mine. However, before that, she like Finola had witnessed the fire that had burned all her wordly goods - - all she had hoped would furnish her home had been reduced to ashes: linen, clothing, books, ornaments. She had saved only her money box with a few gold coins.

In time, the wife of the first senator from California was like an older sister to the sometimes homesick but always optimistic and confident Finola. They shared the unpleasant episodes - the burning of their homes in 1851 which for Jessie was considerably more difficult since she had two small children, but it was this first disaster which really cemented their friendship. Jessie's example and comportment on that occasion were such that many others besides Finola were inspired and took heart, noting how a woman who had been brought up in comfortable surroundings shouldered her own work gallantly in a frontier community refusing to employ slaves.

Finola saw and read with eagerness the first draftings of the now famous work, *A Year of American Travel* and from this intelligent, vivacious woman, she also learned the art of polite yet persuasive conversation on topics domestic as well as political.

Life had become considerably easier for Finola - the long hours of hard work that had consumed their early days in San Francisco were memories now. The hired help did the menial and backbreaking jobs at the stores. Although this leisurely lifestyle suited Frank and afforded Finola a respite from his jealous and guilt-ridden outbursts, yet it did not change his drinking habits or curtail his visits to his favorite bordello on Market Street.

Such was the state of affairs when another Irish woman of great charm, beauty, and controversy arrived in the four year old city, now become a sophisticated metropolis of brick and stone housing over fifty thousand.

Lola Montez or Eliza Gilbert was born to Edward Gilbert and Eliza Oliver in 1805 in the city of Limerick, Ireland. She was a natural beauty with thick black hair and wide-set dark-blue eyes. Although illegitimate, she was proud of her powerful Protestant family background, for her father's father, Charles Silver Oliver was a former high sheriff of Cork, a member of Parliament and the family held great land holidings and controlled most of the public offices in both Cork and Limerick. Charles waited until he was past forty to marry but while he prolonged 'the agony' he had sired four children by his mistress Mary Green of whom Eliza, Lola's mother, was the youngest.

After Eliza's birth, Edward, Charle's son and Eliza Oliver did get married in Christ Church, Cork. At the time Edward was an ensign in the British army and was posted in India where he took his family. So Eliza's early years were spent in that exotic land.

As a young child, she was sent to England to be educated. Upon growing to womanhood, she again met her mother who had come back to England for the purpose of securing a marriage for her daughter with a sixty year old man who lived in India. However, Eliza didn't wait long enough to return to India with her mother but ran off to Ireland with a Lieutenant James who had been her mother's escort and friend. The two married hastily but the union didn't last long.

As a young divorcee, Eliza wasted no time. After several affairs she decided upon a theatrical life. Since at age twenty-two, she was too old to study ballet, she decided to take Spanish dancing lessons, engaging a teacher for this purpose. She then made a trip to Spain spending several months perfecting her skills there. Before her departure from that land she assumed the name of Lola Montez.

Returning to England, she succeeded in supporting herself by her performances on and off the stage so successfully, in fact, that she was seen in the best society. But her appetite for excitement and travel was insatiable - new cities, new countries, new people.

Her conquests during the next few years were, to say the least, impressive. They included Liszt, the world renouned pianist and composer, whose handsome physique and expressive eyes hypnotized his many mistresses, but Lola's words regarding him were: 'Liszt changed my life - I knew love, real love for the first time.'

Writing to George Sand, Liszt was not so gracious towards Lola: 'The Spanish lady was like the wind that unleashes a sea of sand and dirt on the plains of Castile and leaves one red-eyed and spent when it has passed.'

In 1844 Lola joined a group of creative artists in Paris and then became acquainted with men like Eugene Sue, the novelist, as well as the great writers Alexander Dumas and Victor Hugo. She also spent time with George Sand - Aurore Dudevant, in her country estate.

Lola lived openly with Alexandre Henri Dujarier, a man who had half interest in *La Presse*, a newspaper with the largest circulation in France; this man subsequently died in a duel on her account. Lola's words on that occasion were: 'He was the only man I ever loved.'

Probably her greatest conquest was Ludwig I of Bavaria. This relationship was to change the course of European history ending with Ludwig losing his crown while Lola gained a title, Countess of Landsfeld.

That Lola's arrival in San Francisco in May 1853 caused a stir no one will deny but because the city was only four years old there was no settled establishment - nothing like she was used to. It was a classless society, or at least a society where one's individual abilities and ready cash were considered criteria for status.

Finola's place in the community had been acknowledged for quite some time. She was accorded all the respect due her achievements and hard work and was greatly admired by rich and poor alike. So, accordingly, there was no animosity when the Countess was lodged in the Glencarrow Hotel on the Embarcadero owned by Finola.

Within days invitations were issued and tickets sold at the exorbitant price of $5 each, for Lola's appearance at the American Theater in *The School for Scandal* playing the role of Lady Teazle. Finola, like the rest of the audience, was enchanted by the ravishing beauty's performance that first night. However, subsequent presentations, particularly her rendition of her "Spider Dance" left Finola far from enthusiastic - considering the conduct of the actress less than ladylike. But to her besotted husband, the Irish beauty's dark and seductive allure was irresistable.

Finola awoke one morning to read the heading in *The Pacific*: 'I have known all the world has to give - all!' And as she read further, she realized that among the many admirers Lola had known in the city on the Bay was her own handsome if ne'er-do-well husband, who, it stated, had left the evening before with the Countess for Sacramento. And this, despite the fact that she, Lola, was also accompanied by her recently acquired husband, Pat Hull, editor and part owner of another San Francisco newspaper, the Whig.

Not one to bare her soul or wear her pain for others to see, Finola bore well the humiliation and anger she felt by Frank's insufferable conduct but when she eventually heard of his suicide, for his body had been found in the Sacramento River several days after his hurried departure, Finola's strength seemed to weaken. It was then that she realized the true worth and character of her good friend, Rory.

"You'll be taking it easy, Finola," he said. "I'll see to the store an'…

He stopped, interrupting himself as he noticed Finola's drawn face. But there was still beauty in the soft green eyes and the creamy skin was flawless in the morning light. His heart missed a beat when an anxious shadow passed across her lovely countenance.

He lifted her hand to his lips and kissed with evident hunger the pale fingers while his eyes still probed the depths of the glistening orbs trying to fathom the emotions that she was so bravely trying to conceal. For an instant he pulled her close. She felt the throbbing of his loving heart and wanted so much to return his warmth. Emboldened by her seeming acceptance of his advance, Rory lowered his mouth covering hers, and for a moment she was lost in the sweetness and ecstasy of his kiss. But as quickly as she realized what was really happening to her, Finola pulled away. Embarrassed, Rory blushed - a bright red blush. He had taken a liberty he knew he should never have taken. He finished his sentence...

"I'll go pick up the stuff you ordered. *The Mary Anne* dropped anchor early this morning.

"Wait," Finola didn't want him to feel hurt. She knew Rory meant well. He would never hurt her, he respected her too much for that. "I appreciate all you're trying to do to make things easier for me. It seems you are forever doing. Now you want to do more. As if you haven't done everything already an' been responsible for all for so long," she replied. "But it's better for me to keep going now. I need to be busy, Rory. You do understand?" She daren't look into his eyes again. It would be the undoing of her. She was vulnerable at that moment.

"Aye," he answered a little half-heartedly. He had hoped to spare her toil and the embarrassment of those who only wanted to ridicule, but he should have known better. Finola was not one to take idle gossip to heart. She would do her work and get on with her life and perhaps... perhaps, given time, Rory thought, he might again suggest an alliance that he had, so often, been tempted to suggest in the past. "You're right. Of course you're right," he tried to reassure himself and not being able to give further assistance attempted to take his leave on one pretext or another. "I'll be at the store if you need anything."

"Thank you, kindly, Rory." And Finola raised her beautiful eyes full of sweetness to meet his searching anxious gaze. It was at that moment that she realized the full extent of Rory's love. She saw it in the depths of his clear blue eyes and her own feelings responded despite an inner voice which told her to be cautious. He took a step closer. "You know how much I think of you... Finola... a grá." He clasped her to himself once more and held her in a tight embrace. She allowed herself the luxury of feeling his strength, his warmth, his sincerity for an instance. Then she withdrew from his embrace. "Rory... dear Rory... it cannot be... Not yet, please give me time."

* * * * *

Chapter 22

Ambition is the germ from which all growth
of nobleness proceeds.
- T.D. English.

In the days that followed, Finola threw herself even more furiously into her work, staying long hours at the store despite Rory's objections. Still her ardent nature was not satisfied; she wished to accomplish more. Now, freed from the responsibilities of caring for her wayward husband, she had time and energy to spend on other occupations.

During the first weeks after Frank's tragic death, she applied herself with unrestrained and vigorous energy to all the tasks she set herself, but when the initial shock gave way to more acceptable and realistic sensibilities, she grew calmer and tackled the daily grind with composure. Her own unique form of self-confidence and self-assurance returned giving her an air of dignified maturity not often seen in one so young, for Finola was still only in her twenties.

Finola brushed her hair a second time, tied it with a clasp behind, and taking stock of her black skirt and white blouse, she left for the store. A radiant morning bright with the sunshine and blues of sky and ocean that California so generously offers greeted her first look around as she stepped to the dusty road outside. She drew in a deep breath but exhaled a long slow sigh. She should have been happy. Why was her heart not satisfied. She had everything; yet, she felt her life was empty.

Her steps were slow, not her usual brisk self-confident walk. She was dawdling and at the rate she was going would be late to the store. Not that she was concerned about it. Rory, faithful and true as always would be there. He would even be happy that she took her time. How often had he told her to take it easy. No need to overburden herself any longer, 'sure wasn't the businesses doing fine,' he had said. She could afford to stop working altogether, if she wished.

She looked back at her beautiful home the envy of many in the thriving city. In her imagination she compared it with the miserable hovel she had called home in those now far-off days back in Ireland. Yes, she told herself, she had come a long way. She had, indeed, risen in the world. No one looked down on her, no one treated her with disdain or dared to do so. She dined with the best, entertained the elite of the city. Was considered a person of consequence. What would her dad have to say were he to see her now. She thought of her mam, her brothers, especially little Patrick. How he would have loved to live in a fine home - all he needed was food - such a fine wee boy.

"Mornin' Miss Finola" Stuart Hickey saluted her as he passed.

"Good morning, Stuart. How's little Aiden?" Her thoughts interrupted for the moment.

"Ah, sure he's fine - just a wee cold. Strange how even here one gets the cold - ye know what I mean, so much sun and warm weather an' all."

"Aye, seems strange, Stuart. But I'm sure there's sickness everywhere. No paradise on earth." She laughed and pressed on still thinking of Aiden, Stuart's little four-year old lad. The thought struck a vibrant chord in her own heart and it occured to her that without a family to care for, the idea of amassing wealth for its own sake was a shallow and vain achievement. There were better and nobler things to do with ones life and talents.

She had, it was true, left a life of poverty behind. She had bettered herself as she had known she would. Yet, her ambitions to accomplish something more, something for, perhaps, the betterment of mankind was taking shape in her mind. How this might be done she hadn't the slightest idea just then.

Finola opened the main door of the store. The sounds of Rory's singing filled the air. She was reminded of another and her heart was sad… Dara. Oh, Dara where are you - the faint cry from deep within did not find an escape in uttered words.

"Well the top o' the mornin' to ye my fair lady." There was a twinkle in his clear blue eyes as the tones of his baritone voice were interrupted only long enough to salute her.

"An the same to you, good sir," Finola shouted above the strains of - 'When first I met Sweet Peggy', as she removed her fancy bonnet and laid it aside intending to take it to her office later. Her attention was drawn to some pretty scarves which lay in disarray on a rack near the door. As she began to fold them in an orderly fashion, she noticed a young lad about ten years old running down the street. She stopped what she was doing taken by the angelic face behind the grime and was immediately reminded of Patrick. The boy was barefoot; the baggy pants he wore was surely a hand-me-down; his sandy hair tossed wayward curls about his lovely face as he ran.

Probably never saw a comb or a wash since he landed, she remarked mentally. His tattered and torn shirt was also badly in need of soap and water. A regular little rag-a-muffin, she concluded. But the face, the blue, blue eyes, as he stopped to contemplate some candies in the shop window, the slender sensitive nose and the rosebud mouth betrayed a delicacy, a refinement that no amount of dirt or grime could conceal.

"Oh, God!" she cried aloud. He's about the right age. She went to the door and beckoned to him. As he hesitated, she coaxed "Sonny, come I want to talk to you."

The boy thinking he was in trouble started to move away. "Please don't go." her voice was gentle. "I had a little brother like you... but he died on the ship coming to America."

When the child heard her voice more clearly and realized that she, too, was like him, Irish, he was no longer afraid. "What's your name?" she asked as he approached.

"Danny, Danny Lynch." he replied and Finola noticed a broken tooth right in the front of his small mouth.

"Well Danny, tell me, what did you eat this morning?"

"Eat?" he looked at her as if she had lost her mind. "We don't eat anything in the mornin's. Ma has to find something during the day. We eats jus at night."

"I see," responded Finola. Well what do you say to a nice cup of milk and some bread then?"

"Oh, that would be grand." the child answered, as he followed Finola into the shop. "But you won't be tellin' me Ma. 'Cause I must bring home any stuff I gets to share with me little sister."

"Don't fret, Danny. I'll give you some extra for your sister. What's her name?"

"Ashling. She's only three."

"What a lovely name! Perhaps you can bring her to visit me some time."

"Aye, I can do that," was the confident answer as he chewed a large slice of bread, butter and jam, the likes of which he rarely ate.

Finola's heart was mightily touched as she watched him and the thought occured to her that here was the answer to her morning's musings. Danny, poor, ignorant, and dirty needed someone to teach him, so that he, like herself, could rise from squalor and poverty and live a life of dignity. Yes, Danny and all the other little whippersnappers running barefoot and dirty around the streets and down at the waterfront... a school! A school is what was needed, and needed badly. Yes, the future of this great country was here... it lay in the children, all the children.

Dismissing Danny with an ample supply of bread and milk, she asked him to return the following morning with his mother. She would like to talk to her, she said.

For the rest of that day Finola's mind was busy with many things, but they had nothing at all to do with the store, or the restaurant, or the hotel on the Embarcadero. Rory noted the change and was happy but had no time to ask the reason nor did she offer to enlighten him just then; time enough when everything was up and running, were her initial thoughts.

The question of where she would house the children whom she hoped to educate was no problem - her home, her beautiful home was spacious enough to spare a room or two for these deprived little ones. All she really needed was some chalk, a blackboard and a long stick - not for spanking, Finola didn't hold with spanking, but for pointing to what she intended to write on the blackboard. Books - they could come later. She had no qualms about her own teaching ability. Hadn't she taught her own brothers in the not so distant past. Yes, she could teach the children of San Francisco just as well, to read and write and count. Then she remembered she had also learned the rudiments of the Latin tongue from old Sweeney under far greater difficulties. Yes, she concluded, she was quite capable of passing on her knowledge and skills to another generation of Irish but she hoped to include others, in time.

The following morning Mrs. Lynch arrived bright and early, Danny in tow, at the Sheridan & O'Gorman store. A large woman, strong with a no-nonsense attitude, she gave the impression that she was no push-over for the gentility of the city. She bade Finola good morning and then seated herself on the one spare chair and undid the top button of her ill-kept blouse. She was perspiring and was quite obviously uncomfortable.

Finola tried to put her at ease by offering a cool glass of lemonade. For this Eilish Lynch was grateful. She settled back in the chair. Touched her hair with a ladylike gesture. She was being treated well, not looked down upon. She looked Finola straight between the eyes and asked: "An' what can I be doin' for ye, Mam?"

"Well," answered Finola, "it's not so much what you can be doing for me as I can be doing for you." Finola saw the look of confusion on the woman's face. "You see, yesterday when I saw little Danny here, outside my store..."

"Now, he wasn't botherin' ye, I hope." Here she stopped talking long enough to cast a look of displeasure upon her offspring, . . " 'cause an' if he was he'll catch it when I gets him home."

"Oh no, no, nothing of the kind. Danny is a good boy, you can be sure of that, Mrs. Lynch. And it is precisely because of that, that I would like to make you a proposal.

"We'll an' I'm glad to hear that, now." Here she nodded her approval in Danny's direction.

Finola wasn't quite sure how best to tackle the question of Danny's education but not being one to pussyfoot around she said: "Mrs. Lynch, I wish to start a school in this city for youngsters like yours. It's a shame to see such a fine boy as Danny running around the streets when he could be learning to read and write."

Mrs. Lynch was taken aback. She had been hoping that Finola was going to offer him a job. Hoping that it was an errand boy she was needing, for she, herself, was badly needing extra money. Her husband, Joe, wasn't what you would call a laboring man, although, to give him is due, he did try. Seems like the only work available was for strong, broad-shouldered fellows with large muscles and that Joe didn't have. He was a slim, delicate type - a fellow who could use a desk job if he had had the training.

After the idea sunk in, Eilish spoke up. "Well, Miss, now that's a grand idea but as ye can see for yerself 'tis food and clothen' this child needs not learnin'. If you could be seein' yer way to, say, givin' him a job… " she paused to ascertain what effect her words were having on Finola.

"But, Eilish, I may call you Eilish?" The older woman nodded and Finola continued: "You see without an education Danny will never amount to anything. Yes, I could give him a job, but that would only help for a short time."

"Ah," Eilish grabbed the opportunity. "But 'tis now we need the money. What if he dies of hunger in the meantime, then what good will the education be?"

She had a point, Finola had to admit to herself. Then a thought occured to her. "What if I were to give Danny a job and to teach him to read and write at my school also?"

"Now yer talkin," and Eilish sat bolt upright. "De ye hear that, Danny, ye'll be a workin' man like yer da. Can ye beat that now." She smiled at Danny and then back at Finola. "When de ye want him te start?" she asked and then continued: "The sooner, the better."

So Danny began his first day of steady employment. He was put to work delivering supplies. In time Rory made him a cart and bought a half-starved mule, which the boy named Shifty - the animal had a peculiar habit of shifting from one leg to the other when waiting for a load. Thus Danny was in business big time and quite the envy of many another lad. The agreement worked out and verbally assented to by both women assured Danny of half a day in school and half a day of work six days a week.

And so the first elementary school was opened and with the backing and support of Jessie Freemont, Finola soon had the children from the better families applying also for admission, so she was obliged to look for another person to help with the teaching. She placed an ad in *The Pacific* which was immediately answered by three prospective candidates, all female. Two were Irish, the third a Swede. Of the three Eileen McCaffery was the best qualified, but somehow, Finola sensed trouble. However, she also had an ulterior motive for hiring Kirstan Erickson. The student population was mostly Irish. Only one Chinese - a little girl, attended.

Kirstan was a beautiful blond with thick hair plaited and coiled around her ears. She had bright blue eyes and a little tilt to her nose. Her happy disposition and ready smile won all hearts. Finola was content she had made a wise choice. Perhaps now the folks from the other communities would step forward and send their children to the "Irish School".

Rory, never surprised at Finola's ideas and, as usual supportive, spent every spare moment working on projects big and small for the school. Soon rows of forms and small tables allowed the children to vacate their floor spaces. A blackboard imported from back East and carried by stage coach half across the Continent made writing and reading that much easier. The first attempt, again improvised by Rory, was not a great success. The wood proved too hard and the paint difficult to write on. Yet the children didn't complain and the teachers were happy that they saw so much progress. Finola felt she was having a civilizing effect on that raw city - like her forebears, who centuries before had gone forth to educate and enlighten a darkened and illiterate European continent, she hoped to bring light and education to this fledgling western state in North America.

As part of her salary, Finola had made a room available to Kirstan. The young woman was alone, having arrived but lately from Stockholm, so the arrangement suited her very well and she was grateful also for Finola's company in the strange land she now called home. Of her background, Finola knew little except that she was practically speaking, an orphan, her mother having died while she was young, her father had abandoned her to the care of an old grandmother. Kirstan, like Finola had decided to make something of herself and her first step in that direction was to leave home and go as far away as possible from all that she knew up to that ime. 'A new beginning, a new world, a new life,' she often repeated to herself. It took guts and courage, to embark on such an adventure and Finola admired her for it.

In 1854, the situation regarding the evictions in Ireland had become so critical that it was literally a national catastrophy. *The Quarterly Review* declared: "The cabins of the peasantry were pulled down in such numbers as to give the appearance, throughout whole regions of the south, and still more of the west, of a country devasted and desolated by the passage of a hostile army." Again others reported that in a single day 700 people were evicted in Westmeath. In one house there was a person delirious with typhoid fever but that made no difference; the house was pulled down. In another, an eye-witness described how a widow and her three daughters seeing their home leveled to the ground raised such agonizing, heart-rending cries, that strong men burst into tears. Yet a third story told of an old man of ninety, who as he walked from his home, kissed the door-posts, then went with his family to sit shivering in the rain beside a smoking fire which had been built near the doomed house.

Snatches of information about the plight of Ireland reached San Francisco in the weeks that followed as immigrants poured into the Golden State. Thousands were now working in the mines who had recently come from the old country, and, like Finola and Rory, having fled the horrors of their native land, yet left their hearts at home in their beloved Ireland. From the fortunate ones who had survived the ordeals of the Atlantic crossing and the further trials by land or sea to the west coast, those who had preceded them learned the current state of affairs in their poor wasted land.

Hearing also of these atrocities, Finola's heart ached and realizing how fortunate she was to have escaped such a fate, she also turned her attention to activities aimed at alliviating the sufferings in her beloved land. She sponsored fund-raising events and organized gatherings of the most influential in the city for the sole purpose of making as many as possible aware of the state of affairs in Ireland. At first, the response was slow but, in time, she knew, their hearts would be moved to contribute to some charitable organization or other in order to help Ireland.

* * * * *

On St. Patrick's Day, 1858, in a small room in Dublin, James Stephens who had been a tutor both in Paris and Kerry awoke the spirit of nationalism when he founded the Irish Republican Brotherhood by swearing in his friend, Thomas Clark Luby, and, in turn, Luby swore in Stephens. This movement which had such modest beginnings spread rapidly and was to become one of the greatest of Irish movements with far reaching consequences. While Stephens, a man of extraordinary persuasive powers with a strong character, high idealism and powerful intellect, was working to spread the movement in Ireland, John

O'Mahoney and Michael Doheny were spreading it in America where it quickly took roots and became known as Fenianism. Stephens, himself, travelled throughout the United States collecting funds to help carry on the work at home. Upon his return to Ireland, he was ceaseless in his efforts to win men over to his organization.

In San Francisco the movement won many stalwart followers among them Rory. With Finola's help, he raised considerable sums of money which in a short time found their way into the right hands.

It happened in the spring of 1860; one evening a crowd gathered on the corner of Market St. A man named Terence MacManus was speaking. It was soon learned that he had been a Young Irelander. Finola out on her weekly errand of collecting money for the Fenians stopped to listen. She approached a tall slim man of about thirty.

"Did I hear correctly?" she asked. "Is this man a Young Irelander."

"He was one o' them. Indeed one o' the best," came the response.

Finola's heart leaped, her thoughts immediately of Dara. If this man had been a Young Irelander, he surely must know something about her long lost love. She would wait and speak to Mr. MacManus after the meeting.

In the course of the evening, she would learn a lot not only about MacManus the noble, self-sacrificing hero who had been sent to penal servitude in Australia several years before and, who having escaped, found his way to San Francisco where he continued to fight for Ireland's oppressed, with the only weapons he possessed - his oratory, but she also heard tales of Dara. And her heart swelled with pride as she listened in rapt silence.

MacManus accompanied her home and graciously accepted the hospitality she offered.

"But you know come to think of it," MacManus said, "Dara didn't leave Ireland in '47." He scratched his head and rubbed the side of his face as his mind travelled back to the days of O'Brien, Meagher and Mitchell and the many fine men he had known in those times. "Ye know, my recollection of Dara or young O'Rourke as he was called by the older men, is that he hung on, finding a hiding place in the mountains until after John Mitchel was arrested. And then when they caught up with me, I lost track of him altogether." His eyes had a faraway look. And Finola knew he was back in the green fields and the lonely haunts that had been his home, his bed, his only refuge in those days of fear and loneliness.

"It was an unfortunate ending to what had been such a promising start." He added half to himself. Then looking straight at Finola, he said, 'But ye know, if Dara O'Rourke's the man I think he is, he didn't leave Ireland till all thoughts of revolution were dashed."

"You think... you really think that Dara..." It seemed incomprehensible to Finola that her beloved Dara might still be in Ireland. Hadn't he said goodbye to her and told her himself that he intended to go to America... to send for her when he got there. No, Mac Manus was wrong. But hearing her lover's name... listening to the words spoken in his defense by this great man was, in itself, a consolation... a little comfort after so many years of silence.

Following that first meeting, Mac Manus often came to visit Finola. Occasionally Rory joined them and inevitably, at those times, their conversations were of Ireland. And when they had well-supped, they might entertain themselves a few other friends with their singing, for Rory had a fine tenor voice and Finola's soft melodious tones likened to that of an angel's.

But as the year grew old, it seemed that Mac Manus also lost the vigor of his youth and his lively wit and light step grew dull and unsure. Yet, in those days his thoughts were fixed on the same theme... Ireland... Ireland... Ireland. His beloved land... how long would she suffer. The much-loved author Charles Kickham's words were often on his lips:

> "That rake up near the rafters,
> why leave it there so long?
> Its handle, of the best of ash,
> is smooth and straight and strong;
> And, mother, will you tell me
> why did my father frown
> When to make the hay,
> in summertime I climbed to take it down?"
> She looked into her husband's eyes,
> while her own with light did fill,
> 'You'll shortly know the reason,
> boy!' said Rory of the Hill."

And when he died in November, '61, still thinking of his native land and ever true to his principles, the American Fenians felt that the body of this Irishman should find its final-resting place in Irish soil. All across the Continent the immigrant Irish showed their respect and love for Mac Manus', the funeral journey was a veritable triumph, before arriving in New York where it was equally well received. When the coffin arrived in Cork, the crowds were more than impressive and all the way to Dublin the trumphal march continued. People dropped to their knees praying while tears of happiness and grief wet their cheeks - happiness that a native son had come home, grief for his untimely passing.

But he was more than a beloved son, he was a conquering hero. And as a hero he lay in state for a week in the Mechanics' Institute while thousands upon thousands filed passed, saluting and praying for their ideal of a true Irishman. The demonstrations on the day of the burial were such that the citizens of Dublin had never before witnessed. At the graveside, Captain Smith's oration gave voice to the sentiments in the heart's depths of those 'marching myriads'. "'Is there any hope?'" he said, quoting the question so often asked by Mac Manus himself about Ireland when he lay dying. "'Is there any hope?' That coffin speaks of more than hope today, for it gives us faith and firm resolve to do the work for which Mac Manus died."

Back in San Francisco, Finola learned of these happenings some months later, and later still read in the *Daily Alta California* of how a distinguished young businessman from the city of Newark, New Jersey, named Dara O'Rourke had given a firey but powerful speech to a tumultuous and exuberant crowd in that city as his hero passed that way. Echoing the words of another dead hero, Thomas Davis, he reminded his audience of the sorry state of affairs in Ireland.

'Remember that many nations are as well off as the men of cold, rocky Norway. Remember that no people on God's earth are so miserably poor as the 'peasantry' of soft and fertile Ireland. Read and remember this: and then ask yourselves - and ask your neighbors - why it is so? Ask them indoor and out - ask them ere you do your business in the market, and after you have said your prayers on the Sunday - ask till you are answered, 'Why are the Irish so poor, when their country is so rich?' Why are so many foreigners well off on worse land and in a hard climate? - 'Is there no way of bettering us?'

The vast majority of those listening in the chill of that raw November evening were Irish immigrants whose memories were still fresh with the horrors they had recently left behind. Dara's words roused them. They would not abandon the land of their birth. And even as the great New York Cathedral was being built by the generosity, the pennies of the Irish working woman, so these hardworking men and women emptied their pockets as the final words of Dara's impassioned plea echoed in their ears:

> 'Fruitful our soil where honest men starve;
> Empty the mart, and shipless the bay;
> Out of our want the Oligarchs carve;
> Foreigners fatten on our decay!
> Disunited
> Therefore blighted,
> Ruined and rent by the Englishman's sway.'

Finola read the article again. Was she dreaming... could this distinguished businessman be her Dara... Surely there was no other with such a name. "My God! he's alive! He's here... in America!

Part IV
Dara

The certainty that I shall see that lady
Leaning or standing or walking
In the first loveliness of womanhood,
And with the fervour of my youthful eyes,
Has set me muttering like a fool.

W.B. Yeats (1865 - 1939)

Chapter 23

'May Ireland's voice be ever heard
Amid the worlds' applause!
And never be her flag-staff stirred,
But in an honest cause!
May freedom be her very breath,
Be Justice ever dear:
And never an ennobled death
May son of Ireland fear!
So the Lord God will ever smile,
With guardian grace, upon our isle.'

-T. Davis

A miserable day turned into an even more miserable evening when Dara bade Ireland farewell. Cold - a blustering gale that flung sheets of blinding rain in wanton fury on land and sea. All on board *The Elizabeth and Sarah* were drenched to the skin. A pitiful group of Irish emigrants huddled together at one end of the moaning creaky ship.

The vessel of 330 tons had been built in 1762. On board were 276 passengers. There were 8,700 gallons of water stored in leaky casks instead of the 12,532 gallons required. The Passenger Act of 1842 stipulated 7 lbs. of provisions per week for each passenger but no distribution was ever made in *The Elizabeth and Sarah*. There were 36 births, four of which were used for the crew: the 32 left were shared by the 276 passengers while those who were denied access slept on the floor. Absolutely no sanitary convenience of any kind was provided. Perhaps,the whole truth should be told here. There were two privies on deck when the ship set sail, but as soon as it was at sea, these were destroyed. Below deck there were none, even of a temporary nature, as a result the state of the ship was 'horrible and disgusting beyond the power of language to describe.'

As if this insufferable situation weren't enough, the passengers were further aggravated by the weather. The north Atlantic can be very treacherous, especially in winter and spring. A sudden lurch of the ship sent an entire family, in one instance, headlong into the spaces of other passengers and back again, against the flimsy partitiions where they were knocked about, battered and bruised, while the little children were severely hurt. At such times, the cries, the screams, and the chaos that ensued as all the passengers were tossed about like so many straws before the wind, was beyond description. The water poured into the steerage area, their mattresses and clothes were soaked, and with no way of drying them, the plight of the miserable occupants was rendered even more unbearable. Yet they had no recourse to any medical help, no medicines, no comfort, no aliviation whatsoever for all their sufferings.

The *Elizabeth and Sarah* left from Killala on the west coast in July and did not arrive in Quebec until September taking in all eight weeks to cross the Atlantic. Forty-two people died, tortured by hunger and thirst. The 'fever' or typhus was rampant and the number who had contracted it was never actually identified.

Dara's thoughts were continually of Finola. He saw her in the wind and rain, in the golden flected clouds and the blazing sunsets. Her face was etched between the tumbling waves and on the cresting breakers her glorious hair was plain to see. And, as he watched some young women propped against an empty water cask, pale, emaciated, lethargic, having lost the freshness and bloom of their youth, he felt happy that Finola was under the care of Mrs. Mulvaney. She would get enough to eat, at least, as long as she was working at Glencarrow Manor. But he would hasten the day when they would be together. A good job, maybe in time, a piece of land. He had heard that there was land for the takin' in some western states. Aye, he decided, given time and opportunity he would make a future for Finola, little Patrick, and himself.

At Quebec the regulations were such that all ships with passengers had to stop at the quarantine station on Grosse Isle for medical inspection. Those who were sick on board were removed to a make-shift hospital on the island. The facilities at the hospital were totally inadequate; it was built to house only 150 patients and although Dr. Douglas, who was in charge sought assistance and money for improvements, he was given very little help.

Soon the number of immigrants was such that there was nowhere for them to stay. Those ordered ashore were divided into two catagories - those who had the 'fever' and those who were 'healthy'. One priest visiting this latter group who were housed in tents had to give the last rites to fifty dying people.

Each week more and more ships arrived. At one point, over forty vessels were waiting at Grosse Isle and in all the vessels there were cases of fever and dysentery. By the end of August 2,500 fever cases were reported in the hospital.

When Dara arrived conditions were totally and completely chaotic. Dr. Douglas was, most of the time, the only physician. A Dr. Benson from Dublin had arrived and volunteered his services but within six days he was dead of the 'fever'. There was little or no equipment; bed clothing had arrived but no beds, not even planks of wood to place on the ground, so the sick and dying lay in the mud and the bedding was soon soaked. Privies were few and as a result the nearby brushwood was in a 'disgusting' condition.

Dara was still fit, healthy and energetic, when he left Ireland, despite his hazardous, nerve-wracking sojourn of over three months in the hills and caves of Galway and Mayo. By the time *The Elizabeth and Sara* had docked, however, at the isolated island in the St. Lawrence, he was suffering from dysentery and was running a high temperature. Consequently, he was, like so many others, ordered to leave the ship and betake himself to the hospital.

"God Almighty!" were the first words he uttered. He had caught sight of several half-naked creatures lying in the mud and stones of the beach; there was no pier. These miserable starving wretches, scarcely human-like were trying to crawl to dry land using the last ounce of strength left in their emaciated bodies. Dara reached down and despite his own weakness managed to carry a dying woman to a grassy spot before he succumbed himself to dizzyness.

Three days of tossing and turning in the hospital and, fortunately, his fever broke. Weak and ravenous from hunger, he managed to drag himself to where the food was being dispensed. A week later, he was helping the good doctor. But he did not intend to remain on Grosse Isle; his mind was set on reaching the States as quickly as he could.

Like the vast majority of the Irish, at that time, Dara thought his greatest opportunity for employment and hence advancement was to be had in the big city. So New York was his goal. He spent six months as a laborer barely ekeing out a living, then decided to try his hand at construction. He was hired by the firm of Delaney and Corcoran, and, through wit and a bit of 'the fight' wormed his way up to foreman within six months. This meant extra pay and extra pay meant savings and savings would, in time, buy two tickets on a decent vessel plying between New York and Southhampton. For Finola would not cross the Atlantic in a 'coffin ship' if Dara O'Rourke had his way.

Not being one to waste his evenings, what was left of them, in drinking or playing cards, Dara instead sought the company of older men like his boss, Mr. Delaney. For Dara was eager to learn from the source and anxious to profit from the experience of those who had, like himself, come from the old country but who had managed to make good despite the prejudice and discrimination. He had seen the signs, himself - 'No Irish need Apply' or 'Niggers and Irishmen not wanted.' Yes, Dara decided, he would find out what it was that men like Mr. Delaney possessed which enabled them to rise above the average, which allowed them to become successful.

Mr. Michael Delaney was the senior partner. A mild-mannered man, frugal, disciplined, retiring; he was the opposite, in many ways, to his partner. Whereas Mr. D., as he was called, was rarely seen by the rank and file, Mr. C. was quite conspicuous and though many had never heard Mr. D's voice, they were all familiar with the roar of Mr. C's. A burley muscular man with a quick temper, Mr. C. put up with no nonsense, demanding a day's work for a day's pay. Yet, it was well known that 'he had a heart as big as his fist' and many's the one who had benefited as a result.

So when Dara was summoned to Mr. D's office one evening after work, it was with some trepidation and concern that he mounted the rickety stairs to that lofty sanctum.

"Come in," and the soft Cork accent in response to Dara's knock, was barely audible.

"Good evening, sir. I'm Dara… Fergus O'Rourke, you wished to see me?"

"Aye, sit down Mr. O'Rourke. Sit down. I'll be with you in one moment." Mr. Delaney extended his hand and motioned to a chair. He then bent over the ledger on which he was working, finished totalling up a column of figures and closed the book. "Well, that's that, and another day's work." He lifted his head, took off his glasses, rubbed his eyes-lids and then looking at Dara with bright, blue, tired eyes, spoke again. "I sent for you, young man, because I have heard good things about you."

"Thank you, sir." Dara felt at ease. He was appreciated; his work was appreciated.

"Tell me, Fergus, or is it Dara you prefer?" he waited for Dara to answer.

"Dara is the name that seems to have stuck here as it did back home."

"Well, I can see why I'd say you got your fair share of that Spanish blood in you."

"You may be right, sir, hailing as I do from the west coast."

"What part?" Mr. D. asked with raised eyebrows.

"Clare... Aye, from Glencarrow. Beautiful Glencarrow, I may add." And Dara sat back in his chair and smiled at his boss.

Delaney pushed away from his desk and also assumed a relaxed position leaning back and crossing his legs. "Well, Dara, being a Corkman, myself, I'll come to the point. As I said, I've heard good things about you and I've been observing you also, although you didn't know that. Yes, I like what I see and have a proposition to make to you."

Dara listened intently as the older man confided his life story. He soon learned that this kindly man had never married.

"Having come to New York some thirty years ago, I was lucky in acquiring an existing business when the owner, another Corkman, like myself, suffered a heart attack. He had grown to trust me and having no heirs left me the lot. Over the years I've paid off the widow and when things got too big for me, I brought in young Joseph

Corcoran, another Corkorian. He's a good man. You two should get on well together."

"You mean... Mr. Delaney..."

Michael," interjected Mr. D.

"Yes, sir. I mean Michael. But... but do I understand correctly?"

"I think you do. But it's late now and I want you to think about what I've said." Mr. D. rose from his chair. "Why don't ye plan to spend a few hours with me at my apartment tomorrow evening. We'll talk some more then."

"Certainly, sir." Dara extended his hand as he also got up and said goodnight. Then he remembered that he didn't know where Mr. Delaney lived.

"Ahem, I don't know your address sir. Perhaps I could stop by..."

"Not at all. Here I'll write it down for ye now." And as he was talking Michael Delaney hastily wrote the address and a few directions. "There ye are now. That should get ye to the right spot."

In the next few months, the two became close friends and during that time, Dara learned much from the older man's experience and wisdom.

Then one evening in the spring of '49 while they shared the dancing fire which Dara had lit in Mr. D's spacious and comfortable apartment and sipped the heady port his host liked so much as an after dinner drink, the older man spoke in more serious tones.

"It's time for me to be takin' it easy, Dara. Between yerself and myself, I don't really know how long it will be before my Maker calls me home."

"You're not well, then, Michael?" Dara asked with deep concern.

"It's something I've had for some time now and the doctors say there's nothing more they can do..." He looked into the happy flames and nodded his head. Then he turned again to Dara. "But I don't want our evening to be a sad one. Ye know how much I've grown to love you over these last months. You've become more like a son than an employee and I thank God that ye came alone just in the right time."

'Tis right honored I am, Mr. Delaney that you have that kind of confidence in me." Dara was moved by the words of his dearest friend.

"Now, I want to give you a few words of advice. When you take my place, an' I want it done by the end of the month, treat others always with respect. Ye get more with a spoonful of honey, ye know. You're no amadán, as they say in the old country," He took another sip of port. "But, it never hurts to improve your education. Reading. . . reading is the best way. I'm not saying I know everything, but I've spent a fair amount of my time over the years with my head in a book and I consider it the best thing I've done."

Dara glanced around at the stacks of books piled on the floor that the shelves he had filled were unable to hold.

"It would give me the greatest pleasure if when I'm gone, you'd take these, my lifelong friends, and make them yours." Michael Delaney looked at his young companion with the warmth and tenderness of a true father.

"My God Michael! It's too much! You're life's collection must be worth…"

"Yes, Dara, I've spent a lot of money on books, but I consider that money well spent. For what you put into your mind no one can take from you. Its' yours, utterly and entirely yours. And there's no greater treasure than the acquisition of knowledge."

Thus did Dara become junior partner in the firm of Delaney and Corcoran which in due time became Corcoran and O'Rourke. He not only inherited the library and apartment but also the tidy sum that Michael Delaney had stached away over the years. And as his previous employer, mentor, and benefactor had often said: "Success comes not always as a result of brains and talent, but through luck - or destiny. On some the gods smile favorably, if you like. A man has to be in the right place at the right time. You came in the right time to the right place, Dara. Now it's up to you to make good."

Dara prospered and succeeded in the years that followed beyond the wildest expectations of even his benefactor's dreams for him. In time, he moved from the apartment and built a fabulous home in the upper Westend.

Having heard from Ireland that Finola had left and was supposedly now living in New Orleans, he used every means in his power to track her down. In the summer of '50, he journeyed himself to the southern city with the hope of finding her and it was on that occasion that he learned the news of her marriage and subsequent departure for the West coast.

With a leaden heart, Dara returned to New York, threw himself even more intensely into his work by day and spent his evenings absorbed in his reading. This lifestyle continued for another two years. Then in 1852, while visiting a client in Atlanta, Georgia, he met and... 'fell in love' with Caroline Whitney, a debutant of an old and respected family from that city.

Chapter 24

"Who dares think one thing and another tell, My heart detests him as the gates of hell."

- Pope.

Caroline Whitney was not beautiful in the classic sense but her coy ways and husky Southern drawl were irresistable to the male population of the small and exclusive circle in which she moved. It was true she did have some redeeming features; her blond hair fell in soft waves to her waist and her clear-blue eyes were alert and intelligent. She had dainty feet and small hands with long tapering fingers but her nose had an arrogant tilt, and her mouth was too large, although the pearly teeth that shone when she smiled modified, in part, the less desirable feature.

Caroline, like all young ladies of her class, was instructed at home by her English governess, Miss Cosgrove. As a consequence, her education was, for want of a better word, limited. She did acquire the rudiments of reading, writing, and arithmetic, but her progress in French was slow chiefly because Caroline did not like to commit herself to any one thing for any length of time. It was also due to this habit of 'playfulness' that her progress on the pianoforte did not reach an acceptable standard. However, her talent in sketching was significant and her water-colors drew considerable attention much to the pride and delight of her father, the honorable Walter Whitney, Senator, plantation owner, cotton king, and slave trader. It invariably gave him great pleasure to point out to his friends and guests the many framed pictures of his gifted daughter which adorned his home.

In her sixteenth year, Caroline was sent to a finishing school in France where, according to Miss Cosgrave, 'she had learned more than her prayers.' This proper and straightlaced female who had been imported, according to Senator Wallace Whitney, along with a large consignment of English breakfast tea, was palitable only at that time of the day and for as long as it took him to swallow the morning beverage. He never did agree with the idea of governesses, but since that was his wife's domain, he didn't interfer. But he certainly paid little attention and gave less credence to the remarks and assessments the good woman made regarding Caroline's accomplishments or lack thereof. So when his daughter's behavior at the Spring Cotillion held in the Governor's mansion was the topic of discussion at the dinner table the following evening and Miss Cosgrave very politely and demurely spoke her mind, Mr. Whitney left no doubt about his position on the matter.

"The cackling hens are at it again." And he looked straight at the prim governess whose thin lips pursed in a tight firm pose and wide startled eyes reminding Caroline of a frightened pullet, caused a spontaneous giggle which the young lady quickly tried to cover up by placing her napkin over her mouth and coughing politely into it. After a brief glance in Caroline's direction, her father continued: "A fiesty rooster would take care of that situation, I'm thinking. Now lets have no more gossip." Then he turned his attention to Caroline. "You were charming, my dear, and had many admirers." He nodded his approval. Mentally he decided to discuss later the need for continuing the English woman's services with his wife, Lucinda. Her job was finished; Caroline was a grown woman. Time to be done with that inconvenience. "Joe, bring me a claret," he addressed the negro attendant.

"Yes, massa,"

There was a moment of silence; everyone occupied with his or her own thoughts.

The old fool, Miss Cosgrave utterly disgusted and humiliated gave her whole attention to her plate although she scarcely ate a morsel. She knew better than to express herself further on the subject of Caroline and for the rest of the dinner was completely ignored.

Caroline, for her part, was amused. It hadn't taken long for the busy-bodies to voice their opinions. She had been aware of the Howards, particularly Emily from the moment she entered the ballroom. And she knew that buxom matron was more than envious when the very young and very handsome Lieutenant John Dashill escorted her onto the floor not once but five times and the fact that she was seen alone with him during the evening only added fuel to the fire. What if it had been the frumpy Diana Howard who had been thus honored, or Solange Benton, that mousy old maid whom everyone had been trying to marry off for the last five years. Caroline shrugged her shoulders imitating her French classmates, and said: "Quel dommage! And I was having such a good time."

"You go right on having a good time, my little rosebud. If middleaged spinsters and jealous old matrons don't approve it's just pure narrow mindedness. Don't you pay them no heed, now." And Wallace Whitney patted his lips with his napkin, pushed back his chair and arose. "I'll be having my coffee in the library," he said. An hour of peace and quiet was more to his liking at that point.

Caroline smiled sweetly at her father as he left the room and she knew he'd never find fault with her. Left alone with her mother and Miss Cosgrave, she didn't relish the idea of conversing with either. She promptly decided she had several things to do in preparation for the next day's picnic, an annual affair held at the Hamilton estate and to which all Atlanta, meaning anyone who was anyone, was invited.

"Run along then, my dear. I'm sure Ellen and I can find plenty with which to amuse ourselves." Her mother glanced at the governess who nodded stiffly.

Caroline spent the greater part of the evening deciding what she would wear the following day. She would have to have two gowns - one for the outdoor picnic, the other for the ball in the evening. As she pulled out one gown after another tossing them in shimmering heaps on bed and chairs, she found it difficult to decide. She wanted to appear ravishing for both functions. A whiff of jasmine floated into the room through the open window and she was reminded that the summer was just beginning. It would be a glorious time; she would have so much fun playing with the feelings and tantalizing the appetites of all those foolish young men who thought she cared about them, admired and looked up to them. She didn't give a fig for anyone of them but she would use them, all of them for the moment. She would go right ahead having a good time, as her father had advised. She whirled and danced around the room filled with the sheer joy and exuberance of being young and the knowledge that she could, by the mere flicker of her eyelids and the clawing sweetness of empty chatter, ensnare, seduce, nay capture one of those handsome males who in his assumed masculine superiority considered himself Lord of the World. What was it that Mark Anthony said before he met and was captivated by Cleopatra. 'They can't think, they can't fight, they are merely our playthings.' Well, thought Caroline, we'll see who really are the playthings. Then, she posed before a mirror, considered her reflection and ran her hands down her shapely hips. Yes, she would use whatever feminine wiles it took to bring the hounds to bay and when she had them to heel she would slowly and painstakingly crush them under her foot.

She sat on the side of her bed in her lace fringed pantalets, and linen corset. She had discarded several lace and linen petticoats earlier and as she studied the array of finery scattered about, her only objective was to arrange every last detail of her attire for the next day, so as to trap as many flies as possible in her web.

The morning was a swirling of light and color when Caroline awoke. The cream-colored walls glowed, the lace curtains swaying gently at the window were shimmering with light-gold, yellow, and rosy hues. Sunbeams danced and played on the polished surface of her dressing table and then dashed across the surface of the gold-framed mirror. It would be a glorious day; the birds told her so as they squacked and fought for possession of their favorite spots in the oleanders just outside her window.

She looked at the clock on the mantlepiece. Why heavens! It was close to eleven. How could she have slept so long. Then she realized she had to get ready for the picnic. Where was Connie, the colored girl, the new one that had been given to her by her father when she returned home from finishing school. 'The pick o' the litter, she is child.' And then he turned to the wide-eyed mulatto, and sternly ordered her to do whatever her new mistress decreed.

Connie had been bought at an auction some weeks before Caroline's anticipated arrival. She would be one of the many presents Walter Whitney would lavish on his only child.

Caroline got up and went to the bedroom door. Upon opening it, she discovered the little servant fast asleep on the floor outside.

"Well, I never! What are you doing at this time of the day? You know I've got to be ready to leave in an hour."

Then she noticed her morning coffee and what appeared to have been her breakfast.

Connie was wide awake and on her feet. "Yo' wuz so purty jus now w'en yo' wuz sleepin' I…"

"Sakes alive, Connie! You're supposed to wake me up not admire me sleeping," Caroline snapped and then ordered the girl to draw the water for her bath. By the time she had finished her toilette, it was too late for breakfast, so she swallowed a few mouthfuls of orange juice as Connie helped her with the pale-pink organdie she had, finally, chosen for the luncheon. She most certainly would be late… A fantastic idea entered her mind.

"Go tell papa and mama not to wait on me. I'll take the small open carriage."

Connie ran off to do her bidding, while Caroline set her mind to work on staging a most spectacular entrance at the Hamilton gathering. She would order the carriage to be halted directly in front of the main table. Then, before alighting, she would stand up in the carriage drawing attention to her plight and… Voila! She anticipated that half the young men in attendance would come running to her aid. Gloating over the commotion she would cause, she pinned a red rosebud to the front of her dress in such a manner as to draw the eye to the perfect swellings of her shapely breasts. She then pulled the neckline as low as she dared from off her creamy-white round shoulders and snatching a silken shawl as a show of decorum draped it over her arms.

"There I think I'm ready, Connie. What do you say?" She looked herself up and down one more time in the long mirror facing her bed.

"Oh, yas'm," Connie's eyes were wide with excitement and admiration. "Ah guess yo' is de mos' beauful young miss at de pahty."

"I hope so, Connie. I hope so." She tossed the words over her shoulder as she sallied forth into the bright sunshine and the waiting carriage.

The reception that awaited Caroline went far beyond ever her wildest expectations. Her carriage was beseiged by an army of eager young men, all vying with one another for the honor of escorting her when she paid her respects to the host and hostess, Mr. and Mrs. Jesse Hamilton.

The young lieutenant again won out and gallantly lending her his right arm he battled his way through the throng, laughing and threatening the jostling young braves who would rob him of his prize.

"That young woman certainly knows how to make a spectacle of herself," was the snide remark, Caroline overheard as she and her boisterous companions bounced along. But she neither gratified the speaker with a hasty glance in her direction nor pretended that she had heard her insult.

As soon as the formalities were over and done with, Caroline, effervescent, exuding charm, captivated several young men with colorful accounts of her experiences in Paris. Many heads turned, as the group grew noisy and the laughter sounded coarse and not a few matronly high-flown noses sniffed their disapproval.

Drawn in the general direction, from his place beside Mr. Ferguson, a wealthy Scotsman from Virginia who had been a longtime business associate of his, Dara stood a moment on the fringe of the group. But that's all it took for Caroline's sharp eyes.

"And who's the handsome stranger? I don't remember seeing you before, sir," she drawled and held out her delicate hand as she sidled up to Dara.

Rising to the occasion, Dara took the dainty finger tips and gallantly bent to place a kiss. Then lifting his dark brow, his lilting voice and twinkling smoldering eyes were a challenge to Caroline.

"O'Rourke's the name... Dara," he offered and drawing himself to his full height continued to smile at the fledgling coquette.

"Irish! Am I not correct? And without waiting for him to answer, she continued. "Don't deny it, sir, 'your accent doth betray you', she quoted appearing to be clever and causing the bystanders to erupt in rauccous unrestrained laughter. Some, taking her remark to be a slight and therefore an opportunity to give vent to pent-up animosity and hostility against the Irish in general, added their own innuendos and disparaging remarks.

"Sure, 'tis one o' the wee folk we've got," the unsophisticated but sinewy broad-shouldered offspring of Georgia's largest tobacco producer, Clide Hopkins, spoke.

"They say, Paddy is not too far removed from the monkey." The clipped consonants and condescending posture identified the speaker as he stood arms folded, head erect looking down his long nose at all in general and Dara in particular.

"Touche," was the immediate response of the young lieutenant.

A few had the courage to agree, nodding, mumbling... but before another word could be said, Dara spoke calmly and with dignity: 'Give up the idea of being great orators without preparation'. And without more ado turned on his heels and walked off.

The little group stood silent a moment merely looking after the Irishman as he strode with firm determined step towards Mr. Hamilton and was instantly received with warmth and enthusiasm by the older man.

Who was this... this O'Rourke? Where did he come from? were the questions now being asked by Caroline and her admirers. For an instant she was taken aback by his unexpected actions and words but she resolved to fathom the mystery of Dara O'Rourke before the night was spent.

The ball was a veritable triumph. So many beautiful women arrayed as only the ladies of the South knew how. Criolines, a myriad colors, shades, and hues swirling and swaying in time to the music like a field of spring flowers wafting in the breeze. The tingling laughter of the young ladies, the sonorous tones of older gentlemen interspersed by cackling old dowagers as they gossiped over their fans. And of all the subjects of conversation none was so interesting and popular a topic as Caroline Whitney's future.

'That silly young woman will amount to nothing, I tell you,' was Clara Watson's assessment of the matter. Clara had successfully married off one daughter, but the other had run off with an older man who, it was said, already had a wife. So Clara could speak from experience without hinting that such a disgraceful and tragic occurance had ever taken place in her family.

'The young people today have far too much of their own way. Now, when I was...' and Jessica Langtree's panegyric on the society of her youth and the proprieties and observances that were the hallmarks of real ladies and gentlemen was delivered with such gusto and authority and with unbroken lengthy sentences that presently one by one her matronly companions, on some pretext or another found they were needed elsewhere.

The departure of all but the mealymouthed Fanny Horace didn't seem to affect Jessica in the least. She delivered her oration dutifully like Reverend Mann at the Sunday service and with just as much effort, perspiration and ejaculation and, I might add, having the same effect on her listeners; nor did she cease until from sheer exhaustion and the excessive heat of the evening, she slumped back in her chair and with hoarse voice, parched lips, and in a succession of gasps pleaded for a glass of lemonade.

Fanny scurried to grant her wish and then she, too, abandoned the 'sinking ship'.

Caroline by this time, had managed to circulate to within a few feet of where Dara stood tall, dark, and handsome in his dress-suit, white shirt-front, black bow-tie and black velvet waistcoat. She had chosen well her own gown for the evening - a pale blue taffeta that shimmered and rustled as she floated about the room. The low-cut bodice showed off her creamy rounded shoulders and as she had done earlier, she made sure that the firm fulness of her maidenly breasts did not escape the masculine eye; a tiny rose-bud nestled in the cleavage.

She tip-toed to Dara's side and slid her arm into his. "You cannot refuse to lead me in the next dance, sir," she coyly glanced up at him as she spoke.

Momentarily taken aback and off guard, Dara did the only thing a gentleman could do under the circumstances. He bowed, gently took her hand from his arm and led her toward the dancing.

Fortunately for Caroline, the dance did not allow for much conversation, otherwise Dara might have revealed his true feelings, instead he merely answered her questions and continued to concentrate on the dance so different from what he was used to back home in Ireland.

The music stopped, a brief pause as the next piece was selected by the orchestra. Dara was about to escort Caroline to the side of the room and make his way back to the company of the group of older men with whom he had been having a serious discussion when Caroline detained him, and never one to be outwitted, his young admirer declared. "You're not going to desert me now, Mr. Dara O'Rourke when it has taken me half the evening to capture your attention? Why! It seems to me that you might even be avoiding me?" Again Caroline batted her long lashes and coyly cast furtive glances at Dara.

Although Dara was amused, he was also attracted to the sophisticated and worldly manner in which she comported herself especially, as he realized, she was still very young. "And why should you think I've been avoiding you?" he asked. "On the contrary, wasn't it you, yourself, who spoke, quite bluntly I may say, the last time we met, regarding my qualifications, my suitableness to be in your company?"

Caroline bowed her head as if in thought but quickly raised it again and with the most alluring of smiles answered: "Ach, sure you won't be holdin' it against me for the rest o' me life if I made a little fun o' ye, now." The exaggerated imitation of the Irish accent and turn of the English language irked Dara's sensitivities, but he chose to ignore her faux pas.

"I'm able to take a joke as well as any man," Dara replied, "but I have no mind for insult, and insult is the only word that fits your treatment of me this morning. Now what has happened to change your mind, may I ask?"

"I declare, Mr. O'Rourke, it seems to me you're no gentleman." She pretended to be hurt. At least no Southern gentleman would accuse a lady of lying."

The insincerity in her voice was quite obvious and the complete disregard with which she treated his feelings left no room to doubt the depths of her own.

Dara decided to play along. In fact the defiant tilt of the head and the determined tone of voice reminded him of his one and only love - Finola, and his mind drifted across the broad Atlantic to the tiny community of his youth. A dull ache in his heart, a passing, fleeting pang caused him to gasp and blanch.

"Mr. O'Rourke! You're not well?" Caroline clutched at his arm and was about to lead him to a chair.

"'Tis nothing... nothing at all. Perhaps I've been putting in too many hours lately." Dara by this time had seated himself in a large high-backed chair. His color returned and the pain had eased. "Ach, maybe this southern air and the present company have cast a spell on me." He turned to Caroline who handed him a tall glass of 'Southern Comfort'.

"This should give you a warm feeling." As Dara hesitated, she coaxed: "Go on, it's good, I've tasted it myself," and she giggled and sat down beside him.

Several eyebrows were raised and across the room the fans of aggitated matrons fluttered vigorously and irratically. Comments were made; even a few elderly gentlemen puffed a little longer and harder on their smelly cigars as they considered the prospects of such an unlikely union.

'It is unbecoming, unseemly for a young lady to behave thusly. What is her father thinking about, to allow such brazen conduct?' Soon the chatter and gossip turned to Dara... 'Irish, did you say Irish!' The troubled questioner did not conceal her resentment and disgust. 'No doubt married with a family of twelve or more back home, wherever that is.' Some of those listening giggled.

This last remark was overheard by Caroline's father. "Tut, tut, my dear ladies. Allow me to introduce you to Mr. O'Rourke." The Senator, never bashful when an opportunity was offered to make a speech or take the floor, stepped away from his frumpy wife's side and in a commanding voice drew the attention of all in that part of the room. "Since some of our gentle ladies here have not been introduced to one of New York's most promising young politicians and I might add successful businessmen, allow me the privilege: Ladies and gentlemen, Mr. Dara O'Rourke." He pointed to Dara who stood to acknowledge the Senator and the acclaim that followed. "But before you resume your place and the company of my beautiful daughter, Mr. O'Rourke, I want to say a few words, further, about you. For it seems, ladies and gentlemen, we have a rising star that few in this the greatest state in the South, know much if anything about. Yes, Mr. O'Rourke is Irish and proud of it. He came as many others to this country in the late '40's and like others of his race he has, I'm happy to say, done well, in his adopted country, though not without his ups and downs. Briefly, for I see my young friend is getting embarrassed, he's a man of many talents. Well read, he's considered by many of his colleagues as the 'Trinity Man', though he'll tell you, himself, that he never set foot in that illustrious institution. A lover of the arts and," he looked directly at his daughter, "and beauty." Again, the Senator turned to acknowledge Caroline, "And, no doubt, my beautiful daughter has something to offer in this department being a fine artist herself. But over and above all his personal attributes, this young man is now the owner of one of the largest construction companies in the industrial North. As the older gentlemen seemed to be sitting up and taking notice, the Senator concluded his eulogy by drawing attention to Dara's good looks and stressing the fact that he had a charasmatic personality if anyone dared to find out. "So, my friends, now that you have all been introduced to this remarkable young man, you'll be happy to make his acquaintance I'm sure," and he looked directly at the ladies in his immediate circle.

There was little time for Caroline and Dara to converse privately after that. Many of the young women who had not appeared to be interested in the new-comer before, now suddenly seemed to have found some remarkable or unique quality that appealed to them and descended enmasse like a gaggle of geese to the feeding trough. Caroline, however, did not give up her seat beside Dara nor did she dance with any other that evening.

When it was time to say good night, she made sure that her father extended an invitation to Dara to visit and dine with them the following evening.

Chapter 25

**"It is in vain that a man is born fortunate,
if he is unfortunate in his marriage."**

Dacier.

The wedding of Dara O'Rourke and Caroline Whitney took place in early September. It was one of the memorable events of that year in the city of Atlanta.

'Senator's daughter to wed Business Tycoon,' and 'Beautiful Caroline Whitney and Businessman Mr. Fergus (Dara) O'Rourke to wed.' The headlines were eye-catching and bold. Senator Whitney spared no expense to see that his only child had the very best. A honeymoon in Paris and a tour of France, Switzerland, Austria, and Italy followed taking all of four months. The return of the couple to America and their new home in uptown Manhattan was an occasion for another celebration, and one slated to start the young couple off on the right foot. They were, of course, a splendid match. Although she was very young, just seventeen, he was ten years older, all agreed that the union was bound to be a long and happy one.

It was on their homeward-bound journey, before the ship docked in New York that the pact was made. They would go through with the formalities. Follow the appropriate proprieties, but each would go his/her separate way. So Dara had made the greatest mistake of his life. The seventeen year old was not a youthful, vivacious girl fresh from an exclusive boarding school in the French capital, but a woman of the world. He did not ask the details but when she told him about herself and pointed out the fancy houses she had frequented on the Avenue Champs-elysees, Dara was in shock. She had fooled everyone and most of all Dara, himself. And she enjoyed the result - laughing at his perplexed expression, his incredulous, bewildered gaze as he stood, speechless before her.

Then, as if it were the most natural thing in the world, she announced: "Don't worry, Dara, I'll be the most perfect hostess when your friends come a callin'. You'll see how the old windbags in Atlanta will talk; we'll be the envy of all and they'll know that none are happier, more charming, more suited to each other. Oh, yes, and how wrong they were when they thought that giddy Caroline would never amount to much." She enjoyed the image such a discussion conjured up in her mind and laughed her gay tingly laugh that seemed to echo in every corner of the lavish cabin and then return to mock Dara anew.

Unable to fathom the mind of the woman he called his wife, Dara for the first time in his life felt like a cornered animal. He was crushed, beaten, and had been dragged through the slime of the earth. And he knew there was nothing he would do about it or could, if he were to keep his place in society, and at the same time run his business. But worst of all, he knew that she had foreseen and calculated his reactions and had come out the victor.

Dara's heart closed up and his happy boyish laughter, his natural good humor and carefree spirit slowly wilted and within six months, he was not the same man.

Caroline, on the other hand, blossomed. She was hailed as the most charming, interesting, and talented woman, and her sketches and paintings were in high demand. This outlet gave her ample opportunity to leave home, travel and otherwise indulge in her preferred lifestyle.

With the passage of time, the beautiful home, 'Glencarrow', in the finest part of the city was frequently empty. Dara unable to return home during the weekdays stayed in the old apartment in New York, while Caroline always had the excuse that she was at an exhibition or planning one and just had to see to the details herself. On weekends they sometimes ran into each other, but on such occasions Caroline was so inebriated and disorganized that Dara preferred to stay out of her way rather than provoke an argument.

It was June, the time of roses and sweet smelling gardenia. The garden was a riot of color. Dara had come home; he wished to spend the weekend at 'Glencarrow', presuming he would be alone and undisturbed. He had no reason to think otherwise for he had not seen Caroline in over six weeks.

He looked at the clock on the mantlepiece. It was ten minutes to seven. Dinner would be served at seven thirty, so he had about half an hour to strole in the garden. A perfect evening, the sun was still high in the western sky, Dara's heart and soul craved the caresses of nature - a whiff of his favorite rose, a gentle brush of the summer breeze against his cheek, the touch of a velvety leaf and the soft grass beneath his feet. He walked through the grove behind the house and allowed his mind free rein.

"God! What have I done with my life?" he looked up to the azure sky and allowed his heart to speak. Without noticing, he leaned his back against an old oak, closed his eyes, and followed his thoughts back to the beginning. . . his home in Ireland, the little cottage where he was so happy with his mother and sister... A tear fell from one dark eye and ran down his cheek. Then he sent a prayer heavenward for the souls of his loved ones. As he brushed the tear aside, he heard the music of Finola's voice ringing in his ears and saw the fresh beauty of her lovely face as he remembered it that spring before he said goodbye. What would his life have been had he married his first love? Only

God could answer that question. Where was she, the girl of his heart?

"Oh Finola, Finola, a cuisle mo croí," he heard his own words as from afar. Then a tingly silver ring broke the stillness. Like a thunderbolt the laughter struck a vibrant chord in Dara's heart. Caroline! Could it be Caroline? he asked himself. But... but... He walked towards the rose covered bower.

In the golden glare of the evening sun, he saw her in the arms of a man he did not recognize.

A shaft of pain shot through the inner recesses of his broken heart. Without thinking, he rushed headlong at the intruder. In sheer anguish and the heat of the moment, he delivered a blow to the left jaw of the unsuspecting would-be lover and sent him sprawling on the ground. Caroline was aghast and turned pale throwing her hands up to her mouth to surpress the scream that had caught in her throat. Then realizing that the intruder was none other than her own husband, she became abusive, cursing him, threatening him in words so loathsome that Dara, though used to the language of rough workmen in his early days as a laboring man, could hardly stomach her vocabulary.

"Madam, you've said enough. I don't want to hear more. Either you or I will leave this house this very evening. You have betrayed me in broad daylight before my servants. You have broken your agreement. This is the end." Dara turned and left the scene and even when she shouted after him, delivering a volley of expletives unseemly for even a guttersnipe, he did not look back or answer.

Dara went directly to his own rooms and pulling on the silken cord by his bed, rang for his personal man-servant. By the time the young Irishman, Barry MacNamara, knocked on his door, Dara had written a letter.

"I want you to take this, at once, to the Hanson estate. You will deliver it in person to Judge Victor Hanson and no one else. Take my horse." Dara sealed the envelope and having addressed it, handed it to Barry.

"Right away, sir."

When Barry had closed the door behind him, Dara strode up and down the room for some time. He was completely unnerved and unable to comprehend the full import of what had taken place. This was not how he expected things to turn out. He sat down, put his head in his hands and for the first time since the awful day when he beheld the total destruction of his potato crop, Dara O'Rourke - the oak, the strong one - wept, wept bitterly.

How long he remained thus, he did not know but the sound of galloping horses roused him. Thinking it was Barry returning, he tried to pull himself together, but remembering that the Hanson estate was a good five miles away, he realized he must be mistaken. He arose, went to the window and was just in time to see Caroline accompanied by a male companion, he could only surmise was the same he had so recently encountered, ride off into the fading light.

*****

Early the following morning, Dara was awakened by a loud banging on the front door. Before the servant arrived to awaken him, he was up and dressed. A strange forebooding, an eerie sickening sensation, seemed to assail him.

"Sir," the servant hesitated. "Sir, I'm afraid…"

"What is it, man? Out with it." Dara was aggitated.

"It's your wife, sir. She's…"

Dara waited no longer. But dashing from the room ran down the stairs. When he reached the hall several servants were standing about in shock. The women with their hands to their faces, the men awkward and with bowed heads.

"Great God Almighty!" exclaimed Dara. "What has happened?"

Before him on the marble floor lay the lifeless body of his wife, Caroline. Except for a small scratch on her forehead there was no other visible sign of hurt. But when he bent to pick her up, the men who had brought her restrained him saying:

"No, sir."

"Her neck, sir. It's broke. You can't."

Dara looked up at them, bewildered. Then blurted out: "Where? How?"

"About five or six miles away, sir. Seems the horse threw the lady. We shot the animal. It's legs were broken."

"Was there anyone with my wife? Anyone else?" Dara asked but didn't look at the men.

"No, sir. No, we didn't see anyone else. But then we only came upon her about three, three an' a half hours ago and she was... well, sir, she was dead at the time."

"I understand." Dara replied trying to assimilate all that had happened in such a short period.

He ordered the men to take the body to a room close by and then sent for a doctor. The Senator, her father, would have to be told and, of course, Judge Hanson should be notified as soon as possible. Then the thought occured to Dara... The letter! The letter he had sent the evening before... My God! he had unwittingly planted a motive in the judge's mind. He would, undoubtedly, be under suspicion. There were no witnesses to this death. Her companion of the night before had quit the scene of the accident. No, he told himself, he must not panic. Hadn't the men who brought home her body said it was indeed an accident. Yes, the horse... The horse had fallen. They had to shoot him. Dara was letting his nerves get the better of him. After five long years of covering up, he no longer knew what it was like to live in the old way, to be himself with nothing to hide. He realized he was trembling.

"Sir," It was Barry. "Sir, I think you could do with a drink." He offered Dara a brandy. "Take it. It will do you good," he urged.

Dara hesitated a moment but then sat down and took a few gulps.

As he was about to place the glass on the table beside him, Barry spoke again.

"You've had a shock, sir. You should drink the lot, if you don't mind me sayin' so."

"Yes, Barry. Yes, you're right." Dara proceeded to drink the remains of the glass. His color improved and within a few minutes he seemed in control again.

"Oh, by the way, sir. I didn't want to disturb you last night. It was late when I got home. Your horse dropped a shoe so I had to walk most of the way. However, I didn't have any luck delivering your letter, sir. The judge was not home an' as you…"

"You didn't…" Dara's relief appeared too obvious. He tried to cover up. "And the letter?"

"I have it safe, sir. If you like I'll take it over later?"

"No… No, I'll… well, I'll see to it myself. Please bring it to me."

Barry went off to get the letter he had kept in a safe place. When he returned, Dara was more relaxed and having retrieved the document which he feared earlier would have incriminated him, he was able to concentrate on the matters on hand.

However, if Dara thought that he had nothing to fear from the law, that he was beyond suspicion, he was soon to learn the reality of the American Justice System - things don't always work in favor of the innocent.

The local police chief urged on by the Senator, would hold a thorough investigation. The facts of the case as he saw them, were not as credible as they first appeared. And this defender of the law was not known for his affability to Jews, Irishmen or Negroes.

The Senator, could not, would not believe that any man would permit his wife to ride off into the night all alone. Yes, there was more to this gruesome tragedy than he was being led to believe based on the flimsy account of her husband. His beautiful, talented, vivacious daughter, a young woman in her mid-twenties, full of the bloom of youth and, he added, an experienced horsewoman! - it was impossible that such a thing could happen. Then blaming himself he fumed: I should never have allowed her to marry a damn Irishman in the first place.

These comments and others of similar sentiments were common parlance within a few days. The newspapers were ambiguous, however, in their exposé of the story which only added to the sense of mystery, but the headlines were quite explicit: 'Accidental Death or Murder? 'Senator's Daughter found Dead - Circumstances Vague.'

Doctor Stephen Daniels examined the body. His report verified that the deceased had died from a broken neck and lacerated spinal cord, received, he presumed, when thrown from her horse. But the Senator, Caroline's father, was not satisfied. He hired a first-rate lawyer, the best that money could buy and Atlanta had to offer, a Mr. Edward P. Henderson, and the matter was brought before the local court, the presiding judge being, the Honorable Martin Cline.

Dara's attorney, Mr. Joseph Norton, in his defense, shied away from the unpleasant details of his client's relationship with his wife and concentrated instead on the corroboration of reliable witnesses as to his moral character and rectitude.

Only one person cast any aspersions on Dara's integrity, the local police chief when he declared from the stand that in his opinion, 'Everyone has his dark side.'

It was a hot humid afternoon. A mammoth moth too lazy to move lay flat against the corner of the Judge's bench. There, it clung to the polished wood, wings wide, hoping, no doubt, like everyone else in that grim oppressive place to find a little relief from the sweltering heat. As Dara took his place, it slowly moved its wings once, then settled down and was quiet again.

Dara looked around the court room; many of his friends were there, and many of those who considered him an outsider and wanted him humiliated, brought low and put in his place, where also present. One of these was Mr. Henderson, attorney for the plaintiff, Senator Whitney.

Mr. Henderson, true son of the South came from a long line of English landed people - gentry would have been the term given them in Ireland, - and was smug in the knowledge of his birthright and boorish when it came to recent Irish immigrant 'peasants', particularly those who had managed to beat the odds and rise above poverty and ignorance.

"You say you were at home on the night of your wife's m... death?' Mr. Henderson's drawl aggrevated Dara and as he answered the question for the umpteenth time, he could scarcely contain himself.

"Yes, as I said before, I had come home early that week end."

"Any special reason why you should have done so, Mr. O'Rourke? I mean come home early. You were not in the habit of coming home at all... Is that not so?"

"I came home rarely... I do have to attend my business and..."

"Yes, yes, of course. But rarely! I might add that you came home very rarely. Is it not true that you and your wife, although contrary to all outward appearances, were not happily married?"

There was a gasp from some female in the court.

Dara looked startled and hesitated to answer.

"Come now, Mr. O'Rourke, you don't have children. You rarely, as you said yourself, saw your wife. What is one to conclude?"

"Mr. Henderson, I don't know what you might conclude, but I think that the question of whether I have children or not is a personal matter and none of your business."

There was murmuring and general commotion in the courtroom. The judge struck the gavel and called for order, then addressed Mr. Henderson.

"I think you had better confine your questions to... to the essentials, Mr. Henderson. I order that the afore be stricken from the records. Now you may proceed."

"Your Honor, I am trying to establish a motive for the death of Caroline Whitney. The notion that an experienced and youthful horsewoman should have fallen to her death from her own horse seems to me..."

"Mr. Henderson, I again warn you. You are treading on dangerous ground. Please resume your questioning according to my directives."

Mr. Henderson addressed Dara again. "Where was your wife the evening you decided to come home early?"

Dara knew that the sordid details of his life with Caroline would now be noised abroad. He had tried to keep the realities of their relationship from the servants, the local gossips, and the newspapers, but if he were to clear himself he realized that the truth would have to be revealed.

"On the evening in question, I came home, as I told you, and went straight to my room. I had about an hour..."

"Your Honor, I would like to draw the attention of the Court to the words of the Defendant, 'my room' "You may proceed, Mr. O'Rourke."

"I had about an hour to freshen up before dinner."

"I see. You didn't then greet your wife or inform her that you were home? Most men do." Mr. Henderson looked affably at the jurors.

"I didn't think she was home at the time. So I saw no reason to go looking for her."

"Yes, of course. You and she rarely frequented the same house at the same time. So I suppose your statement could be plausable. After you had freshened up, did you then go directly to dinner?"

"No, it was a beautiful evening and I thought a walk in the garden would be relaxing."

"So you took a walk in the garden. Did any of the servants, other than the man who drove you home see you that evening?"

"Certainly…" Again Dara hesitated.

"Yes, Mr. O'Rourke." The attorney urged him to continue.

"Well, no, the servants did not see me. I… I."

"So if the servants did not see you who served your dinner? I'm sure a man of your position does not cook and serve his own meals."

There was a giggle from one of the younger ladies attending.

"I didn't have any dinner that evening," said Dara angrily.

"Ah, hah! So why didn't you partake of something that evening? What happened to change your mind? Please tell the Court." The enthusiasm in Mr. Henderson's voice had the desired effect."Well, when I had walked to the end of the rose garden, I heard laughter coming from the arbor and upon drawing closer wondering who could be there at that hour, I saw that it was my wife and... and a male companion." Here Dara tried to cover his embarrassment by searching for his pocket handkerchief and wiping the perspiration from his brow.

"And seeing your wife was engaged with this gentleman, presumably on some project regarding her art exhibitions, you politely turned on your heel and left? Is that so?"

"No," Dara answered. Here he became agitated and was unable to hide his anger.

"Well, Mr. O'Rourke if you did not leave the spot what did you do?"

"I... I... ran towards the arbor and struck the lout."

"Rather an excessive and exaggerated form of behavior. But then you Irish are hot-blooded and pron to fight. What provoked such rash action? Did you also strike your wife at that time?" the lawyer sneered.

"No, Mr. Henderson, I never strike women. I left as the fellow went sprawling in the bushes. And the rash action, as you call it, was provoked by the fact that... that... the cad had been kissing my wife."

"I see. And then...?

"And then, I went back to the house and spent the rest of the evening in my room."

And you didn't speak to your wife or see her after the encounter in the gardens?"

"Well... well, I did see her later as she rode off. I was working at my desk when I heard the sound of a galloping horse, and when I got up to take a look, she was already at the end of the driveway."

"You said your wife rode off alone?" Mr. Henderson inquired.

At this juncture, Dara seemed to have lost track of time and space. He was far away in another world, another place... The lovely face of Finola appeared and disappeared in his troubled imagination. He heard only the rippling of the crystal spring that danced over the rocks on its way to the broad Atlantic and smelled the freshness of the wild woodbine in the evening air. And his heart cried for his long lost love.

"Mr. O'Rourke... your wife was alone?" The D.A. took a few steps closer.

"Eh?"... the now familiar drawl aroused Dara. "My wife... alone?" The words came automatically; there was no emotion, no inflection in his tone.

The lawyer hastened to ask his next question, delibertly ignoring the slight inflection in Dara's voice and knowing full-well that his mind was not focused. "And it never occurred to you, never entered your mind to follow her. It was by this time almost dark. Were you not concerned for her safety?"

"My wife was a superb horsewoman. I had no need to fear for her safety. And besides, she was used to the terrain and didn't like my interfering in her business."

"I see." Mr. Henderson opened his mouth to question Dara again but thought the better of it.

"Very well, Mr. O'Rourke. I have no more questions to ask right now."

The judge inquired of Dara's lawyer if he had any questions for his client.

"No, your Honor, not at this time."

With that, the session concluded for the day.

The days following were as harrowing as those that preceded them. Dara's health suffered and before the illusive 'male in the garden' was found and called to testify, Dara had become quite ill. Eventually, the jury found him not guilty and he was acquitted. However, the strain had taken its toll. He was suffering from severe pains in his stomach and had difficulty eating and sleeping. He was forced to take a leave of absence from his business, and to pay the legal expenses he had to sell his Manhattan residence. He moved his personal belongings and took up again the lifestyle of a bachelor in the old apartment left him by his friend and mentor, Mr. Delaney.

As the business was still growing but did not demand the constant supervision of the early years, he had time to engage in other pursuits, charitable and political which distracted him and gave him a purpose in life. He was often seen on the docks particularly when the ships from Ireland were disgorging the miserable excuses for humanity that never failed to arrive. He even travelled to Governor's Island to rescue the abandoned ones who because they were sick and penniless were scheduled to be returned to their homeland. Maybe Finola would be among the next batch! Although he knew in his heart of hearts that such could never be the case, he still fooled himself into thinking that the letter from Mrs. Mulvaney had never come. Finola was still in Ireland waiting for him. But when it came time for him to act on his make-belief, to set pen to paper and write, he was brought up against reality and he could only place his head in his hands and cry. Yes, Dara O'Rourke, the successful business man, the orator, the well-read, self-educated Irishman who had dragged himself up by his bootstrings to become one of the country's best, sat alone, dejected, weeping.

It was in the early hours of the morning, the 25th day of October 1858, that Dara, finally, realized what was happening to him. For the first time in his life, he was feeling sorry for himself and giving in to defeatism. He, who could not be beaten down, he, who could rise above all obstacles, who would win despite all odds in his native land, had come to this in the 'Promised Land', the land of opportunity and freedom.

He got up, made himself a cup of tea; then as he sipped it, his eye caught the headlines of the evening paper.

'Fenian Movement gains new membership.' Scanning the column, his heart seemed to swell with new life. Here was something he could relate to - Irishmen, the newcomers and those who had come to this blessed land several generations back, all joining together to support the homeland. This very day, he told himself, he would join their ranks - take up where he had left off so many years before.

So it came about that Dara became a Fenian and soon rose in the ranks to become an inspiring and devoted leader and one of their finest orators.

In the Fall of '61 when the coffin bearing the remains of the great patriot and beloved friend of Dara, Terence MacManus, arrived in New York, the Fenian leader did himself and his country proud with the eloquent oration delivered before a crowd of several thousand Irish sympathizers.

Opening with the words of Thomas Davis: 'A people not familiar with the past would never understand the present or realize the future.' Dara went on to outline the glories of Ireland's ancient past; its sufferings and agony of recent years, but he gave courage and hope to those listening, telling them that Ireland's hour would surely come. She would rise like the phoenix and be counted among the nations of the earth once more. He knew it. The spirit of the Fenians was alive and vibrant; - it was the spirit of Ireland, herself. None could crush that spirit, try as they might.

The acclaim was long and boisterous when Dara concluded and many more came to swell the ranks of the Movement that evening. They pledged whatever they could - the young, their youth and enthusiasm, the old their wisdom and experience, and those who had wealth gave generously.

The following day the papers were unanimous in their praise of Mr. Fergus O'Rourke and soon word traveled across the eastern states through the mid-west and within a week the name was known and reverently spoken of in the mines of Grass Valley and the bars and taverns that slunk down to the swirling waters of the Pacific.

Chapter 26

"Man supposes that he directs his life and governs his actions, when his existence is irretrievably under the control of destiny."
- Goethe.

The morning edition of *The Pacific* was delivered to the shop and lay on the counter for several hours before anyone took notice. It was Monday, an extremely busy time since Rory and Finola, in strict observance of the Sabbath always closed the store on Sundays, the result was a frenzy of activity in the early hours of the first work day of the week.

Around eleven o'clock, things began to slow down; the restaurants and eating houses were picking up customers by this time and consequently relieved the crammed space in the Sheridan and O'Gorman.

On the front page of the newspaper the handsome countenance of Dara O'Rourke was magnificiently displayed. This was no happy chance; the light and angle were perfect; no amateur had taken such a photo; the emotion and fire of Dara's noble soul were captured in that split second.

Finola said good morning to the last of her customers and, reaching to brush back a stray wisp of moist hair from off her pretty face, turned her head so that her eyes rested on the paper. A moment of confusion; then she grabbed the paper for a better look.

"My God! It's Dara!" she cried aloud and folded the paper.

Rory was at the other end of the store and did not hear. He was attending to some man who needed a sack of potatoes.

Finola's heart was thumping. She found a chair and sat down. Dare she look at the paper again. Were her eyes playing tricks on her. She placed her hand on her forehead. It was clammy; perhaps she was ill.

The weather had been sultry, humid, and sticky for the past few days. Not what they had grown accustomed to. And although Finola had experienced much worse changes in climate conditions, for some strange reason, this unaccustomed change in the atmosphere seemed to affect her. She suffered a lethargy, - a lack of physical energy quite rare in her young life.

She pulled herself together, she just couldn't allow such insignificant occurances as a disturbance in the weather to influence her behavior.

No, it couldn't be Dara. It was someone like him - yes, she had been mistaken and her heart-beat quickened as she grappled with the paper in her lap.

By this time, Rory had bid his customer good morning and came walking in his usual brisk manner to the front of the shop. Seeing Finola seated, not a habit of hers especially at that early hour, and noting the ashen hue and paled lips, one hand hanging limp by her side while the other clutched *The Pacific*, he grew concerned. Then, as he approached and she seemed to unfold the paper without success, he stepped up to her and enquired if she were feeling ill.

"You've been overdoing it again, darlin'," he said by way of breaking gently into her thoughts. For, indeed, her thoughts were far away; her beautiful eyes told him so. "Eh? Maybe..." she answered indifferently, unemotionally as she still continued to stare into space.

"I'll make you a cup of tea. Then perhaps you should go home and rest." He started to take the paper from her hand and placing his arm around her shoulder would have led her into the small adjoining room where they ate their noonday meal and where a comfortable chair, purchased by Rory had been installed especially for her. As he did so, she immediately came back to reality and snatching the newspaper from his hand forced herself to look at the face she had not seen in over ten long years.

"It's Dara! My Dara! Look, look for yourself," she said as she pushed the paper towards Rory.

Rory glanced at the handsome face and scanned the heading. Yes, indeed it was Dara O'Rourke, that he had to admit. He knew Finola had once loved a man of that name, a man who had left Ireland promising to send for her and from whom she had never again heard. How often over the past years had Rory hoped and prayed that Finola might forget or might never again hear of him. He had even hoped that she might, in time, even find a small place in her heart for himself. Now, he realized how deep that love really was... Dara would always be there.

"Rory, read the article. I want to know. I want to know for sure," she commanded him.

Rory slowly read the article aloud.

"I knew it, I knew it," she cried almost hysterically when Rory had finished reading. "I must go to him. I must get in touch with him."

Rory's reaction was typical of his magnanimous and selfless heart. "You must do what your heart dictates, Finola, but I don't want you to get hurt. That has happened too often. Remember, it's been a long time and, undoubtedly, Dara has…"

"Married!" she finished the sentence knowing full-well what was in his mind.

"Yes, I would expect so. It's only natural, after all."

"I had thought of that," she answered matter-of-factly, "but I would like to contact him, all the same."

"As you wish... as you wish," and his voice trailed off. What if Dara hadn't married, he mused. Then he, Rory, would most assuredly lose her. But then, he confessed to himself, it were better for both of them to know the truth. He knew she would always be wondering, always be hoping for the day when somehow Dara would turn up, would come looking for her. Yes, Rory boyo, he told himself, 'tis better this way.

"I've been thinking that perhaps a letter to this paper would be the best way to find out about him. What do you think, Rory?"

"Seems a good idea to me," he answered but without enthusiasm.

"Then that's what I'll do. Aye, this very moment." She got up; the old self-confidence and energy had returned and with agile step she procured pen and writing paper.

"Then I'll be letting you to it." And he made for the door which led into the shop thinking as he went. Sure 'twill take months for anything to come of this anyway, and even then only God knew what the outcome would be. "No sense countin' the chickens before they're hatched," he said to himself and turned his attention to the lone customer who had entered.

Finola, pen in hand, considered how she would tackle the letter to the newspaper. She should make it short and to the point... her only objective to find Dara.

Within fifteen minutes, she had composed what she thought was a suitable letter and was ready to send it off post haste. The Pony Express which had just been established by the great freighting company of Russell, Majors and Waddell was by far the best and fastest way to send this important missive. She had recently read Mark Twain's account of this innovative method of transporting the mail. Traveling west by coach, he had seen a rider dash by the doors and then vanish in the distance, and he never forgot the sight. "So sudden is it all, and so like a flash of unreal fancy, that but for the flake of white foam left quivering and perishing on a mail sack after the vision had flashed by and disappeared, we might have doubted whether we had seen any actual horse and man at all, maybe."

She took off her apron, donned a bonnet and left for the mail depot. That accomplished, she felt better and was able to turn her mind to the usual chores that now occupied her time.

America could well boast in the 1850's. The decade had witnessed an expansion of material resources previously undreampt of. The population had grown to 31.5 million. Manufacturing establishments had jumped from 123,000 to more than 140,000 and the number of farms from one and a half million to two million. And perhaps, the most sensational aspect of all, the total railroad mileage more than tripled - from 9,000 to 30,000 miles.

But American productivity and energy was not confined to the material realm. The creative spirit was alive and vigorous - in science, journalism, oratory and above all in literature. From New England great writers like Ralph Waldo Emerson, Henry Wadsworth Longfellow, Nathaniel Hawthorne, Oliver Wendell Holmes were a powerhouse fueling the Union's optimism.

The inventions and discoveries of the previous years - steamboat, cotton gin and the ever extending railroads were the beginning of mass production in industry and the introduction to and shaping of the modern world.

It was May 15th, 1862 - a beautiful sun-drenched day. San Francisco was minding its own business despite the fact that the Eastern section of the country seemed to be losing all sense of reason. The political parties were so divided over sectional issues that it had taken Congress nine weeks and 44 ballots to carry out the routine business of electing a Speaker of the House of Representatives. Six years before at Ripon, Wisconsin, a group of Whigs, Free-Soilers, and antislavery Democrats had called for the formation of a new political party opposing slavery's extention into the territories. At Jackson, Michigan, on July 6, 1854, the name Republican was chosen for this party. Finola's friend and one whom she greatly admired, John C. Freemont, had lost in 1856 when he ran for Presidency of this party chiefly because it was purely sectional in its appeal.

Finola was day-dreaming. It was past noon, a lazy time at best. She was sitting down in the little antiroom off the store supposedly checking some bills, but her mind was several thousand miles away. She was picturing the effects her enquiry might have had on Dara. Apprehensive, she dare not allow herself to think that he might not be pleased to have received news of her after such a long time. No, if she knew Dara O'Rourke, married or not, he would welcome word of the girl he once loved - his first love! For she knew that was, indeed, and without any doubt, her place in his heart.

"Finola... Finola darlin'. I've got a letter for you!" Rory's voice betrayed an excitement and eagerness that it had lacked for some time. It's from back East, a grá." His happiness was genuine as he handed it to her.

"Oh, thank you, Rory," she said and a tremble ran through her body. She looked at the envelope, but the writing though clear and bold told her nothing, she had, after all, never seen Dara's writing.

Breaking the seal, she withdrew the single sheet of vellum. It was not a long letter and as Rory saw how her hand trembled, he withdrew on some pretext or another. Finola didn't hear him go.

432 Washington Ave.
New York
March 2nd 1860

Finola, a cuisle mo croí,
What can I say? Can Heaven have opened her doors and allowed me to glimpse paradise! Words cannot tell; my heart knows no bounds, "I'm walking on a cloud. Finola, Finola, the very sound of your name is music to my ears.
When, oh when can I see you? Only say the word and I'll be at your side, my eternal love.
Dara

Dara! Dara... alive and well and still loving her. He hadn't said a word about a wife. He had spoken only of his eternal, abiding love for her... She reread the note. He was waiting for her, still waiting after all these years. Oh Dara... Dara... Dara... and she clutched the precious letter to her breast.

"Oh God! What happiness. Can it, indeed, be true. "Shall I once again know true love?" she spoke the words aloud.

Then she was jolted back to reality. It would take months, maybe years for them to meet. And she sank deep into the armchair and allowed the tears to flow freely. It was thus that Rory found her a few minutes later.

"An' what have we here, at all? Sure, I thought it was glorious news, I was bringing you. So they didn't find him, eh?" And although his heart reached out to her for the pain he thought she endured, yet, he felt a sudden rush of joy, of hope. Maybe... just maybe he still had a chance. But his fleeting moment of hope was soon shattered.

"Oh, no, Rory. The letter's from Dara, himself! He wants to meet me. He wants..."

Rory interrupted. "Then what in thunderation are you crying for? Sure aren't all your dreams come true, darling'?"

"Oh Rory, sure how can we ever meet? New York's such a long, long way off...

"Now, what on earth are you talking about? Don't you know we're living in times when journeys, no matter how long, are accomplished in no time at all. Haven't you heard of the Stage Coach. Sure, they say it takes only twenty-five days now for it to come from St. Louis to our fine city, here. An' sure St. Louis can't be that far from New York."

Rory's words sounded encouraging.

"You really mean it?" she asked groping for assurance.

"Of course I mean it. Dara could be here in... well in five or six weeks anyway. So you best get busy and write your letter of invitation instead of shedding those precious tears of yours."

Finola looked up at Rory. A tear glistened at the corner of her eye before it dropped onto the precious letter she still held in her hand. "Rory... Rory you're the only... " She flung herself into his arms and for the first time allowed herself to show any real emotion in his strong loving embrace. For a moment, they clung together, then Rory remembering that Finola was in reality another man's sweetheart, gently disengaged himself saying: Finola you and I were not destined to be together. We have worked and succeeded in our many business enterprises, but now the time is come when we must make a decision. How long will our partnership last? And do we want it to last?" He paused a moment. Things were changing too fast. Even his own small world was being swept along in the rush and hurry of the new modern age that was breaking in upon them. Who could tell what was going to happen, what with the war an' all. Who knew what the next day would bring. "Now write your letter and let destiny take control." Rory hurried from the room lest he betray his own deep emotions. He closed the door quietly after him. Finola, it was quite clear now, would never be his. Of course he knew it all along, but he had hoped. Well, he would turn his attentions elsewhere. He wasn't getting younger. His Una would wish it. He needed a family. That very evening Rory made up his mind to pay a visit to the pretty young woman lodging under Finola's roof. Kirstan Erickson would be his wife!

Finola waited a few moments longer, savoring the blessed, unexpected outcome. Dara, her Dara alive and well and wishing to come to her. It was almost more than she could bear. A knock on the door roused her to the reality of the business day.

Rory stuck his head in and told her that a very fine gentleman, was without wishing to speak to her.

"Who is it? she asked but Rory was gone. She checked her face in the small mirror over her desk and smoothed the hair on both sides of her shapely head, then glancing down at her dress, she pulled it into place as she arose and went into the shop. She was hoping it wasn't the parent of one of those new students she reluctantly enrolled a few days before - new neighbors they were and new to San Francisco but they had an air of snobbery about them. She wasn't sure... Oh, well, she told herself, if they're not satisfied, they can take them elsewhere. She raised her head on her proud shoulders and went to face the stranger.

The man had his back turned. He was examining a silk shawl as if he wished to purchase it.

Coming towards him, Finola was about to salute him formally when a toss of the head beneath the black silk hat made her hesitate... there was a familiarity about it... Her brain spun in circuitous routes trying to fathom, seeking an explanation...

The stranger set the shawl back on the rack and turned to face her.

"Dara!" she screamed and was in his arms.

Chapter 27

Epilogue

"The nerve which never relaxes - the eye which never blanches - the thought which never wanders - the purpose that never wavers - these are the masters of victory.

— Anon.

The days that followed were glorious beyond words to describe. Both Dara and Finola, having fallen in love with one another all over again tried to catch up on what had happened in their separate lives up to that point. And when they had exhausted each other with their stories and tales of struggle, hard work, disappointment, sorrow, and finally, success, they began to plan for their own future.

On a knoll high above the tranquil Pacific, he once again asked her to be his bride. "Would that we were sitting high on the Cliffs of Moher and we looking out over the mighty Atlantic," he began. "But at last, at long last, I have the means to make you my wife, Finola, a grá," Dara said as he knelt before her looking lovingly into her deep-green, always determined eyes. "It has taken a long time, much longer than I had ever thought to arrive at this moment. But it has come. Now let us delay no longer." He took her in his strong arms and pressed her close. "Oh, Finola, Finola, I can no longer live without you. Just seeing you has given me back new hope and strength. I'll devote every waking hour to you for the rest of my life, and that's a promise."It was decided that they would make their home in sunny

California. Not in San Francisco, the city had grown so that those who had been among its first pioneers thought it crowded and congested. No, they would build a home in the hills above Monterey where the climate was temperate and, as yet, the crowds had not discovered that natural beauty, alone, would guarantee them happiness. Dara would sell his business and move his books, there was little else he cared about, to the 'Wild West'. Finola would retain an interest in the businesses but Rory would be in charge and therefore make all future decisions.

Dara united with his first love, his only love would return to husband the earth . . . he was, after all - a man of the soil. He would raise sheep and till the fine rich land that God had now given him. He would plant orchards and vineyards and he would raise a family, a new generation that would not only learn the old ways but also what was good and noble about the great land in which they would be born and grow to maturity.

They had come a long way . . . and he thanked God in his heart for what he and Finola had achieved. But in the midst of his happiness, and great joy, he could not forget the past. His mind travelled across the broad continent and over the vast expanse of ocean that divided him from the land of his birth. . . Ireland; it seemed so far away now. If only his children could have been born there . . . in the land that had for untold generations given life to his people . . . to the strong, energetic, intelligent men and women who preceded him. He thought of his mother, of her gentle persistance in the face of utter misery and despair, of her quiet unfaltering trust in God, of her complete and unwavering submission to what she considered His Will. Then he looked around him and crushed a sob deep in his heart as he thought of how she might have fared in the beautiful fertile land that spread out before him, now. "Oh God!" he cried. "I weep for the sufferings of all mankind."

* * * * *

Their union was blessed by Padre Jose at the Carmel Mission, the site chosen by the Franciscans after the initial mission near the Monterey Presidio 1770 had proved to be an unwise choice.

In the quaint old church the work of the skilled hands of Manuel Ruiz, a professional stone mason brought from Mexico in 1791, is still seen. The exterior tower is Moorish in character and the front is adorned with a star window. The statue of the Blessed Virgin which Father Serra, himself, brought to San Diego and then to Carmel stands in a side chapel.

On a sunny morning in the spring of '59 Dara O'Rourke and Finola O'Donnell pledged themselves, one to the other for the rest of their lives.

She wore a gown of green, which according to Dara, paled when compared to the glow of her emerald eyes. On her arm she carried a bouquet of lilies which she later laid at the feet of the Mother of God.

Dara handsome, strong, elegant was at the height of his manhood. In all the years that intervened he hadn't really changed that much - still dashing, debonair, every ready with a joke, still optimistic.

Rory was in attendance and gallantly performed the duties of best man. And to further grace this auspicious occasion, Kirstan in a soft pink gown acted as maid of honor.

Several friends had gathered to wish the ecstatic couple long life and prosperity. But Dara and Finola scarcely heard the felicitations so wrapped-up where they in their own thoughts and with one another.

Finola, still a young woman, radiated a mature beauty - quiet, yet forceful and vibrant which left a powerful impression on all with whom she associated. She had, in a relatively short period, achieved much and risen to an impressive status in the society that was forming the backbone of San Francisco.

After her marriage to Dara, her financial situation was greatly enhanced. She became mistress of a stately Spanish hacienda in the hills above Monterey Bay. Here she managed a number of household servants as well as those who worked without in the manicured gardens. And, as she had succeeded in gaining respect and honor in San Francisco, so in Monterey, she quickly won over those who were already in good standing as well as those of lowlier station.

She did not neglect her activities in the national interest of her beloved Ireland. Besides organizing meetings to keep all concerned abreast of the situation and happenings in that country and among the Fenian members in America, she also faithfully continued to collect funds and in other ways helped to keep the spirit of the organization alive and vigorous in and around the area.

Nor did she forget the school. Her old mansion was turned over completely to housing the children. She no longer taught but there were many others ready and willing to take her place. Kirstan assumed the role of Head Mistress until she, too, chose to become a mother.

In time, Finola and Dara had seven healthy children - four boys and three girls. Starting with the first born - Tara, Finola made sure that the child was from the beginning well instructed in the fundamentals not only of her faith but also in the traditions, culture, and history of the land of her forefathers. She would know from whence she had sprung and she would grow up with a deep pride and love for the land that bore her parents.

It gave Dara no greater pleasure than to hear the silvery tones of his beautiful wife as she sang to her babies at the 'moth hour of eve' songs his own mother had sung when he was a small boy, songs ancient and new about the land they both loved so well:

> I love my love in the morning
> For she, like the morn, is fair;
> Her blushing cheek, its crimson streak,
> Its clouds, her golden hair;
> Her glance, its beam, so soft and kind,
> Her tears, its dewy show'rs;
> And her voice, the tender whispering wind
> That stirs the early bow'rs.
>
> I love my love in the morning,
> I love my love at noon
> For she is bright as the lord of light,
> Yet mild as autumn's moon:
> Her beauty is my bosom's sun
> Her faith my fostering shade
> And I will love my darling one
> Till e'en the sun shall fade.

Between them, Finola and Dara would raise up sons and daughters worthy of their beloved Ireland but also loyal to the country which had given them so much - America.

Soon after Finola and Dara were married, Rory also won Kirstan's hand. It was an ideal union which over the years produced five lively children, three boys and two girls.

The two families kept in touch, Rory and Kirstan finding no greater joy than to spend time on the farm called 'Glencarrow' where their children ran freely with Dara's and Finola's as they would have had they lived in the beautiful valley of the same name back home in Ireland.

One of the greatest pleasures in the lives of both families was the day that Tara O'Rourke married Rory's handsome first born, Fergus in the same little Spanish Mission Church in Carmen where both sets of parents had been married some twenty years before.

The Choice

The intellect of man is forced to choose
Perfection of the life, or of the work,
And if it take the second must refuse
A heavenly mansion, raging in the dark.
When all that story's finished, what's the news?
In luck or out the toil has left its mark:
That old perplexity an empty purse,
Or the day's vanity, the night's remorse.

- W.B. Yeats

Bibliography

Costigan, Giovanne. A History of Modern Ireland. New York: Western Publishing Co. Inc. 1979.

Darling, Amanda. Lola Montez. New York: Stein and Day Publishers 1972.

Edgeworth, Maria. Castle Rackrent. London: Aldine House. 1910.

Edgeworth, Maria. The Absentee. London: Aldine House. 1910.

Gallager, Thomas. Paddy's Lament. New York: Harcourt Brace Jovanovich Publishers. 1982.

Keegan, Gerald. Famine Diary. Dublin: Wolfhound Press. 1991.

Kickham, Charles J. Knocknagow. Dublin: James Duffy & Co., Ltd. 1887.

King, Joseph A. From Ireland to North America. Washington, D.C.: Elliott and Clark Publishing. 1994.

MacManus, Seumas. The Story of the Irish Race. Connecticut: The Devin-Adair Co. 1979.

Miller, K. and Paul Wagner. Out of Ireland. Washington, D.C.: Elliott and Clark Publishing. 1994.

Murphy, Ignatius. Before The Famine Struck. Irish Academic Press. 1996.

Murphy, Ignatius. A People Starve. Dublin: Irish Academic Press. 1996.

O'Flaherty, Liam. The Famine. New York: The Literary Guild, Inc. 1937.

Rees, Jim. A Farewell To Famine. Arklow: Arklow Interprise Centre. 1994.

Seymour, Bruce. Lola Montez. New Haven: Yale University Press. 1996.

Woodham-Smith, Cecil. The Great Hunger. New York: E.P. Dutton. 1980.

Glossary

A cuisle mo croí — beat of my heart
A grá — love
A mhic — son
Boithrín — narrow road, lane
Mo Croí — my heart

* * *

Emancipation Act
　　A few years prior to this time, the great Irish leader, Daniel O'Connell had succeeded in obtaining a passage of the Emancipation Bill thereby, in theory, restoring to Catholics many of the civil and religious rights they had lost during the Penal Laws.

Cover Artist
John Pirva

John Priva was born May 21 1962 in Balsa, Romania, a small town in the foothills of the Apuseni Mountains. Third of five children, he developed the talent for Fine Arts early in his childhood, and followed courses in The School of Fine Arts and The Fine Arts High School in Deva and Sibiu. In 1981, at the age of 19, he escaped communist Romania and crossed the border to freedom. In the US, he continued to pursue an Art career, went to Portland State University as an Arts Major for four years and now works freelance in the Arts field. One of his most fulfilling surprises was a letter from his son, Adrian, which contained a beautiful drawing and the assurance that his most precious inheritance from his father was his art talent.

About the Author
Louise Gherasim

Born and raised in Ireland, Louise Gherasim came to this country in the 1950's. She is a successful novelist, writing for adults, teenagers and children. Louise now makes her home in Oregon with her Romanian husband, after spending over thirty-five years in the classrooms of the world, teaching everything from art, music, history and philosophy to English Language and literature.